PENGUIN BOOKS

A Mask of Shadows

Oscar de Muriel was born in Mexico City and moved to the UK to complete his PhD. He is a chemist, translator and violinist who has worked all over England and Scotland, and now lives in Cheshire. *A Mask of Shadows* is his third novel, following *A Fever of the Blood* and *The Strings of Murder*.

A MASK OF SHADOWS

OSCAR DE MURIEL

PENGUIN BOOKS

PENGUIN BOOKS

UK | USA | Canada | Ireland | Australia
India | New Zealand | South Africa

Penguin Books is part of the Penguin Random House group of companies
whose addresses can be found at global.penguinrandomhouse.com.

First published 2017
001

Copyright © Oscar de Muriel, 2017

The moral right of the author has been asserted

Set in 12.5/14.75 pt Garamond MT Std
Typeset by Jouve (UK), Milton Keynes
Printed in Great Britain by Clays Ltd, St Ives plc

A CIP catalogue record for this book is available from the British Library

ISBN: 978–1–405–92622–5

The third one is for the Hanburians and Mr Akhtar,
who gave Frey & McGray a fighting chance

Author's Note

The real lives of Bram Stoker, Sir Henry Irving and Dame Ellen Terry – the darlings of Victorian theatre – were far more intriguing and complex than any of their plays.

As I will detail in my final note, nearly all the backstories, love affairs, family disputes and on-going tribulations mentioned in this book, no matter how anachronistic they might seem, are historical fact – and an irresistible treat for the crime writer.

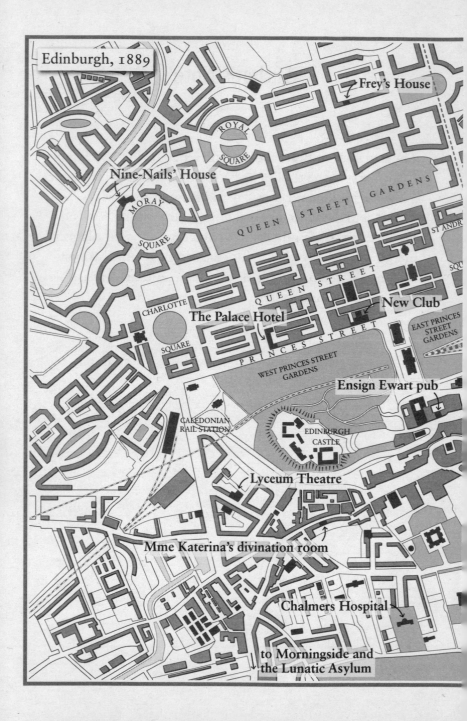

Edinburgh, 1889

Frey's House

ROYAL SQUARE

Nine-Nails' House

MORAY SQUARE

QUEEN STREET GARDENS

ST ANDR

SQU

QUEEN STREET

CHARLOTTE SQUARE

New Club

The Palace Hotel

EAST PRINCES STREET GARDENS

PRINCES STREET

WEST PRINCES STREET GARDENS

Ensign Ewart pub

CALEDONIAN RAIL STATION

EDINBURGH CASTLE

Lyceum Theatre

Mme Katerina's divination room

Chalmers Hospital

to Morningside and the Lunatic Asylum

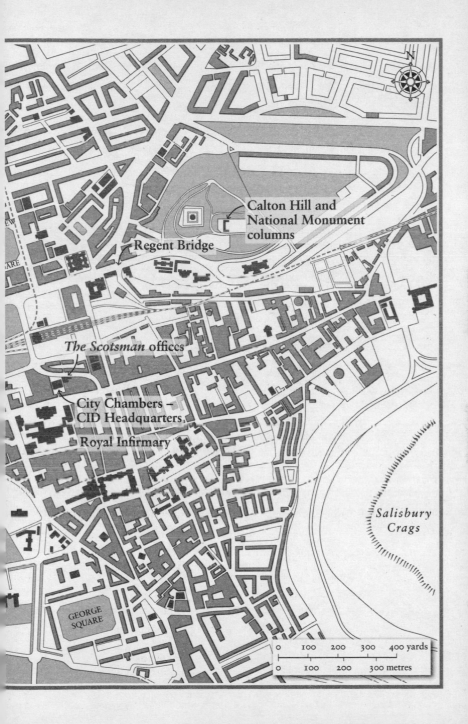

Calton Hill and
National Monument
columns

Regent Bridge

The Scotsman offices

City Chambers –
CID Headquarters

Royal Infirmary

Salisbury
Crags

GEORGE
SQUARE

| 0 | 100 | 200 | 300 | 400 yards |

| 0 | 100 | 200 | 300 metres |

OVERTURE

BANQUO
> The earth hath bubbles, as the water has,
> And these are of them. Whither are they vanished?

MACBETH
> Into the air, and what seemed corporal
> Melted, as breath into the wind.

Bram Stoker's Journal, 1889

Fragment filed by Inspector Ian P. Frey

30 June. London – *The Lyceum Theatre is still in turmoil. Nobody can tell for certain what happened last night, and there is little I can deduce from the morbid accounts. Mrs Harwood is still a wreck and Irving will not tell me much.*

The police arrived timely but refused to investigate any further. The officers told us we were all insane and left without even looking at the desecrated set. Irving had to snarl, curse and threaten before the cleaners agreed to mop up the ghastly mess.

I will have to call Mr Harker, as a matter of urgency, before we set off for Scotland. I would not trust this deed to anybody else: he will have to patch and repaint the entire lower section of the castle scenery. The canvas cannot be salvaged. It is drenched in blood.

London, 29 June 1889

Thunder struck, startling the crowd, and the hazy stage glowed under blinding lightning. Then a spear emerged from the thick mist, bearing the severed head of King Macbeth.

The ladies gasped, covered their mouths with lace handkerchiefs or clutched their feathery fans to their chests. Some of them were moved, but most were sickened by the sight of dark, viscous blood dripping from the dead king's neck.

Sharp voices were heard among the high notes of strings and trumpets, just as three shadows ascended, spiralling like scavengers around the ghastly stake. These were no vultures but three black ravens, flapping their wings and cawing in mockery, as their sinister call became mixed with the choir.

'All hail Macbeth! All hail! All hail!'

It all ended in horror, tragedy and death. Their eyes were wet and their hearts were heavy. They all assumed there was no redemption, but then a slender, shy figure emerged through the thick fog. The swirls seemed to retreat and the spectators saw the golden hair and the wide blue eyes of a teenage boy. The darkness gathered around him, his frame lit only by a little taper he'd brought with him – but then a single, sharp ray of light appeared, cutting right through the haze. The beam grew and widened, bouncing off the bejewelled crown that the boy carried in his other hand.

'Fleance,' a gentleman murmured.

Future father of kings. The seed of justice, peace and glory. The promise of a kingdom restored.

The boy looked up, and the choir instantly shifted into a sweet, angelic note, which faded as the curtain gently began to drop. Long before the velvet touched the floor an explosion of applause and cheering flooded the theatre, so loud Henry Irving thought he could feel the sound vibrating in his chest.

He clenched the canvas, peering on one side of the painted scenery. He knew people might see him but he did not care now. London's Lyceum Theatre reverberated to the deafening cries of acclaim, and he lived for these moments. His eyes panned the auditorium as the people began to clap on their feet. In a moment the main cast would join him. He'd hold Ellen's soft, beautiful hand and raise it in the air, and . . .

His heart skipped a beat, all the joy vanishing in a blink.

Well into the rows of seats there was a pair of piercing eyes, fixed on him. He knew whose they were, even before he could make out the features of the face.

'Florence!' he cried, but amongst all the clamour nobody heard his voice.

Irving wondered how he could have missed her until then: the woman's skin, vinegar-bleached, was so pale she glowed amidst the rows of seats like a ghost with a deep frown that was visible despite the distance. And she looked much thinner, as if recently ravaged by a consuming disease.

The actor fancied himself in full command of his

features, his breath and eyes the very tools of his craft; however, at that instant three decades of acting served him only to realize his utter loss of self-control. Florence lifted her chin, defiantly, and her eerie smile grew wider when she saw Irving's expression.

'What are you doing here?' Irving mouthed, livid, just as the curtains blocked his vision, but the woman's ominous stare seemed to have scarred into his retinae.

And then they all heard the banshee's cry.

Ellen Terry rubbed her hands again and again.

It was strange that the syrup and cochineal dye concoction, which vanished from clothes with a little rinse, would cling to her nails and cuticles so stubbornly.

'*A little water clears us of this deed,*' she'd say on the stage, only to spend the rest of the evening trying to clean her own skin.

Miss Ivor, her sour understudy, held the porcelain basin in the middle of the corridor and watched as the grand Miss Terry spruced herself up.

The ageing actress had good reason to be upset: Ellen Terry had not missed a single performance since December, and with the London season ending tonight, poor Miss Ivor had not had a chance to play her Lady Macbeth.

'I hear the battle's *lost and won*,' she said. 'You should change now, Miss Terry.'

'I'd better do,' said Ellen, drying her forearms and handing the towel to Miss Ivor. 'Thanks, darling. And sorry again. You do know I hate to treat you like a servant!'

Miss Ivor concealed her resentment very poorly, but Ellen Terry had no head to worry too much: she was still wearing the white nightgown from her sleepwalking scene, which was utterly inappropriate for thanking the public. She liked to change back into her main outfit: the majestic green gown, bejewelled and embroidered with real beetle wings, which had been the talk of London throughout the year.

The door to her dressing room was ajar, but Ellen thought nothing of it. It could have been one of the seamstresses, or little Susy, coming to borrow a book and read herself to sleep after her performance, or Bram bringing flowers or presents from one of her avid admirers.

'Fussie!' she exclaimed as soon as she saw Irving's beloved fox terrier on top of her dressing table, wagging its tail. The dog had once been hers, but Irving had stolen its affections with courses of lamb chops, strawberries, ladies' fingers soaked in champagne, and a beautiful fur rug of his very own. 'What are you doing here?'

Fussie did not hear. He was facing the mirror, his head half buried into a bundle of wrapping paper, munching loudly.

'What is that, dear?' Ellen asked. The dog was a glutton, always sniffing the air for treats he could steal. 'Your little stomach will be the end of you, you know that?'

Ellen reached for her dress, too busy to even glance at the bundle, but then she perceived an odd smell. Meaty and slightly sickening.

She looked back, and the eagerness with which the dog was devouring it suddenly repelled her.

'Oh, Fussie, what are you eating?'

Many sheets of brown paper were crumpled all around the dog. Ellen held a corner with her now quivering fingers and gingerly pulled the wrapping aside.

At first she thought it was a pile of slugs, their slimy grey skins sodden in a ghastly red fluid. Then she blinked and felt as if life itself slipped from her body, leaving only an icy hollow in her chest. Fussie had been chewing on blood-soaked brains.

And just as Ellen Terry rose to scream, the banshee's cry was heard.

'My God, who turned all the lights off?' Bram Stoker asked, looking into the darkened corridor.

'Mr Wheatstone,' the first witch prompted.

Her weird sister added, 'He was bringing in that white powder and said a little spark could kill us all. He cut the gas himself.'

Bram peered into the thick blackness. 'And this is where you last saw her?'

'Indeed. We asked her where she was going but she said nothing. She was having one of her – moments.'

Bram felt a draught of cold wind. Mr Wheatstone must have left the back door open. Anyone could have come in – or gone out.

'Here,' said the third witch, bringing a small oil lamp. Its amber flame projected sharp shadows on the crones' faces.

For the first time in history the Weird Sisters were being played by women, and these ladies looked the part, still wearing their dark rags and with their twisted face prostheses still in place. As Bram took the lamp he thought they looked like monsters in a cave, as eerie as on the stage.

'We need to go now,' said the first witch. 'Get our ovation.'

Indeed, since the opening night they'd received acclaims dangerously close to those for Terry and Irving.

'Do you want us to help?' asked the third witch.

'No,' Bram answered, a little too keenly. 'No, it is all right. You go and thank the public. You deserve your moment of triumph.'

It did not take much to convince them. Bram saw them rush back into the theatre, just as a second draught made him shiver.

He turned on his heels very slowly, wielding the lamp like a weapon as he stepped into the darkness.

He had never liked dark places. Bram had spent the first seven years of his life bedridden, with a lamp or candle always within reach, and Mother in the next room. Now, even though he'd grown into a six-foot-tall, broad-shouldered theatre manager, Bram could not walk into a shady room without taking a deep breath first.

'Mrs Harwood?' he called, too conscious of the slight tremble in his voice, and baffled by his groundless anxiety.

He clenched the cool brass of his lamp more tightly and forced himself to move on.

Bram took a turn, approaching the Lyceum's back door, but just as he saw the silver moonlight delineating its frame, he heard a revolting squash, felt his shoe slide on something, and his heartbeat quickened.

He looked down and spotted something dark on the floor. He squatted down to have a closer look, but just as he recognized the intense red of blood, the wind came again – this time stronger, directly from the back alley, and it swirled into the lamp's glass chimney, extinguishing the flame.

A howling began somewhere far down the road. As his

eyes adjusted Bram saw a dark trail emerge: a nasty dripping, running from underneath his feet and all the way to the door, ending in a puddle on the street's flagstones.

Then a black shape came into view.

It dragged itself slowly, creeping towards the puddle as if to drink from it. It was a dog, enormous, dark and foul smelling: a massive black wolfhound with matted fur, veiny eyes and a long muzzle that dripped blood. The animal still licked it noisily.

Bram dropped the lamp, the chimney shattered on the floor and he fell backwards from the fright. The dog started, and its long, white fangs glowed under the moonlight.

And then the banshee's cry was heard.

It was a horrible wail, rising quickly until it became a drilling, unbearable blast that injured the ears and curdled the blood.

Irving released the canvas, covered his ears and closed his eyes in agony. He noticed the sudden silence from the crowd, and pictured the shocked faces of the audience, aghast at the infernal cry.

The terrified screams of the cast were like whispers compared with that otherworldly shriek, which held itself on and on, as if drawing air from the most powerful lungs.

It stopped as suddenly as it had begun, but Irving could not react for a moment. Still stunned, he groped through the scenery. Whoever had made the noise must be standing behind another two canvases.

It was like crawling through lines of bed sheets left to dry, only these were gigantic pieces: twenty feet tall and thirty feet wide. The glow of the stage lights did not reach the full depth of those canvas passages, and the narrow gap ahead of Irving blurred into blackness.

The last canvas was heavier, with thick layers of paint depicting Dunsinane Castle. Irving had to kneel down and crawl to pass through. He placed his hand on the floor, only to plunge it into something viscous and repulsive.

His heart nearly stopped as the dim lights silhouetted a crouching woman.

'Mrs Harwood!' he exclaimed, not believing his eyes. The usually gentle seamstress was on her knees, her hands stretched forwards and her nails scratching the floorboards. She looked up, so suddenly that Irving thought her neck had snapped.

'You heard her too!' she babbled, trembling from head to toes. There were dark stains all over her skirt.

Irving drew a hand to his face, but before he covered his mouth he saw that his fingers were tainted too, the same colour as Mrs Harwood's.

'Tell me you heard her!' she implored, reaching for him with her red hands, *'Tell me you heard her too!'*

'We all heard!' Irving shouted, just as someone came through the canvases, bringing a heavy oil lamp.

On the floor, surrounded by scratches on the wooden boards, there was a smear of blood – red letters as crooked as the words they spelled:

All hail! These tragic marks await Macbeth
All hail! The Scottish stage shall see your death

Edinburgh, 17 July 1889

[. . .]

We were all warned that murder would take place, and whilst particulars such as the date and the place were accurately foretold, the one detail that was purposely omitted was the name of the eventual victim(s).

As they developed, the events that led to the ghastly deaths at Edinburgh's Lyceum Theatre appeared utterly disjointed and incoherent [. . .]

The murderer's actions became evident only once the accounts of various unconnected participants were put side by side. I have endeavoured to collect all the relevant documents and testimonials that support this statement.

How these papers have been gathered and placed in sequence will be made manifest in the reading of them.

[. . .]

Inspector Ian P. Frey
(Fragments of his foreword to the documentation
presented at the Irving–Terry inquiry)

ACT I

MACBETH

    Cure her of that:
    Canst thou not minister to a mind diseas'd;
    Pluck from the memory a rooted sorrow;
    Raze out the written troubles of the brain;
    And with some sweet oblivious antidote
    Cleanse the stuff'd bosom of that perilous stuff
    Which weighs upon the heart?

DOCTOR

    Therein the patient
    Must minister to himself

Bram Stoker's Journal

Filed by Inspector Ian P. Frey

9 July. Edinburgh – *Left London at ten o'clock on the Scotch Express. Service left punctually from King's Cross, but we were in very real danger of missing it. As soon as I opened my cab's door, a hive of reporters huddled around and I had to elbow my way to the platform.*

They all shouted, even the ones standing right by my ears. 'Is it true, Mr Stoker? Is the play truly cursed?'

Miss Terry wisely used me as a decoy. Her carriage had been waiting around the corner, and she sneaked through while the journalists stalked me. I cannot imagine how persistently those men would have pursued her.

Glad all sets, wardrobe and equipment left three days ago; we couldn't have possibly managed the logistics with all the press in the way. The good Mr Howard and Mr Wyndham sent me a very opportune telegram, telling me that all the props arrived safely. Some beetle wings in Miss Terry's dress were crushed on the journey, but fortunately I heard in good time. Mrs Harwood managed to source enough material, cannot tell where from, and she has been working on it. Assured me the dress shall be ready before the first performance. Must admit she is still in a sorry state, and I think she welcomes the meticulous work; it must keep her mind from such a terrible memory.

Unfortunately, Irving has not managed to find solace. He is hugely distressed, and not only because of that horrible prophecy — the unexpected presence of his Florence left its mark on him.

Upon our arrival he urged me to seek aid from the police, thinking that perhaps the Scottish authorities would see our plights with more sympathetic eyes than their London counterparts.

I was exhausted from the eight-hour journey and the sleepless nights that preceded it, but Irving is so troubled I could not refuse. I had his luggage, as well as Miss Terry's and mine, sent to the Palace Hotel, and immediately inquired for the police.

The station officers recognized Miss Terry — her open carriage was leaving, and she blew a kiss to the besotted sergeants. At once they told me I should see a certain _Superintendent Campbell_. One of them kindly guided me to their headquarters.

I was received by that very man, whom I found extremely disagreeable.

He seemed about to leave, and whilst he listened to my statement his eye kept checking the time on his mantelpiece clock. I told him everything, showed him the London papers, pleaded for their protection — and the man sneered! He then had the audacity to request two box tickets for the opening night, and suggested that the investigations might be carried out more quickly if he got hold of a programme dedicated to him by Miss Terry. To these requests I had no other choice but to agree.

He had '_just the man_' to deal with this sort of matter, he said.

Puzzling statement. I was further intrigued when he scrib-
bled the address of one Inspector McGray and said that,
should I become lost, I had but to inquire any passer-by for
the abode of 'Nine-Nails McGray'.

He gave me an envelope with a note for said man, allegedly
instructing him to take full care of our case – he sealed it
before I could read a word. He then dismissed me swiftly,
all too eager to go home and have his tea.

One of the officers was kind enough to summon a cab, which
swiftly deposited me on the northern side of Edinburgh. I
had but to mention the name McGray and the driver at
once knew my destination.

I have been to this city several times, mostly on Irving's tours,
but never explored much. The cab took me through a
sumptuous neighbourhood, beautiful Georgian mansions
on both sides of the road, and then to a crescent, the elegant
façades surrounding a very well-kept garden. We halted at
number 27.

A rather coarse, wrinkled butler attended. He informed me
that I had called at the correct residence, and pronounced
rather warmly the name McGray, but to my frustration the
man himself was not at home.

Told him I must see him right away. The old servant was
reluctant to tell me the whereabouts of his master, and only
obliged after I mentioned that I brought word from the
superintendent, regarding urgent police business.

He gave hasty directions to my driver, and upon hopping back
in I asked the young chap whether he'd understood the
instructions.

'Aye, master,' he replied. 'The auld man sent us to the lunatic
asylum.'

Off we went, crossing back and further south. By the time we reached the infamous institution the very long summer day was coming to a close. However, the sky still glowed, for the Scottish nights in this season are rather a permanent dusk, so the driver and I had a fair view of the asylum's front lawns.

It was the worst possible moment to arrive: the place was in uproar. A black stagecoach was riding away, driven by a strongly built orderly. Passed so close to my cab I thought we would clash. Caught a glimpse of a young lady travelling in the back seat, dressed all in white, and even though I saw her less than a second, the soft outline of her pale face will stay fixed in my memory. A middle-aged man accompanied her, but of him I glimpsed little more than a dark, bushy beard.

My cab slowed upon approaching the building's main entrance, where stood a scrawny policeman, a pair of nurses and two tall gentlemen embroiled in a heated argument.

They were the most contrasting sight I had yet encountered. One wore a black, very elegant overcoat, a bowler hat and a bright white shirt; the other, the taller of the pair, I can only describe as gaudy, wearing mismatched tartan trousers and waistcoat, and a baggy raincoat of cheap material.

That man sounded wild. His Scottish accent resounded throughout the grounds. He looked at my cab with a fierce face, shouted a very clear curse at the other gentleman and then strode away, closely followed by a pale golden retriever I had not noticed before.

As soon as I alighted the policeman and the nurses intercepted me.

A middle-aged woman (confident gait and manners; she must be the head nurse) asked me if she could be of any help.

I told them briefly what my business was: I _must_ talk to Inspector McGray.

Their faces lost what little colour they still had. The nurses looked fearfully towards the eccentric Scotsman, who now stood on his own by the far end of the lawns, looking up at the sky, back turned to us. More than twenty yards separated me from him, but I could nonetheless see his shoulders rise and fall in deep frenzied breaths. Put me in mind of a caged circus lion.

The young officer was just as uneasy. Advised me to speak to <u>Inspector Frey</u> instead, but in a tone that suggested I should expect very little.

He led me towards the thin, narrow-shouldered fellow with the bowler hat. The man turned to me and I had a clear view of his lean face. He had an angular jaw, brown eyes that looked at everything with suspicion, and a deep fold right in the middle of his brow.

He had heard my accent, for he cast me a severe stare and barked an even harsher remark.

'Jesus Christ, get rid of the bloody Fenian.'

The words caught me by surprise and I could not say a word. It was the young officer who answered. Tried to say my business was important, but the arrogant man interrupted.

'McNair, do you not know the nightmare we are going through?'

'Aye, Inspector, but this lad says he was sent by Campbell. With instructions for Inspector McGray.'

If everyone around was tense, this Inspector Frey appeared to be carrying the weight of the world. He snorted irascibly and then rubbed the bridge of his nose, forcing himself into patience.

Then he looked at me with proper attention for the first time. Inspector Frey was somewhat shorter than I, and much thinner. I would have easily beaten him in a fist fight.

'What is your name?' he asked me.

'Stoker. Bram Stoker, Inspector.'

He stared at me for another moment, his brow quizzical. 'I believe I know your name . . .'

'Perhaps from Henry Irving's Theatre —'

'Never mind,' he interrupted. 'What are these instructions you bring?'

Given his curt manner, I thought it better to present his superior's words first.

'They're in this note,' and I produced the sealed envelope. 'Mr Campbell said quite clearly that Inspector McGray was _just the man_ to look at my request.'

My last remark had the entirely opposite effect I expected. Inspector Frey let out a mocking chuckle, and then looked at the taller man; that Scottish chap who, with his outlandish clothes and frantic breathing, could have easily passed for an inmate. The Londoner sighed wearily before looking back at me.

'I am afraid that Inspector McGray's brains are — otherwise engaged at the moment. I am his next in command, however. You can give me that note and I shall attend to it at my earliest convenience.'

Inspector Frey extended me a gloved hand, but I refused to put the message in it.

'Sir, you don't understand,' I protested. 'This is a matter of life or death!'

Inspector Frey laughed most insolently. 'We have had _plenty_ of such matters of late. You can have my word; I will look into your case.'

'Excuse me, this is urgent.'

'Is anybody injured or dead?'

'Why, no, but . . .'

The shadow of Inspector McGray was too temptingly close to give up. I made the foolish attempt to walk past the infuriatingly conceited Englishman and deliver the note myself.

Inspector Frey took a firm hold of my arm. His grip was much stronger than his thin frame suggested.

'You do not want to talk to him right now,' he hissed. 'Not if you wish to maintain your skull intact.'

His tone was fittingly dark; not a warning, but actual concern.

'Give me that note if you want it seen at all,' he added. I would not call that a request, for he was pulling the paper from my hand as he spoke. I had to release my grip else the message would have ripped. 'Leave your card with McNair and I will contact you as soon as possible. Now get away.'

He released my arm and shoved the note in his breast pocket. I believe I looked miserable, for Inspector Frey cast me a final stare, in which there was a brief hint of empathy.

He said, 'It is a murky day for us all.'

Side note by I. P. Frey:

I have only a faint memory of the conversation – I certainly do not remember having called him a *bloody Fenian*, though it does sound like something I would say. I may have behaved harshly, but Mr Stoker could not have arrived at a more fraught moment.

Nine-Nails McGray had just seen his young sister, a patient at the asylum, being removed from Edinburgh – a necessity he has not yet come to accept.

1

It displeases me to begin this narrative by trumpeting the most tragic and intimate affairs of a colleague. However, I believe I must explain the sad background of the McGray family, and the sooner the better, before I move on to the nightmare brought upon us by Mr Stoker.

Inspector McGray is the son of a self-made ... wait, what did his late father do? I believe the man owned some farmland, and I am *sure* he ran at least a few distilleries in and around Dundee; whichever the case, the McGrays were once new money moving into Edinburgh, and unsurprisingly not very well regarded by the upper classes – who in turn would not be very well regarded in my own London circles, if I may say, but I digress.

Their disgrace befell them quite suddenly, on the summer solstice of 1883, while they holidayed in their country house near Dundee. Miss Amy McGray, then a girl of sixteen, lost her wits quite inexplicably and just as suddenly. On that night she butchered her mother and father with a fire poker and a kitchen cleaver; and then, as her brother tried to restrain her, she severed the ring finger on his right hand. People almost instantly began calling him 'Nine-Nails' McGray.

Amy, nicknamed Pansy by her parents, was deemed a dangerous mad person and locked in Edinburgh's Royal Lunatic Asylum. It was a roaring scandal. Before the terrible episode she'd been a beautiful, vivacious girl, with very good chances of stealing the hearts of the Scottish well-to-do. But that was not all.

From the last words she uttered (because, with one nasty exception, she has never spoken again) she hinted at – well, having been possessed by the Devil.

The entire affair was shrouded in mystery, and is likely to remain for ever so. The only witnesses were the late Mr and Mrs McGray, and their daughter, but her ever speaking again does not appear to be on the cards.

Naturally, the tragedy of the McGrays caught people's imagination, exaggerated and embellished with each telling. It has become part of local lore, undoubtedly told around Edinburgh's bonfires, and Inspector McGray has unwittingly kept the interest alive.

He became obsessed with anything related to the Devil, the occult and the supernatural. He has gathered an encyclopaedic knowledge of the field, and ultimately instigated the creation of a police department devoted to investigating such nonsense: the – take a deep breath, Ian – Commission for the Elucidation of Unsolved Cases Presumably Related to the Odd and Ghostly (in due course I shall recount the curious circumstances that threw me into serving such a preposterous subdivision).

Six years have passed, but McGray's determination has not faded. He still harbours the irrational hope of bringing Pansy back to sanity. Everything he does is for her, the only family he has left.

A part of me understands him and his clinging despair. Another side of me, the more rational, fears and resents the recklessness of his drive, which has dragged many – myself included – into the most dangerous and distressing situations.

It was rather late, well past ten o'clock; however, the thin strip of sky that was free from clouds still glowed in a blueish twilight. It reminded me how far away from London I was: Edinburgh was so far north that on these midsummer nights the sky never went completely dark.

The air felt oppressive, unmistakably announcing a heavy storm. Indeed, the skies broke as the carriage took me back to Edinburgh's New Town, and I congratulated myself for having called a cab instead of riding.

I had recently leased new lodgings on the very fine Great King Street. Sumptuous and comfortable as my Georgian townhouse was, I could not yet look at it without wincing a little, for I had been forced to rent it from one of the most despicable characters in the city: Lady Anne Ardglass, appropriately nicknamed 'Lady Glass' because of her notorious drinking.

I stepped down from the cab, swiftly opening my umbrella. The rain glimmered around the golden light from the street lamps, lashing my face as I saw a single light coming from one of the first-floor windows. My young brother was still waiting for me. I would delude myself thinking he'd be worried; I knew he wanted all the gossip.

'Mr Frey!' Layton cried from the door. 'Do walk out of that wretched rain!'

He was already at the entrance, bidding me in and

taking my drenched umbrella, coat and hat as soon as he shut the door.

'My, that is a downright tempest out there,' he said with his stiff Kentish voice.

Layton was my new valet. Forty-eight, his body long and bony, and with an aquiline nose, he always reminded me of an overgrown fire poker. The man had served my uncle Maurice for more than ten years, and before then he'd served some of the finest households in London. Now, much like me, he detested his new situation in Scotland. Unfortunately for him, I was so pleased with his presence I would not let him go any time soon: he was efficient, well mannered and mindful of the etiquette (most importantly, he knew exactly how I liked my clothes and my morning coffee). With his refined training, he was entirely the opposite of my former housekeeper, Joan, whom I had recently lost to . . . McGray's blasted butler.

'I hope the affair did not trouble you exceedingly,' he said, as I changed into more comfortable footwear.

'*Exceedingly* is not descriptive enough.'

'Why, I am sorry to hear – oh, sir, would you like to keep this?' He was showing me the now crumpled envelope handed in by Mr Stoker.

'I would not, but I must,' I replied, taking it from him.

'You may have already seen that Master Elgie is waiting for you in the smoking room. Shall I bring you some supper?'

'Indeed. Something hearty. I am famished.'

I climbed the mahogany stairs, relishing the slight scents of leather and bergamot I'd come to associate with that house. For the past few months I had learned to embrace the little pleasures of refined life: the warmth of the fire on a rainy day, the scent of a good glass of brandy, my brother playing his violin on Sunday afternoons . . .

As I stepped into the little smoking room I regarded it as one of the most civilized spots in *Edin-bloody-burgh* (as my father calls it) with its dark oak panelling, a small marble fireplace, a fine bearskin rug and three leather armchairs set around a mahogany table that was usually overladen with books, cut-glass tumblers, violin strings and stacks of sheet music.

Elgie, the youngest of the four Frey brothers, was lounging in the chair farthest from the fire, perusing the pages of a shabby tome by Harrison Ainsworth. He was a slender chap about to turn nineteen, although his wide blue eyes and blond curls made him look younger, and everyone in the family seemed to treat him accordingly. Elgie's mother – my father's trollop of a wife – had been appalled when her baby son announced he wished to move to Edinburgh, where he would play first violin at the Royal Lyceum Theatre in the upcoming production of *Macbeth*.

Our father had said he'd rather Elgie played *third triangle in the bloody Whitechapel parish*. I believe the only reason they allowed him to come was my being already here, although at the time I was staying at – it still makes me shudder – Nine-Nails' house.

When it became impossible to share lodgings with Inspector McGray – largely because of his sister's worsening condition – and I secured my current property, I had insisted my brother moved in. I'd alleged that the house was too big for a single tenant, and that he'd be more comfortable here than in rented rooms at the New Club, but in reality I had come to genuinely appreciate Elgie's company. He and my uncle Maurice are the only relatives whose presence I enjoy, and I appreciate them even more after closely witnessing the misfortunes of the McGrays. Now Elgie and I frequently dined together, or I would meet him at the theatre and listen to his rehearsals, and if the weather permitted it we'd walk back home in the evening, talking of everything and nothing in particular.

He'd been looking at the pages with sleepy eyes, but as soon as he saw me he became fully alert.

'So?' he urged. 'What happened? Did they take that girl away?'

'Good evening to you too,' I replied, helping myself to a well-deserved brandy and lounging in my favourite chair. I realized the envelope was still in my hand. I shoved it distractedly into my shirt pocket, still unwilling to read it. 'I thought you'd be practising,' I said, nodding at the abandoned violin and bow by the music stand.

'I know that Sullivan backwards and forwards by now,' he said hurriedly. 'Pray tell me, what did Mr McGray do? Was he very upset?'

'Upset, raging, homicidal . . . I cannot think of a suitably emphatic term.'

'Was the girl screaming when they took her away?'

'Elgie, do not be morbid! It was a very sad scene, but if you must know, she was perfectly calm – her usual self.'

Indeed, after her initial burst of murderous frenzy six years ago, Pansy McGray had become a catatonic creature, completely mute and barely aware of her surroundings. She had thus spent the interim years, until last January, when her condition began to deteriorate steadily.

'Do you still believe,' Elgie began, 'that it was all triggered by . . . ?'

'The Lancashire affair? But of course! The poor girl witnessed a murder, Elgie, and a very shocking one too. It would have been terrifying enough to disturb a sane, stout head; now imagine what it must have been like for a girl whose mind is already unbalanced.' I sighed. 'Yes, Miss McGray must have been shaken to her very core.'

As I spoke, Layton had come in and displayed an assortment of cold meats, cheese, bread and chutneys. His eyes did not even flicker upon the mention of murder or insanity. He simply bowed and quit the room.

Elgie had already dined, but he still helped himself to the best of my cheese. 'Is Mr McGray still of the opinion it is all – witchcraft?'

I could not help but smile at his roguery. 'You could not wait any longer to ask that question, could you?'

'Of course not! The gentlemen at the New Club talk of nothing else these days.'

'I had a chat with Dr Clouston,' I said. The good doctor had appeared at my door a few hours earlier, begging that I helped him talk some sense into McGray – as if I, of all people, were capable of such a thing. I have a very high opinion of the doctor and his entirely professional approach to mental illnesses, so I could not refuse. Since I have some medical training myself, we were able to discuss Pansy's case on our way to the asylum. 'He agrees with my theory,' I told Elgie. 'The girl's mind simply was not able to cope.'

McGray, on the other hand, attributed his sister's relapse to something far more sinister.

'Capital fellow, Dr Clouston,' I said. 'He is taking her by coach.'

'Is he travelling all the way to the Orkneys with her?'

I shushed him, then whispered: '*I told you not to mention that out loud!* Yes. I assume he feared she might have another fit on a moving train. And I was not supposed to tell you where she is going in the first place.'

'Will she spend a long time there?'

'I cannot tell. He might send for her as soon as there are signs of recovery, I suppose.'

And that was the truth. Clouston thought the reclusion in the asylum was the very thing that had been torturing Pansy. Those walls, those corridors, the very people looking after her would be a constant reminder of the terrors she'd seen and heard. She needed a new environment, to be taken away from the distressing memories, and after very careful deliberation Clouston decided to take her to the Orkney Islands. They were as remote as one could conceive of, six miles above the northernmost tip of Scotland, but Dr Clouston had been born there, and now sponsored a small retirement house for the islands' elderly. In the care of his most trusted pupils, Pansy would be well looked after there. And most importantly, she'd be safe – safe even from her own brother's eagerness.

McGray now suspected Pansy's insanity had been caused intentionally – quite understandable after the dreadful Lancashire affair, which I have described in detail elsewhere. Consequently, McGray mistrusted the medical staff and everyone around her: throughout the spring he had showed up in the asylum at ungodly hours demanding to see her, to inspect her room and food, to watch over people preparing her meals and washing her linen . . . Clouston and I discussed those episodes a few times, and we have come to believe that McGray's attitude, though kindly meant, might well have worsened his sister's condition.

Distance, it appeared, would be the best balm for both. Convincing Nine-Nails was, of course, an entirely different matter, and tonight he'd made one last, desperate attempt to talk Dr Clouston out of his plans.

These grim thoughts were lessening my appetite, so I turned my attention to the tray and ate silently for a moment, hearing the torrential rain battering the window.

'We are finally playing *Macbeth*,' Elgie said, also trying to brighten the mood. 'Next week!'

I chuckled. 'Are you sure now? How many times have they postponed the bloody thing?'

'Twice. They were supposed to come on tour in February, and then around Easter.'

Elgie shook his head. He had initially come to Edinburgh to perform in that play, but it seemed that every time the orchestra was ready the production had to be postponed. The first time it had been apparently at the whim of the leading lady, the celebrated Ellen Terry, who did not fancy travelling to Scotland at the end of winter.

The second rescheduling was a little more justified: the theatre company had been summoned by Queen Victoria herself, who had requested a private performance.

The musicians, in the meanwhile, had been kept on for other productions, which had given Elgie the chance to play some beautiful and challenging pieces, but not everyone shared his enthusiasm. Disillusion had been followed by cynicism, and then boredom.

'People are sick of waiting,' Elgie went on. 'They were saying the other day that the play would never happen; that it was all because of the curse of *Macbeth*.'

I sneered, for lately I had been learning plenty about curses.

'Also,' said Elgie, 'three musicians have quit and more than two-thirds of the tickets have been returned. It is a real shame. The music is terrific, and Laurence told me he read some wonderful notices for the performances in London.'

I almost grunted at the mention of my estranged eldest brother.

'Well, I hope they do manage to present it this time,' I said. 'You have worked really hard on those pieces.'

And I knew it too well. I had heard him play 'Chorus of Witches and Spirits' so many times I now hated every single bar.

'It will definitely happen this time, Ian. Mr Irving and Miss Terry must be already in Edinburgh. I heard Mr Wyndham say their train would arrive today. He spent all day boasting very loudly he'd be having luncheon with Miss Terry tomorrow. He will miss the Saturday premiere; he has some conveyancing business out of town, I believe.'

'Well, then you shall finally have your big performance – in just five days! I am sure your mother will be very proud.'

As soon as I said so, Elgie's mouth opened a little, like the beginning of a gasp he had scarcely managed to contain.

I tilted my head. 'Elgie?'

His eyes had suddenly turned sheepish. I knew what was about to happen, but I did not want to pronounce it and thus make it real. I had a sip of brandy instead, and Elgie finally spoke.

'Mother and Father are coming. With our brother Oliver, I presume.'

34

It felt as though the spirit soured in my mouth. I savoured the drink, my jaw and lips tense, trying not to spray the very expensive brandy all over the carpet. I swallowed, and Elgie read the rage in my eyes. His lip was quivering; he was not done.

'And?' I grunted.

'And . . . Well, I told them they were welcome to stay here.'

'*Damn it, Elgie!*'

I jumped up and threw my cheese knife on the plate, crumbs falling all around, and the rattling made Elgie shrink in his chair, very much like a turtle's head retreating into its shell. Right then there was a frantic knocking at the main door, which I barely noticed.

'*Are you completely out of your mind?* Do you want your crazy mother, our cantankerous father – *and me*, all of us under the same roof? It will take five minutes for the house to become a bloody Bosworth Field!'

'Well, I could not invite them and not offer them a room! They would have struggled to find decent lodgings on such short notice!'

I became aware of my dangerously firm grip on the tumbler. I put it on the table before I crushed it.

'And when shall I expect the gentle pair of doves to arrive?' I asked, and Elgie stammered. 'Oh, for goodness' sake, you can hardly tell me anything more shocking.'

'The day after tomorrow. They telegrammed this afternoon.'

I took a few deep breaths, trying to keep myself as composed as the news allowed. Then I spoke through my teeth. 'And for how long are we to be *privileged* with their presence?'

'Well . . . at least a fortni–'

'*Damn it, Elgie!*'

Layton knocked right then.

'*What?*' I yelped.

Layton entered, completely unaffected by my shouting, merely arching one of his eyebrows in puzzlement.

'I do apologize for the interruption. Master Frey, there is a young constable at the door demanding your presence. I may have misheard, but he claims that . . . a *banshee* has been spotted under Regent Bridge.'

I exhaled noisily, feeling utterly spent. 'You have not misheard, Layton. You had better get used to delivering that sort of message.'

2

'Who was the man, again?'

'Some southerner, sir,' said Constable McNair. 'Theatre type. Really odd-looking. Wheatstone, I think he said. Ye'll meet him soon, Inspector.'

'Is Inspector McGray at the scene?'

'Nae, sir. We cannae find him.'

I sighed bitterly as the cab took us east, towards Waterloo Place and the craggy outlines of Calton Hill. Of course, nobody could find Nine-Nails. Not tonight. He would be either crying or drinking his sorrows away in some dreary place. I might have had an idea of where, but preferred not to say just yet – he'd need his solitude.

The rain had not receded, the tempestuous winds hitting the side of the carriage with such strength I thought it would capsize. A reminder of how close we were to the unruly North Sea.

We took a sharp turn to the right and entered Calton Road, which descended steeply south. The cab rattled along the street, which was flanked on both sides by alarmingly tall tenement buildings, all begrimed with soot.

There, ahead of us, was the solid, imposing arch of Regent Bridge, which connected the opulent Princes Street to the harbours, and which ran above the dingy, reeking Calton Road.

The bridge's upper section was decorated with the lavish Greek-style columns that made Waterloo Place such a pleasant promenade. The bottom arch on which they rested, however, was a firm, plain, solely utilitarian structure, as grime-caked as the slums around it. Regent Bridge could not have been a better allegory of the city's upsetting class differences.

As we approached I saw that the road had been closed. Half a dozen police officers stood around a spot under the arch, in the very centre of the road. Most of them carried bright bull's-eye lanterns, silver beams flickering in all directions. A cart, heavily loaded with coal, had stopped in front of them, and an indignant driver was arguing heatedly.

'*Let me through!*' I heard him yell in an almost incomprehensible Glaswegian accent. 'Youse bastards, Ah've a delivery to complete!'

My cab halted right next to him and I jumped down swiftly. I opened my umbrella but it gave me little protection; the wind, funnelled by the high buildings, carried the rain in horizontal swirls all around us. The carter whistled as he saw me wrap my fur-trimmed collar more tightly around my neck. 'The pretty laddie in charge?'

I gave him my fiercest roar. 'Get away! *Now!* Or your sorry bones spend the night in a cell!'

I did not give him time to reply. I turned to the small cluster of policemen and elbowed my way through. One of them was shedding light on the cobbled road.

'What on earth is that?' I asked, my eyes instantly attracted by four crimson stains on the wet stones, which the streams of rain were slowly washing away.

'There was some writing on the road,' one of the chaps told me. 'We tried to save it for yer eyes, Inspector. This is the best we managed.'

'Good job,' I said, but merely as a courtesy. Despite

their efforts, the message was now unintelligible. 'Is it what I think it is?'

'Blood?' McNair said. 'Aye, we think so.'

I kneeled down to inspect. It indeed looked like blood, dark red and more viscous than the water running between the stones of the road. I took off my leather glove and prodded the stain with my little finger, then tasted it with the very tip of my tongue. It had the unmistakable ferric hint of blood. I spat it out at once, a sudden retch reminding me why I had abandoned my career in medicine. I recalled how blood seeps into everything – clothes, skin, porous stone – leaving persistent marks that only vigorous brushing or caustic powders can remove.

'Did anybody take note of it?' I said, rising swiftly and trying to hide my repulsion.

The young officers looked nervously at each other, but McNair jumped in before I had a chance to scold them. 'The weird auld man who found it kept babbling the words.'

'The idiot who claimed it was a banshee?'

'Aye, I'll take ye to him.'

I followed McNair to one of the nearest tenements. We had to walk around the spurts of mucky water that fell furiously from the top of the bridge, spat out by the drains that collected the runoff from the road above our heads. I wondered if that was the destiny of our ever more crowded cities: to become clusters of cheap, claustrophobic dwellings stacked vertically as the land ran out.

We made it to a decayed door that led into a narrow, damp, darkened corridor. There was some light coming through the cracks on a tattered door, upon which McNair knocked.

'Constable?' a woman asked.

'Aye, hen. The inspector's here.'

The door opened and a slender woman received us, wrapped in a ragged shawl and carrying a sleepy toddler swaddled in blankets. She looked to be in her early thirties, around my own age, but her skin was so weather-beaten she seemed a decade older. She had wide, alert eyes that examined me nervously. I felt a twinge of compassion; she seemed the kind of woman who would have been bright and smart and beautiful, had she been born within the right circles.

'Come in,' she said, stepping aside. 'There's yer man.'

I walked into the single-room dwelling. A hard bed, a battered table and two chairs were the only furniture. There was not even a stove or a fireplace, the only light coming from a blackened oil lamp on the table. I saw a – blessedly empty – chamber pot half concealed under the bed, and thought how hard that woman's life must be.

Sitting at the table was a middle-aged man leaning forward, one hand wrapped around a pewter mug and the other pressed against his forehead. He was a short, compact sort of fellow, clearly experiencing a nasty hangover, but other than that he seemed incongruously respectable: he wore an expensive tweed suit and half-moon spectacles, and I noticed the shiny gold chain of a pocket watch. Thick, stiff curls of grey hair grew on each side of his balding head, his overall image reminding me of one of my eccentric professors of anatomy. His hands supported that impression, for his thick, stumpy fingers were dry and calloused.

'I assume you two are not connected,' I said.

The woman shook her head. 'I've never seen him

before. The other peelers asked me to shelter him here while youse arrived. I only went out there to have a look after I heard all the hurly burly.'

The man groaned as she said that.

I sat in front of him. 'What is your name?'

He cleared his throat and massaged his head. 'Wheatstone,' he said, in an undoubtedly upper-class English voice. 'John Wheatstone.'

'Mr Wheatstone,' I said, 'Constable McNair here tells me you claim to have seen a banshee.'

I did not bother to hide my incredulity, and he gave me a bitter look in return.

'Do you want me to lie, Inspector . . . ?'

'Ian Frey.'

'Do you want me to lie, Inspector Frey, simply to avoid your mockery?'

'What makes you think you saw a banshee?' I could certainly guess, given the unpleasant scent of stale alcohol that the man gave off.

I did not get an immediate answer. He hesitated, rubbed his forehead hard and fixed his stare on the greasy table.

'Mr Wheatstone, do you want me to investigate this matter or –'

'I've seen one before!'

His outburst made us all start. The little girl burst into tears and her mother wrapped her more tightly, rocking her in her arms.

Wheatstone snorted. 'Well . . . not *seen*. But heard. Tonight's the first time I've actually laid eyes on one.'

'What did she look like?'

'A petite woman, all covered in white rags – I could not see her face. She was crouching in the middle of the road, washing a nasty bundle of bloody clothes in the street puddles.'

I pondered on those words. Even for the rational mind, someone cleaning up blood is never a good omen.

'I would have thought she was just a beggar, but then I saw she had written those lines on the road . . . and then she let out her cry.'

'Which you recognized, since you have heard a banshee's cry before,' I said, attempting to sound more sympathetic. Unsuccessfully.

Mr Wheatstone arranged his spectacles. 'Inspector, I'm a man of science. I trust my eyes and my ears and my nose. I know what I heard and I'm not the only one.'

He looked at McNair, who took a step forward.

'Quite a few people from along the street have come to us, Inspector Frey,' he said, 'to ask what that scream was. They all described the same thing. Some o' them saw her too, from their windows.'

I nodded. 'So all we know for certain is that there was a shrieking female under the bridge.'

'It didnae sound natural,' the woman said from a corner of the room. She was rocking her daughter rather spasmodically, as if trying to calm herself rather than the child.

'How so?' I asked, seeing the tension grow in her.

'It was drilling in our ears, sir. My poor Josephine was terrified. I've heard wolves' cries, I've heard . . .' she shuddered, 'I've heard folk bein' murdered down these alleys . . . But I've never heard anything like this.'

Mr Wheatstone nodded slowly, casting a dark stare at the sleepy child. Despite their clearly different backgrounds, he and the penniless mother had one thing in common: their intelligent, watchful eyes, glimmering with the same spark of fear.

'Very well, I believe you saw and heard something untoward,' I said, trying to sound as reassuring as possible, 'and it shall be investigated. Mr Wheatstone, can you remember what was written on the road?'

'I scribbled it down when it began to rain again,' he said, producing a small notebook from his inner pocket. He truly must be a man of science, for the small pages were filled with tiny writing and all manner of diagrams. He tore one out. 'Here.'

I folded it neatly and shoved it into my pocket, noticing that Mr Stoker's message from Superintendent Campbell was still there.

'Will you not read it?' asked Mr Wheatstone.

'I have poor eyesight,' I lied, 'but I would like to ask you one more thing before I leave – I need to fetch our specialist on this sort of matter.' I could already see the enthusiasm in McGray's eyes. If anything could bring him out of his depression, it would be this.

'You mentioned this is not the first time you have heard a banshee,' I said. 'Can you elaborate?'

Mr Wheatstone cleared his throat. He explained that he'd worked as an effects expert in the London theatres for the past twenty years, and then told me everything that had happened in the capital but a few days ago, in as much detail as I could take in.

I could not believe my ears.

🪲

Showing my full astonishment, I jotted down Mr Wheatstone's contact details – he was lodging at the Palace Hotel with the rest of the theatre company – and then rushed back to my cab. As my feet splashed in the puddles, I pulled out Campbell's note, which was now very badly crumpled. Fearing that the rain would make it illegible, I tore the envelope open only once I was in my sheltered seat.

'McGray is going to revel in this . . .' I said out loud.

McNair had trotted behind me, rather befuddled. 'Inspector Frey, are ye all right?' he asked, his bony hand resting on the cab's door.

'Indeed,' I replied, stepping out again. The rain was still hard, and I realized that in my haste I had not opened my umbrella. Doing so, I headed back to the lines of blood, now a mere smudge on the road.

'That blood came from somewhere,' I told the officers. 'Try to find any source in the vicinity.'

'D'ye want someone to stay round here?' one of them asked. 'To preserve the writing?'

'No. There is nothing you can do about that any more.' I turned on my heels, McNair following my every step. 'Take some statements from the neighbours,' I told him, 'the ones who appear more sensible to you. And if those chaps find anything of use, either bring it to the City Chambers or fetch me from Great King Street.'

'Aye, sir. May I ask . . . where are ye heading?'

I hopped on to the cab as I spoke. 'To find Inspector McGray, I know exactly where he will be.'

3

The Ensign Ewart was a dire public house, a few hundred yards from Castle Rock.

The rain was lashing its weatherworn sign, the wind flapping it violently as my carriage approached. Despite the hour – now well past midnight – the place was a lively hive: all its windows lit up, the shadows of many merry customers visible through the steamed-up glass, loud music and roaring laughter coming from within.

'Shall I wait for ye, master?' the driver asked me.

'Yes, please, and not too far away,' I replied as I stepped in, eager to escape the downpour.

As soon as I opened the door a blast of damp heat and human stench hit me, almost as solid as a wall. The frantic notes of a flat fiddle and a bagpipe led the steps of a dozen drunken dancers, while a chubby woman, as ginger as a ripened carrot, passed around refilling their tankards.

'*Madam!*' I called, forced to shout amongst the music and cheering. '*Madam!* Is Mr McGray here?'

'Eh?'

I repeated my question.

'Och, aye! But I wouldnae trouble him tonight, if I were ye!'

'I shall take my chances.'

'Eh?'

'Never mind.'

I had to elbow my way forwards, the dancers hitting me as they dashed about in their clumsy dosey-does. A drunken man tripped and spilled half a pint on my chest.

'What an appalling display of debauchery,' I grumbled, wiping the drink away with my gloved hands.

I found McGray rather easily, for it was not a large establishment. He was sitting in a corner, away from the crowd, his boots up on the small table and his fingers interlaced, in deep thought. In that pose the stump of his missing finger was all too evident.

There was a large bottle of whisky on the table, some of it poured into a greasy glass, but from its level I judged McGray had not taken more than a few swigs.

He'd always been a far from immaculate gentleman: his jaw was ever shadowed with unkempt stubble, his dark hair was messy and peppered with premature grey strands, and I could devote many a paragraph to his tasteless choice of tartan clothing. His broad shoulders and thick wrists were a warning of his fiery temper; if he rose to his full height and spoke at his full volume, he could be genuinely frightening.

Tonight, however, he showed none of that spirit. His blue eyes were lost, looking at nothing, with an empty stare that very much reminded me of the eternal expression on his sister's face. He seemed utterly broken, completely out of faith, and it affected me far more than I expected.

I cleared my throat.

'How now, Nine-Nails.'

He barely moved his pupils, studying me for a moment, and when he spoke his lips barely moved. 'Sod off.'

'May I have a word?'

'I said *sod off.*'

Another drunken lowlife crashed against me, but instead of apologizing he put his sticky arm around my shoulders in the most disgustingly familiar fashion. As he raised his limb an overpowering waft of body odour nearly brought tears to my eyes.

'Och, don't ye upset Nine-Nails McGree!' he cried, spitting with every consonant.

'Move your slimy tentacle away,' I snapped. 'I am CID.'

'He works fer ye?' he asked McGray, who did not even attempt a reply. 'Helps ye hunt spooks?'

The drunkard stumbled towards Nine-Nails, the contents of his pint glass slopping on the table. Had he been a slightly less annoying man, I would have warned him he was stepping on to a hornet's nest; tonight I was only sorry I had no cigars to enjoy the spectacle. And I was not the only one who thought so; some of the less intoxicated dancers were already craning their necks to have a peek.

'Oi, are ye deaf today?' the brown-toothed man asked after McGray's silence, but nobody in his senses would think his impertinence had gone unheard. Nine-Nails was glaring at him, his eyes burning with uncontainable rage.

'Another mute McGree!' the drunkard cried. 'Och, what d'we have to do to make a crazy McGree speak?'

In a startling move, as swift as a chameleon's tongue, McGray thrust forth his hand and grabbed the man by the face. His four nails – he was using his maimed hand – dug into the wretch's skin so deeply I thought he'd puncture it. The man howled in dread as if all the alcohol had suddenly deserted his blood, his pint smashing on the floor.

There was a general cry, the fiddler stopped and the dancers halted; all their eyes on McGray. A dying note from the bagpipe was all that could be heard, as the instrument slowly deflated in the hands of the embarrassed player.

'Say yer sorry, laddie,' said McGray.

The man's yelping had not stopped, and he was throwing blows about. McGray shook him, as one shakes a matchbox to hear if it is empty.

'Come on,' he said, sounding rather bored. 'Just say yer sorry.'

If anything, the drunk grunted something that sounded like 'lemme go'. McGray sighed with the resignation of a grandfather disturbed by little children, and stood up, never letting go of the man's skull.

'To beat or not to beat ye,' he said as he dragged him across the pub, '*that* is the fucking question.'

People scurried out of Nine-Nails' way, and someone even opened the main door for him to throw the drunkard out.

A few people clapped and cheered – the rascal must have been annoying more than one – but when McGray turned his head back everyone went silent. His heavy steps resounded amidst the tense hush, until he sat back at the exact same spot I'd found him. Not really regarding anybody around him, he interlaced his hands once more.

The strident, even more off-key notes of the fiddle broke the silence, making some people jump, and in a moment most of the customers were dancing as merrily as if nothing had happened.

There was a chair near McGray's table, all splattered with ale. I wiped it thoroughly with a handkerchief which

48

I then threw away – I seemed to do that every time I set foot in that pub – and as I sat down, the ginger landlady came around.

'Adolphus, I'm so sorry ye had to –'

McGray waved a hand dismissively, sparing a rather affectionate glance at the plump woman.

'Here, share a dram with yer friend.' And she banged another greasy tumbler on the table. I picked it up, touching it with only the very tips of my fingers, and then produced a second handkerchief to wipe the glass methodically.

'The ethanol will sterilize it, I suppose,' I mumbled to myself, thinking I'd rather boil the thing.

'What the hell brings ye here?' McGray asked. 'I s'pose yer not here for the drams – or for the pleasure o' my company.'

'Of course not,' I replied, sniffing suspiciously at the whisky. 'I have not yet forgiven you for that incident in the Forest of Bowland . . .'

As I said that I felt the bridge of my nose – it had looked slightly crooked since that ghastly January in Lancashire. I shook my head, casting those thoughts aside, and had a cautious sip. 'Mmm! This is not bad Not bad at all.'

'Course it's bloody damn good. It's from one o' my auld man's distilleries.'

Knowing the tragic fate of his late father, the unabashed pride in McGray's voice was poignant to say the least.

I relished the notes of oak and vanilla, and the fiery warmth as I swallowed the drink. I was now ready for business.

'Ironic that you should misquote Hamlet tonight,' I said. 'Campbell has some Shakespearean work for us. He has called specifically for you and your ... singular talents.'

'Campbell can sod off too.'

'This appears to be a rather fanciful assignment; one I am sure you will enjoy. And you could definitely use some distraction.'

McGray said nothing, which I took as invitation enough to continue.

'As it turns out, a ...' I bit my lip, hearing my next words in my head and then saying them with as much conviction as possible. 'A banshee has been spotted under Regent Bridge.'

For a brief moment there was no reaction, and I could not tell whether my words had been lost under the raucous music.

Very, very sluggishly, McGray's pupils moved in my direction. He would not speak, but again his silence was the only cue I needed.

'Apparently, everyone along Calton Road heard her, and a few claim to have seen her. All their statements match. However, that is by no means the most intriguing part.'

I consciously stopped there, attempting to tease his curiosity. The racket of the dancers was beginning to wear my patience thin.

'I'm listening,' he said after a moment, a shadow of his former self beginning to alight in his stare. I had to dig my nails into my thigh to repress a triumphant grin.

'Another banshee was allegedly heard in a London theatre about a week ago,' I went on, 'under similar circumstances: many people heard the cry and they all agreed on its "eerie" nature. Tonight, unlike last week, there are eyewitnesses who claim it was a woman in white, crying the same sort of lament. And these banshees left threatening messages, both written in blood.'

I finally had McGray's undivided attention.

'What sort o' messages?' he slowly reached for his drink.

I did not repress my sly smile any more, as I produced the two notes and flung them across the table. 'Something very fitting for the play on stage.'

McGray stretched his arm so suddenly I flinched, thinking he was going to punch me, but he simply seized the sheets. I could see his eyes devouring the words I had already memorized, his pupils running from side to side as quick as the reeling notes of the violin.

'Interested?'

He raised his gaze, and I could tell that at least part of him was back.

'Very.'

Original note handed over by William A. Wheatstone

Filed by I. P. Frey.

29 JUNE OMEN

Added by the eyewitness at my request

All hail! These tragic marks await Macbeth
All hail! The Scottish stage shall see your death

9 JULY OMEN

On the night the blood runs thick and freely
Some fiend here comes, replete with too much rage
Announcing death and doom and infamy
Like a poor player, sentenced on the stage

4

Defying all reasonable odds, all expectations and all common sense – Edinburgh was sunny the following morning.

It instantly improved my mood, and I may even have whistled a Mozart's minuet while putting on my cufflinks.

The delicious aroma of coffee welcomed me into the small breakfast parlour, where Elgie was already helping himself to jam and toast. I consciously avoided mentioning the banshees and the threatening notes linked to the very play for which he was rehearsing, although I knew I could not protect him for long; by now people would be talking of nothing else.

'Would you like to see today's papers, sir?' Layton asked.

I was about to say no, for I had to make my way to the City Chambers as soon as possible. As I turned to him, however, I saw the newspapers already in his hand, and *The Scotsman*'s garish headline screaming:

MACBETH'S CURSE ON HENRY IRVING!!!
Cryptic Prophecies Loom over his Lavish Production

My jaw dropped and I did not even register what Layton said next. I must have read the long article in a flash, my eyes widening as the paper described the previous night's events in striking detail.

'How could they know all of this?' I looked up, my eyes fixed on the blue sky as the events arranged themselves in my head. Then I smirked. 'Of course! I should have known better!' I rose to my feet swiftly. 'Layton, my coat.'

'Right away, sir.'

As I readied myself I thought I would probably have the whole matter sorted before lunchtime. McGray was going to be so disappointed.

Philippa, my snow-white Bavarian mare, seemed to rejoice in the sunny morning as I rode towards the Old Town. Princes Street Gardens were a carpet of bright green grass and leafy chestnuts, their gentle canopies bordering the craggy drops of Castle Rock.

Unfortunately, the joy did not last. As soon as I approached the narrow, crowded Royal Mile, the stench of a myriad puddles and sewers, gone septic under the full sun, hit my sensitive nostrils.

In what has become a tradition, I dodged the contents of a few chamber pots being emptied on to the road, their nasty contents jettisoned from the tall tenements on either side of the street. This was, of course, illegal, but it was impossible to enforce the law: with fourteen-storey buildings, where everyone blamed everyone else, it was impossible to track the source of each discharge of filth.

I spurred Philippa on and thankfully she took me to the City Chambers in no time at all.

As if trying to outdo the messy road, our so-called office was one of the most depressing spots in the police headquarters. An old cellar, deep underneath the Royal Mile, was the only space the CID was willing to spare for McGray's hokum. It was a moth-infested, damp-plagued pit, which I endearingly called 'the dumping ground', thinking of what my present post was doing to my career.

To make the place even grimmer, McGray had recently told me that our office might be just a wall apart from the buried remains of Mary King's Close. Centuries ago people infected with the bubonic plague were thrown there and walled up alive in order to contain the outbreak. Legends about their ghosts abounded, particularly amongst the officers who had to do night shifts. I had once caught McGray listening at the walls with a stethoscope.

My mind engaged in such thoughts, I started as the grotesque face of a monster received me. McGray had been recently sent a large Peruvian sculpture, and he'd planted it right by the entrance, for there was little space left in the room: the place was overflowing with countless books, amulets, formaldehyde jars containing horrendous things, along with all manner of odd artefacts. Everything was crammed on unstable shelves or teetering in precariously balanced towers. Last month I had tried to put some order into the room, but McGray threw an epic tantrum, telling me he could no longer find anything. Indeed, he somehow knew the precise location of each book, specimen or sheet of paper in that chaos.

I found him already there, part of me glad he was back at work, part of me already bored by his obsession.

Standing by one of the tallest piles of books, he was holding an ancient tome in one hand. In the other he had the thickest sandwich I'd seen in a while, bits of bacon and fried egg sticking out, all wrapped in a sheet of newspaper now drenched in fat.

'Yer late,' he said, his mouth so full of food I had to guess the words.

'No, McGray, you are early.'

'I don't sleep much, ye ken that. Thought I'd come and do some reading on banshees. I don't have much literature about . . . Wait, why are ye looking so bleeding cocky?'

My deformed reflection on a formaldehyde jar informed me I was smiling in my most contemptuous way. I tried to control my features while tossing *The Scotsman* before McGray.

He frowned, put his dusty book down and picked up the paper.

'Those laddies are quick!' He read through the article at staggering speed. 'Is this shite accurate? Ye were there last night.'

'Accurate to the last word. They even mention the exact writing that Mr Wheatstone scribbled down.'

McGray arched an eyebrow. 'Might've been a whistle-blower in our lines? Which officers were there?'

I shook my head. 'McNair, Millar and a few of their chaps. I doubt the story leaked through any of them. I know them by now, and they have seen far stranger, far juicier stories.'

'Yer still grinning.'

'Yes. Do you not see why?'

He took a huge bite before speaking, bits of egg yolk spurting on to my collar. 'Another smug remark like that and I'll break yer legs.'

I thought I'd better get to the point. 'McGray, this is all a very predictable, very convenient publicity stunt.'

I was expecting McGray to smack me in the face with his fried eggs and bacon, and then defend most passionately the theory of a banshee visiting from the netherworld to announce impending doom.

He did not, however. He chewed on, pensively looking at the headline, and his frown deepened.

'Aye, ye might be right.'

I blinked, utterly confused. Then again, even McGray refused cases from time to time, like the one of the stout lady who'd come two months ago claiming a poltergeist was stealing lard from her pantry – and the lady was *very* stout.

'Did . . . did I just hear . . . you say I might be right?'

Very carefully, very neatly, McGray folded the paper in half, and then in half again, and then rolled it firmly and used it to bat the top of my head. 'Aye. *Might.*'

I grunted in frustration, telling myself I should be used to all this by now.

'Nine-Nails, this is bloody obvious. Only last night Elgie was telling me about the poor sales of this play. He told me it has been postponed twice. People are angry, and according to Elgie more than two-thirds of the tickets have been returned.'

McGray looked at the rolled-up paper. 'So they're creating a wee bit o' scandal and telling the papers themselves?'

'Precisely; a little supernatural touch for a play that is already reputed to be cursed. Make people believe something sinister might happen and that will guarantee a morbid crowd queueing to see.'

I could almost see reason creeping into McGray's mind, and then his enthusiasm leaving him, like air from a punctured balloon. Without a case to occupy his thoughts he'd probably go back to his depressive state, and all of a sudden the softer side of me regretted my haste in convincing him it was all a hoax. I thus have mixed feelings as to what happened next.

I heard a tapping coming from the steps behind the office door: the instantly recognizable sound of Superintendent Campbell's walking stick. In the police headquarters that sound was more effective than a bell tied to a cat's neck.

The man pushed the door open, looking furiously at us. With his bushy mane and beard, I have always thought of him as a wild, grey lion, and that morning he did not disappoint. His vicious eyes and his gnashing teeth were as eloquent as his very presence down here, for the head of Edinburgh's police force had never ventured into our Dumping Ground before. I was about to ask mockingly to what we owed the honour of his visit, but McGray took a slightly more direct approach.

'What the fuck ye want?'

Campbell took a little step back, surely reminded of the time McGray had punched and half-strangled him – something I had witnessed from mere inches away. After that the superintendent's face had bruised awfully, and stayed purple for so long everyone now called him Peach-Skin Campbell.

'Watch your mouth, McGray!' he roared, regaining his ground. He looked around with a disgusted, yet not surprised stare; our office must look exactly as he had imagined it. 'I sent you direct orders last night, only to find that your English secretary sent Mr Stoker away!'

'Sir,' I said, 'with all due respect, I am not a secre—'

'*Shush, Frey!* I'm sick of your stupid English pomposity. Mr Stoker says you didn't even read my blasted note!'

As he spoke, Mr Stoker himself came in, his full ginger beard the first thing that caught my eyes. I'd not looked at him with much attention the night before, but even if I had I would have never guessed he was a theatre manager: tall, brawny and solidly built, he rather looked like a rugby player. His eyes, a little too close together, had an air of benevolence, even of slight fright at Campbell's shouting.

'I see you two have read *The Scotsman*,' Campbell said, pointing at the roll of pages in McGray's hand.

'Sir, McGray and I were just discussing the implications of —'

'*I said shush, Frey!* I did not think much of these ridiculous apparitions' — Mr Stoker seemed quite offended — 'but now that it's all gone to the press we have to look as if we're doing something — justify the bloody budget of this damned department for once!'

'Aye, yer vast budget!' McGray ruminated. It was no secret that he funded most of the investigations himself. The large collection of ancient books and his many 'research trips', for instance, had all come from his own pocket.

'If you're unhappy, pack up your rubbish and leave,' said Campbell. 'In the meantime, you'd better attend to this case as a matter of urgency. These are murder threats. I don't want the press crying we won't get involved.'

'If we do get involved,' I said, rushing the words before

Campbell hushed me again, 'we only will be implying we think these apparitions are legitimate.'

'You too are welcome to go to hell if you don't like my orders,' Campbell snarled. 'And make sure the door doesn't hit your royal English arse when you leave.' He turned on his feet and barked at Mr Stoker. 'These blithering idiots will hear you now. Come to me if they don't.'

First letter from the partially burned stack found at Calton Hill

All letters undated. Their placement along the narrative is conjectural. – I. P. Frey.

My dear,

I am so sorry things couldn't go as planned!

But I left them presents. Something wicked you did not intend, but I am sure it would have gone with your blessing.

I wish you could have felt the silky blood on your fingers. Oh yes. I wish 'I' had seen their faces writhing in disgust, but then that scream – [charred fragment, illegible]

Oh my dear, how they have wronged us! Your heart shattered and my bones broken. Your dreams wrecked and my insides forever flayed.

But my dear, I am glad, I confess. I am glad it all failed just now, for it means I will have plenty more chances to see you again before the inevitable end.

We shall meet again, my dear, as soon as my stupor has worn off, and I confess – yes! – I confess I will try, again, to make you change your mind.

Love,
X

5

'Is this . . . the department assigned to the investigation?' Stoker asked, casting a dubious stare at the dusty witch-craft books and the little sepia monsters floating in formaldehyde.

McGray took the hint. 'Aye. Like Campbell said, if ye don't like it ye can sod off.'

'Mr Stoker,' I said, 'what did you expect? You are asking the police to investigate threats from banshees.'

He tensed his lips. By now he must have really disliked me.

'Have a seat,' I offered. 'Mr Stoker, the first thing I want to know is how on earth the papers heard about yesterday's sighting in such exquisite detail.'

Stoker chuckled. 'I came to ask you the same thing. It must have come from one of your officers, surely.'

McGray raised a hand before I scolded the Irishman.

'Nae, laddie. Our boys are beyond suspicion. It must have leaked through *yer own* side.'

'Well, that cannot be! I didn't know anything about it 'til today. I had it from Mr Wheatstone himself over breakfast. He mentioned *you*, Inspector, and pretty much every word the newspapers reported. But he returned to the hotel right after the incident.'

I nodded. 'Did he mention he was quite intoxicated when he strolled around Regent Bridge?' Stoker's eyes opened in bewilderment. 'I guessed not; a very convenient detail to omit, just like disclosing the entire matter to a bloody reporter.'

'You are speculating.'

'Perhaps, but a quick questioning will clarify it all. See, Mr Stoker, we believe these banshee apparitions are a little too convenient, given your plummeting ticket sales.'

That left Stoker open-mouthed. 'How – how do you know that?'

'Doesnae matter now,' McGray jumped in. 'How d'ye think this scandal will affect yer numbers?'

Stoker stammered, his chest swollen. 'I . . . I had not given a thought to that!'

'Had you not?' I probed.

'Of course not!' Stoker leaned forward. 'Everyone in the theatre heard the cry, Inspector. And two people told me they were certain it was a banshee – that they could swear it on the Bible. One of them was our most reliable seamstress; the second was – well, Irving himself!'

'In that case,' I said with a half-smile, 'what precisely do you want us to do, Mr Stoker? Execute the banshee or just incarcerate her?'

'I beg you stop insulting me! I am an educated man! I have an honours degree from Trinity College in Dublin. I have worked and written pamphlets on public service. I have published literature: *Under the Sunset*, *The Primrose Path* . . .'

I chuckled. 'Well, I have never heard of those, so they cannot be any good.'

That made him explode.

'Gentlemen, I came to the police for *help*!' He rubbed his face with both hands, forcing himself back into composure. 'There might be people in danger – people I care for most dearly. If you don't want to help me I don't know what else to do!' Prone to melodrama as the Irish can be, Stoker's distress seemed genuine.

McGray approached him and patted him brusquely on the back. 'There, there, laddie. As much as I like the odd banshee story, I can tell something else is worrying ye. Am I right?'

Stoker struggled to swallow.

'Yes . . .' he said in a whisper and then cleared his throat. 'There are two other very ugly matters I must tell you. Horrible things the press doesn't know yet.'

He was so anxious I could not mock him again. 'Yes?'

Stoker gathered breath. 'Our leading lady, Miss Ellen Terry, might be in great danger.'

'Brains?' I said, almost feeling a foul taste in my mouth.

'Indeed, Inspector. Sheep brains. She found them at the exact same time the banshee cry was heard.'

McGray stopped chewing, lifted his face, and I saw his pupils slowly roll sideways, like he does when his mind works at full speed. He jumped from his seat and went straight to one of his quackery books.

'Why did you not report that to the London police?' I asked. 'If Miss Terry is being stalked, this should have been taken to a proper CID department, not our sad little basement.'

'She insisted, most emphatically, that I told nobody. Not even Mr Irving knows about this yet.'

'How so?'

'Miss Terry feared that the news would trickle through the press and she doesn't want to upset her children. They are studying in Germany, and if this reaches them they'd be distraught.'

I instantly remembered my stepmother's indignant voice, remarking how Britain's beloved 'Miss' Terry was in fact twice a divorcee, and also had a son and a daughter out of wedlock. Shocking.

'That was a reckless decision,' I remarked.

'Indeed,' said Stoker, 'but we never thought the nightmare would follow us here. I convinced her that the police needed to know now. Thankfully, this second banshee didn't bring any more little presents for her.'

I nodded. 'Do you suspect anyone, Mr Stoker? Can you think of anyone with privileged access to Miss Terry's dressing room?'

'I'm afraid not. It's purposely out of the way – for her privacy. People do try to sneak in with flowers or letters, but we always spot them. There are, of course, some corridors that could be used to gain access unseen, but only people who know the theatre like the back of their hand could . . . could have . . .'

Like McGray, Stoker looked sideways, as if having a sudden realization.

'What is it?' I asked.

'Well . . . I was about to tell you: I found one of the doors to the backstreet wide open. There was a trail of blood, and then I saw the d–' His eyes went down all of a sudden and the man bit his lip. His next statement, however, distracted me altogether: 'But I've just remembered . . . somebody had been in that corridor only minutes before . . . and had turned all the lights off!'

'Do you know who?'

'Indeed. And you know the man already. It was Mr Wheatstone.'

McGray came by right then, holding a very thick, very dusty tome. 'Laddie, regarding banshees –'

'*Oh, not now, Nine-Nails!*' I shrieked. 'Mr Stoker, have you said Wheatstone? The very man I suspect told the press?'

'Yes, Inspector. But . . . but then he couldn't have written the message . . . He might have gone down that corridor in the darkness – he manages explosives, you see – but he spent the rest of the play in plain sight. This is a very complex production with all manner of visual effects; Mr Wheatstone coordinates an entire team who would have noticed his absence.'

'I definitely want to question him again,' I said. 'He might have had an accomplice. At least now we know there is an entry point through which the blood and brains –'

'Can I speak now, yer royal bloody majesty?' McGray said.

I snorted. 'If you must . . .'

'Mr Stoker, going back to banshees, ye, of course, are as Irish as a poorly rhymed limerick . . .'

I laughed out loud. 'Said by Nine-Nails McPorridge.'

'Och, shut it, Hairy-Back Mary.' He looked back at Stoker. 'I believe banshees are only s'pposed to announce the death of the most ancient Irish families. Isn't that true?'

Stoker opened his mouth slightly, as if to say something, but then he looked at me (I was rolling my eyes in utter disbelief) and only nodded.

'Now,' said McGray, 'can ye think of any other person in the theatre who might be of Irish descent?'

Stoker whistled. 'Lord, I would need to go through my books. There are plenty! Miss Terry's father is a son of Irish immigrants. Mr Howard – Edinburgh's theatre manager – is from Ireland. A couple of seamstresses, one of the ladies playing the Weird Sisters . . . My – myself . . . I hadn't paid much attention 'til now, but this play is packed with Irish blood.'

Again I chuckled. 'Mr Stoker, *the world* has been packed with Irish blood since the potato famine.'

McGray's eyes had opened wide.

'Mr Stoker,' he said in an undertone, 'd'ye mind if I have a private word with my sorry excuse of a colleague?'

As soon as Mr Stoker stepped out McGray grinned like a little boy.

'Ye almost convinced me to drop this, Frey. But now I think there might be more to it . . .'

'*More to it!*'

'Indeedy. And those brains really worry me. Didnae ye hear Miss Terry is Irish too?'

'I did, Nine-Nails, and a sadistic stalker is indeed a matter of concern, but it also proves that when these people want to keep things quiet – they *keep* them quiet. Unlike this bloody clamour about the banshees, which was clearly orchestrated by people who know very well how to mount a good show.'

'Ye think ye can prove it?'

'I will bloody well do! I bet I'll only need to question a couple of dim-witted actors and stagehands to find out who is behind this limp masquerade.'

McGray closed the book in a swift thump, a cloud of dust bursting towards my face. 'I might take that bet. See if yer wits are worth yer bloody mouth.'

I cast him a derisive look. 'What could you possibly stake that I might want?'

It was indeed a difficult question and it took McGray a rather long moment to answer. 'What about ten years' supply o' my dad's single malt? And it'll *really* bleed me. I ken how much ye drink.'

'Ten years!' I said, not believing my luck. 'It does sound tempting.'

'But if ye cannae find an explanation,' McGray said, 'I'll keep yer Bavarian mare.'

I felt a twinge. '*Philippa!* Are you mad?'

'Well, if yer not so sure about yer theories . . .'

'Bloody hell I am sure,' I cried with blind obstinacy, and then I stood up and stretched a hand. 'Let us shake on it. It will be the easiest winnings of my life.'

I instantly regretted my impulse, for McGray squeezed my hand so mightily I heard my phalanges crack.

Nine-Nails did not have time to mock me though. McNair knocked at the half-open door and came in like a gust of wind.

'Sirs, some o' the lads found this thing near Regent Bridge.' He held up a large leather bag, the material old and cracked, covered in all manner of dirt. What caught our eyes, however, was a filthy rag sticking out and soaked in something dark red. 'It was in a ditch on the side of Calton Hill. Not a hundred yards from the scene.'

I let out my most earnest '*Ha!*' and headed to the door. 'I am already savouring that whisky, Nine-Nails.'

He had snatched the bag and was inspecting the blood-stained cloth but an inch from his face. 'This proves nothing yet. This could've been – Where the hell are ye going? This needs examination!'

'To the theatre, of course.'

'I thought ye'd be running with this to our mortician.'

'To what purpose? I already know there is blood there. Dr Reed will not be able to tell you much more.'

'We might find out where the rags and bag came –'

I did not hear the rest. I was already rushing through the corridor, where Bram Stoker cast me a befuddled look.

'Will you keep me informed, Inspector?' he pleaded after I babbled where I was heading to.

'Of course. If I find anything conclusive you shall be' – I glanced at McGray's door – 'the *second* person to know.'

Bram Stoker's Journal

10 July, 2 p.m. – *Can finally get brief rest and record this morning's events.*
Found Mr Wheatstone at the breakfast parlour, where he told me all that took place last night. Immediately rushed to the police headquarters [. . .]

Note by I. P. Frey: I have omitted Mr Stoker's account of our first meeting in order to avoid repetition (and some unnecessarily punitive remarks he may have penned about my character).

[. . .]

After Frey left, Insp. McGray allowed me to follow to the morgue. Of great interest to me; I had pressing business at the theatre, but thought I could spare an hour or two. I took copious notes – might be useful for future story.
The inspector asked me what we use in the theatre to resemble blood (have spent the best part of my life attempting to modulate my regional lilt, yet this man appeared to show it off with pride). Told him we use lightly diluted corn syrup for consistency, dyed with cochineal powder – washes very easily from the costumes. Old trick; otherwise we'd have to buy new garments for each performance.
The inspector at once dabbed some of the horrible substance on

his fingertip and quite nonchalantly had a taste of it. Said
he was absolutely sure that it was not syrup.

I noticed his missing finger. Decided not to ask.

A few notes on the morgue: air cold, with a chemical scent and
the disturbingly acrid whiff one might find at a butcher's.
Tiled walls were jaded, the general feeling the room inspired
was bleakness.

A very, very young doctor attended on us – blond, childish
features, ungainly. Inspector McGray introduced me. The
young pathologist said plainly he was glad Inspector Frey
wasn't around – I agreed and the young man smiled at me.

Young chap, very accommodating; took a smear from the cloth
and examined it under a small brass microscope. I remem-
ber his remark: 'This is definitely blood, sir; I can see the
cells clearly. But I'd need to be God to tell you whether it's
animal or human.'

Told them I knew it had to be real blood, just like the puddle
we found on the London stage – we couldn't wash it off the
scenery.

Told them how efficient Mr Harker had been at repainting the
canvases just in time for our tour.

Doctor and inspector were a little surprised when I asked if I
could have a look at the microscope, but they obliged. I spent
a couple of minutes marvelling at the little globules of blood
cells floating under the lens. Blood itself is a yellowish liquid.
It is the millions of little cells that give it its red colour!

Inspector McGray asked to spread the bag's contents. Dr Reed
did so, on a clean mortuary table. The splatter of the wet
material when the two men stretched it out – repulsive.

The cloth was a long, rectangular sheet, only a little larger
than the table itself.

Inspector McGray ventured it might be bed linen, and began looking meticulously at the weaving and the turn-up stitches.

I asked him what he might be looking for. He said there might be some initials embroidered, or a merchant's name. He said it was good linen. Expensive.

Unfortunately, there were no revealing marks at all. He asked for scissors and cut out a small snippet from a corner. Put it in his pocket, blood and all.

He also looked at the inside of the bag – thoroughly soaked in blood. Said it looked like someone had used it to carry the blood to do the writing. 'Like a wine boot. Then they had to get rid of the thing. Nobody wants to be caught with such damning evidence.'

I asked him if he now thought it was all faux. His response made me laugh:

'Can't rule it out. But don't you dare tell that [censored by I. P. Frey] *Londoner I ever said that.'*

The Insp. scrutinized the bag. Found a little merchant's stamp in a corner. It seemed very 'upper-class-wifey' acc. to him. The young doctor said his fiancée was a keen shopper and might know the manufacturer.

The Insp. also asked the doctor to find something to wrap the bag and sheet, something that could withstand a trip across the city. Said he was taking it to the premises of some 'madam'. I asked him where he was going and he grinned. 'Have you ever met a gypsy clairvoyant?'

Side note by I. P. Frey:

Dear, oh dear . . .

6

The day being so bright and warm, I'd headed to the theatre by foot, utterly enjoying the walk along the southern cliffs of Castle Rock. Looking up to its jagged stones covered in moss and ivy, and the ancient castle walls rising higher above, I fancied myself promenading along the same heaths once trodden by Macbeth. The illusion was broken by the rumble of a steam engine; I looked down and saw the locomotive disappear into the tunnel that ran under the graveyard of St Cuthbert's Church. I could not help picturing the dust inside the buried coffins, disturbed every time a train passed underneath the tombs. How could the dead find rest in such a rickety place? I shook my head – the day was far too nice for such morbid thoughts – and taking the next turn I reached my destination.

The Royal Lyceum Theatre – named after Henry Irving's own venue in London – was a very pleasing, sumptuous building on Grindlay Street, just one street south-west of Edinburgh's Castle and a few steps from the enduring eyesore that was the provisional Caledonian Station. The theatre had opened only six years ago, so the smut of Edinburgh's countless chimneys had not yet stained its stucco walls, and the snow-white façade even hurt my eyes under the summer sun. The place was already a bedlam.

There must have been at least a hundred people clustering

around the ticket windows, shouting, elbowing and shoving each other, all in a frantic attempt to reach the two poor cashiers. I saw Scottish banknotes being waved in the air, hats flying off heads and being trampled on, as well as jackets and shawls being pulled and torn. A lady pushed her way out of the crowd, clutching her precious tickets to her chest; her face was flushed and her hat dangled by a half-undone lace. She grinned at me. 'Och, ye better hurry, sir! They only have some gallery tickets left! My lady's goin' to be thrilled I got her the last circle seats.'

I nodded politely and marched ahead, thinking that the banshees were certainly serving the theatre well.

I saw a young man standing just a few yards apart from the crowd, scribbling frantically in a small notebook. He had sunken cheeks, his neck was as thin as a pencil, his head slightly too big for his narrow shoulders, and his black moustache was so stiff with grease it looked like two solid spikes. Our eyes met for an instant, and I immediately realized he was a blasted reporter.

I looked away at once, suddenly irritated by the puerile scandal, and stepped briskly into the silence of the main foyer.

A very polite porter came by. I showed my credentials and he rushed to fetch one of the two theatre managers, a Mr Howard.

As I waited I was surprised to see Elgie, coming from one of the back doors and holding a kitchen cloth. His already pale skin seemed even whiter, except for his neck, which was quite chafed from playing the violin too hard.

'Ian! Have you heard about . . . ?'

'The banshee? Of course. That is why I am here.'

'People were showing around the newspapers,' he

whispered. 'There have been threats. Blood messages saying someone will die, but not telling who. It is quite frightening.'

It was only natural he'd be so alarmed. I will not delve into the detail here, but my poor brother had already witnessed horrible things in Edinburgh. I thought I'd better not mention the bundle of brains.

'Elgie, I am here to demonstrate it is all nonsense, and it will all become clear very soon. This will be by far the quickest case in my entire career.' I now cringe at my own foolishness. To change the subject, I asked, 'Have you been playing without your cloth? Your neck looks ghastly.'

'Yes. I left my neckerchief at home. I had to borrow this from Mr Howard's cook.'

Catherine, his mother, still protested about Elgie's chosen instrument. She had allowed him to take lessons only under the strict condition that he always protected his skin, horrified that the violin could mark her little son's neck.

'I have to go back,' he said hurriedly. 'Will I see you for dinner?'

'Certainly,' I said, trusting the entire investigation would be over by then, and Elgie rushed away.

He crossed paths with a man whom, unlike Mr Stoker, I instantly recognized as the theatre manager. Short, medium-built and on the last brink of his forties, he looked quite the businessman: cleanly shaven and sporting an impeccable three-piece suit. He carried pronounced bags under his eyes, surely after countless nights looking over his ledgers.

'Inspector, thank you for coming! Mr John Howard, at your service.' He spoke in a sprightly manner, although I could tell the man conducted himself with calculated, well-rehearsed joviality. As Stoker had mentioned, Mr Howard was Irish, but with a much softer accent than his countryman. 'I assume you're here to investigate the – erm, the sightings?'

'Quite correct, Mr Howard. I am Inspector Frey.'

He led me through a delightful rotunda with polished marble floors, which a young girl was mopping at the time, and then on to the first floor. Mr Howard opened an oaken door that led to his wide, elegant office.

I saw that the adjacent door had a little plaque that read w. p. wyndham. I remembered Elgie mentioning that name. 'Is that your associate's office?'

'Indeed, but I'm afraid you'll not see him. He is attending some urgent business' – lunching with Miss Terry, I thought, remembering Elgie's words last night – 'and tonight he is to travel.'

'Is he? I would expect him to be keen to oversee the play.'

'You see, the theatre was not supposed to be open. We had to rearrange the entire month's schedule to accommodate this staging. Last week was supposed to be the beginning of our summer holiday.'

Mr Howard did not sit behind his large desk, but invited me to a couple of very comfortable leather armchairs by a generous hearth – surely used to entertain his most important clients and associates.

There was a thick photograph album open on the low table, which Mr Howard leafed through distractedly. The black card pages were crammed with very artistic portraits of old theatre productions.

'I want to show this to Mr Irving and Mr Stoker,' he said proudly. 'I found this very old photograph of the good Irving dressed as Hamlet – from the first time he played him, back when he still worked for the Theatre Royale in Manchester. He has hardly aged at all in the past twenty years! Look, sir.'

'Oh, yes,' I said mechanically, hardly even looking at the image. 'Mr Howard, I am afraid I need to question a number of people, and the sooner the better.'

'Oh, yes, yes,' he said, putting the album aside. 'I understand. We are also quite keen on solving this matter; our most impressionable employees are extremely frightened by these ludicrous threats.'

I nodded, pressing my fingertips together and scrutinizing the man's posture.

'It has, however, given you quite a surge of sales,' I said. 'You must be very glad.'

He was not, I could tell. 'I wish it was *art* instead of morbidity that brought people in.'

I arched an eyebrow. 'Do you not care for the attractive profits?'

'Oh, Inspector, those profits are of no consequence to the theatre. Unless it's our own production, we merely rent out our premises for a fixed fee. The profits from ticket sales, or the lack thereof, go straight to Irving's company.'

'I see,' I said, discreetly pulling my small notepad from my breast pocket. I spoke as I took note of that detail. 'Mr Howard, I am a man of reason. I do not believe for one minute that there is something otherworldly involved here. What I do believe is that this production of *Mac*–'

Mr Howard hushed me at once; then he cleared his throat, blushing.

'I – I do apologize, Inspector, but we do not speak that

name in the theatre; only the actors on the stage. I hope you understand.'

'Why, of course. The curse of "The Scottish Play".'

'Indeed. It's one of the oldest legends in this business. Some say Shakespeare inserted real witches' spells into his text, and they became angry and cast a curse on the play. Horrible things are said to happen to the production companies when the name is spoken. I can remember that terrible incident in New York, back in the forties: two rival companies staged The Scottish Play simultaneously. There was such animosity between them and their respective followers that it all ended in a riot; over twenty people died.'

'I see,' I mumbled, starting off one of the lengthiest reports of my recent career. 'Mr Howard, would you consider yourself superstitious?'

He smiled. 'I am Irish, Inspector. I cannot pretend I've gotten rid of all my lucky charms.'

And according to McGray he might need them, if those banshees had come to announce the death of an Irish person. I opted not to mention that.

'I believe the curse also has a more mundane explanation, does it not? It is Shakespeare's shortest play and therefore attractive for a theatre manager to fill a vacancy quickly. I would imagine that the haste would increase the risk of accidents, particularly since the play ends in a swordfight.'

Mr Howard assented. 'Indeed, that is sometimes given as the rational explanation.'

'And speaking of mundane,' I continued, 'there are more mundane interests involved here, which should not take long to prove. Would you mind guiding me to a few people I need to question?'

'Of course. Do you have any names in mind?'

'A Mr Wheatstone,' I said at once.

'Oh, yes, the effects manager,' said Mr Howard, quite surprised that I knew that name. Apparently Mr Wheatstone had not yet told anyone it had been *he* who saw last night's banshee. 'A very eccentric man. Who else?'

I pondered on Stoker's words and what Mr Howard had just told me. 'Well, I would like to see the two people who claim to have been closest to the first banshee; apparently, a seamstress and Henry Irving himself.'

'The lady would be Mrs Harwood. I can show you to the workshop we've allocated for her. She has been stitching since very early, I believe. As to Wheatstone and Irving, well . . .' he cleared his throat, 'I'm afraid they are at today's rehearsal. Mr Irving stressed most emphatically that he is not to be interrupted.'

'Mr Howard, this is a police investigation.'

'Of course, Inspector, but Mr Irving is very particular . . .'

'Very well, take me to Mrs Harwood first, and then show me the way to Mr Irving. If they are not done by then I shall persuade him and his effects man to talk to me.'

'Very well, though I must warn you: I don't know the lady well, but people have been whispering odd things about her.'

'Odd things? How?'

'Well . . . of how she went missing for about half an hour. Just before the "banshee" was heard.'

I am now glad I questioned Mrs Harwood first. Her story would add a shocking line of inquiry to my investigations.

Bram Stoker's Journal (continued)

Was __so__ compelled to follow Inspector McGray on his visit to that mysterious fortune-teller. I offered my cab to make it a quick trip, which in the end took us no more than a few minutes.

Must again describe the events in some detail.

Mem — Short story about a gypsy prophecy.

__Madame Katerina__ has her establishment overlooking a long empty square. From the smell and the animal droppings must be the site of the city's cattle market. Edinburgh Castle can be seen above the humble dwellings surrounding the square, so it's but a few blocks from the theatre.

Insp. McGray told the driver to stop in front of a quite rustic beer stall, set on the windows of a two-storey terrace. Reminded me of one of the taverns I frequented while at Trinity College.

I asked with some incredulity whether this was the right place. The inspector sneered in reply. He grabbed the jute sack in which he had wrapped the bloodstained leather and sheet, and enquired for Madame Katerina at the stall. The large, rough man that sold the beer told him with some familiarity to make his way upstairs.

The inspector asked whether I was joining him or not, and I followed him across a dimly lit storage room which smelled strongly of yeast. They brew nice beer there. Inspector

McGray led me upstairs to a most bizarre little room. All its walls lined with old tapestries. No smell of yeast, but incense and herbs. Even the one window was covered, and instead of sun the room was lit by countless small candles. The flames cast bright reflections on a multitude of crystal balls.

I looked around intently, trying to take in every detail mentioned, and the inspector enquired with some harshness whether I had lost something (the language he used impossible for me to write down). I told him — rather recklessly — that I had an interest in the occult, after which his general attitude towards me softened considerably — I might even tell him . . .

The woman herself, Madame Katerina, is _quite_ a character, ripped from the pages of a folklore guide: swathed in richly coloured veils, adorned with all sorts of cheap jewellery, pierced on the ears, nose and eyebrow, her round face painted with make-up thicker than what we use for the Weird Sisters. Middle-aged and robustly built. I shall not describe her bust; sufficient to tell that it was most indecently sported.

She and Insp. McGray greeted each other most fondly. She looked at me quizzically and said, 'Adolphus, what did you do to the London snob? This ginger gentleman doesn't look like his replacement.'

Insp. McGray laughed and said with much animosity that the 'London lassie' was busy elsewhere, but that he could come round for tea if she so wished. Madame Katerina roared.

When she offered us seats — by a small round table at the centre of the room — she showed her very long, curved fingernails painted in black, like a raven's talons.

Inspector McGray introduced me and began to explain the

banshee affair, but Madame Katerina had read the news-
papers (which indeed surprised me) and said she had been
expecting us all along.

'Is that what you want me to see?' she asked, and she pointed
at the bundle which Inspector McGray had placed on the
floor. She asked him to put it on the table.

'You don't want me to do that,' said the inspector. 'It's a wee
bit disgusting.'

The clairvoyant's response was positively intriguing. I may
have misheard, but think she said: 'Don't be ridiculous,
Adolphus. It can't be more disgusting than that severed
hand you brought last November.'

'True. When you're right, you're right.'

The Gypsy woman bent down to have a closer look. Mme
Katerina was not daunted even when the inspector opened
up the sack. She opened and closed her hands, warming up
her fingers, and then sank them into the sticky mess.

Her face underwent a most shocking transfiguration.
She lost all colour; her green eyes, framed by encrusted
mascara, were fiery beacons. Drew in a hissing breath and
dug her nails into the cloth, squeezing it so hard some of the
still damp blood began to ooze, as though she were wringing
a living thing.

She shuddered, lightly at first, but her quivering grew and grew
until the very floorboards beneath her feet shook. She fal-
tered and nearly fell backwards, but Inspector McGray
jumped up and caught her, then carefully placed her on his
own chair.

She raised her hands and stared at them. She was careful not
to touch anything. She couldn't have looked more upset had
she submerged them in acid.

I asked what the matter was, and Inspector McGray explained *that this woman had <u>the eye</u>. He was quite surprised when I nodded in perfect understanding.*

She looked intently at her stained palms, opened her mouth and tried to speak. Managed, but with broken voice. My hand trembles even now, as I write down her horrid words: 'At least <u>one</u> will die on the thirteenth, my son. There's nothing you can do about it. You might be able to save most . . . but spare one and you'll doom the other.'

7

The auditorium and foyer represented only a small fraction of the Lyceum building. The rest of it, behind and around the stage, was entirely dedicated to prop rooms, scenery, dressing rooms and storage, all interconnected in a maze of corridors through which I soon became lost. The place was dusty and smelled like an amalgam of train station and carpenter's workshop.

We walked along a passage crammed with lighting pieces, which must run right behind the stage, for I heard the muffled echoes of the orchestra, from time to time accompanied by the sound of thunder.

'They're rehearsing one of the most complex scenes,' said Mr Howard. 'Lots of fire and mist and light effects involved. And the witches singing. We pride ourselves on having equipment for effects as sophisticated as any you could see in London.'

We entered a wide storeroom that smelled of naphthalene and damp. There were rows of racks where an extensive collection of costumes hung: wide Elizabethan gowns, Ancient Greek robes, Marie Antoinette wigs, Nefertiti headpieces, swords and weapons for every war from the Roman to the Napoleonic.

In a corner of the room, close to the battered double doors that opened to the street at the rear of the building, there were several brass racks quite different from the rest. These were reserved for medieval costumes. Most of the garments were coarsely woven shirts painted in metallic grey, which from a distance appeared quite convincingly as chainmail.

'The costumes for The Scottish Play,' said Mr Howard. I calculated there must be at least a hundred of those, along with a few more extravagant outfits.

Mr Howard nodded at a little door nearby. 'Mrs Harwood is working there . . .' before knocking he whispered at me, 'I don't know her well, Inspector, but I must warn you. She does seem – a little odd.'

'I have seen my share of oddities,' I assured him.

He knocked then and a female voice, rather lethargic, bid us in.

The place looked more like a wide wardrobe hurriedly adapted as a workshop, with a large sewing machine and rolls of lustrous material piled around it.

Standing in the centre of the shabby room, and radiant like a jewel amidst rags, was one of the most beautiful dresses I have ever seen. Dark green wool cascaded in gentle folds, the yarn crocheted in an intricate pattern that made it look like a delicate fishing net. The borders were all embroidered in Celtic designs: knots and thistles embellished with red and white gems, yet the most striking feature were the countless beads sewn all over the garment. I could not quite tell what they were, for their emerald tones had a metallic, iridescent quality, which made me think of dragon scales from the illustrations in my childhood books.

Mrs Harwood was kneeling on the floor, meticulously stitching more of those thumb-sized scales to the skirts.

She instantly struck me as an extremely nervous woman. Her hands, gnarled and roughened by work, quivered visibly as she handled the needle, and with every movement I feared she'd prick her own skin. I could not quite guess her age; besides McGray, I had never seen a face so mercilessly marked by premature wrinkles, cut deeply around her mouth and forehead, and forming long crowfeet that extended all the way to her ears.

She looked at us without lifting her face, her eyes studying us in a rather mousey attitude. 'Can I help you, sirs?'

I raised a hand, not wanting Mr Howard to tell her the reason of my visit straight away; she looked quite apprehensive already. I took a step closer and admired the frock.

'Impressive work, madam.'

'Thank you, sir. This is Lady Mac– Miss Terry's main dress.'

'Are those beads made of . . . ?'

'Why, they're no beads, sir. They're *real* beetle wings. Very fragile. At least a few get crushed or fall off every time the dress is worn, so I have to retouch it before each performance.'

I nodded in awe. 'That is quite a task.'

'It surely is, sir,' she said with a clear note of pride, 'especially after the poor thing was handled like a fishwife's rag on the trains.'

She combed the last few wings she'd attached so that they fell gracefully across the woollen mesh. They seemed precious to her.

'May I ask you a few questions, Mrs Harwood?'

Her face became stern, her wrinkles deeper. 'You're a policeman, are you not?'

'Yes, Inspector Ian Frey.'

She looked away. 'I don't wish to talk about that.'

'I am afraid I will have to insist. Troubling as I am sure it is, your statement is crucial to my investigation.'

'I still hear her in my head!' she said, fidgeting with her fingernails, pulling at the cuticles and biting off bits of dry skin between sentences. No wonder her hands were raw and chapped.

I made an effort to speak as soothingly as possible. 'I understand that it was the last performance.'

'Indeed, sir.'

'And that you were – out of view for a while.'

'Out of view? Well, I was doing my job, running round like a headless chicken! I had to pack all the gowns. As soon as the actors took them off I'd collected them and began preparing them for transport. They wouldn't have arrived here on time otherwise.'

'Did you happen to go into a dark corridor, by any chance?'

Her chest swelled a little. 'Why, I saw that horrible, wretched man, Mr Wheatstone, cutting the gas for some reason. I shouted at him; told him I couldn't do my job like that, but he took no notice. He just ignored me and walked into the dark! He's such a –' the woman covered her mouth.

'You clearly dislike him,' I said, thinking I could learn more about the man, but Mrs Harwood said nothing. I moved on. 'I hear you and Mr Irving were the first ones to find the – prophecy.'

'Yes.'

'Tell me how it happened. Please, omit no detail.'

'I was getting ready to pack this very dress – I had to

87

do it at the end. Miss Terry likes to wear it for the last ovation – but I'd left its cover on the opposite wing of the theatre. I ran behind the scenery, which was the quickest way, and then . . .'

Mrs Harwood wrapped her arms around herself, as if struck by a sudden draught.

'It has all passed now,' I said softly. 'What did you see?'

She gulped. 'Just a white shape, sir, sneaking through the canvases. Looked like a woman, only – well, there was something in her, in the way she moved . . . I can't explain it, sir! I just know it was terrifying. *And then she screamed!*'

Mrs Harwood's face became utterly distorted, copious tears rolling down her wrinkled cheeks. 'I dropped on my knees. I couldn't stand her cry. It was painful, *painful* to hear. My face was touching the floor, and it was then when I – I touched that mess!'

I remembered Mr Wheatstone's detailed statement. Her hands *had* been dripping blood when Irving found her.

She looked at me with frenzied eyes, recognizing my suspicion. 'I didn't mean to, sir! I just happened to drop there! *It was hell!*' The woman shuddered from head to toe, losing all self-control.

I asked Mr Howard to fetch her some brandy. In the meantime I leaned closer to calm her down, and realized she could not be much older than thirty-five. The brandy arrived very soon, and I jotted down my impressions as Mr Howard and a theatre maid assisted the poor seamstress.

Things were beginning to look bad for her, and it

would only become worse in the following minutes. As soon as she'd recovered a little, I asked about her whereabouts the previous night.

'I was . . . here, sir. I've been here since last night.'

I tilted my head, wishing this had been my first question. 'By yourself?'

'Yes.'

'How so?'

Mrs Harwood sniffed, pressing a borrowed handkerchief on her nose. 'There was work to be done. Didn't you see Miss Terry's dress?' She looked at Mr Howard. 'You knew about this, didn't you, sir?'

He nodded. 'I can vouch for her in that, Inspector. My associate, Mr Wyndham, in fact telegrammed Mr Stoker, telling him the green dress had arrived in a shocking state.'

I pondered on those words. 'So, Mrs Harwood, you arrived in Edinburgh . . . yesterday, on the evening train, with the rest of the company?'

'Yes.'

'And you simply came here to work?'

'Yes, sir. I only went to the Palace Hotel to leave my two children there. Then I came back here and began my mending. I had some bread and cheese and a big pot of tea,' she pointed at the leftovers. 'I haven't left the room since.'

If she was telling the truth, I thought, she could not yet know about the banshee story in the papers. She had indeed spoken as if she did not know; I gathered she would have been – if possible – even more distressed.

'So you have not slept in more than a day?'

She assented, and I examined her face under that light.

The skin around her eyes was indeed puffed and bluish, but amidst her haggard features the fact could have gone unnoticed.

'Was anybody else in the theatre?' I asked.

Her eyes moved in circles. 'One of the clerks knew I was coming back to work, so he stayed to let me in, but he left as soon as I arrived. After that I didn't hear anyone until the cleaners came, just before six o'clock this morning. I heard them, you see, because the back door is right next to my workshop.'

I sat back, stroking my chin. This woman had no alibi, no witnesses, and she'd just volunteered the fact that an exit from the theatre was very handy to her. She'd been alone for at least nine hours; plenty of time to make her way to Regent Bridge and set up the spectacle – it would have been a long walk, but by no means impossible. And then she would have had time to return and clear all evidence – blood on her hands or clothes – at leisure.

'If I needed you to give me evidence of your whereabouts,' I said, 'what could you offer me?'

She looked at me in utter confusion. Either she ignored the fact that a banshee had been sighted last night, or she was acting quite convincingly. 'Why would you need proof?'

'Let us simply assume I need it.'

Mrs Harwood looked nervously around her. 'Well, I – I don't know. Where else could I have been? My boy and girl can tell you I wasn't with them last night.'

'I am more interested in proving that you were *here.*'

The woman looked around for a moment, and then her eyes shone. '*The dress!* Of course, the dress. Miss Terry's gown was an absolute mess yesterday, but now it looks as good as new. It couldn't have been done so quickly unless someone stayed here all night working on it.'

It struck me that she said 'someone', rather than 'I', but perhaps I was reading too much between the lines.

Mr Howard again assented. 'I saw the dress myself last night. I think Mrs Harwood is right. I'm no expert in haute couture, but I can tell you it did *not* appear a task that could be done in a few minutes.'

I took a deep breath. I had just thought it was all a solved matter, but now that dress stood in my way. I looked at its hundreds of beetle wings, which seemed to mock my impasse with their arresting iridescence.

I wondered if Miss Terry ever felt the urge to scratch, knowing that she covered her entire body with dead insects' carapaces, pretending they were precious stones. A macabre illusion, yet perhaps one of the mildest I'd confront. I was about to meet the legendary Henry Irving, and then the leading lady herself, and I would learn of all the treachery, deceit and tragedy that crept behind the velvet and the gilded stage.

ACT II

BANQUO
    And oftentimes, to win us to our harm,
    The instruments of darkness tell us truths,
    Win us with honest trifles, to betray's
    In deepest consequence.

Second letter from the partially burned stack found at Calton Hill

The best preserved sheet of the lot. – I. P. Frey.

My dear,

I am so, so sorry! I was only trying to make you happy. I did not think. Yes, I should have told you. I knew I should but I was reckless.

Last night I swallowed all my little pearls and all my silky locust-ale, and went to bed thinking of all the things I've never told you. All the things I will never have the time to tell!

I never told you I spent weeks sleeping under the stars in the slums of Angel's Meadow, begging for farthings, scavenging for food from the rotting heaps behind the market stalls.

I never told you I did see the angel. The merciful angel that all the other dying beggars talked about. She had a beautiful face, shining white and silver under the moon, and she wrapped me with her wings, and they were feathery and soft and warm.

I never told you I have a little coffin. It's beautiful. It fits in the palm of my hand. And it's full of lies. And every time I open it the lies escape and fly and when I can't catch them back they become ashes – like these letters will. All the lies we've told, my dear. All the lies that have been told to us. I have collected them all and treasured them, and every day I see them go a little drier, a little colder, and lose the lustre and the perfume that once seduced us.

Oh, why did the limelight seem so tempting back then? Why did we all despair so much to catch it? The struggle, the pain, the humiliation we suffered — so gladly. The horrors, the back-stabbing, the things we did so willingly. The things that were done to us!

And what is the limelight in the end? Nothing but lies!! A lying crowd of fickle temper, cheering for a moment and then getting bored. Leaving you, forsaking you the moment you can entertain no more.

Oh, my dear, how these questions must haunt you — You, my dear, of all people — <u>you</u> —

Love,
X

8

My footsteps were concealed by the roaring orchestra, as a dim light rose very slowly upon the witches' cavern.

The music was undoubtedly by Sir Arthur Sullivan. The chords were powerful, dark, martial. With the harsh basses and the shrilling strings, the prelude had a barbaric ring to it, instantly making me think of a warlike, undeveloped age.

The dark, jagged rocks that dominated the scene heightened that sense; the sky, in lurid red, was visible in only a little upper corner of the stage, and the witches' cauldron was at the centre of it all. It was not the usual iron pot, but rather a natural cleft in an outcropping of rock. A cloud of steam and an orange glow emerged from it, as if it were a crater connecting the stage with the deepest pits of hell. The light increased gradually, like a sunrise, slowly turning from indigo to mauve, and then to red. It was an astonishing effect.

And there came the three Weird Sisters: thin and misshapen crones, swathed in dark shrouds from which only their weathered faces and bony arms protruded. Each of them held a long wooden staff, their tops forked branches sharpened like lances, which they used to stir their potion.

Flashes of lightning and a roll of thunder shook the auditorium. The music reached its climax and then the hags began to chant their famous *Double, double, toil and trouble.*

Their wailing voices filled the theatre as they listed the ingredients for their noisome broth, the vapours now rising higher and higher. I had never paid much attention to the rhymes, so when I did, I winced at the most morbid lines: *toad's sweltered venom . . . Liver of blaspheming Jew . . . Finger of birth-strangled babe . . . Cool it with a baboon's blood . . .* The word 'grimorium' crept into my head, and I shivered.

Hecate, the witches' goddess, hovered above the stage. A bright light shone on her head, glittering on sharp spikes braided into her hair. It was as if she wore one of those halos one sees in biblical paintings, and I could not fathom how they'd crafted that effect.

Any of those tragediennes could have passed for a convincing banshee!

I took a few steps ahead – just as the second witch uttered *something wicked this way comes.*

I then saw the man himself, Henry Irving.

Treading on to stone steps in full medieval costume, silhouetted against the crimson sky, tall, helmeted and carrying a sheathed broadsword on his shoulder, he looked as grand and terrible as the ghouls themselves. His face was undeniably suited for the theatre, as even from a distance I could make out his striking features: aquiline, clean-shaven except for a reddish moustache; his thick, bushy eyebrows framed a pair of cruel-looking eyes, whose black pupils were like wells against the pale skin; his chin was broad and firm, and the skin was tight around his sharp, protruding cheekbones. His was a face fierce enough to demand answers from the witches, and he did so in powerful, commanding tones.

The Weird Sisters readily obliged, cackling and stirring their cauldron with renewed power. There were majestic balls of fire erupting from the cleft, illuminating the entire theatre and making me take a small step back.

A triad of invoked apparitions came to them, ascending from the underground through thick, rolling fog. Of the three spirits, it was the second that caught my eye.

A young blonde girl, dressed in a pearlescent white gown, her wavy hair golden and shiny, as if reflecting the glow of lava. She had the most angelic face, with plump cheeks and bright blue eyes. The girl turned slowly, as the music rose with staccatos that announced doom, and my heart jumped when she revealed the other side of her face: red, blistered, ruined skin, made up with the most upsetting prostheses to resemble terrible burns.

The overall effect was grotesque. I felt a violent chill creeping up my spine as the girl delivered her part of the omens:

> Macbeth! Macbeth! Macbeth!
> Be bloody, bold and resolute; laugh to scorn
> The power of man, for none of woman born
> Shall harm Macbeth.

A cold hand clutched my arm, and I jumped and gasped, only to hear the mocking laughter of McGray. Mr Stoker stood next to him.

'Dandy, aren't ye supposed to be working?'

I pulled my arm free, still feeling my quickened heartbeats.

'I *have* been questioning people,' I retorted, and quickly briefed him on the interview with Mrs Harwood. McGray, in exchange, told me about the reading from Madame Katerina.

'The big opening of – our Scottish Play is, of course, scheduled for this Saturday,' Stoker jumped in rather keenly, 'the thirteenth of July.'

I covered my brow in frustration. 'So the full-breasted, swindling enchantress *accurately* predicted something that has been in the newspapers all day! Oh, and the date of the opening night, which has been scheduled for at least a week!' I did not let Stoker speak. 'Nine-Nails, I need to question Mr Wheatstone and Henry Irving. The former must be backstage, fuelling the witches' pot, and Irving is up there soliloquizing.'

'Oh, I would *not* interrupt him right now,' said Stoker. 'He wants this scene –'

But McGray was already walking ahead with decisive strides. He jumped into the orchestra stalls, where the music instantly went discordant, and then he climbed on to the stage itself, pushing aside witches, apparitions and the parade of eight ghostly kings that had just emerged.

There was a roar, higher and more powerful than any instruments or even the thunder effects: the deep, bellowing voice of Henry Irving.

'*Who the hell is this clown?*'

Everyone and everything came to a halt. Only the floating haze remained in motion, spiralling as the towering Irving strode across the stage to face Nine-Nails.

Stoker ran forward in a rather pathetic way. 'These are the CID inspectors, Irving. They've come to –'

'*Get your filthy boots off my stage!*' As he bellowed, Irving pointed the heavy-looking sword at McGray's face.

My colleague was not impressed. '*Oi!* Point yer wee toy-stick somewhere else! I'm bloody CID.'

'You are but a sad fool,' Irving spat, 'trespassing on my premises!'

'*Yer prem*– I don't give a toss whose *premises* these are. Did ye nae hear? We're the fucking *police*!'

'You mouldy rogue! *Away!* Don't you see we have work to do!'

I could not tell which man had the upper hand: they were of equal stature, and each sounded as imposing and determined as the other.

McGray took a step ahead, and with one swift movement knocked the sword from Irving's hand.

'I'm not moving until we've talked. Don't force me to question ye at gunpoint.'

Irving would not move, and for an instant I feared McGray would indeed have to unholster his weapon.

Stoker shared my fears. He raised both hands, cold sweat already rolling down his temples. 'Irving, *please*. These gentlemen are here to help us with the threats. And we have news to tell you.'

I felt as though I was watching a farce: the King of Scotland standing proud against the ludicrously attired McGray, the three witches whispering and giggling in the background, and about ten other ghouls scratching themselves and witnessing the quarrel.

Irving cast Stoker a petrifying look, but in the end he spoke sense.

'You are not worth another word,' he snapped, ripping

the fake ginger moustache off his face, and then roared at his crew. *'Everyone take half an hour rest!'*

Before anyone could say a word, Irving vanished through the stage wing, and as soon as he left, a heavy gloom was lifted from everyone's faces. Actors and actresses suddenly moved and talked at ease, their curious stares still on McGray and me.

I marched to the stage, catching a quick sight of Elgie. He was the only amused one; all the other musicians looked either weary or downright bored. Our interruption meant they'd surely be going home late.

'Inspectors,' Stoker said to us as we jumped on to the stage, 'please, give Mr Irving a few minutes. He needs to take the edge off his temper.'

'I'll cut the edge o' something else if the bastard doesnae come back soon,' McGray replied, fanning away the fake mist.

I looked at the trapdoor through which the apparitions had emerged. A rudimentary timber staircase descended to the darkened basements, from where steam was still puffing, making my eyes water.

As if hearing my thoughts, McGray yelled, 'Would youse turn that bloody thing off?'

Up came the squat figure of Mr Wheatstone, wearing a leather apron, his grey hair even more dishevelled than the witches', and dripping sweat as if he'd just stepped out of a Turkish bath.

'What on earth is going on?' he demanded, but then he saw me. I recognized his shock even through his steamed-up spectacles.

'*You,*' I said, pointing directly at his face, 'are the first person I would like to question.'

9

Mr Wheatstone begged us to talk away from any curious ears and eyes, and we had to climb down – quite literally – through the witches' cauldron, as he led us into the dingy understage.

It felt as if we were walking through the insides of a ship: rough timber beams, ropes and pulleys everywhere, and a plethora of ingenious machinery to produce the spectacular from the mundane: the 'magic' vapours were nothing but water ladled on to a crateful of red-hot charcoal; the explosions of hellish fire were clouds of lycopodium powder, thrown by hand and ignited with a long torch; and the mysterious light that had appeared like a sunrise was achieved with regulated electric current, as I would discover shortly.

A dozen sweating men and a few boys – most of them as lean and worn out as the enslaved rowers in a Roman warship – stood around awaiting orders, their body odours making the place a thousand times more foetid than the changing rooms of the gymnasium where I practise fencing.

'Shall I keep the generator going?' asked a little cockney man who'd come running. He was very short, incredibly thin and entirely covered with soot. The theatre must have its own coal-fired electricity generator. Such a production would soak up incredible amounts of power.

The man saw us and somehow recognized us as police inspectors, for he took his hat off with deference. I smiled at his clean, shiny bald head, which looked almost bleached against the rest of his blackened face. 'Sorry to interrupt you, bosses.'

'Yes, keep it going,' replied Mr Wheatstone, 'but turn it low. We're supposed to restart in half an hour.'

The smoked man bowed and left quickly. Mr Wheatstone looked at the other men.

'Go and have a drink, chaps, but I want you back in twenty minutes.'

There were a few claps but one of them, a particularly sweaty man, protested.

'You said it won't start for half an hour!'

'Fifteen to you,' McGray snapped, and the hireling left, saying no more.

Mr Wheatstone sat on a stool right next to a large artefact that instantly caught my attention: on a wooden base there were two large cylinders of identical dimensions, one mahogany and one brass, sitting in parallel, each with a crank to turn it. A thick, uninsulated electric wire was wound around them, like two bobbins sharing the one thread. It looked like something materialized from Mary Shelley's novel.

'Is that a rheostat?' I asked.

'Yes, Inspector. My madcap uncle, Charles, rest in peace, invented it. He was quite shocked when I told him I wanted to use it for such a ludicrous application.'

I had read about the older Wheatstone's invention a few years ago. The more windings on the wooden cylinder, the more resistance to the electric current and the dimmer the light would be. By turning those cranks, Mr

Wheatstone, or one of his men, would be able to regulate the intensity of the light with unmatched precision.

I was quite impressed – Irving's company was using state-of-the-art technology – and also a little worried. Wire-wound rheostats could be made with ratings up to several thousand watts.

'Is it not dangerous to keep all that current exposed?' I asked, looking also at the buckets of water, the burning coal, the explosive powders and the wooden beams all around us. The place was an inferno in waiting.

Wheatstone simply pointed at his thick soldering gloves and his apron. 'Minor details. I do protect myself, and nobody but me is allowed near the rheostat.'

McGray, always so eager to know everything about the supernatural, was congruently uninterested in those scientific tricks. 'So, this is the lad who saw the banshee,' he prompted.

'While intoxicated,' I remarked, but Wheatstone was already too flushed to look further embarrassed. I asked my first question: 'Mr Wheatstone, what were you doing in a darkened corridor, all by yourself, on the night the first banshee was heard?'

His face twitched. 'Ex– excuse me?'

'You were seen cutting the gas supply to a corridor that led to the theatre's back door. And I had it from the seamstress Harwood that you were not too keen to be followed.'

Mr Wheatstone threw his head back to laugh. 'Mrs Harwood! Yes, I am sure she would offer such fiction. The poor woman is not well in her head, did anybody tell you that?'

'Were you or were you not in that corridor?' I pressed.

'Yes, I was!'

'To what end?'

'To fetch another few sacks of lycopodium.'

'What the hell is that?' asked McGray.

'A very special explosive we use on stage. It doesn't ignite when it is lying still, but it does, and tremendously, when it is suspended in the air. That's why I had to turn all the gas lights off: if a sack fell from the wheelbarrow and burst into clouds of the stuff –'

He explained in detail the chemistry of the powder (a spore, apparently), but I did not pay heed. His story tallied with Stoker's statements – and Mrs Harwood's too.

'I assume that's why you didn't want anybody in the vicinity,' I said.

'Of course.'

'Did you leave the back door open?'

'I – I must admit I don't recall. It was a very tense night.'

'Did you see any trails of blood?'

He had to take his spectacles off. 'Blood? No . . . Do you – do you think it was through the back door that they brought – the stuff they used to write those omens?'

McGray intervened. Like me, he probably thought it better not to disclose too many details, and Mr Wheatstone was clearly a very clever man. 'Did ye see anybody around when ye were fetching the explosives?'

'No, not a soul. As you know, the corridor wasn't lit, and I had warned everyone to stay away until I returned.'

I took note of that. 'How long before the "banshee's cry" was this?'

'Oh, a good while! I always replenish the stock after the beginning of Act IV. We use up a batch during the witches' scene, but we need more for the climax towards the end of Act V, when the forest is on fire. There must be between twenty or thirty minutes between those two scenes.'

I massaged my temples. Anyone could have made their way to the backstage if the door had been open and the lights had been off for so long.

McGray was equally frustrated. That did not help his banshee theory either.

My next question came out quite bluntly.

'Mr Wheatstone, can you tell us now why you revealed all of this to the papers?'

It was as if I'd pushed the man in the chest, for he nearly fell backwards. He composed himself quickly, though. 'I knew you would ask that question.'

'Then answer the dandy,' said McGray.

Wheatstone mopped the sweat off his face with a soiled handkerchief.

'It wasn't me.'

My earnest '*Ha!*' must have resounded throughout the building. 'Mr Wheatstone, my colleague here would be prone to believe that a little green fairy was following you during your drinking spree and that it was *she* who alerted the press. I, on the other hand . . .'

'*I swear!*' Wheatstone snapped, tossing his handkerchief on to the floor. 'I didn't tell anything to the press . . .' he raised his voice before we could interrupt him. '*However* – I did speak to someone else last night.'

McGray smiled. 'And?'

Wheatstone, unexpectedly, sounded rather meek now.

'After I spoke to you, Inspector, I went back to the Palace Hotel. There was someone still awake, protesting about something or other in the lobby. When he saw me so troubled, he forced me to tell him everything.'

'And the man was . . . ?'

'Mr Irving.'

'Of course!' I exclaimed as McGray and I rushed to Mr Howard's office. 'I have just been told that if anybody is to benefit from ticket sales, that would be Henry Irving. He has a number of actresses who could have played the part of the banshee, and there is also a good chance that Mrs Harwood simply saw the impostor and thought it a true apparition.'

'Don't picture yerself drinking my whisky with yer pinkie all stuck out,' McGray grunted. 'There's something that really worries me. If Madame Katerina's right, the prophecy is true and someone is going to die by the end of the week. And the banshee didnae tell us who.'

We made it to Mr Howard's office, only to find the door wide open and the man engaged in a heated argument with a very anxious Mr Stoker.

'*Oi!*' McGray barked to catch their attention. 'We need to talk to that hosiery-wearing prancer o' yers.'

Stoker was appalled. 'Do *not* call Mr Irving that!'

Mr Howard raised a conciliatory hand, 'I am afraid Mr Irving has left the building.'

'*What!*' McGray shouted. I, on the other hand, had to repress a belly laugh.

'As we warned you, he was very distressed by the interruption,' Stoker added. 'He said he needed some fresh air to recollect himself.'

'How convenient,' I muttered.

'Where did he go?' McGray demanded.

'He didn't say,' answered Stoker.

'When's he coming back?'

'He – he didn't say, either.'

'*Damn!*' McGray roared, making us all jump.

'I thought these rehearsals were crucial,' I added ironically. 'He undoubtedly has an artistic temperament, to flounce off like that.'

Stoker looked at me as if he could strangle me. He had to leave the office, quite unable to contain his pique.

Mr Howard again tried to ease the mood. 'Mr Stoker is very loyal to Irving. You must understand.'

Nine-Nails was not sympathetic at all. He punched the wall, leaving cracks on the paint, and then stormed out.

'Where are you going?' I asked him.

He would not stop, snapping over his shoulder, 'I cannae sit round here with a cup o' tea 'til the bastard deigns to come back.'

10

Just as McGray disappeared I told Mr Howard I needed to question everyone who claimed to have heard the banshee.

My request, as expected, proved most unpopular. Everyone thought they had gained a free afternoon (and on the sunniest day in Scottish history too) but I had just ruined their prospect.

I was lucky to find a quiet and well-appointed office to carry out my inquiries, and I summoned the Weird Sisters first.

As I waited for them I found a box full of freshly printed theatre programmes sitting on the desk. The little booklets were made of very fine paper, with beautiful illustrations of the various scenes, and on the first page there was a list of the entire cast. I thought it would be useful when organizing my notes, so I placed a copy in my pocket.

Just then I heard the persistent laughter of the witches coming from the corridor. The three women, all of them in their sixties, had high-pitched voices, and giggled with the volume and energy of fifteen-year-old girls, colonizing the office's sofa like three unwise monkeys.

I saw they had changed out of their costumes, but that was not really an improvement. With their fake jewellery, their bright red lips and their thick mascara, they clung desperately to a youth long gone.

'Oh, such a handsome gentleman!' cried the first witch, Miss Marriott, and I let out the weariest sigh.

'They must think we're the banshee!' cried the second witch, Miss Desborough, amongst frenzied cackles.

'Ladies, would you please let me ask the questions –'

'Well, we're ugly enough!' said the third witch – Miss Seaman, I think. I would struggle to memorize their names.

A deep voice came from the door then. 'Are you honestly this silly or are you just pretending?'

It was the woman who played Hecate – Miss Ivor. She would have been just a little younger than her comrades, but without the vulgar make-up and wearing sensible clothes, she looked at least ten years their junior. I could tell why she'd been selected to play a dark deity and not a witch: there was an elegant poise about her, and she conducted herself like a lady at court. Visibly annoyed, she too sat on the long leather sofa, but keeping her distance from the other women.

They were mumbling simultaneously: 'We were only joking' – 'what a bore' – 'no wonder she never married, the Southampton witch . . .'

'Ladies, please,' I insisted. 'Your whereabouts last night?'

The first witch, who happened to have a long nose that would not need any retouching for her performance, spoke. 'We were all at the hotel. Where else?'

'Can anyone vouch for you four?' I asked.

'I don't like where this is going,' said one of them.

'We just went to bed,' said Miss Desborough. 'We're not in the habit of announcing it like a fox hunt. Gone are the days when anyone would be interested.'

Hecate – Miss Ivor – stepped in. 'We can all vouch for each other; our rooms are adjacent and the walls are paper thin. Because we play witches, people think we like to be together all the time.'

I assented. 'So there is nobody but yourselves to verify your whereabouts?'

'I *really* don't like where this is –'

'Then, for my own sake,' I said curtly, 'I will get to the point. Has Mr Irving asked you to play any parts other than witches of *Macbeth*?'

The women shrieked at the word, and this time even Miss Ivor opened her eyes wide. The third witch jumped to her feet, ran out of the office and came back within the minute, bringing a saltshaker that they all used to sprinkle their shoulders. Even Hecate.

'*It's The Scottish Play*!' the first witch spluttered. 'Call it The Scottish Play!'

I was tempted to say it again, simply to see if the repetition might wreak just the same havoc; however, I could not bear that infernal racket a second time. I snatched the saltshaker and banged it on the desk.

'Ladies, I want you to answer my question, and think carefully. It would not be a crime if Mr Irving asked you to play the part of a banshee and create a scandal to help his sales. If, however, I find that you have lied to me – then everything changes.'

All four women raised their chins, suddenly as dignified as the dark messengers they played on the stage. None of them spoke.

'I need an answer,' I insisted. 'And you are not free to go until I hear it from your lips. Did you or did you not act as the banshee under Regent Bridge?'

One by one, they all denied it. There was no artifice left in their faces.

'I hope for your own sakes that you are telling the truth,' I murmured, and then let them go.

Miss Ivor, however, lingered by the doorframe, waiting for the witches' outrage to fade in the distance.

'Do you have anything to add?' I asked her.

Miss Ivor hesitated, but then came back to the sofa and whispered. 'I do, Inspector, but I did not want them to hear this.' She leaned closer to me and lowered her voice even more. 'Do you know about Miss Terry's . . . *finding*?'

I did not want to reveal too much. 'Could you be more specific?'

'Yes. The bundle of . . . oh, I shudder just to think of it!'

'Very well, we are speaking of the same thing. What about it?'

'Well, sir, I have reason to believe . . . Please, do not tell anyone you heard this from me. If Mr Irving hears this I might lose my job. And I'm an ageing actress – old women are usually played by men!'

'You can trust me, Miss Ivor.'

The woman took a deep breath. 'I have reason to believe . . . that Miss Terry placed that there herself.'

11

'Herself! Miss Ivor, that is a bold accusation.'

'I know! And I would not even mention it if my suspicions were unfounded.'

'Pray, explain.'

'Well, I saw Miss Terry come in that night carrying a large handbag. I remember it very well because it was a very expensive one – blue silk, beaded in black, with beautiful drawstrings. It looked full.'

'Continue.'

'Well, Miss Terry had just finished her sleepwalking scene and came back to her dressing room. I was there because we share some cosmetics, and we usually chat before the end of the play. I am her understudy, you see. But that night Miss Terry asked me to fetch her a jug and basin to wash her hands. She said she still had stains of fake blood, from the scene in which she wields the dagger.

'When I came back she wasn't in her dressing room, but in the corridor just around the corner. And she insisted on washing there and then, in everybody's sight. And she was very agitated.'

I sat back, pressing my fingertips together. 'I see . . . What happened then?'

'She went back to her dressing room, asked me to get rid of the dirty water – she does treat me like her maid sometimes, I must tell you – and it was right then that we heard the cry. I was close enough to hear Miss Terry screaming at the exact same time. I rushed back and I found her with that – horrible mess on her vanity table.

'Mr Stoker came very soon. He was also very frightened. Miss Terry made us swear we'd tell no one, and Mr Stoker later on made me swear again, in private.'

'And you think that she carried it in that blue bag?'

'Yes. I saw her leave the theatre with it, but by then it was empty. It was one of those pouch-style bags, so it was easy to tell.'

I sighed. 'You do realize she could have been carrying anything.'

'Yes, sir, but . . . is it not too much of a coincidence?'

I took comprehensive notes, realizing I'd need to question Ellen Terry herself very soon.

'Miss Ivor,' I said, 'why do you think Miss Terry would do something like that?'

She only smirked.

'Oh, I could not even guess, sir. That woman is a mystery – to everybody.'

It was very difficult to focus after that revelation, but I forced myself to do so.

I questioned the entire cast, letting them go home as I took their statements. Most of them gave me useless or repeated information, and even though I kept my inquiries as succinct as possible, people unavoidably volunteered their own theories and suspicions.

From Mr Black and Mr Carter, the two beefy young men who played Macbeth's assassins: 'Poor Mrs Harwood. Her husband died only a couple of years ago. Left her with vast debts, we've heard. Not even a place to live, and two little mouths to feed.'

From Mr Wenman, the weather-beaten man who played Banquo: 'Mr Stoker would do anything to help Irving. And I mean anything. He even named his eldest son Irving!'

From Mr Haviland, the ancient and regal-looking gentleman who played King Duncan, and who seemed to have a particular taste for prurient gossip: 'Miss Terry and Mr Irving have not been . . . well, I should only say that their idyll has gone cold of late. Irving will never divorce his wife, no matter how much Miss Terry would have liked that . . .'

Mr Haviland gossiped on and on, and just before I kindly asked him to leave he was saying: 'Irving's been very helpful to Miss Terry's children. She has a son and a daughter, you must have heard, both out of wedlock! The girl, Edith, joined the company last year, and now she is training as a pianist *and* costume designer in Germany. The boy, Ted, is to spend the rest of the summer with Irving in Ramsgate, preparing for this autumn's season. Both schemes were instigated by Irving himself! He's not shown *that* much devotion for his own sons!'

I took copious notes, half my notebook full of compact writing by the time I was done.

I was tired beyond belief, and just as hungry. Thank goodness Elgie burst into the office with a large loaf of bread, cheese, cold beef and apples. I could have told him I loved him, but I'd better save that for the day he actually saves my life.

'I saw your boss Nine-Nails leave the theatre,' he said as we indulged in the food. 'I could swear he was reciting

Shall I compare thee to a summer's day whilst counting with his fingers. The ones he has got left, that is.'

'The man *is* a little insane, had you not noticed?'

'And I assume he has some strange theories for this case?'

'He believes someone *will* die,' I said with some scorn.

'And you are certain he is wrong?' I could not possibly reply to that, and Elgie frowned. 'Could not someone – a real person, I mean – be acting the banshee whilst planning a murder?'

I shook my head. 'Elgie, if you wanted to kill someone, would you tell them beforehand? Would you make a spectacle of it? Or, rather, would you attack stealthily and by surprise?'

My young brother pondered. He looked sideways for a moment and then spoke with a cool, analytical tone I rarely saw in him.

'That depends, Ian. What if I were trying to implicate someone? Or just throw the scent away from me?'

My hand halted before I could bring my cigar to my lips, and I considered his words. There was some sinister sense to that statement.

'That is why you would not give an actual name,' I murmured, nodding, 'but only vague hints ... so you would still have the element of surprise ...'

The torrent of names and statements flooded my head, in particular the stern eyes of Miss Ivor as she told me about Ellen Terry's empty bag. I drew some breath. 'What if –'

I did not have a chance to finish, for we heard a woman's desperate shriek coming from the street.

Elgie jumped towards the window much faster than me, and pressed his hands against the glass.

'Ian, look at that!' he cried, as I peered over his shoulder.

Mrs Harwood was running along Grindlay Street, her hands still clenching some piece of stage costume, which she jerked madly as she yelled *There he goes! There he goes!*

I looked to the end of the road, but managed to see only the folds of a dark overcoat turn around the corner. Mr Stoker came out from the main entrance, but I barely caught a glimpse of him. I was already running to the door, telling Elgie to stay put, and then ran down the wide stairs and into the foyer.

By the time I'd reached the street Mr Howard and Mr Wheatstone had joined the crying seamstress. Thankfully, the crowd had dissipated – the red sign SOLD OUT now prominent across the ticket office window – for the woman was throwing a mighty tantrum.

'Are you sure?' Mr Wheatstone asked her, but the woman's reaction was utterly unexpected: she pushed Mr Wheatstone with all her strength, tossed the garment she'd been holding at his face and then hit him repeatedly on the chest, shouting, 'Don't even talk to me, you swine!'

Mr Stoker held her by the shoulders and pulled her back easily. 'There, there, Mrs Harwood, this is not the time for that.'

I was about to ask what was afoot, but Stoker saw me and spoke at once.

'Mrs Harwood just saw a man trying to get into Miss Terry's dressing room.'

'Good Lord, is that true?' I asked, but the woman was still glaring at Mr Wheatstone. Stoker told him he had better leave and the man agreed.

'What did he look like?' I asked, thinking I might still

have a chance to catch him – if she gave me a good enough description.

It took Mrs Harwood a seemingly endless moment to catch her breath, and I had to exert all my self-control not to shake her by the arms.

'Very thin,' she finally panted. Her eyes, for some reason, were shedding tears of fury. 'Very, very thin. Young. Dark hair. Stank . . . and he had this silly, very stiff little moustache all greased up.'

'Darn!' I hissed. I instantly recalled the moustached man with sunken cheeks who had looked at me as I approached the theatre. 'I saw him too,' I told Stoker. 'He looked like a journalist.'

The box-office clerk approached us then, wearing a quizzical brow. 'Aye, boss, the lad was a reporter. I saw his stupid tash too. Came asking me questions as soon as we opened this morning. Stood here on the road taking notes for hours.'

'Did he mention which newspaper he works for?'

'Not to me, but I heard him boasting in front of a very pretty lassie that he wrote for *The Scotsman*.'

Saying no more, I turned on my heels and darted north.

12

Instead of running aimlessly on the surrounding roads I went directly to the offices of *The Scotsman*, on Cockburn Street.

The most winding lane in the Old Town – both horizontally and vertically – it ran as an S shape, ascending from Waverley Station towards the Royal Mile, and it was a good compromise between the Old and the New Towns: full of trade and bustle, but not yet subject to the offensive odours that surrounded the police headquarters.

The paper's name, written in large gilded letters, along with the gothic façade, spoke of a thriving business. Its busy reception room, however, was not glamorous, with plain wooden flooring, people hurrying in every direction and the persistent, chemical smells of inks and glue.

It was not difficult to find the man. I simply enquired for the reporter responsible for the Henry Irving story, not needing to mention a name at all – only the fact that I was a CID inspector – and a young assistant guided me to the second floor.

Along the narrow corridor there were many doors to small offices, separated by flimsy-looking wooden partitions. The sound of typewriters and shouting nearly overwhelmed me.

'That's his office,' the young man said, pointing at one of the furthest doors. I saw that the name of its occupant was not written on a plaque, but scribbled on a yellowed piece of paper inserted in the slot.

Alan Dyer.

The door opened and I instantly recognized the overly greased moustache I'd seen at the Lyceum. The skinny man's face went ghastly pale, his mouth opened wide and the cigarette he'd been chewing fell from his lips. He then slammed the door wide and sprinted down the corridor.

'*Stop!*' I howled, but right then someone pushed me sideways. I crashed against the wall, just as I saw the ghastly brown overcoat that could only belong to Nine-Nails.

It took him two strides to reach the sleazy hack. McGray grabbed him by the neck and arm, which he twisted behind the man's back.

'This the rascal ye've been looking for?' he asked, dragging him back, Dyer grunting and screaming all manner of insults. The hammering of typewriters had stopped all of a sudden, and the heads of curious reporters popped out from their office doors.

'Yes,' I said. 'But – how did you know I was here?'

'Went back to the theatre, Frey, looking for ye. Stoker was still trying to calm down his seamstress. He told me everything.' He pulled Dyer's arm up, making the man squeak in pain. 'This lanky piece o' shite has a lot of explaining to do.'

'You must have run like the wind to get here so quickly,' I said as Nine-Nails pushed the reporter back into his office. 'What were you up to?'

'Tell ye as soon as we're done with this heap o' dung,' he said with a mysterious grin, and then barked at all the onlookers. 'None o' yer fuckin' business!'

He closed the door behind our backs and threw Dyer on to the chair behind a messy desk. A copy of the day's paper lay amongst the disarray of crumpled sheets and shorthand notes; I picked it up and confirmed that Mr Dyer had penned the grim headline.

'Well, well,' I said, sniffing uncomfortably – added to the smell of ink, this cubicle also stank of cheap tobacco. 'So you have been in charge of the whole story.'

Mr Dyer grinned, his teeth stained by relentless smoking. 'I'll take your visit as a compliment. Nice to know I'm being read!' he glanced at Nine-Nails' hand. 'And it's always nice to have a local celebrity visit my workplace. Nine-Nails McGray! No one better to work on a case like this.'

McGray pounded the desk. 'Why were ye sneaking into the theatre?'

'I wanted an interview with Miss Terry. I assumed she'd be at the rehearsals. I saw all the cast leave, except her, so I thought she'd be easy to find.'

'Were you planning to leave anything for her?' I asked.

'What do you mean? Flowers? I am not the sentimental type.'

McGray was already rummaging through the man's desk drawers, but found nothing. It did not surprise me: if Dyer had been carrying anything gory he'd probably just dropped it on the street.

His expression, though blank, did tell me that he must be an expert at concocting lies on the go. I tried to throw him off balance with my next question. 'Mr Dyer, have you been to London recently? Within the past week, to be precise?'

The man looked at me intently, a slight quiver in his

pupils. He moved slowly, reached for a pencil and began tracing shorthand characters on a notepad. McGray snatched it from his hand and threw it into the mess of paper next to me. *'Answer the question!'*

Dyer held his open hand in the air. 'I have not,' he said with mocking deference – and a challenging spark in his eyes.

'Can you prove it?' McGray pressed.

'Aye. I've been at work every day for the past fortnight.'

'No breaks, laddie?'

'News never stops. I take no breaks. Everyone here can confirm that.'

Or lie for you, I thought, and moved on to a more promising lead.

'Who is your source?' I asked, nodding at the newspaper.

'That's confidential.'

I chuckled. 'Would it still be confidential after you spent the night in a cell?'

'Oh, Inspector, I would *hate* having to write a story about how I was victimized by the police.'

I could not believe how much I welcomed McGray's presence. 'Nine-Nails, this man is being uncooperative.'

I might as well have thrown a bloodhound on to Mr Dyer. McGray strode ahead, lifted him by the collar and pinned him against a wall, as if he were one more note on the crammed corkboards.

'Talk, ye bastard!' McGray roared. 'Who's the bloody whistle blower?'

Dyer could barely speak, McGray's hands pressing his chest mercilessly.

'This will be on the front page tomorrow!' he managed to hiss.

'Aye, ye publish that, ye bastard! I want to read it, so I can make ye eat every single copy with a knife and fork!'

'He *means* that,' I told Dyer. 'And once he is done with you we can also prosecute you for obstructing police affairs.'

I realized I was developing a disturbing affinity for Nine-Nails' methods.

'And our superintendent is crazy about Ellen Terry,' McGray said. 'He'll see that ye go down and deep.'

Dyer shook his head in despair. 'Put me down!' he snorted.

'Nae.'

'I need to reach my papers!' he insisted, now rather pleadingly.

McGray pressed him a little harder. 'All right. But if ye don't tell us what we need I'll pluck out yer silly tash hair by hair.'

He put Dyer down. The man rearranged his shirt and adjusted his tie, trying to erase any trace of rough handling. He began searching in one of his drawers, produced a piece of paper and shoved it in his breast pocket.

'I will tell you everything . . . but not here.'

To my dismay, McGray decided to take us to the Ensign Ewart, which was within a ten-minute walk.

'I assume Irving was nowhere to be found,' I said as we headed to the public house.

'Course not,' said McGray. 'The bastard vanished. But I didnae spend much o' this time looking for him. I'm on something else. Tell ye as soon as we get rid o' this wag.'

Fortunately, the establishment was deserted at this hour. The only person around was Mary, still sweeping last night's wreckage, but as soon as we arrived she brought two ales and for me a whisky.

Dyer had lost his bravado, and he stared at his drink with trembling hands.

'I lied to my chief editor,' he whispered as soon as the ginger landlady was at a prudent distance. 'I said I had the story from a very reliable source who wished to remain anonymous. The truth is . . .' he looked around again, and his voice became even softer as he pulled a sheet of paper from his pocket. 'The truth is – I only received this.'

I unfolded it. It was a rushed letter written in spidery, smudged lines. I struggled to make out some of the sentences, but it was definitely a detailed, accurate account of the sighting under Regent Bridge.

'This was written by a very eloquent pen,' I said. 'It has all the drama and embellishment of a gothic horror.'

'Who gave ye this?' asked McGray.

'I never saw the person. I was working very late in my office. Other than the chaps in the presses I was the only person there. Someone slid this underneath my door, knocked and then ran away.'

'And ye saw nothing?'

'I tried. I looked everywhere, but whoever left it was gone – and we don't have eyes on every corridor.'

'Youse leave all yer doors open at night?'

'Yes. The newspaper never closes.'

'Such an important story,' I said, 'yet all you had was an unsigned note as evidence. How very professional!' I looked at McGray. 'If the office never closes somebody else might have seen that messenger, either another employee or people on the adjacent streets. We could start an inquiry –'

McGray snatched the message from my hands. 'We're seizing that note, laddie. And this conversation never happened.'

'That is exactly what I was going to suggest.' Dyer made to stand up, but McGray pushed him back on to the seat.

'Frey, what d'ye think we should do with this one? Put him in a cell anyways? Just to keep him safe from his own eagerness, of course.'

I knew he was only joking.

'We'd better let him go,' I said, knowing that McGray would be thinking the same, 'so he can tell us if another note like this should arrive.'

Nine-Nails nodded. 'Ye heard the dandy?'

'Yes. I –'

'Ye publish *nothing*. Did ye hear me? Ye come to us immediately and show us anything they send ye.'

I gave him my card. 'Here, and if you cannot reach me –'

'Don't worry,' said Dyer, taking the card as he left, 'everybody in Edinburgh knows the house of Nine-Nails McGray.'

'Ye happy?' McGray asked me.

'Why, not at all. I am none the wiser than an hour ago.' I was going to have a sip of whisky, but the murky glass, now under the clear daylight, put me off. I put it back on the table. 'What was it you said you were on to?'

McGray savoured the moment along with a swig of ale. 'I can tell ye, no clairvoyants involved, that there will be two more banshee sightings. And very soon.'

13

'Without omens! Nine-Nails, I am astonished!'

McGray was searching his pockets and produced a transcript, in his own shabby hand, of the banshee's two warnings. He had memorized them.

'It's going to be a very fancy riddle,' he said. 'Look at the first warning. It's a two-line rhyme, as a pentameter.'

I looked at him with amazement. 'McGray, how is it that you know the meaning of the word *pentameter*?'

'Och, don't ye give me all that condescending shite as if ye had no passage to fart through! I don't speak like youse all-michty Southrons – as if I had a boiling spud in my gob – and ye just assume I cannae enjoy some culture.'

As soon as he said that he downed his pint and let out a loud belch.

'It is not only the speech,' I said laconically. Then I recalled McGray misquoting Hamlet at this very table last night, and that was not the first time I heard him bastardize Shakespeare (he'd once done it whilst facing an actual witch).

'Well, I used to read a lot o' poetry,' he said, 'before I –' he halted and bit his lip, looking at what remained of his ring finger.

I realized I had never stopped to wonder what he'd been like before becoming Nine-Nails. The obvious struck me all of a sudden: McGray had had a childhood, a youth, an entire life before his family tragedy. Now I knew he had enjoyed poetry, but how many other things I'd never be even close to finding out?

I tried to lighten the mood. 'Say what you may, I will never be able to picture you walking around turning the pages of a little sonnets book. At best I expected you to believe that *Titus Andronicus* was some kind of chest disease, or that *Coriolanus* is something you get after – never mind. Now, let me see . . .'

I leaned over the paper and counted the syllables in the first verse. I remembered Elgie seeing him counting with his fingers as he left the theatre. 'Pentameters,' I said, 'ten syllables in each line, yes. What about the second warning?'

'It's the same. All lines have ten syllables.'

'But the second is a four-line stanza. Could it be . . . ?'

McGray smiled. 'Aye, these are part of a sonnet, Frey. In Shakespearean style.'

I sat back. 'It has been a while since I last read my Shakespeare. Remind me of the sonnet's metrics.'

'Four stanzas. The first three with four lines. The final one with two.'

'So you think the first warning was, in fact, the *final* stanza?'

'Aye. It sounds odd, but there's two hints at that. First, if they're following the classic structure, the rhymes in the long stanzas are A-B-A-B.'

'Freely – rage – infamy – stage. I see.'

'Aye, they alternate. But in the first warning they put Macbeth and death together.'

'Very well, Nine-Nails, that sounds reasonable. What is the second clue you mentioned?'

'In a classic sonnet the final stanza is . . . how can I say it . . . the conclusion. The punchline. The twist.'

'In this case, somebody's death.'

'Aye, perhaps delivered first for more impact. And it means that, if these two are part of a sonnet, there are two missing stanzas.'

'To be delivered by the same banshee.'

'Aye. Ye finally listen!'

'I shall not wait on the edge of my seat, McGray. If anything, you have strengthened my case. The theatrical effects, the showmanship, the melodrama – it is all in there.'

'I kent ye were –'

'Excuse me, you what?'

'*Kent!* Knew! Knew ye were going to say that. And next yer going to ask why all the riddles; why not a plain statement.'

I would have, had I not heard Elgie's words at the theatre. Someone striving to throw attention away from themselves for some dubious, unknown purpose, was not entirely irrational. I thought McGray would entertain the same theory, but as usual he had something more extravagant in mind.

'Now, this is speculation,' he said, 'but I think the other two missing stanzas will give us the final, crucial clue, about who's going to snuff it. Unfortunately, I fear we won't get the true meaning 'til it's too late.'

'Do you mean, after the death has taken place? Like your ridiculous Madame Katerina suggested?'

'Aye.'

I laughed. 'A prophecy that is evident only in hindsight is not worth the ink it is penned with.'

'My point precisely, Frey. Banshees don't warn. They *announce*.'

Bram Stoker's Journal (continued)

Should have told the inspectors about the dog. I mentioned it to Florence on the night but she mocked me – the woman can be rather cruel sometimes. Now I fear to bring it up.

[. . .]

Something wrong with Irving. I can tell. I know his face so well. I have seen it so perpetually, under almost all possible phases of emotion – the weakness of Charles I; the vulture grip of Shylock; the fossilized age of Gregory Brewster; the asceticism of Becket – that I can now notice any twinge, any tension, any sign, no matter how insignificant, that is not related to his acting.

[. . .]

Must leave. Note from Irving arrived.

Wish I'd heard from him sooner. I cannot even guess what he has to tell me, if he asked me to meet him at [line completely obscured with ink]

14

Irving was now my prime suspect, and even McGray agreed he could well have sent the note to Dyer. Rather than chase him, we decided to leave him a message at the Palace Hotel: if he did not come to our office at eight o'clock the following morning we'd send a team of officers to fetch him at gunpoint – the latter McGray's idea.

The Palace Hotel housed the most fashionable lodgings in all of Edinburgh, and its location was certainly advantageous: the six-storey building graced the corner of Princes Street and Castle Street, the upper rooms looking directly over the castle and the most transited road of the city. Within easy distance from the train stations, the wealth of New Town and the road to the harbours, the hotel was also very close to a crucial landmark: Regent Bridge.

I took note of it, and calculated that it would take but a few minutes to walk there and back. Very handy if one wanted to impersonate a banshee in the middle of the night, even if carrying a bundle of blood-dripping rags.

I whispered this thought into McGray's ear as we walked into the lobby. In the same way that I wrinkled my nose at his beloved pub, he frowned in disgust at the well-appointed room. The lobby was a grand hall with red velvet carpets and large oil paintings depicting idealized Scottish landscapes: romantically ruined castles and implausibly sunny lochs. All those lavish frames led the eye towards a grand mahogany staircase.

The rather snobbish manager immediately came to us, perhaps to throw McGray out, but his attitude changed as soon as we showed our credentials.

'I do not know Mr Irving's whereabouts,' he said, somewhat offended. 'It is not my place to question my guests as to their daily plans.'

'Fetch us pen 'n' paper, will ye,' McGray told him, visibly annoyed by the man's conceit. I nearly blushed as I read the words he wrote for Irving.

'One more thing,' McGray told the manager. 'What type o' bed sheets do youse put in the rooms?'

The manager spoke proudly. 'Egyptian cotton, of course.'

'Right. Bring us one.'

'May I ask –'

'Ye may nae. Do as I said, else I'll punch yer snooty face.'

I feared what McGray was about to pull out of his pocket, and with good reason. He had cut out a corner of the bloodstained rags the officers had found nearby Regent Bridge.

'We should not do that here,' I said. 'You might alarm –'

Too late. The manager had returned with a clean, neatly folded sheet which he laid on the counter, but then his eyes fell right on the reddened cloth.

'Give me that,' said McGray, pulling the bed sheet.

'Will you need a magnifying glass?' I asked.

He would not: the fine weaving, the small stitches, the neat way the edges were folded at the sheet's corner, everything matched.

'The bloody rags came from here,' I mumbled.

McGray took a deep breath and shoved the dirty rag back into his pocket. He looked at the manager. 'What's yer name?'

The man gulped. 'Cla— Clarke. Josiah Clarke.'

'Hear me, Clarkie, we need ye to ask all yer maids if any o' their sheets went missin' in the last couple o' nights. Don't tell them the reason. If they did, find out from which room and when. As soon, and I mean *as soon* as ye get news, ye tell us. Frey, give him one o' yer sissy cards.'

I passed one to Mr Clarke, along with the note for Henry Irving.

McGray then whispered harshly, poking firmly at the man's chest. 'Ye tell no one about this. Ye understand?' The poor man only nodded. 'And ye better see that Irving reads that note the minute he comes back.'

Mr Clarke looked quite intimidated, but his countenance became illuminated all of a sudden, and as if we had vanished into thin air, he raised his hand and yelped most gleefully.

'Oh, Miss Terry!'

He ran like a dart towards the carpeted staircase, where a small crowd was gathering.

An elegant hourglass figure, wearing a dress of white damask, was descending with slow, dignified steps.

Miss Ellen Terry.

An older gentleman offered her a rose, while others waved and called her name. A second gentleman planted himself at the foot of the stairs, babbling loud compliments. Miss Terry, used to the attention, returned the greeting and expertly glided around him, shielding herself behind the hotel manager.

At some point she looked directly at us, her eyes

perhaps drawn to McGray's garish tartan trousers, and then Mr Clarke pointed in our direction, surely telling her who we were. Gracefully and kindly, she kept the people at bay as she approached us, a wide smile on her face, and I very soon had a close look at Britain's most cherished living celebrity. I decided I'd block all my preconceptions of her; I could have never questioned her whilst thinking that she had performed for Queen Victoria not three months ago, or that in her younger years she'd posed nude for Watts's scandalous painting *The Wife of Pluto*.

With that canvas in mind, I soon realized that Miss Terry had to be seen in the flesh, for photographs and paintings did not do her justice. She could not be called classically beautiful, her nose rather large, her chin a little too manly, but there was an arresting quality to her; a certain radiance that made it difficult to look away.

She had smooth, alabaster skin, and blonde curly hair framing her plump cheeks, but it was her pale blue eyes that set her apart. There was a sharpness, an intensity to her stare that invariably drew one's gaze.

Though she was not short, I had expected her to be taller, and although she looked her age (forty-two) she conducted herself with an elegance I could never expect to see in a twenty-year-old belle.

The manager introduced us and Miss Terry offered us a magnolia-white hand to kiss.

'Mr Clarke tells me you are looking for dear Irving,' she said in a clear, musical voice, each consonant and vowel enunciated beautifully.

'Indeed,' I said before McGray could spit out one of his prosaic *ayes*. 'We have left a message for him. It is urgent that he comes to see us.'

'I am sure he will oblige,' she replied, placing her light hand on my arm. 'We are all so grateful you are involved. This ghastly affair is like poison poured on to our little play.' She studied Nine-Nail's attire, especially his tartan, but not once did her gestures show the slightest judgement. 'That pattern is a brave statement, Inspector.'

I could not tell whether she was being coquettish or simply very kind. Whichever the case, she managed to bring an earnest laugh out of him.

'I like ye already, hen!'

They smiled at each other one second too long, until I cleared my throat.

'Miss Terry, I am glad you found us. We need to ask you a few questions; about the banshee affair and – that unwelcome present you received.'

There was a flash of apprehension in her eyes, which I would have missed had I blinked. She recollected herself just as quickly and smiled warmly. 'Oh, of course, gentlemen. It might be best to talk in a more private place, don't you think? I will call for some tea.'

The lady was staying in a large suite with its own sitting room, all tastefully decorated in bright creams and ochres, and all the rooms had a rather heavy scent of camellias. When we arrived a chambermaid was already displaying the cups and plates, in anticipation of the tea.

'What a speedy service,' I remarked as Miss Terry and I sat on cushioned mahogany chairs.

'Oh, it's been the best,' Miss Terry said, smiling at the young woman. 'Bring us some of those delicious lemon tartlets, darling. I'd like the gentlemen to try them.'

McGray was pacing, his threadbare clothes and unkempt stubble completely at odds with the marble mantelpiece and the brocade curtains.

'Will you not have a seat, Inspector?' offered Miss Terry.

'Nae, I'm all right.'

'Oh, I do insist,' Miss Terry said, standing up and, rather too forwardly to my taste, taking McGray's arm. 'Do it for me, sir.'

McGray was shepherded towards a seat and at least some of his uneasiness seemed lifted. Miss Terry noticed his mutilated hand, and again I could not see a trace of discomfort in her.

'What a terrible accident that must have been,' she said with what seemed genuine interest.

McGray looked at his stump and waved his hand dismissively. 'Meh, it's all right. I always say I can still give people the two fingers.'

I blushed, thinking what a shocking thing that was to say in front of a lady, but Miss Terry seemed most entertained.

She smoothed the folds of her dress. 'Perhaps one day you might be able to tell me about all your adventures.'

'Och, this was no adventure,' said Nine-Nails, looking down.

'And there is no time for such stories right now,' I said before the woman distracted us further with her niceties. 'Miss Terry, can you tell us, in as much detail as possible, what happened around the time you found those brains?'

I was expecting Miss Terry to recount the ordeal with tears, yelps and beating her chest with all the abandonment of a

138

professional tragedienne. Quite the contrary: she told the facts clearly and succinctly. She was obviously affected, but in perfect control of herself. And her version matched those of Stoker and Miss Ivor.

'So whoever placed that bundle in your dressing room must have done it while you were washing your hands,' I said.

'Of course, Inspector. It must have been a matter of minutes.'

'And neither you nor Miss Ivor could see anything.'

'No. We were standing just around a corner from the door.'

McGray shifted in his seat, stroking his stubble. He'd initially looked at Miss Terry with some lasciviousness, but now he was back to his brooding self. 'Miss Terry, how come ye were washing yer hands in the middle of the corridor? Sounds a wee bit unusual.'

The tea came in right then and Miss Terry turned her face to the waiters, so I could not gauge her initial reaction.

'Well – I had just gone out to look for Miss Ivor. She was taking her time and I needed to change for the final ovation. Shall I be mother?'

'Miss Terry,' I said, pushing my cup to welcome the brew, 'I understand you were in a hurry, but how long would it have taken you to go back to your dressing room and wash your hands there? Seconds, perhaps?'

She put the silver teapot down with a rattle. 'I beg your pardon?'

'Well, I am sorry to put this out so forwardly, but washing in plain sight seems to me a very unladylike thing to do – for a woman of your refinement, I mean.'

Her eyes narrowed a little, fixed on mine, and I felt as though she were reading into my mind. 'The things that are seen behind the stage would shock you, Mr Frey. But I understand how a woman scrubbing her hands in a corridor might be scandalous in your mansion at Gloucester Square.'

I raised my eyebrows at her curtness, but in a blink Miss Terry was all smiles again.

'Oh, do excuse me, Inspector; that was quite uncalled for. You must understand how distressing this has been. Pray, try these lemon tartlets. They're a menace to my figure!'

I did so, initially to feign I did not mind her remark, but the blasted things were so delicious it annoyed me. I still wanted to ask a few more questions, but with my mouth full I could not keep Nine-Nails from moving swiftly on to the banshee issue.

He mentioned the legends, his 'reliable' source telling him there might be a real threat, and the possibility of it all being about Irish blood. While he spoke I savoured the tartlets and the excellent Darjeeling. Surprisingly, Miss Terry listened to him with undivided attention.

'I have trouble believing it was something supernatural,' I said as soon as the sweet treats allowed. 'Miss Terry, would you say that was a cry worthy of a banshee?'

She shook her head. 'I myself was screaming right then. I could not possibly tell you.'

I looked through my notes. 'I understand the first person to find the writings was your seamstress, Mrs Harwood . . . and that Mr Irving found her with her fingers covered in –'

'Mrs Harwood could *not* have done it,' Miss Terry jumped in, her eyes wide open. This time she was not apologetic about her agitation. 'I know you might find it all very suspicious, but I'd put my hands in the fire for her. I've known her for four – no, five years, and she would *never* do anything of the kind.'

McGray sighed deeply. 'I've met people who've done terrible things . . . Things nobody would've thought them capable of.'

I had not intended to ask much about the dressmaker, but Miss Terry's reaction piqued my curiosity.

'Miss Terry, it would not be such a dreadful thing if Mrs Harwood turned out to have done it,' I said, being as conciliatory as possible. 'She has not committed any crime . . .' I stopped myself before saying *yet*. 'But from my brief conversation with her, and seeing the way she attacked Mr Wheatstone on the street, I do believe she might be . . . unwell. Perhaps this is a cry for help. She might be in need of treatment.'

'She's had her tribulations, certainly, but from that to insanity! I cannot believe it. I *refuse* to believe it.' Miss Terry drank her tea slowly, once again covering part of her face, but I saw it had been difficult for her to swallow. 'I'm afraid I can't offer you any more information about her,' she said in the end, 'neither to absolve her, nor otherwise.'

She put her cup down and said no more, perhaps expecting the silence to invite us to leave. I wanted to ask her about the green dress alibi, but it was clear her statement would be biased.

'Miss Terry, *if* we assume that Mrs Harwood can be ruled out, there is only one alternative –'

'There's a real banshee announcing someone's death,' McGray interrupted, and I could only roll my eyes.

'That is *not* what I was about to offer. Miss Terry, how is Mr Irving handling the situation?'

I realized too late how keenly I'd spoken.

'Is he your other suspect?' asked Miss Terry, now with a hint of derision in her tone.

There was no point in denying it. 'I suspect he has orchestrated all this, yes. You had difficulties with ticket sales in Scotland, did you not?'

'Why, yes, but Henry would *never* –'

'Is Mr Irving not the most passionate actor of our times, miss? Would he not be willing to do *anything* for the success of his plays?'

She looked sharply at me, her pale irises buoyant with outrage. Those eyes were definitely fit for Lady Macbeth.

'Why do you ask me? You seem to have reached your own conclusions already.'

Her defensive attitude did not come as a surprise. Everyone in the land – even I, who consciously avoided paying much attention to gossip from the stage – knew that Ellen Terry and Henry Irving had had an on-going love affair from the very start of their joint careers. Theirs was a torrid romance that sparked and died out several times a year, even more scandalous since Irving had always been a married man.

That thought was rather premonitory, considering what McGray's next question unleashed. 'Was Irving very upset about the banshee?'

Miss Terry was about to bite a tartlet, but Nine-Nails' words put her off eating.

'He was *very* upset, yes, but not so much because of the banshee.'

McGray leaned forward. 'Oh! Why, then? Did anything scarier happen that night?'

Miss Terry's perfect smile was now twisted with bitterness.

'Far scarier, Inspector. His wife was there! Uninvited.'

15

McGray and I were astounded, to say the least, and Miss Terry was now keen to tell us more.

'You may be aware – it has been common knowledge for quite a while – that Irving is estranged from his wife. He hasn't seen his two sons for years. However, on the night of our last performance, she was there.'

'There where?'

'In the audience. Seated with the *pittites*!'

'The who?'

'Oh, in the pit, the cheap area, surrounded by the middle-class tradesmen she despises so much. Irving saw her and was petrified. It was at the same time as the banshee episode.'

'No one had mentioned that wee detail,' McGray said. 'Not even Mr Stoker.'

'Do you know, erm . . .' I cleared my throat, 'the reason for the estrangement?'

Miss Terry threw her head back and laughed hard. 'Something in your tone,' she said, all sarcasm, 'tells me you already have a theory!'

I blushed profusely. Fortunately, Miss Terry showed some mercy. 'Their marriage was never meant to succeed, and not because of me. Mrs Irving dug her own grave long before my time.'

McGray spoke. 'So that was before ye and Irving . . .'

'*Years* before,' Miss Terry went on. 'The poor lady

could never come to terms with Irving's passion for the theatre. Irving does as he wishes; he always has, and responds to nobody. That silly Florence, with her whims and her demands of attention, could never compete with that, and Irving was wise enough to walk away from her.

'It was on the opening night of *The Bells*, gosh, ages ago . . . How old is young Sydney these days? Seventeen or eighteen years ago. Florence was pregnant with Sydney, their second son, you see. She saw the play, was not terribly impressed, and I was told she waited for Irving in their brougham carriage for quite a while after the performance, in the cold of November, being seven or eight months into her pregnancy. But it was Irving's opening night and the play had been a roaring success – people still write to him evoking his rendering of Mathias. Irving could not detach himself from the crowd.' Miss Terry chuckled. 'I can easily imagine Florence, her anger rising as she heard the adulation; she must have thought that her husband had completely forgotten her, and forgotten that she was with child and exhausted.

'Despite her protests Irving dragged her on to a supper in his honour, where even more people praised and praised him. When they finally went home she broke her silence. Irving himself told me that it happened as they crossed Hyde Park Corner, the very spot where he had proposed to her.'

I looked up, for that was not too far from my childhood home.

'Apparently,' Miss Terry said, 'Florence's very words were: *Are you going to make a fool of yourself like this all your life?*'

Her smile then was scornful. She would not hide how much she revelled in that story.

'What a thing to say on such a night,' she continued. 'Irving was at the peak of his career. *The Bells* was his big breakthrough, and it had taken him twelve years to get there – *twelve* years of struggle, of constant training, fighting his old speech impediment, knocking at doors, being criticized and sometimes laughed at, living in the cheapest lodgings and surviving thanks to moneylenders. And when he finally succeeded, when he had his moment of greatest personal glory, his own wife called him a fool! What an irony: he got respect and recognition from colleagues and strangers everywhere, yet he could not find them in his own home, from the very person who claimed to love him the most!' Miss Terry sighed, a sideways smile creeping up her face. 'They have never lived together again. Sydney was born within a month, but Irving was drinking a lot and didn't even go to his christening.'

'Sounds like she'd hate Irving's plays,' McGray said.

'She *abhors* the theatre. But she still demands to have the royal box for every opening night – only because those are the nights we have the most illustrious guests and she loves to be seen. She considers our profession useless and shameful, yet she has no scruples to enjoy the perquisites – or to live extravagantly on Irving's wealth.'

'So what was she doing there?' McGray asked.

'We have no idea, Inspector, and there was no chance to confront her. The banshee was heard just as Irving spotted her. When he looked again the woman was gone.'

I nodded. 'That closing performance was last week, was it not? Has there been any communication between Irving and his wife since then?'

'Not that I'm aware of. But Irving never tells me much about his dealings with that woman . . .' again she chuckled, 'for reasons you two can imagine. I only overheard him mumble that she looked sickly thin, as if she'd just gone through some ravaging disease. Her own bitterness consuming her, I would say.' She cleared her throat. 'I believe Mr Stoker would be in a better position to answer that.'

Indeed, I would like to know why Stoker had omitted that piece of information.

As I took a note on that, there was a soft knock on the door, in an irregular rhythm. Miss Terry seemed to recognize the petitioner immediately, for her frown softened and her lips relaxed into a wide smile.

'Yes?' she said, her voice as warm and charming as it had been at first.

A juvenile voice came back. 'May I come in? Mr Clarke says you're mighty busy.'

'Of course you can, don't be a goose.'

The door opened slowly, and I first saw the small hand of a young girl, bejewelled with three golden rings with very shiny stones. Then, as shy as the knocking, a clump of blonde curls emerged, and I saw the right-hand side of a very sweet girl's face – the young girl I'd seen on the stage, playing the apparition.

'Don't be timid, Susy,' said Miss Terry. 'Come and greet these handsome gentlemen.'

The girl Susy did hesitate, and when she took her final step in my heart skipped a beat. I first thought she'd not washed off the make-up, and was about to comment on how realistic it was, but all too soon I realized my mistake. The ghastly scarring, those reddened, horrible blemishes, shining and bulging like molten wax, showing where the tissue had at some point burned . . . that *was* her face.

A shudder crept all over me. It was not the shock of the face itself (sadly, I have seen many a defaced youngster in the London slums) but the surprise of her disfigurement being real.

'Susy, meet Mr McGray and Mr Frey,' said Miss Terry, but the girl was rather paralysed by shyness. She was around twelve, and it saddened me to think that she would have to carry such a burden for the rest of her life.

McGray kissed the girl's hand, as if saluting a very grand lady. 'Nice to meet ye, lassie. First time in Scotland?'

Susy smiled with endearing shyness, and covered her face with a little book she'd been carrying. I managed to read the golden letters on the cover: *Alice's Adventures in Wonderland*.

'I read that same book when I was about your age,' I told her. 'Do you like it?'

The girl nodded but again remained silent.

'I assume you have finished it?' asked Miss Terry, and Susy nodded again and handed her the small book. 'That was very quick! I have just discovered a collection of fairy limericks you're going to love. I'll leave it out on this table for you; come and take it whenever you want.'

The girl smiled, still quite flushed, and immediately curtsied and left.

'She was one o' the spirits,' said McGray. 'It's quite cruel to parade her on stage, don't ye think? No wonder the poor lassie's so shy.'

Miss Terry sighed deeply, staring at the book. 'It was Irving's decision to cast her. At least the girl has a good income.'

An uncomfortable silence followed, which I tried to break with what I thought was an innocuous sentence.

'A rather unusual choice of literature,' I said, and I pointed at the children's book. 'For a grown-up, I mean.'

Miss Terry's mouth twisted in a melancholic grimace, and I knew I'd somehow made matters worse.

'I *used* to be very good friends with Mr Carroll. He sent me this a few years ago.'

She opened it on the first pages and I saw a long dedication written in a beautiful hand, followed by a flourished signature and an exquisite sketch of the White Rabbit.

Miss Terry's expression was that of someone who'd been slapped in the face.

Used to be, I repeated in my head.

I imagined that a gentleman as respectable as Lewis Carroll, renowned academic, author and mathematician, had considered it impossible to maintain any kind of connection with a woman such as Miss Terry. She might be wealthy, beautiful and adored by the public, but she was still a divorcee with two children born out of wedlock. And those were just the tip of the iceberg of secrets I'd soon learn about her.

16

Miss Terry showed us the way out herself, the actress in her quickly taking over with wide smiles and soft laughter.

'We are holding a little soirée tomorrow night, here at the hotel's ballroom. Would you care to join us?'

McGray frowned. 'Black tie 'n' so forth?'

'I'm afraid so, Inspector.'

'Nae, but thanks for the thought, hen.'

'Are you sure?' Miss Terry insisted, squeezing McGray's arm in a scandalously forward way. 'The most illustrious names in Scotland will be there.'

'Och, that's what I'm trying to avoid! I'm not exactly popular in those circles.'

Miss Terry nodded. 'Very well, but I will keep you on the guest list in case you change your mind.' She looked at me, still very kindly but not even nearly as coquettishly as she'd addressed Nine-Nails. 'Inspector Frey, you will surely enjoy the evening. And you can bring Mrs Frey, if you wish.'

McGray cackled. '*Mrs Frey!* This virginal English rose got left at the altar.'

Miss Terry laughed as well, and it was only my utterly mortified face that made her realize Nine-Nails was not joking. She covered her mouth in embarrassment.

'Oh, I am so, so sorry. I had no idea . . .' But then she

looked back at McGray and resumed her shameless flirting. 'My, oh my! How can you tease your colleague so?' and she playfully smacked his shoulder.

I, however, had the perfect revenge at hand.

'I will most likely be busy,' I lied, 'but would it be terribly improper of me to forward your invitation to my father and his good wife?'

'Oh, by all means!' Miss Terry said at once, if only to compensate for her laughing at my disgrace. 'In fact, I will only list you as *the Freys*, in case you find yourself free as well.'

I smiled. Poor Miss Terry had no idea of the curse I'd just unleashed upon her.

And since we were talking frivolities, I found the perfect chance to bring up the dress matter as casually as I ever could.

'I had the opportunity to see your Lady Macbeth costume,' I said, choosing my words very carefully.

Miss Terry smiled. 'Why, the green one with the beetles?'

'That very one; it is a remarkable piece of craftsmanship. I wonder – how long did it take to make it?'

'Well, the dress itself took no time; it's very simple crochet in yarn and tinsel, but I tried it on stage and Irving thought it didn't look *regal* enough, despite the jewels on all the hems. My friend, Miss Comyns Carr, came up with the idea of the beetles. She's a genius. I would never have even thought about them. Poor Mrs Harwood was not that impressed, I'm afraid. The dress needed more than a thousand wings – it took her three full days to have the darling ready.'

I nodded, exchanging looks with McGray. To my

frustration, Mrs Harwood's alibi *did* ring true. I would need to look for other suspects.

I followed McGray to the City Chambers, where Philippa was still tethered.

'You should get yourself a horse,' I said as we reached the front courtyard.

'What for? That Bavarian beauty will be mine before Monday.'

I did not comment further. Before leaving I saw McGray heading straight to the narrow corridor that led to the Dumping Ground.

'Are you not going home?' I asked, looking at my pocket watch. It was well past six, yet the sun was still high in the clear sky.

'Nah. I'll stay in the office. I could use a wee bit more reading on Irish spectres. And I want to be available in case there's another sighting.'

I was too tired to even mock him. 'Do you think it might happen again tonight?'

'Could well be. It's just three nights before the opening.'

I only sighed. I also could have gone to the office to review my notes, but I remembered that my dear father and his even dearer wife were to arrive tomorrow, thus leaving me one last night of peace and quiet. A tranquil supper, followed by a couple of relaxing hours with a book and a brandy sounded most tempting.

Sadly, I was not so lucky, and it was all Elgie's fault. The little rascal had invited the entire bloody orchestra for drinks, which I would not have minded, had they not brought along at least another twenty drunken musicians and a handful of young trollops I had never seen in my life.

Layton, whose face looked as if someone had bleached it, received me with a quivering voice. 'Sir, Master Elgie has . . . organized a little gathering.'

'Little!' I could hear the frantic notes of *Orpheus in the Underworld*, so loud it was as if the entire house had become a dingy ballroom in Montparnasse. And then roaring laughter. And then I saw a trio of young men, cackling and waving fat glasses of whisky, spilling it on the carpets as they swayed across the corridor and on into the dining room, where yet another little noisy group had gathered.

Layton's voice came out as if the poor man were constipated. 'The young master said you would not mind, sir.'

I pushed my hat into his hands. 'I am sure he did . . .' and I stormed into the main parlour, where two cellos, a viola and three violins shrilled merrily. Elgie stood at the centre, one of his colleagues feeding him red wine as he played on.

I elbowed my way forward, and when my brother saw me he dropped his bow, which fell at the foot of a fat dancing man, who tripped on it and fell on to a lady, who in turn fell and pushed another guest, who spilled half his drink on me.

'What the hell is this?' I roared, but even though the music stopped, the chatter and laughter went on. Elgie appeared to be the only one who recognized the extent of my anger.

'Ian!' he said, as he approached me with a nervous smile. 'I hope your investigations have gone –'

'*What the hell is this?*'

Elgie tried to pull me away, not to be embarrassed in front of his friends. I repeated my question nonetheless.

'We have been working to death in the past few days,' he whispered, 'and it will only get worse before Saturday –'

A swaying middle-aged man, whom I recognized as the conductor of the orchestra, pushed both of us as he chased a giggling woman.

I snorted. 'What kind of scoundrels have you invited, all of them drunk by six? And who are those – *ladies*? Are you turning the house into a bloody brothel?'

A young woman heard me and began to give me abuse, first telling me I'd not been invited. I had no patience to deal with that, and without even glancing at her I dragged Elgie out of the room.

'I simply told them they could bring company,' Elgie said. 'It never occurred to me they'd bring ladies! Mr Horrax just arrived with two –'

'*I want all your drunken friends out!* I will have my dinner in my room and will come downstairs within the hour. And if a single one of them is still here –'

By then I was already climbing the stairs, and I locked my door thanking providence for the thick walls and ceilings of Lady Anne's house.

Layton must have heard me or divined my intentions – or simply wanted to escape the mayhem himself – for he soon came by, bringing me a bowl of steaming oyster soup and a fresh-baked loaf.

'I cannot apologize enough for the infernal rattle, sir,' he said, cutting thick slices of crusty bread. 'I could do little to stop them.'

'Do not worry,' I assured him. 'I doubt this will happen again while our parents are visiting.'

He searched his pockets. 'Sir, that brings to mind this correspondence, which arrived this afternoon.'

He handed me an envelope: a telegram from London, for Elgie. The sender's address, though close to Hyde Park Gate, was not that of my father.

'Are you all right, sir?' Layton asked. I realized I'd clenched my fist around a slice of bread and the crumbs were making a mess on the tray.

I put the telegram on the table, face down, for I could not stand the sight of that address while eating.

※

I have explored McGray's turbulent past in detail, so it is only fair that I devote some paragraphs to mine.

The telegram had come from Laurence, my elder and only whole brother. Just thinking of his name brings fire to my gut, a discomfort that only seems to worsen as life goes on: I have disliked him since we were children, but our boyhood scuffles are nothing compared to the loathing that now exists between us.

Our exacerbated enmity was caused by Eugenia Ferrars, my erstwhile fiancée. Contrary to the gossip that Nine-Nails loves to drop around so casually whenever he has the chance, she did *not* leave me at the altar. There is no need to embellish the tale, for it was bad enough in reality: she summoned me one day – the same day I'd been dismissed from my post in Scotland Yard – and with no forewarning announced that she wished to end the engagement.

Not much later, on that very night, I'd been dispatched

to Scotland to end up under the authority of the disgraced McGray. It was only weeks later that I found out the reason she'd jilted me: Laurence had proposed to her . . . and she had accepted on the spot! And as none of my family members had dared give me the news, I'd first heard it from Sir Charles Warren, the CID's former commissioner. The news had obviously travelled faster than the plague, and that was the main reason I'd not been to London since. I would never admit it, but the mere prospect of people's mockery infuriated me – my brother's most of all.

He and Eugenia were having one of those long, fashionable courtships, parading themselves and their chaperones at every possible social occasion, where my name was surely whispered as soon as they were in sight. The peak of my humiliation would come on their wedding day – the date had not been suggested yet – but even after that, the entire affair would remain there, forever floating around us like a foul smell.

While I am not sure I'd really *loved* Eugenia, I had certainly loved the idea of our future together. Our flawed personas would have complemented each other, and we had definitely enjoyed a plethora of sweet moments. Sadly, even the happy memories were tarnished now, for I could no longer think of her without bitterness, disappointment and unbridled anger.

The months had passed and I'd forced myself to keep the matter out of my head, but occasional reminders, like that telegram sitting on my table right now, were impossible to avoid.

The door opened slowly after a meek knock, and I saw Elgie's face peeking in. He did not dare enter, but just smiled nervously.

I closed my book with a thump that made him jump. 'Come in, for goodness' sake.' So he did, his hands folded behind him. 'Are they gone?'

'Yes.'

'Good. How ruined is the house?'

Elgie bit his lip. 'Do . . . do you think Lady Anne would have been very attached to that Imperial Ming vase that was on the – ?'

I raised a hand. 'On second thought, I do *not* want to know right now.' I handed him the telegram. 'This is for you.'

Elgie's already wine-blushed face became a ripened currant when he saw who the sender was. He opened the envelope with nervous hands, nearly tearing the message itself.

'What does he want?' I grunted after a moment.

'Well . . . he is coming for the play.'

'Laurence and *that* woman will not set foot in this house,' I said promptly. 'And you'd better bloody tell them so.'

'Laurence assumed as much,' said Elgie. 'Says here they will probably go to the Palace Hotel, and Eugenia asks if I know in which suite Henry Irving is staying.'

'The trollop,' I muttered.

'Ian!'

'What? Even father calls her that!'

Elgie had to cover his mouth to conceal a hint of a laugh, surely remembering our last Christmas at our uncle's.

'Tell me as soon as you know their plans,' I said. 'I'd rather a real banshee appeared and painted messages with my own blood than see them.'

'Do not tempt fate,' said Elgie. 'What would Mr Mc-Gray say of your disbelief?'

I believe I threw something at him before locking myself in my bedroom, where I distracted myself by reviewing my notes from the day – incredible that the possibility of a mortal curse was preferable to the idea of seeing my stepmother and my former sweetheart.

I thought it would be a quiet night, but at twenty minutes past twelve, just as I was finally beginning to drift, there came a frantic knocking on my front door.

17

Layton was somehow fully dressed when he opened the door. I could not tell whether he'd been sleeping in his clothes or had not yet gone to bed, but there was no chance to ask him: my attention was caught by the shadows of what could have been two towering, broad-shouldered twins.

'Nine-Nails!' I said, and then had to rub my eyes to believe who stood next to him. 'Mr Stoker?'

'Would the gentlemen like to come in?' asked Layton.

'This yer dad?' McGray said, albeit not giving a chance for an answer. 'We've no time for formalities. Irving wants to see us.'

'Irving . . . at this hour . . . Why?'

'Told ye he wisnae too smart at night,' McGray muttered for Stoker, who looked ghastly pale.

'You need to talk to him,' the Irishman pleaded to me. His accent was stronger than ever and his brow was wrinkled in apprehension. 'Please, I know it's the most inconvenient hour, but –'

'*Inconvenient!* That is not even close to –'

'*I beg you!*'

Stoker's anguished voice echoed throughout the deserted street. As he took a step forwards I saw the ghastly, dark rings under his eyes. He'd probably not slept more than a few hours in the past two days.

'Very well, I will come,' I said, and less than ten

seconds later Layton was handing me a change of clothes. Not five minutes after the initial knocking, I was sharing a cab with Nine-Nails and Bram Stoker.

We must have looked like overgrown sardines: three men taller than average, two of them rather generously built, all crammed up shoulder to shoulder in that little carriage. Fortunately, the streets were deserted, and even though the clean sky glowed in the eternal midsummer dusk and the almost full moon, there was nobody around to laugh at us.

The driver took us east, and for a moment I thought our destination was the now infamous Regent Bridge. Indeed, we rode across it, but the horses moved on without slowing down. The cab ascended the steep slopes of Calton Hill, towards the towering shapes of the Royal Observatory, the Nelson Monument and the Greek-style columns of Scotland's forever unfinished National Monument.

The moon came and went behind the blackened pillars as we rode round them, the wheels leaving the road and now rolling on damp grass.

I had not realized how tall and imposing the structure really was: each column must be six feet in diameter, and the foundation stones on which they stood were taller than McGray standing on Stoker's shoulders. No wonder the monument had never been completed, and now it stood atop the hill looking as ominous as any ancient ruin.

There, in between the thick pillars and perfectly delineated against the dark blue sky, was the figure of Henry Irving, swathed in a black cloak that waved with the soft wind. He looked down at us, as if from a gigantic stage.

I heard the soft neighing of a horse, and saw a second carriage – Irving's luxurious landau – parked nearby.

Stoker jumped down as soon as we halted, and we followed him to a promontory and then the unfinished steps that ascended to the columns.

Irving waited patiently, and as we approached the moonlight played a macabre transfiguration on him: his pasty skin glowed in almost silver tones, and his sharp cheekbones and his deep brow were outlined by clean, straight shadows, making him look like a spectre.

'Good evening, gentlemen,' he said as a sudden wind made me shiver, his voice as clear and penetrating as ever.

'I think ye've heard we're looking for ye,' said McGray.

'Mr Stoker has advised me to see you,' Irving hissed, and Stoker held his breath, a rather pathetic expression on his face. 'Here I am. Ask whatever you intended to.'

'Did you divulge the story of the banshee under Regent Bridge to the newspapers?' I asked at once. I did not want to spend much time in front of such a man.

Irving clasped the lapels of his cloak and raised his chin even further.

'Yes.'

Another sudden breeze, and this time I had to wrap up more tightly in my overcoat.

'Why, that was *much* easier than I thought,' I said, instantly turning to McGray. 'Nine-Nails, you owe me some drink.'

'Hold yer horses, lassie! Irving, did ye mount up the banshee spectacle?'

Irving smiled a sardonic, arrogant smile, his wet, sharp teeth so white they seemed to shine.

'No. I did not.'

My shoulders fell an inch. 'Dear Lord! And I thought this was going to be easy. Could you please stop telling lies, Mr Irving? You have already confessed –'

'*I have confessed to telling the tale!*' he roared, pointing at me with a long, gloved index finger, his imperious voice bouncing across the hill. 'I have *not* said that I took any part in its creation!'

'I find that a little hard to believe,' I said, standing my ground. 'Your company is already benefiting from the scandal. Your play was not doing as well as it did in London and now it is sold out. You employ several well-trained actresses who could have been instructed to play the part. *You* yourself were one of the prime witnesses of the first so-called apparition. Shall I continue?'

Irving sighed. 'If someone is playing the apparition it is not my doing. Yes, I saw the advantages of the scandal. I did, and I used it. As soon as that clown Wheatstone told me everything, I saw the possibilities.'

'So you wrote this?' I asked, unfolding the letter that Mr Dyer had given us.

Irving was only slightly impressed. 'Yes, disguising my hand a little. And I sent one of my footmen to deliver it. He found the one man still working at that hour. I *did* use the story, but, as I said, fashioning such a farce for the sake of selling a few more seats is beneath me.'

'Would you be prepared to declare everything you have just said under oath?'

'Of course I would.'

I could not see a hint of nervousness, or guilt, or anything that betrayed his statements, yet I felt I could not trust him; he was after all one of the most gifted actors of our time.

'Do you also admit,' I asked, 'that a mysterious banshee announcing death in cryptic verses is something very hard to swallow?'

'Of course. I'm as confused as you are. This whole affair is very alarming.'

'Yet you had no hesitation to use it in your favour! You certainly deserve to be dragged to jail, at least for a couple of days.'

Stoker jumped in like an angry housewife. 'Mr Irving hasn't done anything illegal. It's no crime to give information to a respectable newspaper, and his report was neither false nor libellous.'

He uttered those words as if memorized from a solicitor's guidelines, and I remembered the man had worked in public service. This was probably not the first time he had aided Irving out of legal trouble.

'I'd only be committing a crime,' Irving added, 'if I failed to tell you the truth. I have done so now. I should be free to go.'

I snorted bitterly, glaring alternatively at Irving and Stoker. 'At least you are well advised.' I looked at McGray, who had been suspiciously quiet, stroking his prickly stubble. 'Anything you would like to ask?' I wondered.

His eyes, I then saw, showed that impish spark that usually unnerves me. Tonight, however, I was not his target. He was looking straight at Henry Irving.

'What can ye tell us about yer wife?'

Irving seemed to lose his balance. He looked at McGray with blazing eyes, dropping his gloves, and slowly closing his bony fingers into tight fists.

'That doesn't concern you!'

McGray chuckled. 'We're CID, lad. If I think it concerns us, it bloody well does.'

Stoker tried to place a hand on Irving's shoulder, which the actor pushed away in an angry move.

'She was at your London theatre when that first banshee appeared,' I reminded him.

'You are very well informed,' Irving said.

McGray said something I had not at all considered until then. 'Would yer wife be interested in sabotaging yer wee play?'

Irving's brow arched with eerie plasticity.

'She would not dare . . .' he whispered. 'She . . .'

'Likes her theatre money far too much,' concluded McGray.

'Crudely put,' Irving mumbled bitterly, 'but accurate. Besides, my two sons –' Irving stopped himself. His dark pupils looked sideways. 'Their education depends on me. And they are Florence's darlings. She would *die* before doing anything to their detriment.'

I studied his face carefully, and Stoker's. To my frustration, the situation made perfect sense: if Irving was not behind the apparitions, he was indeed doing the sensible thing now by confessing to his opportunism.

'Very well,' said McGray. 'We'll take our leave.'

'I must . . . beg you to keep this strictly between us,' said Irving, making McGray laugh earnestly.

'Why should we do that? We'll tell if we want to tell. Och, and by the way, we might need to question youse again as things develop . . .' McGray approached Irving boasting his most insolent face. 'And if we ask ye to talk, *ye* talk to us, no matter which sodding tights ye happen to be wearing or which bloody declamation youse are rehearsing. And if ye do another silly runner like today's, we'll not warn ye again; we'll just send the peelers to get ye to a cell.'

Stoker jumped in. 'That's preposterous! You cannot arrest a man without charges.'

'I am afraid that is not entirely true,' I said. 'We can hold anyone for as long as we want if that suits our investigation. There is no law limiting our powers in that respect.'

'Your superintendent would not allow it,' said Stoker.

'Perhaps not, but we can make sure it takes at least a few hours before he finds out and orders a release.'

McGray was smiling. 'What d'youse reckon even a few hours in the dump would do to the reputation of the famed Irving? And we've just met a savvy reporter of flexible morals who'd *love* to write the exclusive.'

Irving was going to interject but Stoker spoke in time. 'That shan't be necessary.'

And he grasped Irving's shoulder, whispering something in his ear. Whatever it was, Irving picked up his gloves, wrapped himself tightly in his black cape, and retreated. His eyes were fixed on us one second too long, and I felt an inexplicable shudder. Irving was a man used to having his way, to feeling powerful and revered, and we were acknowledging neither his talents nor his fame. The ultimate insult.

Bram Stoker's Journal

Fragments collected by Inspector I. P. Frey.

11 July, 2 a.m. – Can barely keep myself awake, after the ghastly ordeals I have witnessed tonight. A much needed measure of single malt sits next to me and has much relieved my overworked senses; I could easily doze off into a blissful slumber, but I must register all this before the memory fails or – worse still – twists the facts.

[. . .]

Finally found Irving in [Obscured in the original] *Needless to say how distressed he was. He told me everything.*

I was convinced the good Irving would smack me when I suggested he confessed his involvement with the newspaper. It was the best choice, the <u>only</u> *choice for him, so I insisted. Don't mind taking his rage this time.*

[. . .]

The inspectors are as suspicious as expected but I'm proud of my intervention. At least Irving is now covered.

After we left them the cab returned us to the Palace – but the trip was not peaceful.

To avoid prying eyes I instructed the driver to go through some patches of wilderness that grow on the south-eastern side of the hill, then turn west.

There, at the foot of the mound, the horse became agitated,

refused to tread on, even after a good lashing from the coach-
man. The cab jerked and Irving swore.

The coachman shouted there was something on the road. I
stuck my head out the window but in the commotion only
managed a fleeting glance.

A willowy figure in a glimmering shroud.

I turned to Irving but when he looked out the vision was gone.
I've been trying all this long to recollect what my eyes
glimpsed. I must have imagined it, but can't take it out of
my memory: the sight of that pair of red eyes, and then the
glint of —

Side note by I. P. Frey:

Another paragraph must have followed, but the rest of
the page was deliberately flooded with ink.

Mr Stoker wrote those final lines applying a lot of pressure. From the marks on the back of the paper I only
could make out the words *enormous dog* and *my doom*.

18

I only managed to have a very light sleep, so when Layton came to open my curtains I received him with a savage grunt.

'A note for you, sir,' he said, handing me a neat envelope. 'From Lady Anne; your fine landlady.'

'Oh dear Lord,' I sighed, 'I do not want to know . . .'

I read it as I got dressed, hearing Lady Glass's arrogant chimes in every sentence. Though quite drawn-out, her message could be summarized in four sentences:

All my more <u>respectable</u> tenants on Great King Street are complaining of the hellish noise, the dubious characters and the jezebels that invaded <u>my</u> house last night [. . .] You are not turning my property into a house of ill repute! [. . .] I shall promptly send a clerk to inspect, and bill you for any wreckage caused.

And she concluded with the charming:

If all you want is a brothel, I suggest you move to St Julia's Close!

I hurried to the breakfast room and tossed the note next to Elgie's fried eggs.

'See what you have done, you little imp!'

Elgie struggled to swallow his buttered toast. He had but to read the first couple of lines to know what it was all about.

'I am sure you had entirely forgotten the charms of the Ardglass family,' I said.

'Of course not! You forced me to dance with Lady Anne's horrible granddaughter.'

Quite bizarrely, Elgie describing Caroline Ardglass as *horrible* made me feel a twinge of irritation.

'I would not call her that,' I said. 'That girl has been through . . . very hard times . . .' I cleared my throat, casting those thoughts away. 'I have a lot to do today, so you will have to see that the house is fit to receive the all-mighty Mr and Mrs Frey. Coordinate everything with Layton.'

'*What?* But I need to go to rehearsals!'

'*I do not give a damn, Elgie!* I have an investigation pending. The last thing on my mind right now is cleaning up your mess. You wrecked this place, now you shall help fix it. And see that we have a decent dinner too. Good spirits for father. And *no* Scottish food.'

'Very well,' said Elgie, somewhat crestfallen. He tried to lighten the mood. 'I cannot imagine Mama even looking at those Scottish black puddings . . . sausages . . . what do you call them?'

I massaged my temples, my patience absolutely spent. 'You are thinking of haggis. Black puddings are an *English* abomi—'

Then, as if a heavenly beam of understanding descended upon me, I stood up.

'I just had an epiphany . . .' I mumbled, walking out of the breakfast room as if floating in a cloud – or so I was later told by Elgie, for I did not hear a single word from anyone as I set off.

🐞

I soon made it to 27 Moray Place, McGray's home.

'Och, the master's not in,' barked George, Nine-Nails' old butler, as soon as he opened the door. I had forgotten how wrinkled and – well, how *Scottish* he was. 'Went to his office in the wee hours.'

'I am not here to see McGray,' I said, making my way in. 'I have come to see Joan.'

'*Whah!* Yer nae taking the lass away, ye smug Soothron!'

I had to compose myself, for George was the very reason Joan no longer worked for me (my retinae were still scarred from the sight of those two . . . frolicking in a wardrobe).

'That is not my intention, good man,' I assured him. 'For both our sakes, please tell her I am here to see her. The sooner I speak to her, the sooner I can leave.'

I was left in the corridor and had a good look round. This had been the house where I'd first stayed in Edinburgh, but it had looked quite different back then. McGray had not paid much attention to the state of his abode since the death of his parents, and given the eerie tales that still surrounded him, and – let's face it – his garish, intimidating appearance and manners, he never received visitors.

It had been left to Joan to set things right, and she'd done so astonishingly quickly. Now they had new rugs, the furnishings were polished, the walls repainted, and there were even fresh flowers displayed in vases that had probably been gathering dust in the cellars for years, or used only as drinking vessels by McGray. I thought that even I would be quite comfortable living there now.

I could not suppress my curiosity and distractedly took a few steps towards the entrance to McGray's library, the door being ajar. Tucker, his golden retriever, was sleeping peacefully by the fireplace. I was not surprised to see that Joan's storm of cleanliness had not reached that large room. It was still crammed with towers of books and queer artefacts (the formaldehyde specimens, it appeared, were reserved for the office). It was in stark contrast to the entrance hall, which now boasted its polished wood panelling and a chandelier I'd never thought could be so shiny.

When I saw Joan emerge I felt the warmth reserved only for good friends. She was as stout as ever, and with her double chin, her ample bosom and wide hips, she was the very image of plenty. The tray of tea and biscuits she brought only added to that impression.

'Master!' Joan said in her loud Lancashire accent. 'How very good to see you. Do come into the small parlour and have a nibble.'

I followed her to a side room that I vaguely remembered being used to store trinkets. Now it was freshly painted, and it had a dainty rosewood table adorned with more fresh flowers.

I sat and saw Joan make my tea strong and with just a drop of milk – exactly as I liked it. I would only have time for a few swigs, though.

'Joan, I have a seemingly strange question for you. It is related to my work.'

'Indeed, sir. Ask away, if you think I can help.'

I put my cup down. 'Joan, is it possible to buy . . . blood from the butcher's?'

She seemed puzzled, but replied at once. 'Oh, of course, sir. My mam used to make the best black puddings in all Burnley. She got the blood from Mr Swift, our butcher . . . I'd say at least once a month. She said it was good for people who caught tuberculosis. Oh, and she also used it to thicken them beef stews.'

I felt my stomach churn. 'I am sure you thoroughly enjoyed such delicacies. Joan, how much blood would your mother usually buy at one time?'

'Well, *pints*, sir. We were a big family.'

'I see . . . so, if I went to a butcher's and ordered, say – half a gallon of blood, nobody would think me odd.'

'Oh well, if it was *you*, sir, with your bowler hat and your leather gloves and your starched collars . . .'

'Joan!'

'I know, I know what you mean, sir. Yes, it would be perfectly natural.' She started squeezing her apron, as she used to do when she wanted to ask me something I might consider impertinent. 'If I may, sir, why do you need to know this? Anything to do with them apparitions I read about in t'papers?'

There was no point in lying. 'Yes, but you are not to say a word. Do you understand?'

Joan assented, although I was sure she'd be talking in a matter of minutes. She led me to the door, and as I passed the pristine corridor I wondered what miracles she could work in Lady Glass's house.

'Joan, can you possibly spare any time today? My young brother got himself into something of a pickle yesterday . . .'

And I was indescribably relieved when I saw her grin.

Joan can definitely haggle, but in all fairness I would have gladly paid her twice the first amount she requested.

Happy to have struck two birds with one stone, I went straight to the City Chambers. I found McNair there, so I sent him, with a couple of officers, to make inquiries at all the butchers that served New Town. I also told them to inquire at the cattle market. Perhaps someone would remember a suspicious-looking customer buying pints of blood. It might be a lost cause, but I should at least try. Once that was sorted, I'd go through that cast list and – I sighed – start a brand new list of suspects.

Little did I know then that McGray was having a very interesting conversation with Bram Stoker.

Bram Stoker's Journal

11 July, afternoon – *Can hardly focus on duties at the theatre. While I ate breakfast, the waiter told the most extraordinary stories regarding Inspector McGray.*

[Mr Stoker has narrated McGray's past in a most disgustingly sentimental manner. He definitely has a talent for melodrama. I am also editing out his lengthy description of our office at the City Chambers, which he decided to visit whilst I met Joan. Stoker transcribed his dialogue with McGray with astonishing detail – if this is at all accurate. – I. P. Frey.]

BS: I'm sorry to disturb you . . .

McG: What you want?

BS: May I sit?

McG: Aye, but there's just that old chair I keep to torture the London dandy.

BS: Jesus! How can anyone . . . ? Inspector, I wanted to give you some additional information. Something I'm afraid I have been keeping to myself.

McG: Oh? Well, I'm listening.

BS: Before I do, I must confess that – you'll excuse my intrusion – I've heard certain facts about your past.

McG: (Laughing) Hadn't you noticed this? (Raises his mutilated hand)

BS: I had. But it's not something one comments on. Given your profession, I just assumed . . .

McG: Aye, aye. A fair assumption. Go on.

BS: Well, I have been told that you have a deep interest in the . . . supernatural.

McG: Och, if you're going to mock me, you can —— off!

BS: No, no! On the contrary. I have to tell you that I . . . (whispering) share that interest.

[Lengthy nonsense, mostly from McGray]

BS: I see that you, unlike your colleague, _do_ contemplate the possibility of a real threat, possibly a future death.

McG: You sound like you have something very interesting to tell me. If someone in Scotland will take you seriously, that's me. _Believe me._

BS: Thank you, I thought so. There are two things I wanted to tell you when I came here yesterday, but I was afraid you and your colleague would ridicule me. See, I have read extensively about banshees . . . and the undead. Not from academic books, that is, but the kind of references that you keep in this very room. The kind of references other people would deem ridiculous.

McG: Continue.

BS: You mentioned yesterday how banshees seem to announce _only_ the death of certain illustrious Irish families. Remember?

McG: Aye.

BS: Well, there are two people who I'm sure share that ancestry. The first one is Miss Terry.

McG: You're joking!

BS: I've sketched her family tree. See for yourself.

[I suppose Mr Stoker showed McGray such sketch. Unfortunately, the document was not reproduced in his journal]

McG: *O'Grady on one side and Cavanagh on the other. How do you know her family history in so much detail?*

BS: *I came across her story by mere accident. We are all good friends with Oscar Wilde, the playwright. He's written some very pretty sonnets for Irving and Miss Terry. A good while ago we were toasting on a particularly good review. It was for Faust, I believe, so four years ago. Miss Terry must have made some sort of joke, which only Mr Wilde and I laughed at. Mr Wilde – well, you don't know him, but he certainly has his share of wit – he remarked that it was our Irishness coming to the fore. He made Miss Terry tell us the story of her family in detail. Her grandfather, one Benjamin Terry, was an innkeeper in Portsmouth; I believe his tavern was called the Fortune of War. He claimed to have a glorious ancestry, which declined slowly but steadily for centuries, until they ended up ploughing their own vegetables. That grandfather of hers sold whatever land they had left, and then moved to England. Miss Terry assumes he was escaping huge family debts.*

McG: *So you think the banshee could be announcing Miss Terry's death?*

BS: *Well, as I said, she is one of the two possibilities.*

McG: *And who's the other?*

BS: *Me.*

ACT III

DOCTOR

 Foul whisperings are abroad: unnatural deeds
 Do breed unnatural troubles: infected minds
 To their deaf pillows will discharge their secrets.

Bram Stoker's family tree

Sketch found amongst Mr Stoker's possessions at a later date; identical copy to the one shown to Insp. McGray. Inserted here given its relevance. – I. P. Frey.

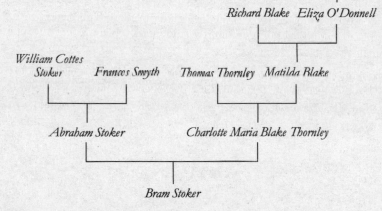

Bram Stoker's Journal (continued)

McG: What the ———! You're ———!

BS: I've also made you a sketch. You can see my direct connection to <u>Colonel Manus O'Donnell</u>. His grandfather, another <u>Manus O'Donnell</u>, was a true war hero, killed in action during the Irish Confederate Wars. And his grandfather was <u>Niall O'Donnell</u>, the very last chieftain of the O'Donnell clan. From him you can trace the lineage back to the eleventh century.

McG: Are you telling me that . . . ?

BS: My documented lineage goes back more than a thousand years. I'm not simply a member of the O'Donnell clan; I'm a direct descendant of its chieftains.

McG: You are ——— joking!

BS: I wish I was! The O'Donnell banshee is a very old family legend. My mother told me about it when I was a child, and said she heard her shortly before my grandfather died.

McG: How long have you thought the theatre banshee is your family's?

BS: It's been in the back of my mind from the very start, but I didn't consider it seriously – until last night. I believe I saw a black dog. Red-eyed. And it's not the first time. Do you know that in Nordic folklore that is a sign of –

(It was then that we were interrupted by the English Inspector)

19

As soon as McNair and a couple of other officers headed off to the local butchers and the cattle market, I headed to the Dumping Ground. There I found McGray and Mr Stoker in deep conversation, and they both cast me the kind of stare that I'd find on Joan whenever I caught her drinking the cooking sherry. I managed to see McGray folding two sheets of paper and shoving them into his breast pocket.

'Good morning, Mr Stoker,' I said. 'I see last night's activity has not stopped you from an early rise.'

He said nothing in reply. In fact, he looked ghostly pale. I noticed that his fingernails were blackened, as if he'd plunged his hands in ink and had failed to wash it away.

'Are you here to give us another confession?' I asked.

'Nae,' Nine-Nails said promptly. 'He came just to ask if we were making any progress.'

I could tell McGray lied, but I also knew I'd get nowhere if I asked further questions.

'I also need to give these to your superintendent,' said Stoker, showing us two tickets and a theatre programme. 'If you'll excuse me . . .'

He left quickly, and I saw a flinch in McGray's face. I had no chance to speak, though, for he flattened a piece of fine paper on his desk. It was embossed on the top with the emblem of the Palace Hotel.

'That Mr Clarke worked quickly,' said McGray. 'Says they did lose a few bedsheets, but not from a room; they came out o' the laundry.'

'That is a dead end,' I said, looking at the message myself. 'Did anyone see anything?'

'Nae, sadly. But the sheets did go missing on the evening o' the ninth, so two to three hours before the banshee appeared.'

I chuckled. 'So we know for fact that the banshee is lodging at the Palace Hotel. Expensive taste for an apparition.'

Right then I heard boisterous steps and saw the young Dr Reed storming in.

'Sirs, I've just found that – !'

He bumped his face against McGray's ugly Peruvian totem, and the voluminous relic knocked over a pile of books that rained on the poor doctor. We had to help him to the hard chair.

McGray patted him on the shoulder. 'Ye all right, laddie?'

'Yes, sir, it was just a wee –' He blinked hard and shook his head, still slightly stunned.

'You have to stop hoarding trinkets,' I told McGray. 'This place is a landslide waiting to happen.'

'Aye, I'll start with ye, Frey. Reed, what was it ye came to tell us?'

'Oh . . . right! I think I know where that leather bag comes from.'

Nine-Nails almost did a little dance, and for once I could have joined him.

'Really? Did yer lass tell ye?'

'His *lass*?' I echoed.

'My fiancée, sir,' Reed told me with a certain acrimony. He knew I had requested his dismissal merely hours after I first met him, and it would take more than time for him to forgive me. 'Inspector McGray found a tradesman's seal on the leather bag found in –'

'I know which bag, go on.'

'I thought my Sophie might know the manufacturer. She directed me to the manager of her favourite shop, a Mr McRye. I've just been to his place on the High Street.'

'And?'

'He has a very long directory of leather merchants from all over the British Isles. He half recognized the emblem and went through his catalogues. He found that the bag came from a chap who sells very fine custom-made pieces. The establishment is called Richmond & Sons. Good news is, they only have the one shop.'

'Where?' McGray prompted.

'Southampton.'

I raised my head like a hound after a scent, and repeated the word a couple of times.

'What is it, Frey?'

'I – I think I heard that town yesterday . . .' I mumbled, producing my little notebook with increasing excitement. 'No, I am sure I did, but I cannot remember when, or the context.' I began turning pages at full speed. 'I only hope I wrote it down . . .'

McGray looked over my shoulder, wrinkling his nose. 'Ye take too many notes.'

'That is nonsense, you can *never* take too many notes,' I said stubbornly, though while going through pages and pages of endless scribble I could see his point.

Luckily, the word caught my eye sooner than I expected.

'Of course! Miss Ivor. Plays Hecate, the witches' dark goddess, and I believe she is also Miss Terry's understudy. It was mentioned she comes from Southampton!'

'I assume she denied being involved at all,' said McGray.

'As did they all, but now we have a trace to follow. We should go to the theatre and confront her.'

McGray again patted Reed, almost sending him off the seat. 'Good job, laddie. I'll get ye a dram as soon as this is over.'

'By the way, there were three alleged banshee sightings last night,' McGray was saying as he led us through narrow, malodorous closes; a very twisted shortcut to the Lyceum Theatre.

'Alleged!' I laughed. 'I thought that word was not in your vocabulary. What makes even *you* admit they were false?'

'One was a very drunk –'

'Mr Wheatstone again?'

'*Och, shut it!* A very drunk *male* lowlife that frequents the Ensign Ewart, shouting nonsense. The other one was "seen" by this fat lass that asked if she could get free tickets – in case she recognized the banshee at the bloody theatre. The third one was just some stupid inscription in red ink someone left a couple o' blocks from the theatre. Atrocious spelling, no metrics, no rhymes. Clearly a hoax.'

We made it to Grindlay Street in no time. The theatre was mayhem, since nearly every single actor and actress was on call. We went to the auditorium and as we approached the stage I saw, with certain satisfaction, that most of the musicians were bleary-eyed – they had surely continued their drinking spree somewhere else after wrecking my place.

On the stage there were two horses, stomping their hooves on the wooden floor amidst a painted Scottish landscape. Macbeth's assassins stood around the beasts.

'We need Fleance!' one of the two burly actors yelled as soon as he saw Stoker. 'We've been calling him for the past ten minutes!'

Stoker had no chance to reply, for right then we heard a voice resounding throughout the theatre like a gunshot.

'*Leave me alone, you stupid cow!* I've been called.'

The voice came from a rangy adolescent, who strode crossly towards the stage. He must have been around thirteen or fourteen, but his features were already very handsome: strong chin, high cheekbones, fiery blue eyes and wavy blond hair. Within a couple of years he'd be one of those young men so attractive they are in fact annoying to behold. And he already sported his good looks with unmitigated arrogance.

Mrs Harwood came running behind him clenching her sewing kit, holding pins in her mouth.

'I know, I know, dear. But I'm almost done. Just a couple of stitches and –'

'You had plenty of time!' the boy interrupted, and I saw the thread and needle that still dangled from his medieval doublet (of the wrong period, if I may say). He tore them off, taking with them a good piece of material, and threw the small bundle at Mrs Harwood's face. '*There!* That'll teach you to have my clothes ready on time.'

His insolence angered me as much as if he'd directed it at me.

McGray stepped in front of 'Fleance' before the boy climbed on to the stage. 'Och, treat the missus with some respect!'

The boy smirked. 'What do you care? Stupid Scotch.'

'Oh, dear Lord . . .' I murmured to myself. Thankfully, McGray's reaction was quite mild for his standards. He simply smacked the boy around the face – only once on each side. His very white skin swelled instantly and he looked around in as much pain as disbelief.

'*Stoker!*' he shrieked, rubbing one of his cheeks. '*Do something!*'

McGray slapped him again. 'He's *Mr Stoker* to ye, wee maggot. Now apologize to the missus.'

Mrs Harwood's cheeks looked redder than if she'd been slapped herself. When she spoke the pins fell from her mouth. 'Oh, sir, I appreciate it, but it's not necessary. I had all night to –'

McGray raised an assuaging hand and she went quiet. 'Apologize, laddie!' he snapped.

The boy glared at McGray, defiant beyond good sense.

'These gentlemen are CID, Freddie,' Stoker grumbled. 'You are going to have to.'

'Freddie!' McGray laughed and then looked at me. 'The laddie's called Freddie! Just out o' yer nappies, boy?'

I could see more than one man in the orchestra covering their mouths to contain their giggles.

Nine-Nails grabbed the boy by the arm and planted him in front of Mrs Harwood, who seemed about to burst into tears. 'I won't wait for long,' McGray grunted.

Freddie bit his lip, trembling with rage. He looked at all the mocking faces around him before he finally spoke.

'I'm sorry – you lazy baggage.'

And he ran away before McGray could strike him again.

Mrs Harwood ran in the opposite direction, pressing the torn piece of costume against her face.

Wasting no time, the actors began the scene where Fleance, son of the murdered Banquo and future father of kings, manages to escape Macbeth's assassins.

'Will she be all right?' McGray said, his eyes looking at the side door through which Mrs Harwood had disappeared.

Stoker nodded. 'Yes. Sadly, this is not the first time something like this has happened.'

'Who is the spoiled brat?' I asked, just as Freddie mounted one of the horses with regal movements, shed real tears, and made his dramatic escape.

'Never mind him,' replied Stoker. 'Irving's promised him Romeo when he turns sixteen. A hollow promise, I think, but may the Lord have mercy if that time comes.'

'I'll still talk to her before we leave,' said McGray, his face a little sombre.

Fortunately, Miss Ivor *was* at the theatre and happy to talk to us. Again we used Mr Wyndham's office, since the man was now out of town.

'Didnae recognize ye without the wee halo,' said McGray.

Miss Ivor smiled. 'It's a nice effect. Tiny electric lights. Mr Wheatstone designed it himself for our production of *Faust*.'

'Oh, that is how it works,' I said. 'I was curious.'

Thinking those pleasantries were enough, I asked the pressing question. 'Miss Ivor, yesterday one of your fellow actresses implied that you have a connection with Southampton. Is that correct?'

'Yes. I spent a good part of my life there. I was well known in the local theatres.'

'I see. I need to ask you – have you recently lost a leather bag?'

Neither McGray nor I blinked, studying the woman's reaction. She arched her eyebrows; puzzled, certainly, but not exceedingly so. 'No, not that I recall . . . Is this related to –'

'I'm afraid we cannae give you more details,' McGray interrupted, 'but we do need ye to tell us if yer familiar with the company Richmond & Sons.'

Miss Ivor actually gasped. 'Why, yes! I am astonished you know of Mr Richmond! He's very skilled, but he has only the one premises – a little shop in –'

She halted then, slowly lifting a hand to cover her mouth.

'What's the matter?' McGray asked.

Miss Ivor's eyes had opened wide. 'I *did* buy a leather bag from him . . . but it was almost a year ago. And I gave it away – as a present.'

'To whom?' I asked, leaning forward and almost falling from the seat.

I could not help notice a hint of a bitter smile on her face.

'Miss Terry.'

20

'I was originally cast to play Lady Macduff,' Miss Ivor was saying, 'but Mr Irving decided to omit her scene altogether.'

'Did he?' I asked, producing my copy of the programme and looking at the cast list.

Lady Macduff – the woman Macbeth has savagely murdered, along with her children and entire household – was not there.

'Intriguing choice,' I said. 'Her murder is one of the cruellest scenes in the entire play; one the theatre directors like to make the most of.'

'Mr Irving didn't want anyone to eclipse Miss Terry's performance,' Miss Ivor said, and from then on she was unable to repress her bitterness. 'Although it was all Miss Terry's idea. I heard her when she requested the change. She told Mr Irving that my scene came right before her sleepwalking monologue; that people would be thinking of my death instead of paying attention to the nuances of her lines; that she had worked on that soliloquy for months and the gore would overshadow her.' Her voice came down a tone. 'And the mighty Miss Terry demanded yet more glory.'

'I can see that made ye really mad,' said Nine-Nails.

'Of course, sirs. You must forgive my bluntness, but that was my only scene. Perhaps the last important scene I'd ever get to play before I'm ditched for being too old – I am two years *younger* than Mr Irving, yet my career is effectively over. How is that fair?'

Miss Ivor forced a deep breath, followed by a very uncomfortable silence. I could understand her perfectly, but this frustrated side of her was intriguing to say the least.

'I did not know you felt such – animosity towards Miss Terry.'

The woman looked up at once. 'Oh, I try not to, sir. I try hard. She's forty-two. She'll be in my same situation very soon, and she must know it. No wonder she is squeezing her last years in the theatre as much as she can.' Miss Ivor attempted a smile. 'And she did put in a good word for me afterwards. She probably felt guilty and persuaded Irving to recast me as Hecate. It was then that I gave her the leather bag.'

McGray shifted in his seat. 'Ye gave her a pressie *after* she cut yer scene out?'

Miss Ivor nodded. 'It's curious, isn't it? I was the aggravated one, yet I had to be the one reassuring her everything was all right. Just in case they ever need an old crone for another play . . .'

'Did ye see Miss Terry use that bag lately?' McGray asked, making Miss Ivor laugh.

'No, Inspector. Not lately, not ever.' Again she could not conceal her resentment. 'Well, she can afford much nicer things, I suppose. And she gets presents all the time. What is to her a cheap trinket given by a nobody like me?'

We lingered in the office after we let Miss Ivor go, McGray pacing restlessly next to the marble fireplace.

'So they carried the blood in a bag that belonged to Miss Terry,' I said.

'It *still* belongs to her,' McGray pointed out.

I looked at my notes from Miss Ivor's first statement. 'I must say her statements ring true to me ... It simply makes sense: Miss Terry either puts the bundle of brains in her dressing room, or has someone bring them in –'

'While she keeps an eye on the corridor pretending to wash her hands.'

'Exactly. And then, a week later, she uses a "cheap" leather bag to carry blood to Regent Bridge – or again she gives it to someone to do the deed for her. Miss Terry creates it all; Miss Terry "squeezes her last years in the theatre as much as she can". It is a simple answer; and the simplest answers tend to be the correct ones.'

Nevertheless, I could not pronounce those words without a hint of disbelief. And McGray was thinking exactly the same:

'Aye, but the two statements that incriminate Terry come from the same source – a woman with a clear grudge against her. That's all a wee bit too convenient. And I saw Miss Ivor rehearsing; as ye said, she could have played a convincing banshee.'

I could not help grinning. 'My oh my, you are suspecting a real person now. How many years' worth of whisky did you say you'd – ?'

'Och, sod off. There's work to do. We need to confront Terry right away.'

'Indeed. With everything running behind schedule she should be here today.'

Just as McGray was going to place his hand on the doorknob we heard a desperate, insistent knocking.

When he opened the door we had to look down. It was Susy, the young girl, her little fists still in the air. I felt guilty that my eyes should fall first on to her scars, for the child was distraught.

'Sirs, please!' she sobbed. 'Help me find my mother!'

McGray placed his thick hand on the girl's shoulder with surprising gentleness.

'S'all right, lassie. We'll see ye get help. Who's yer ma?'

I could not believe her answer.

Cast as listed in the 1889 Edinburgh souvenir

Underlined and annotated by Inspector I. P. Frey.

Duncan	Mr Haviland
Malcolm	Mr Webster
Donalbain	Mr Harvey
Macbeth	Mr Henry Irving
Banquo	Mr Wenman
Macduff	Mr Alexander
Lennox	Mr Outram
Ross	Mr Tyars
Mentieth	Mr Archer
Angus	Mr Laccy
Caithness	Mr Leverton
Fleance	Master Harwood ←◊
Siward	Mr Howe
Scyton	Mr Fenton
Two other Officers	Mr Hemstock
	Mr Cass
A Doctor	Mr Stuart
A Sergeant	Mr Raynor
A Porter	Mr Johnson
An Attendant	Mr Roe
Murderers	Mr Black
	Mr Carter

Gentlewoman	Miss Coleridge
A Servant	Miss Foster
Lady Macbeth	Miss Ellen Terry
Hecate	Miss Ivor
1st Witch	Miss Marriott
2nd Witch	Miss Desborough
3rd Witch	Miss Seaman
<u>Apparitions</u>	Mr Baird
	<u>Miss Harwood</u>
	Miss Holland

21

'Son of a bleeding whore!' McGray whispered at my ear, as the young Susy led us to Mrs Harwood's workshop.

Even before looking at their names in my copy of the souvenir I began to remember. Yesterday, Mrs Harwood had mentioned she had two children, whom she'd dropped off at the Palace Hotel before coming back to the theatre to work. Apparently, Nine-Nails had just smacked her son.

'When was the last time ye saw her?'

'After rehearsing my scene,' Susy replied through sobs, the despair overcoming her shyness. 'She was mending my brother's costume. She said she was very busy and asked me to leave. I just went back and –'

She could not say more. McGray patted her gently and we rushed down to the storerooms.

We found her workshop crammed with sumptuous court attires, surely for the banquet scene. She'd been busy ironing and adjusting them, and there was a particularly grand dress – white silk as fine as a cobweb, richly embroidered with silver threads – that seemed to require particular care. The green dress with the beetle wings, I noticed, was not to be seen.

As we stepped in, our attention went to a single piece of cloth: the brown doublet her son had been wearing. Curled up on the floor, the thread and needle still attached to a half-finished seam. The thread, originally white, was now stained in red, and a tiny drop of blood hung by the tip of the fine needle.

'Step out, lassie,' McGray told Susy.

'What is going on?' asked Miss Ivor, who was just coming in with some garment under her arm, perhaps to ask for some mending.

'Take care o' Susy,' McGray told her. 'Take her to Mr Howard's office and give her some tea or something.'

'Is anything the ma—'

'Please, just do it,' I urged. Miss Ivor held Susy's hand and led her away with motherly care. As they walked, the girl's reddened eyes remained fixed on the workshop's door.

'We'll find her,' McGray assured her, and as soon as they disappeared we went back to inspect the place.

McGray picked up the needle almost tenderly, examining it so closely I thought he might pierce his eyes.

'Looks like she injured herself,' he said.

I lifted the garment and found several drops of blood on the floor. A few were getting dry.

'A little badly,' I mumbled, 'and then she kept on working, even —'

We heard a mad scream from one of the corridors: a woman's desperate cry. We jumped to our feet and darted towards the sound.

Just then a man began to shout. 'Don't let her near the understage! *We'll all be blown to pieces!*'

McGray found his way to the voices with astonishing speed. I followed him to a dimly lit hall, where we found a panting Mr Wheatstone surrounded by half a dozen technicians. He was bellowing commands and the men ran swiftly.

'The seamstress has gone mad!' Mr Wheatstone gabbled

when he saw us. His grey hair was stuck to his sweaty temples, his thick spectacles askew. 'She went after me!'

'Again?' I asked, but there was not time for explanations.

'Yes,' said Mr Wheatstone. 'We had to usher her away from the rheostat and the lycopodium. They're rehearsing the forest fire right now. We have ten people handling explosives and electricity all over the place.'

'Lord!' I let out.

'I just sent these chaps to keep anyone away from the rheostat,' said Wheatstone, 'but I'm afraid she might go to the stage and get burned – get others burned!'

'They need to stop the rehearsals,' said McGray.

'Then you must tell Mr Irving yourselves,' Wheatstone urged. 'He'll listen to nobody here.' McGray and I were already running as we heard Wheatstone's advice. 'Go directly to the stage! Irving will be there!'

***

The auditorium was like a window to hell. The stage glowed in every shade of crimson, flames arising from trees ablaze like torches. Dozens of soldiers, all carrying burning fir branches, roared madly at the walls of a brooding castle. They were rehearsing the scene when Dunsinane Forest, fulfilling the witches' prophecy, rises to attack Macbeth.

Irving, in his full royal attire, looked at the flames from a turret. His frown was as deep and worried as the one I'd seen the previous night. This was the instant Macbeth's determination began to shatter; when the idea that the spirits had tricked him first crept into his twisted thinking. And when he saw us come in, running past the empty rows of seats, his thick brow warped in a gesture fitting for that scene.

'*Stop!*' McGray howled. '*Police orders!* Put out all the fires!'

Even his booming voice could not get through the roaring flames, the sound effects and the frantic orchestration.

Only a few extras and musicians looked at us, but then Irving waved a command, and when he bellowed '*Go on, you fools!*' his long-trained voice did reach every corner of the enormous vault. For a moment he did not seem to be acting: he was indeed the cruel, tyrannical lord, staring at us threateningly from the heights of his besieged fortress.

Stoker had been there all along, and he ran to us looking as pale as a corpse. 'What is going on?'

We had no time to reply. The soldiers' synchronized cries of war halted, replaced by confused murmurs as their orderly lines parted and gave way to a solitary, small female figure.

The staggering Mrs Harwood was right in the centre of the stage, grasping her right hand and shouting with anguish.

Even from the distance I could see her fingertips stained in red. With her lined face and pleading stare, she could not have looked more like an actual witch.

'*Run away!*' she was crying at the soldiers. '*He'll burn you all! You'll all die!*'

McGray jumped on to the stage and went straight to her.

I was expecting Mrs Harwood to shriek, to struggle, to try to scratch out his eyes, but instead she dropped bonelessly into his arms.

By then the orchestra had stopped and the clouds of fire had faded, and I could hear her pleas with clarity.

'Go away, sir! He'll burn you too! Tell them to go away! *Please!*'

'She needs a doctor!' Nine-Nails said, dragging her aside.

Stoker and I reached him, dodging the still-blazing fir branches held by the soldiers.

I looked at Mrs Harwood's spent face. She was not unconscious, her eyes still half open, but she looked like an empty shell. I lifted her hand carefully and felt a twinge when I saw it: she'd been biting her nails and cuticles until they bled.

'Is she dead?' Irving shouted from his turret.

'No,' answered Stoker, 'but she looks like she needs –'

'Then get her out of my stage and let's resume! *Now!*'

McGray shouted at him something I cannot possibly transcribe, but he stepped off the stage just as soon.

'Stoker,' said Nine-Nails, 'I'm taking her to yer hotel. Send someone to the Lunatic Asylum in Morningside. Tell them I need either Dr Harland or Miss Smith, the head nurse.'

'Of course, Inspector. I will –'

'And send her children to the Palace too,' McGray added. He shook his head with weariness, staring at the poor woman's face. 'Tell them we found their mother, but don't tell them what's happened. Not yet.'

22

I could only guess what was going through McGray's mind as a cab took us to the Palace Hotel. He was facing the narrow window but looking at nothing, his stare lost somewhere in the distance.

Mrs Harwood's episode must have been like salt on his still fresh wounds. Though it felt like weeks, McGray's own sister had been taken away only two days since.

And what a terrible night that had been. I will never forget the sight of him standing there, tall and broad shouldered, yet crushed and powerless in the circumstances. Dr Clouston had tried hard to talk some sense into him, but McGray had roared, kicked about and punched the walls. He had been holding a small bouquet of white roses he'd brought for his sister, and despite the commotion and his seemingly brutal hands, he managed to keep the flowers intact for her.

Amy had appeared down the corridor like a floating ghost; wrapped in a thick shawl, with her dark hair netted tightly into a chignon, and flanked by two nurses who guided her gently by the arms. Everything in that image spoke of constraint.

McGray offered her the flowers, and it was the one moment the girl acknowledged her surroundings. She received the blooms with a very slow yet very steady hand, and dreamily brought them close to her face to breathe their perfume. McGray rested a hand on her back with unexpected gentleness, and perhaps meant to tell her something, but in the end he simply nodded at the nurses and Dr Clouston, who resumed their sad march.

When Miss McGray passed closest to me I could not help feeling a quiver, as if the very air around her carried a chill. I caught a glimpse of her thick eyelashes, as dark as her eyes, and her youthful features, which even madness has not managed to harden. I have always thought her a pretty sight, but the tragedy of her situation, imprisoned in her own broken mind, had never struck me with all its harshness as it did right then.

And as they took her away, my mind began to wonder. What would have become of her had she not needed to be confined to a mental institution? What would she be doing with her life, instead of forever sitting by the window, looking at the sky and counting the clouds? Would she have married? Would she have friends? Perhaps right now she would be looking forward to seeing Ellen Terry, going through all her pretty dresses, looking for the one ideal for the theatre halls. Or perhaps she would be spending those nice summer days in the Scottish countryside, rejoicing in the cool breeze and savouring the ripe wild berries without a care in the world.

If only.

Mrs Harwood had only a small room at the back of the hotel, very close to the kitchens. We had deposited her there about half an hour before, and asked two chambermaids to look after her. Her children had arrived right behind us, Susy insisting she remain close to her mother, Freddie looking quite put out, as if tending to his parent's fits were an utter nuisance. He soon ran to the kitchens, shouting out that he was starving.

McGray and I thought it better to stay present until someone from the asylum arrived. We went to the hotel's tearooms and found a table a little away from the others.

A small part of me wanted to cheer, since Mrs Harwood could not have looked more like a banshee: up there on the stage, unsteady and eerie, and shouting about everybody's impending death. However, this was no moment to gloat.

'Why would she break down like that?' I whispered instead. 'She seemed a little unbalanced, but nothing to suggest this would happen.'

McGray only nodded, unable to say something back. Somebody would (partly) answer that question very soon.

'Inspectors, is Mrs Harwood well?'

I saw it was the bearded, stately old man who played King Duncan. He noticed I struggled to remember his name.

'Mr Haviland,' he said.

'We are waiting for medical help,' I told him. 'Thank you for your concern.'

I looked away, trying to make him leave, but he only stepped a little closer, clearly in search of gossip.

'It is only logical that she would try to attack poor Mr Wheatstone. I don't know which party deserves the more pity.'

McGray and I turned our heads to him in a perfectly coordinated movement.

'What d'ye mean?' McGray asked, and Mr Haviland instantly blushed.

'Well, I assumed you would know by now – after all your inquiries, I mean.'

McGray kicked a nearby chair. 'Have a seat, Yer Majesty. Tell us everything.'

Mr Haviland began to squeeze his bowler hat. 'I – I do not want to get myself in trouble, gentlemen . . .'

'Too late for that,' said McGray, snapping his fingers at a waiter. 'Oi, laddie! Bring us a dram for King Duncan.'

The man sat slowly. 'I suppose you don't know the circumstances of little Susy's – mishap.'

'Is that relevant to our investigation?' I asked.

Mr Haviland shrugged. 'Well, it explains a lot.' Then he shook his head. 'Terrible accident; really terrible. There was a fire in the last performance of *Faust*. Little Susy was only eight or nine years old and she played an angel. An angel! Can you believe she is now playing a witches' ghoul? She was the most beautiful of all the angels in that play.'

I remembered that fleeting moment during the previous day's rehearsal, when I was only able to see the unharmed side of the girl's face and thought her so very sweet.

'Irving called it a *laddor of angels*, and that is precisely what it was: a group of girls suspended from this ladder-like structure, painted black, so that against a dark background and under the appropriate lighting it looked as though they were floating in mid-air. I didn't act in that play but I was a spectator – though fortunately not on that final night; I can tell you, it was the most beautiful, most impressive effect I've ever seen in the theatre. And you need but look at me to tell I have had a long career!

'When the fire burst Susy got entangled in a harness – or so I've been told. People managed to free the other girls. But Susy, being the prettiest . . .' Mr Haviland looked down, 'she was the one on the apex. People couldn't get to her in time. They managed to save her, but only after the fire had . . .' The old man shuddered, and I shared his discomfort.

'A lot of people felt guilty,' Mr Haviland continued. 'In particular Mr Wheatstone and, I am afraid, Miss Terry.'

His drink arrived then but he did not even attempt to touch the tumbler.

'Was Mr Wheatstone in charge of those stage effects?' McGray asked.

'Indeed, Inspector. Has been for years. And Mrs Harwood never forgave him. It was right after that accident that she began to fall apart. Her husband died only a few months later, and then she had to take up work as a theatre seamstress. And her children had to work too. Miss Terry had a lot to do with that.'

I nodded. 'You just mentioned Miss Terry also felt very guilty.' I remembered her treating Susy as though she were her own daughter. 'Why is that?'

'She was instrumental in hiring the Harwood children. She spotted them in the audience during a performance of *Henry VIII*. On that very night she invited them backstage – Mr Harwood was still alive then and apparently was a very greedy man. It was not difficult to convince him to allow his daughter on the stage. He died, as I told you, soon after Susy's tragedy . . . It was as though the entire Harwood family had been cursed as soon as Miss Terry set her eyes on them. She must feel terribly guilty. Not that she could have known any of that would happen, but still . . . I understand her chagrin.'

McGray and I nodded in agreement. It all made sense now: Mrs Harwood's aggressive behaviour towards Mr Wheatstone (whom I determined to question again at some point), her unhinged expression when she saw fire on the stage . . . her warnings that everyone would burn.

A very uncomfortable silence followed, and I could only nod at Mr Haviland, indicating he could go. McGray said nothing, staring at the table and feeling the stump that was his finger.

I realized with a flinch all the sad stories that surrounded me. Perhaps the weather was casting its spell on me – through the windows I could see that the day was very quickly turning from sunny to grey, with thick clouds coming from the north-east. By the time Cassandra Smith arrived from the asylum, Edinburgh looked its usual self. It was not raining yet, but a storm was indeed brewing.

23

Miss Smith looked as out of place as did McGray. Her simple, faded navy dress, her washed face as lacklustre as unvarnished wood and her hair hastily tied in a simple plait instantly caught the eyes of the well-to-do guests of the Palace Hotel.

The nurse, however, was undeterred, sporting her simple clothes and her medical bag with self-assurance, and looking defiantly at the richly attired ladies who walked by, carrying nothing but parasols.

Mr Clarke did not like her presence in the hotel one jot, or McGray's. The manager had received us with a grimace and showed us the way to Mrs Harwood's room with unprecedented speed – surely thinking we were spoiling the ambience of his lobby.

'Thanks for coming so quickly,' McGray said as we guided her. 'I couldnae think of anyone better.'

'Oh, that theatre clerk told me everything,' said Miss Smith. 'You did well. I'm glad I can help you, but I'm afraid I can spare only an hour or so.'

'Aye, that should be fine,' McGray said. In Dr Clouston's absence (he'd still be ensuring that Pansy made it safely to the Orkneys) Miss Smith had been left in charge of the asylum – later I'd hear that she did so with an iron fist, and that even the arrogant Oxford graduates turned to her for advice.

I knocked gently at Mrs Harwood's door, and it was the soft voice of her daughter that bid us in.

We saw that Mrs Harwood shared the lodgings with Susy, for whom a tattered chaise longue had been adapted as a bed. They were not enjoying the opulence we'd seen at Miss Terry's apartments, but their place was clean, tidy and spacious enough.

Susy was sitting on the floor, her back against the foot of her mother's bed. The girl's pale blue dress was spread around her and her hands were busy turning the pages of a book. I heard Mrs Harwood mumble in her troubled sleep, and I felt a pang of sorrow for the child.

'Good day,' she said, quite shyly, never looking up from the pages.

'What happened to the maids?' McGray asked.

'I asked them to leave,' said Susy in such a low whisper I had to guess the words. 'Mama was sleeping already and they made me uncomfortable . . . they were looking at her like –'

She could not finish, her lips trembling.

Miss Smith had all the motherly delicacy that the situation demanded. She kneeled by Susy, asked her name and age, and complimented her beautiful eyes. The girl eventually replied with more than monosyllables.

'Mr Frey tells me he's seen you on the stage,' Miss Smith said then. 'Do you like doing that?'

'Yes.'

Miss Smith smiled, expertly concealing her doubts. 'That's very good. What do you like best about it?'

Susy drew a hand to her scarred skin. Her fine fingers followed the shiny bumps and rosy furrows; the fire marks carved all across her cheek and around her right eye. However, she did so rather distractedly, as if the whole matter did not really mean that much to her.

'People think it's a mask,' she said. 'They don't point at me like they do on the streets.'

I thought that was a harrowing statement, only worsened by the dreamy way in which she had said it.

Miss Smith asked a few other questions at random, but then threw in: 'Do you miss your father?'

Susy looked at her straight in the eye. 'No, miss.'

We were all staggered by how natural, how matter-of-factly the girl had spoken. Miss Smith again asked for her reasons, but just as Susy was about to speak the door was flung open and we all started.

'Where's that lazy – ?' It was Freddie, eating a large slice of melon – an expensive treat – pulp smeared across his face. His eyes fixed on Miss Smith. 'Oh, who's the ugly wench? Looks like a scarecrow with that hair.'

'*Out!*' McGray bellowed, pushing him away with one hand and shutting the door with the other. Freddie began to yell something, but McGray banged the door with an irate fist and we only heard the boy run across the corridor.

The noise awoke Mrs Harwood, who instantly sat up and stared at us in confusion. 'What's going on? Why are you here? What – ?'

'Shhh, it's all right,' Miss Smith said soothingly. '*I'm* the one who's come to see you. I'm worried about you.' She looked at the girl. 'Susy, could you bring us some fresh water?'

Susy looked uneasy – perhaps fearing she'd stumble across her brother in the halls.

'Here, I'll go with ye,' McGray offered, which made her only a little less anxious. As they left the room he cast me a look that undoubtedly meant *pay attention to everything they say*.

The first thing Miss Smith did was take one of Mrs Harwood's chapped hands.

'What happened here?' Again she spoke in a motherly tone, as if addressing a child. 'Have you been biting your nails?'

Mrs Harwood nodded. 'Can't help it, I'm afraid.'

'Oh, I'm sure you can. Let me help you with those.'

I whispered in Miss Smith's ear. 'Could you please ask her why she did —'

The nurse cleared her throat, commanding me quite unambiguously to step back. She then produced bandages, a little bottle of ethanol and some cotton wool, and began cleaning Mrs Harwood's fingers.

'Many people do this,' Miss Smith said, 'when they're very worried or afraid . . . Are you?'

In response, Mrs Harwood began weeping and covered her mouth with the hand Miss Smith was not treating.

'It's all right,' said Miss Smith. 'We all have our mishaps. Some more difficult than others, but such is life. Tell me, what worries you?'

Mrs Harwood sobbed, looking at me with distrust.

'Mr Frey is a friend,' said Miss Smith. 'He's worried about you too.'

I was so glad Miss Smith was here. I would not have been able to set Mrs Harwood at ease with such kindness.

'Tell me about your husband,' Miss Smith encouraged. 'I know he's not with you any more. Did you love him very much?'

Not a very difficult question, yet Mrs Harwood vacillated. Miss Smith waited patiently for a reply.

'I . . . well, yes,' Mrs Harwood said at last, conscious of her hesitation. It took only an inquisitive look from Miss Smith to make her go on. 'My late husband was . . . very difficult to live with – God forgive me for speaking ill of the dead. But he liked to mock me in front of the children – told me I was ugly, stupid, that the house was neglected, that I couldn't control the servants . . . I'm not perfect, of course, sometimes I deserved his scolding, but . . . I only wish he hadn't done it in front of the children every time. He used me as an example; told them he didn't want them to grow into daft geese like their silly mother.'

Miss Smith could not conceal her anger at those words, yet she spoke kindly. 'Nobody deserves to be disparaged like that, my dear, especially not by those who are supposed to love us.'

Mrs Harwood began chewing on her knuckles, but Miss Smith swiftly pulled her hand away.

'I've never told this to anyone,' Mrs Harwood continued, her eyes now flickering in distress, and spitting the words out as if she'd repressed them for years. 'But part of me was a little – relieved when he was gone.'

And Freddie had taken after the father, I now could see, abusing the family's women.

'When did it happen?' asked Miss Smith.

'It will be exactly three years next month,' was the instant reply. I wondered if the poor woman kept count of the days. 'It's good the theatre company won't be working by then. Susy and I are going to take some flowers to his grave on the anniversary.'

Miss Smith asked the next question as if standing on eggshells. 'He didn't leave you in a very good position, did he?'

Mrs Harwood frowned and blinked away a renewed wave of tears, but when she spoke there was more spite than sorrow. 'No. He liked to gamble. A lot. He left us in debt, and after selling the house and the carriages we still owed money. We are paying to this day, my children and me. With our combined wages we barely have enough to maintain ourselves and pay the interest.'

'Don't you have any family you might appeal to?' I asked this time.

'Not in England. I have a couple of distant cousins in New Zealand, wherever that is. I would have had to send my children to them, if Miss Terry hadn't managed to get us work.'

Miss Smith was now applying some unguent. 'I want you to try and stop doing that biting and chewing. Your hands are precious. You need them to work. Look after them.' Then she began bandaging each finger.

'Yes, nurse, miss,' said Mrs Harwood, although she probably did not believe her own words.

'Can I ask you . . .' Miss Smith added, still quite cautiously, 'how your husband died?'

'He fell down the stairs,' Mrs Harwood said soon enough, but with a tremble in her voice that grew steadily with each word. 'We had just been arguing – I can't even remember why. He was seething! He gave me a smack and left the room. Next thing I heard was him rolling down the steps and my Susy shouting. My poor Susy saw it all –'

Mrs Harwood could not say more. She pouted,

suddenly looking like a scolded child, and then buried her face in her bandaged hands, abandoning herself to misery.

I was going to speak, but Miss Smith shook her head, patting her patient's back as the poor woman wept.

The talking was over.

Third letter from the partially burned stack found at Calton Hill

Sheet almost torn into quarters, as if folded and unfolded compulsively. – I. P. Frey.

My dear,

Large black dogs can be a dark omen, did you know that? They foretell death, just like banshees do, and they follow you, and if you but look at them in the eye you are condemned.

Still, I'd rather see a dog when my time comes. The soft fur and the glassy eyes and the friendly bark of a playful hound, to take me gently to the realms of heaven. Not a shriek to curdle my blood, or the ghastly sight of a tormented soul from purgatory.

You might have seen one these days. A massive, beastly hound. Have you, my dear?

If you do, I beg you, if you do –
Shut your eyes to it
Look not upon it
Turn away and run, even if you doubt what your eyes see
Escape from it

Don't leave me

Love,
X

24

We found McGray in the corridor – he'd asked Susy to go and order us some tea at the hotel's breakfast parlour – and we told him all that we'd heard from Mrs Harwood as we headed there.

'I'm afraid she's at the brink of collapse,' Miss Smith said in a whisper. 'She's obviously been through years of strain.'

'So ye think she needs proper help, I imagine.'

'Yes, Mr McGray, and the sooner the better. Do you mind if I arrange it with the doctors?'

'By all means,' McGray said. 'Do what ye think is necessary. We can discuss the bills later.'

Miss Smith assented. 'Thank you, sir. And it might be good to look at the child too.'

'Are you certain?' I asked. 'The girl seems quite composed to me . . . all things considered.'

Miss Smith winced. 'I meant the boy. He's driving them both insane.'

'He's just a bully,' said McGray. 'Cannae abide the stupid brat.'

'Mr McGray, bullies usually are the most fragile people you could think of. They simply use bravado to hide their own anxieties. I'm afraid that boy's head might be the most disturbed of all.'

That would give me food for thought for a good while.

Miss Smith, unfortunately, said she had to leave very soon after that – she'd already devoted plenty of her time to us. All the same, she took a moment to bid goodbye to Susy and assure her she'd be back soon. Just as we saw her leave the hotel, Miss Terry herself was coming in, led by the arm by Henry Irving.

They were whispering to each other, for once ignoring all the greetings and the waving from everyone they stumbled across. It was as though they were locked in a bubble nobody around could possibly burst.

McGray, however, approached them with huge strides, the stomping of his boots resounding throughout the lobby, and he planted himself right in front of the celebrated couple. I will never forget the way Irving glared at him.

Miss Terry jumped a little, but her coquettish eyes and radiant smile immediately concealed whatever emotion she might be feeling.

'Inspectors!' she said warmly. 'What a delight to see you again so soon.'

'So youse finished yer rehearsals,' McGray said, smiling at Miss Terry but casting mocking looks at Mr Irving. 'I thought it would keep youse busy well into the evening. What changed? Did ye tear yer tights?'

Irving snorted like an angry bull. 'I do not talk to vulgar clowns.' And saying no more he let go of Miss Terry's arm and walked away. Just before he disappeared into the corridors I saw him push a footman so hard the unlucky chap nearly fell.

Even Miss Terry realized her smile would be out of place now. 'Gentlemen, I must apologize for him. Irving has been under a lot of stress and he's always been a very driven man. If you needed to talk to him I might be able to persuade –'

'Actually,' McGray interrupted, 'it is *ye* we want to question now.'

Her lips parted in genuine surprise. 'Me? Well, of course, if you think I could be of help. Would you like to come to my suite?'

'Nae, it's just a very quick question, Miss Terry.' McGray leaned closer to her and lowered his voice. 'Can ye remember losing, within the past few days – a wee leather bag?'

Not a muscle, not an eyelash, nothing moved in Ellen Terry's face. And I studied her reaction without blinking once. I remember the dark blue specks in her pale eyes, her curly blonde hair moving because of the draught that came from the open doors, her soft neck that never gulped, and the fine golden locket that rested on her perfectly calm chest.

Calm she was, but perhaps just a little too much.

'A leather bag?' she echoed.

'Aye.'

'I'm afraid I . . . I don't know. I don't think I have. Why? Have you found something?'

'No idea,' McGray said swiftly. 'We were expecting ye could tell us more.'

Miss Terry brought a hand to her locket and fidgeted with it. The piece was encrusted with exquisite rubies that caught the light from the chandeliers.

'I'm afraid I don't understand,' she said.

'Are ye sure?' McGray pressed.

'I am *sure* I don't understand,' she retorted, now quite uncomfortable.

McGray lowered his voice a little more, leaning closer to Miss Terry. 'Has anyone given ye a leather bag as a present?'

She laughed, but it was a nervous sound this time. 'I often receive gifts. From all sorts of people. This locket came from Her Majesty herself.'

'D'ye ken Miss Ivor?' McGray asked. 'She plays one o' the witches.'

Hecate, I nearly said, but that was no moment to correct McGray.

Miss Terry looked blankly at him. 'Yes, of course I do. She is a very charming la—' and then she looked sideways, her eyes widening. When she glanced back at Nine-Nails her expression was an entirely new one. 'How did you know that?'

'So the penny dropped,' McGray said with a grin.

'She did give me a leather – purse. It was a drawstring purse. But that must have been nearly a year ago!'

'Where is that purse now?' I asked this time.

Miss Terry shook her head. 'I . . . I don't know. London, perhaps . . . I'm sorry to say this, but it was a dreadful, cheap little thing. I only accepted it to be polite, and I don't even remember what I did with it afterwards.'

Miss Terry sounded completely honest, and she *was* wearing jewellery presented to her by Queen Victoria. It was no wonder she saw the gifts from a minor actress as mere tat.

'Can you remember the last time you saw it?' I asked.

'Why, no! But it must have been months ago.' She bit her lip. 'Have you found it?'

She asked that question with a hint of desperation, and I purposely avoided answering.

'What do you think might have happened to it?' I asked.

'Well . . . From time to time Mr Stoker clears out the presents from my dressing room. He has to; otherwise I'd be flooded with bric-a-brac. But he would have asked me before disposing of something like that.'

'And did he?' Nine-Nails jumped in.

'I honestly cannot remember, Inspectors.'

'Could anyone have taken it?'

Her cheeks lost a shade of colour, and her voice a little of its brightness.

'May– maybe. But I need to think about it . . . It's been a long . . . long time . . .'

She went on fidgeting with the locket. For once, the actress was out of words.

'Aye, ye try and freshen yer memory,' McGray said. 'And make sure it happens before the opening ni–'

He did not get to finish the word.

A shriek – a horrible, drilling holler – came to our ears, and everyone's attention went to the other side of the building.

'*Another banshee!*' somebody shouted, unchaining a general gasp, and then there was frantic shouting and people running about like ants.

I saw McGray's eyes searching desperately for the source of the noise, his legs ready to sprint and his hand on his gun. I feared that his predictions were finally becoming true.

I would, however, have preferred to see a hundred banshees than what was really happening.

One of the waiters came running from the tearooms, carrying in his arms the distraught creature responsible

for the anguished cries: Susy Harwood, the girl screaming and kicking about.

My heart jumped when I realized that her small hands
and her blue dress were splattered with blood.

25

I felt for the young Susy more than I can tell. We very soon realized she was experiencing . . . well, her first rags week, but as it so commonly happens, nobody had ever told her about the tribulations that puberty had in store. I cannot imagine what might have passed through her mind, finding herself in that situation just as everyone around her had been talking about dark omens, curses and horrendous messages spelled in red. No wonder she'd howled like that.

Fortunately, Miss Smith had been waiting for a cab by the entrance, from where she heard the commotion and immediately returned. She was thus able to explain to the distraught child what was truly going on, but we had no occasion to see Susy again. Miss Terry offered her lodgings, a bath and a change of clothes, and the women locked the doors behind their backs.

Just before Miss Terry vanished, McGray caught her by the arm.

'We'll be back tonight to finish our wee chat. D'ye understand? And don't ye dare disappear on us like Irving.'

Miss Terry turned to me as if looking for help, but she found none.

'Your soirée tonight will be a perfect time,' I said. 'I *will* take your invitation after all.'

Fuming, Miss Terry pulled her arm away and slammed the door.

Stoker stopped us just as we were turning on our heels. His cheeks were flushed, almost as bright as his ginger hair and beard.

'Inspector McGray . . . I happened to hear that you will be joining us at the ball?'

Nine-Nails grimaced at the question. 'Aye, why?'

Stoker bit his lips, and moved the tip of his shoe as if struggling to crush a bug on the carpet. 'Erm, please don't misinterpret this question, but . . . Do you . . . do you own a black suit?'

He was looking straight at McGray's gaudy tartan trousers.

'What made ye think I don't?' he said after a loud cackle.

Stoker's cheeks blushed even more.

I laughed too. 'Mr Stoker, I can assure you that this shabby Scot owns no decent pair of trousers.'

Stoker checked his pocket watch. His embarrassment had instantly turned into anxiety.

'Inspector, if you don't mind, please allow me to lend you one of my suits. We seem to wear the same size. And we may be able to do something about your stubble as well.'

'Och, sod off. I'll just wear this!'

Stoker might as well have made the sign of the cross. 'Inspector – quite frankly, I'd rather you quit the case.'

'Should I see you back here tonight?' I asked McGray as I made my way out. Nine-Nails did not seem to hear me, though. He was lighting a cigarette, looking pensive, and I had to pat his shoulder with the back of my hand. 'Is something bothering you?'

He shook his head. 'I think we might have another sighting tonight.' As he spoke he produced the crumpled piece of paper where he'd scribbled the banshee's prophecies. 'On the night the blood runs thick and freely / Some fiend here comes, replete with too much rage . . .'

I brought a hand to my frustrated forehead.

'Are you not reading too much between the lines?'

'Perhaps, but I want to be near, just in case. I'll stay around.' He looked sternly at me. 'And ye better bring some officers. That's an order, dandy.'

'And a very stupid one,' I added, leaving him behind.

Even if he had not wanted officers fetched, I still needed to go back to the City Chambers, since my mare was still there.

As soon as I arrived McNair came to me, looking jubilant.

'Inspector Frey, we have news!'

'News?'

'Aye, about the butchers.'

I nearly gasped. After all the ordeals of the day I'd completely forgotten that errand. I recognized a couple of those sleazy reporters snooping around, so I took McNair to the Dumping Ground.

'We went to every butcher in town,' he said as he closed the door behind us. 'They all told us the same story: no blood was sold on the day the banshee appeared under the bridge.'

I blinked in confusion. 'Nothing at all?'

'Right. They're sure. Not a wee drop.'

'How can they be so certain?'

'They told us that too, sir. It wisnae market day.'

'Cattle market, you mean?' I asked.

'Aye, sir,' said McNair. 'Most o' the slaughtering is done on market day, or the day after. The chaps at the abattoir had done their last slaughtering on the sixth.'

'So three days earlier.'

'Aye, so there was nae blood to be sold; apparently the stuff goes bad very quickly, especially in summertime – they have to cook it very soon.'

I went to McGray's chair, sat back and pressed my finger-tips together. 'That makes an awful lot of sense . . . but . . .' I thought of Susy and the prophecy, and then a disturbing thought came to me. 'By any chance did they tell you when the next market day will be?'

'Aye, but it already *was*, Inspector.'

'Please, do *not* tell me that it was –'

'Aye, sir. Today. All the slaughtering has been done and the blood's been sold; most of it gone in the early morning.'

I covered my brow, grunting. When I looked up I saw that the young constable was as worried as I.

'Were there any unusual customers? Strangers?'

'Aye, but they said that's quite normal these days. The city has grown quite a bit.'

'That is not good enough, McNair. We need to know exactly what was sold and to whom.' Butchers, like most tradesmen, lived above their premises, so I thought we could send some of the officers to ask around. The dwellers would not be happy, but this was a police affair.

'And we also need some of the chaps to mount guard at the Palace Hotel,' I told him.

'Really, sir?'

'Yes,' I said wearily, my eyes slowly moving towards a

large formaldehyde jar which contained a thick, repugnant snake coiled on itself. 'If Nine-Nails is right – and gosh, now I think he is – we might have another sighting tonight.'

26

As I arrived in Great King Street I saw there were two large carriages parked in front of the house. One was a wide landau, with a foldable roof that, in view of the impending weather, had been set up. The other was a simple cab, but instead of carrying passengers, its whole interior was crammed with chests and cases of all shapes and sizes. Two men were busy unloading them and taking them into the house.

'And so it begins,' I sighed.

By then the light drizzle had become a proper storm. It was as though Edinburgh itself was having an allergic reaction to the Frey family.

I stepped into the corridor and dodged piles of luggage, but still saw that the house had been thoroughly cleaned. There were no traces of wine on the carpets, or shattered vases, or ladies' forgotten shoes. And I was impressed by the smell too: the stench of cheap tobacco had been completely replaced by rose and bergamot.

Just as I thought so I met Joan, who was bringing a tray brimming with tea, pastries and my best decanter full of brandy.

'Master,' she said before I could compliment her efforts, 'your visitors have —'

'Why, there you are!' cried the familiar voice of Catherine Frey, née White, my less than beloved stepmother, coming into the corridor.

Not yet thirty-nine, so scarcely seven years older than me, she carried her age outstandingly well, which I hate to admit (then again, when your only mission in life is to be a rich man's decoration . . .). She still had an elegant hourglass figure, a long neck slightly titled backwards, and only mere traces of wrinkles on the sides of her mouth. She had the bright blonde hair and blue eyes she'd passed on to Elgie and Oliver, but unlike my youngest brother, her face never showed the slightest trace of humour.

'Ian,' she said, looking at Joan with her eternally haughty manner, 'this good woman claims to have worked for you the best part of eight years, yet I have never seen her in my life.'

'Good evening to you too, Catherine,' I said. 'Joan kept my rented lodgings at Suffolk Street, back in London.' *My golden days*, I thought.

'Why, that explains it! Your father told me never to venture into such a dreadfully dangerous area.'

My stepmother had the talent of stressing just the right words to set my father's temper on fire, and tonight it would work as effectively as ever. He came from the main parlour, armed with a fat glass of spirit that was nearly empty.

'At least you managed to get a place that is not in the middle of a rat-infested slum,' he said reprovingly.

I'd not seen my father in six months, and in that relatively short period of time he'd done an excellent job at expanding his waistline. The buttons on his shirt were dangerously outstretched, and I feared one of them would soon eject like a bullet. He seemed to be ageing faster these days, the wrinkles becoming deeper, and blotches appearing on his skin as suddenly as blossoms in spring. Twenty-seven years older than his second wife, the old Mr Frey no longer looked like her father, but rather her grandfather.

He snatched the decanter from Joan's tray and went back to the main drawing room, where Elgie sat, looking rather tense. This was the very room where I'd found him fiddling and drinking and partying the day before; tonight, however, with the immaculate rug, the puffed-up cushions and the fresh flowers on the mantelpiece, the place could not have looked more different.

I was about to comment on how I liked the room, but Catherine spoke first.

'We did not know where to sit, Ian. This room is awfully draughty, and the only thing worse than the shabby décor is that all the windows face southwards; I would tan and freckle like a field hand if I had to spend all my afternoons here. Thank God the Scottish weather is ghastly.'

'So, Father,' I said, turning to him, 'how long are you planning to stay?'

At least the food was no matter of complaint.

Joan and Layton had prepared some delicious beef fillets, and even my fussy stepmother enjoyed them with unprecedented gusto.

I thought the conversation would be terribly dry, but Catherine turned out to be a bottomless fountain of theatre gossip. She could recite everything there was to know about every liaison, adultery and love affair involving every actor and diva the United Kingdom has ever seen.

It made me realize how little attention I'd paid to anything she had said in the last twenty years or so.

Ellen Terry, I soon realized, seemed to be her pet hate.

'Oh dear, it would take me half the night just to go through the names of her lovers!'

'Then don't,' Father grumbled, but went unnoticed. Catherine began the very long list.

'George Frederic Watts, for instance. They married when she was sixteen and he was in his forties!'

A rather hypocritical remark, I thought, since Catherine herself had been sixteen when she married my father, who was forty-three at the time.

'The marriage didn't last a whole year,' she went on, 'but people whisper that he paid her a pension for the next *twelve* years, even though she was already having sordid affairs with Charles Reade, Tom Taylor, Lewis Carroll, Edward Godwin ... Oh, the *scandal* with the wicked Earl Godwin! They lived together, *never* had any intentions to marry and thus produced two illegitimate brats. I heard Godwin built her a dream house, but it was so lavish he had to mortgage the property and run away from his creditors. By this point *Miss* Terry left him – what use was a penniless man to her? – and I believe he died not long ago, still calling for her, some papers claimed.

'Then she married Charles Wardell, but he eventually lost his mind. The poor man also died, I believe three or four years ago – alcoholism! It was in every paper.'

Catherine only stopped for a moment to catch her breath. Even Joan was not capable of such incisive gossip.

'And in between all those men,' Catherine resumed, 'she has always been Irving's little toy – not that *his* wife is that innocent; I heard people have seen her on the arm of a pauper-looking scarecrow,' she laughed. 'Oh well, Irving is not doing much better himself. Honestly, how can any-one think Ellen Terry is a beauty? With that jaw and that nose – she looks like a Trojan mare. And so old these days! Forty-two and still playing the little dove on the stage! In a couple of years she will be playing Juliet with a walking stick.'

I had to bite my lip not to remark that Catherine was only three years younger.

'Will you tell her so at tonight's soirée?' Father asked. I had told them about the invitation, which was not received quite as I expected: Father complained about not having a chance to catch his breath, and Catherine moaned about not having her best frock ready for the night. She could not bring up the subject enough times.

'I would have loved to have the chance to parade my green silk dress in front of that tasteless woman. If only we'd known with a little advance.' She sighed deeply. 'At least I can save it for the premiere night. Laurence man-aged to get us the most wonderful seats available. A raised box! And at the perfect distance from Oscar Wilde's: close enough to see what he is up to, but not so much so that he might spill champagne on my frock.' Catherine stretched a hand to pat mine. 'Oh, Ian, it is a shame you shan't be with us, but good that Laurence had the tact to avoid you meeting Eugenia –'

'Don't overdo it, Catherine,' Father grunted.

Catherine usually submitted if my father protested, but this time she would not have it.

'My dear, I do not know why every time I mention the name of the poor girl I seem to get a good scolding . . .'

'You know perfectly,' Father said gravely. 'You know what I think of the situation, yet you prattle about it day and night. Don't you remember our Christmas?'

I wish I could have jumped across the table and hugged my slightly inebriated father. After Eugenia had ended our engagement, the old Mr Frey had, against my wildest predictions, supported me fully. He'd even thrown Laurence and Eugenia out of my uncle's house on Christmas Day, and he'd forever refer to my former sweetheart as *the trollop*.

'I am still bloody mad at the pair of them,' Father went on. 'If I am joining you it is only because I want to see what my youngest son has been doing in this bloody dump of a city all these months. But don't expect me to be all smiles and chatter.'

Father gulped down the rest of his wine and then a tense silence fell on the table.

Elgie speedily tried to change the subject. 'I was thinking we could go to the new Scottish Portrait Gallery. It will open next week and it is a very impressive building.'

'A Scottish Portrait Gallery!' our father cried with contempt, sending breadcrumbs all across the table. 'To see *what*? Scottish faces? I can see those from your brother's bloody south-facing window.'

'There, there,' said Catherine, her taming powers on my father unequalled. 'Elgie is just trying to make your stay a little more bearable. Thank goodness Oliver is not here.'

Somehow, only then did I realize that the elder of my half-brothers was not around.

'Where is he?' I felt quite guilty for asking that so late, but Oliver's contribution to the conversation would have been the same whether he was in London or in Scotland. The poor chap has always been sickly, quiet and – it pains me to say it – a little slow-witted. He'd been Catherine's first child, born when she was only seventeen, and for years I have suspected that something odd might have occurred during that pregnancy.

'Oh, *thank you* for asking,' she replied, for her husband's mouth was too full of food. 'Poor Oliver caught a nasty summer cold and he is only just recovering. He could have made the trip, I suppose, but I didn't know in which dire conditions you might receive us, so I'd rather not risk a relapse.'

Layton came to me with a little tray and I realized I had squeezed my bread roll into scraps. 'More wine?' I offered, brushing the crumbs off my hands.

'Do not take this the wrong way, Ian,' Catherine said, stretching her glass to have it refilled with my best Merlot. 'But you still work at that dreadful place, interacting with thieves, prostitutes, policemen and the rest of the criminal classes.' She looked around. 'It is a decent little lodge you have secured here, but there is only so much you can stretch what God has given to this side of the land.

'Which reminds me,' she added, looking directly at Elgie. 'Once this little *Macbeth* charade is over, I am taking my son back to London.'

Elgie dropped his cutlery and I nearly crushed my glass in my hand. Catherine, however, took a demure sip as innocently as if she'd but remarked on the shape of a cloud.

I put my drink carefully back on the table. 'Father,' I said in my most composed attitude, 'do you have anything to say?'

He only chuckled. '*Two* of my sons in Edin-bloody-burgh, or *one* of my sons in Edin-bloody-burgh? Do I need say more?'

Elgie looked livid but I discreetly raised a hand.

'Perhaps this is something we should discuss *after* the play,' I said, for once acting as peacemaker. 'We do not want these paltry domestics affecting your performance, Elgie.'

He barely managed to compose himself, but Catherine was not done.

'Well, it is not a very discerning audience you'll be playing for, is it? Provincial theatre. And mucky Terryphiles for that matter! I doubt people will be much concerned with the music when Ellen Terry appears wearing an indecent cleavage.'

Elgie could not stand his mother's bluntness any more. He sprang upwards, hitting the table and making every glass clatter, and then he stormed out of the room as heated as a whistling steam engine.

I stared daggers at my father and his wife, who resumed their dinner as if nothing had happened.

'*What?*' said Father, noticing my reproachful stare.

I drew in a deep breath. 'What shall we talk about now? Elgie is usually the oil between the sharp Frey pegs.' I received no reply, so I asked Layton to bring my dessert to my bedroom, and then swiftly left the table.

I enjoyed pastry and coffee in the privacy of my chamber, and then managed to have a short nap before getting ready for the ball, for which I now thanked providence. That night I would not sleep at all.

Fourth letter from the partially burned stack found at Calton Hill

Middle paragraph smudged and barely readable. Hand much clearer towards the end. – I. P. Frey.

My dear,

It feels all so real now. Now that the wheel has begun to turn. Your inescapable end.

Oh my darling, are you really sure you are going to a better place? Or will it be only the corruption and the maggots feasting on your flesh, staining the satin lining of an icy coffin?

I cannot bear the thought, my dear. Before that happens, you must know, I will cut locks of your beautiful hair, and make bows, and deck all the knobs to all my doors, so that each time I walk into a room I shall think you might be there. And then, when I'm convinced you'll not come back, when I'm resigned I'll never see your face again, when even my stupor is not enough to deceive my senses . . . then I shall go to your grave, and dig out your bones, and pluck out all your teeth and make myself a necklace, and wear you until I too can join you there, in the quiet earth.

Forgive me, my love, if I falter. I shan't fail you. I swear. I shall see you tonight, with the ghouls and the dark spirits. I shall fetch them all, as I said I would.

Do not worry. Your message will be sent. Even if it means your doom. And my own ruin.

Love,
X

27

I felt surprisingly rejuvenated after a good shave and putting on my finest suit – the impact that a nicely starched shirt, some cologne, a bow tie and a pair of gold cufflinks can have on the mood is unbelievable. Even Father, who had lately relaxed his etiquette, seemed quite pleased in his finery. After our argument he had been set on not going, but the combined pressure from Elgie and Catherine proved too much for him.

The rain had receded a little and become a light yet still persistent drizzle; the clouds, partly gone, were black patches on an indigo sky. I did not remember whether the moon was supposed to be full, but it certainly looked so: white and shimmering, and casting a persistent silver light that competed with the street lamps.

The ride was quite short, but our carriage had to join a slow-moving queue in front of the Palace Hotel, since all other guests were arriving at the same time. It seemed as though Irving had invited half the city to this reception.

I had time to see the officers guarding the main entrance and the corners of the building. There were five that I could see, and perhaps there would be more inside. I could not find McNair, whom I assumed would be visiting all the butchers in the Old Town.

I recognized Millar, one of the men who'd been sent to investigate the first sighting under Regent Bridge. I approached him and asked discreetly, 'How many of you have come?'

'Eight, sir.'

'That many?'

'Aye. Superintendent Campbell overheard McNair and he sent us all.'

'What about Inspector McGray?'

'He came round to tell us to be vigilant, and then a couple o' times to get updates, but we've not seen him for the past half hour.'

'Very well. Keep up the good work.'

And I headed back to my relatives, feeling sorry for the officers who had to patrol the building under cold drizzle, while I shared drinks and canapés surrounded by the city's elite. I would follow McGray's example and get them all a dram after this ordeal was over.

As the Frey family walked en masse into the Palace Hotel, its ballroom welcomed us with a parade of black suits, glittering dresses and clinking glasses. The kitchens had done an impressive job, boasting multicoloured fruit jellies and piles of seafood so splendid they looked like offerings to Neptune. Their pièce de résistance, nevertheless, was an enormous replica of Dunsinane Castle entirely made of marzipan, the rocky hill carved from chunks of dark chocolate and its hills covered with green icing. I saw Miss Ivor pinching out a little piece of parapet, a mischievous look on her face.

I recognized most of the people I'd interrogated so recently: the three Weird Sisters with their wide, utterly unfashionable skirts from the sixties, moving around in a tight pack and holding large glasses of red wine – the assassins, Mr Black and Mr Carter, one on each side of the room, wooing the young females – Mr Howard, the Lyceum's manager, by the wide staircase, staring at the general splendour, his chest swollen with pride – Freddie Harwood whispering something in some girl's ear, the poor creature instantly running away from him – and Mr Stoker, whose ginger head stuck out above everyone else's. It was he who first approached us, smiling yet unable to conceal his fatigue.

'Inspector Frey, thank you for coming. Won't you introduce me to your good family?'

So I did, yet Mr and Mrs Frey did not seem too impressed, squinting at Stoker's thick Irish brogue. As soon as the most basic formalities were met, they both disappeared amongst the crowd.

'I had not realized you two were related,' said Stoker, looking at Elgie. 'Your brother is very talented.'

Elgie blushed ever so slightly. 'We have had a lot of time to practise.'

'He *is* quite talented,' I said, 'but try not to flatter Elgie too much, Mr Stoker. It tends to go to his head.'

Stoker smiled. 'Elgie, would you be interested in working in London? Mr Sullivan is always looking for new musicians.'

Completely at odds with my young brother's usual character, he went speechless.

I had to pat him on the back and answer for him. 'That might work. He is apparently going back to London after this play, whether he wants it or not.'

'Well, at least you will have something to look forward to back in the city,' said Stoker, producing a card he offered to Elgie. 'Make sure you contact me when you are there. I shall make the proper introductions.'

I waited until Elgie was beyond hearing distance. 'Mr Stoker, I hope you have not given him your card simply to get rid of him.'

'Of course not, Inspector. I meant my words. But I do need to talk to you . . .'

One of the Weird Sisters, Miss Desborough, happened to be walking nearby, and she recognized the concern in Stoker's voice, her eyes suddenly widening in expectation. Stoker gently pulled my arm and we went to a quieter corner.

'I've seen the officers outside,' he whispered. 'Are you and Inspector McGray expecting . . . trouble tonight?'

'I cannot lie to you. We are not sure, but if something were to happen –'

'Does it have anything to do with Miss Harwood?'

I arched an eyebrow. He too had made the connection between the girl and the prophecy.

'It might,' I said. 'But as I told you, we are not sure.'

Stoker pressed his back against the wall, stroking his beard as if kneading hard dough.

'Is something the matter?'

He gulped, his forehead shining with perspiration. 'I . . . I am just worried about the people around.'

I cast Stoker an inquisitive stare, but whatever was troubling the man, he had buried it deep in the back of his mind.

'That nurse from the asylum – I hear she had a good chance to assess Mrs Harwood's mental state.'

'Indeed.'

'There is something wrong with her, is there not?' To that I nodded, but I had no time to explain the details before Stoker blurted out: 'I *do* hope it's her.'

'Excuse me?'

Stoker looked intently at me, his mind in turmoil, and very slowly – so slowly I could not tell when it happened – his eyes switched to somewhere behind my back.

'Your colleague is here,' he said as if out of breath, pointing towards the entrance.

I thought he'd just said it to change the subject, for I could not find McGray amidst the crowd. But Elgie came around to confirm it.

'Ian, I hardly recognized your boss.'

I had to blink thrice to believe it. Indeed there he was: Nine-Nails McGray, perfectly shaven, his dark hair cut and combed neatly, sporting a black suit of the finest cut. It secretly annoyed me that the garments should fit him so well. Still, he frowned as if the world's most expensive wools were tar and feathers, and he kept pulling the collar of his shirt.

Catherine, my stepmother, came behind Elgie, looking rather flushed and fanning herself vehemently. 'Ian, is that the madman Elgie told us you work for? He looks – quite dashing.'

'A monkey dressed in silk is still a monkey,' I grunted, my words oozing bitterness. 'Catherine,' I said with a raised voice, so that my father – who was nearby, helping himself to a liberal amount of canapés – heard clearly, 'you should sit down. You look as red as a beetroot. We do not want you to *faint*.'

Father turned and found her even redder. 'Gosh, Ian is right. Let's find you a seat.'

'*Elgie*,' I pleaded like never before, 'keep those two away. The last thing I need is Catherine and Nine-Nails teaming up against me!'

So he did, and just in time.

'I hate this fuckin' penguin jacket,' Nine-Nails grumbled as a greeting, 'and the fifty-five sodding pieces o' shite ye have to assemble just to keep the top together.'

'Oh, I do appreciate your efforts,' said Stoker, shaking McGray's hand most effusively. 'My barber told me you didn't quite enjoy the shave, but surely you'll understand. We have la crème de la crème here tonight. Investors and – even Edinburgh's Lord Provost is over there!'

I saw the old Mr Boyd in the distance, his expression and his wife's soured by the conversation of the three Weird Sisters. McGray, however, was not impressed.

'Where's Miss Terry?' he asked. 'I've been looking for her for a while. We couldnae finish our questioning after Susy's incident.'

'Oh, I mustn't tell,' said Stoker. 'She is preparing a spectacular entrance. You will see her soon enough.'

McGray hardened his tone. 'D'ye ken where she is or no?'

Stoker had to snatch a napkin from the arm of a passing waiter, and used it to wipe the sweat from his temple.

'But of course I do. It's just a little trifle she's putting together . . .'

'Och, for goodness' sake . . .' McGray interrupted, exasperated, but not because of Stoker's words. He was not looking at him, but somewhere behind me. 'See, Frey. There's the man we need to question!'

Stoker and I followed his eyes, and we saw a short, thick figure lurching about, crossing the ballroom in a zigzagging route. I recognized the bushy hair and beard of Mr Wheatstone, his golden spectacles now hanging precariously from a single ear. His legs were as flimsy as a garment sent from the wash without being starched; he had to grab people's arms and shoulders for support, and more than once did he place his hands on unmentionable spots of ladies' bodies. One of such affronted ladies was a Weird Sister, the one with the hooked nose, and she was pounding him on the back with her feathery fan when we approached.

'Mr Wheatstone!' cried Stoker. 'You left the theatre but an hour ago! Look at yourself now!'

The man groped about for another supporting point, but people by now strove to avoid him, and he nearly fell on his face. McGray leaped forward and managed to catch him.

'We needed a statement from him,' I grunted. 'Now it will be hours before he can put two sensible words together!'

'Not necessarily,' said McGray, snatching a large champagne cooler – bottle, ice and all – that stood on a nearby table. 'But we need some privacy for this.'

Mr Stoker led us to a small side chamber, perhaps a private meeting room, furnished with a small table and a few velvet-upholstered chairs. McGray threw Mr Wheatstone on one of those, banged the silver cooler on the table, took the bottle out, and in its place plunged Mr Wheatstone's head right into the icy water.

Nine-Nails had a leisurely swig of champagne directly from the bottle, while holding Mr Wheatstone's head in place with his other hand. The poor man thrashed and kicked about, grunting with a desperation that tore the nerves, but McGray remained as collected as if reading the morning news.

'This bubbling brew is nae bad,' he admitted.

Stoker winced. 'Is this really necessary?'

I shrugged. 'Perhaps not, but I dare you to stop my colleague.'

McGray let go of Mr Wheatstone, whose face had gone blue. His spectacles, surprisingly, were still on his face.

'Ready for a chat?' asked McGray, but Mr Wheatstone was only partially aware of his surroundings. McGray had to repeat the operation twice, each time asking the same question. 'All right, lad, ye better speak now. My own hand's getting numb.'

Mr Wheatstone rubbed his face, dropping his spectacles and spilling cold water all around. His eyes were red and he looked at McGray with loathing.

'*You're a beast!*'

'And ye, my lad, are a bloody drunk! Were ye drinking like this when that lassie got her face all burned? I bet ye were.'

Mr Wheatstone leaned one way and I thought he was going to fall from the chair, but he grabbed the edge of the table. It was impossible to tell whether it was the impact of McGray's words or the remnants of intoxication. The man sniffed and then let out the loudest, most roaring sneeze.

'What does that have to do with you?' he hissed.

'Does Mrs Harwood see you as responsible for it?' I asked directly.

Mr Wheatstone shook his head, unable to meet our gazes. 'Of course she does! Alas, she's mad.'

McGray took a small step forwards; very small, but he looked like a dark cloud looming over Mr Wheatstone.

'I ken plenty about madness, lad. The seamstress is unwell, o' course, but it cannae be without reason . . .' He bit his lip at this point, unable to keep his eyes from the void where his ring finger had once been. 'Madness . . . *almost* always . . . can be explained' – he allowed himself a deep sigh. 'In this case, it can. She blames ye; that's clear. She thinks ye'll burn everyone on stage. Would ye say she has any reasons to think so? However faint – or even imaginary?'

Mr Wheatstone stared into McGray's eyes – a sad, doomed look in him. It was the kind of stare I have seen in convicts who have been cornered into confession; when they realize there is no point in hiding things any more. He pinched the bridge of his nose and blinked hard, then rubbed tears from his eyes with his sleeve. I had to offer him my handkerchief, and he blew his nose stridently.

'It was my fault,' he said at last, his eyes flickering around the room, again unable to meet anybody else's. 'Of course it was my fault. I designed the blasted ladder of angels! Mr Irving wanted the most spectacular ending for *Faust*. He knew exactly what he wanted, and I had to deliver!'

Stoker cleared his throat, visibly uncomfortable.

'It was a challenging production,' Wheatstone continued. 'Full of experimental effects – it was the first time anyone used electric flashes on the stage. And then there was this sword scene where electric sparks burst whenever the blades clashed – I even worked with one of Edison's partners to design the mechanism. It was all so spectacular, and we had word that the Prince and Princess of Wales meant to attend the premiere, which only added more pressure. Mr Irving wanted something almighty for the final scene, when his lead lady lay dead at the foot of the cross. He wanted the most ethereal illusion: a line of angels descending from heaven, floating in the air. I worked very hard on it, and in the end it *did* look the part. I have created sea storms, battlefields, herds of faeries . . . but people have never reacted like they did for that effect. People bought tickets for *Faust* just to see those angels hovering above the stage with their plumed wings.

'It was all very simple, in fact: a black steel frame against a black starry background, which became virtually invisible under the proper lighting. And I designed it to avoid any redundant support: a single steel backbone, hung from the flies with steel rope. It had to be strong enough to bear the weight of twelve souls, between little girls and young women – the daintiest Irving could find, with the prettiest one on top, of course – and using steel the entire structure could be very thin. Attached to this backbone there were thin rungs to support the angels, and their robes and wings were made to cover most of the steel. One of my technicians would strap the girls with either rope or leather belts. I added pegs in the back of the main structure, pointing backwards, so that they couldn't be seen, and the girls used these as steps to climb up to their positions. That all helped create the illusion, but it also meant there was only one way up or down . . . Only *one* girl could descend at a time . . .'

Mr Wheatstone covered his brow with a shaking hand, his voice breaking.

'The top angel . . .' he resumed after a couple of long, deep breaths, 'had to be the first one to climb up and the last one to come down.

'And the lighting . . . the – the lighting had to be very

strong; not only to show the angels glimmering in pure white, but also to use that shining to obscure the black steel support. Electric lights would not do; they're not contrasting – well, *white* enough. We had to use limelight.'

I raised my eyebrows. 'Dear Lord!'

'I was going to use electric light, but on the night before the opening Irving suggested we try limelight. Once he saw the effect he would not look back. I did protest against it, but Irving was adamant –'

'Remind me how that works,' said McGray.

'You direct a flame to a block of quicklime – calcium hydroxide – until it becomes incandescent. It is a beautiful effect, but . . .'

'Terribly dangerous,' I added. 'Quicklime only ignites at thousands of degrees.'

Nine-Nails whistled.

Mr Wheatstone struggled to breathe in. 'I know! And with the wooden rafters and rope . . . and the girls sitting so high up, so close to the ceilings . . . Still, Irving insisted –'

'Don't try to blame it on Irving!' Stoker hissed.

'Oh, but I should,' said Wheatstone, in a coarse, poisonous growl. 'He bursts into rage, hollers and punches people whenever he pleases. George Alexander came out of the *Faust* production with bruises all over him. And before him, Irving ruined John Tarvin's career – Tarvin broke his hip after Irving pushed him into the orchestra pit, just because the poor fool always forgot his lines; the man was in such pain he became addicted to his medications. Mr Stoker, your great Henry Irving *loves* to be feared.'

Stoker turned away, his chest heaving. By then I was taking comprehensive notes of everything being said.

'And yet,' sighed Mr Wheatstone, 'I am guilty. I should have prevailed. Do you believe I don't feel terrible about –' he swallowed '– about what happened? I do! I know what people whisper behind my back and I deserve it. But people also forget it was *I* who rescued the little girl from the fire. It was on the last performance, when we were all relieved and thought the whole thing would be over; the flies and the rafters caught fire just as the curtains were closing down, and I climbed to the girls and cut their belts, but we weren't fast enough. Poor Susan was fastened at the top, screaming her lungs out. She was held so firmly she could not jump even if she'd wanted to. I climbed up to her and cut the ties. No one but *me* had a closer sight of her face as . . . it burned . . . I saw it. I smothered the flames on her little face with my bare hand. I *felt* the –'

He shuddered. We all did.

'There was a period I had nightmares almost every night. I would see her standing next to my bed, still burning and blistering, shouting at me! Telling me I should have left her up there to die, rather than let her spend the rest of her life looking like that.' He looked at the bottle in McGray's hands. 'Before that I only drank a little glass of port at Christmas . . .'

'Is that the reason you got yourself intoxicated tonight?' I asked.

'What else, Inspector? The first thing I heard upon coming back was what happened to the girl this afternoon. On top of her mother slowly losing her mind and her boor of a brother . . . It will sound silly to you, but until today I'd never contemplated the thought of her . . . well, growing up into womanhood. And what a future awaits her . . .'

It was a looming thought indeed, and it left us all in an eerie silence. McGray was the first to break it.

'Does the lassie blame ye as well?'

This was what completely shattered Mr Wheatstone's spirit. He buried his face in his hands and whimpered.

'No!' he mumbled. 'She's a true angel . . . the little girl thinks I saved her.'

He said no more after that, or brought his face up again, but the way he dug his fingernails into his scalp was more eloquent than a thousand words. His own hands were the claws of unmitigated guilt; the man himself his own tormentor, forever unable to forgive himself.

'Stoker,' said McGray at last, 'please bring some strong coffee for the lad. I've shaken him enough.' Stoker bowed and went out, while McGray approached Mr Wheatstone to pat him on the back. 'There, there. Ye seem a wee bit too passionate for an Englishman. Are ye sure yer not part Scottish – or Irish?'

He could not have concealed the spark in his eyes. I wondered if he'd sent Stoker away on purpose before asking the question.

'Must be my drop of Irish,' said Wheatstone, making me draw in a deep breath. 'From my mother's side.'

McGray nodded, looking more pleased than surprised. I thought he would press more about the Irish ancestry, but he would follow an entirely different thread. 'Mr Wheatstone, we've heard about another person who seems to feel guilty about that lassie. Miss Terry.'

Wheatstone let out a bitter laugh. 'Of course. She is the one who discovered the girl. During the run of *Henry VIII*, about a year before *Faust* premiered. Miss Terry insisted and insisted she be top angel. She must believe she passed the poor girl's sentence, and she has clearly tried to get some atonement.

'Miss Terry was the one who had Mrs Harwood and the children hired when the family went into debt. I myself heard her once appealing to Irving. That Harwood boy now thinks he's invincible; he must know the guilt that Miss Terry feels and takes advantage of it, the little turd. He does as he pleases and insults whomever he wants, yet he'll never be dismissed as long as Miss Terry is around.'

McGray paced for a moment. 'Ye saw the banshee under Regent Bridge,' he said, coming closer to Mr Wheatstone. 'And ye saw Mrs Harwood's fit at the theatre . . . D'ye think that . . . perhaps . . . ?'

Mr Wheatstone rubbed his temples. 'Before today I would have said it was impossible.' He sighed as if he carried all the worries of the world. 'After today . . . I'm not so sure.'

A footman came round then, bringing a tray with steaming coffee and telling us Mr Stoker had gone back to greeting guests. We left Mr Wheatstone to compose himself and told him we'd be around for a while in case he needed to tell us anything else. Before we left the small room, McGray whispered in the footman's ear.

'Don't leave the lad on his own. Ye understand? If anything happens, come and fetch us.'

The young man nodded and I saw Nine-Nails slide him a handsome tip.

'Do you fear for him?' I asked McGray in a low voice.

'Indeedy. If Mrs Harwood's really acting as a banshee . . .' He did not bring himself to finish the sentence. 'We should keep an eye on her too.'

We summoned two other officers, who came in dripping rain all over the red carpets. One of them was Millar (who barely recognized McGray in his finery). We asked the other chap to look after Mr Wheatstone. Millar was to guard Mrs Harwood's corridor, but to keep a low profile – the last thing the woman needed was to know that the police suspected her.

Back to the ballroom, I let out a weary sigh. 'I should feel a little more at ease with those two being watched.'

'Aye,' said McGray, turning down champagne from one of the waiters, 'but I cannae help feeling all this is so fuzzy – like looking out through a grubby window. Can we even tell for sure what we are pursuing? A prophecy that might not even –'

'Sirs . . .' a voice called us from behind.

It was a soft, meek voice, and when we turned our heads I could not believe my eyes. It was none other than Freddie Harwood.

'What d'ye want?' McGray snapped at once, but then we realized that the boy was ghastly pale, as if he'd seen a ghost.

'What is the matter?' I asked.

The boy spoke fast and with little breath. 'I need to talk to you. But I don't want *her* to know.'

'Who?'

'You know who,' he said, a hint of his usual insolence ever present. 'Can I see you before you leave? I'll be waiting in the music room. Tell no one!'

And he ran off immediately, becoming lost amidst the crowd. We were, of course, going to pursue him, but before we moved two steps ahead, all the lights in the room went off.

Fifth letter from the partially burned stack found at Calton Hill

Unlike the others, this sheet has no salutation. – I. P. Frey.

Dead beetles for dragon scales, stencilled Bolton sheeting for cloth
of gold, coarse salt for glistening snow,

> *wooden crowns, wooden thrones,*

> *wooden goblets, wooden swords,*

> *and then painted pine for ebony,*

cut up wrapping paper for autumn leaves,

bleached cock feathers for angelic wings,

a lady of easy virtue for a mythic queen –

28

There was a general cry and I felt my heart skipping a beat, instantly regretting not having brought a weapon. McGray had, and he elbowed me as he pulled it from his breast pocket. I heard him stride forward, pushing people aside, and I groped after him in the pitch black, but then we heard several awed voices.

A small yellow glimmer appeared at the top of the stairs, not much brighter than the flame of a single taper, but it grew slowly, shedding light on the graceful figure of Ellen Terry. Holding a little oil lamp up high, she was wrapped in a white linen shroud that made her look like a phantom.

'Oh, for goodness' sake,' I mumbled.

After a well-measured moment to let us catch our collective breath, Miss Terry dragged herself down the stairs with restless, animal-like movements, grasping the banister with a trembling hand, her legs twisting at seemingly impossible angles. With her frenzied eyes and the sharp shadows projected by the lamp, she was a disturbing thing to behold.

She stopped halfway down, curling up around the light. Amidst the darkness her bright clothes appeared to be floating, as she reached for imaginary water and began rubbing her hands in desperation.

'Out, damned spot! Out, I say!'

I could feel her madness and despair, her voice hissing

and quivering at the precise moments, and her pale eyes flickered in every direction, as if haunted by voices all about her. I felt the impulse to run to the side room, fetch Mr Wheatstone and ask him if that was what he'd seen under Regent Bridge – Would he have seen Miss Terry's performance at all, being always at the backstage running the effects? – However, the crowd had packed up closely around us, and I soon realized I could never get the man in time.

And there was something else that caught my attention.

McGray looked stricken, like a dam about to burst. His hand was still stuck in his breast pocket, the Scot frozen to his very core. His body moved only in an involuntary tremor, as if Miss Terry's lines had injected ice into his veins.

'. . . *who would have thought the old man to have had so much blood in him?*'

I also trembled, realizing exactly what was going through Nine-Nails' mind.

Was that what young Amy McGray had looked like six years ago? Had she been thus torn? Had she appeared so much a deranged, tormented creature? She must have, and only then did I realize the nuts and bolts of that ghastly moment; McGray *must* have found his sister in the most dreadful state imaginable, the then sixteen-year-old girl still covered in their parents' blood.

Miss Terry descended a few more steps, stumbling quite artistically as she mentioned the death of Macduff's wife, and she crouched again but a couple of yards from the spectators. McGray was on the frontline, and his whitened face gleamed under the lamp's light.

He caught Miss Terry's eye, and for an instant the actress lost her focus. They stared at each other for a split second that seemed to stretch for ever, and I could not tell who was the more affected. McGray's mind I now knew fairly well; Miss Terry's, on the other hand, was a mystery.

She looked away, trying hard to concentrate on the little flame, yet suddenly looking confused. She took a deep breath, and with her next lines everyone else must have thought that was all part of her act.

'*Here's the smell of the blood still*,' she whispered, hissing like a snake, and then turning to despair. '*All the perfumes of Arabia will not sweeten this little hand . . .*'

And then she wailed. What a piercing, devastating sound that was; anguish itself, like a steel blade running on glass and drilling into our ears. She let out a second wail, and a third, the last one diminishing and quivering as her lungs ran out of air.

She petrified us all. Not a murmur, or a cough, or the ruffle of clothes could be heard. Miss Terry had us all hanging by a thread until she decided to speak again. As she concluded her soliloquy, her voice gradually faded into an eerie whisper, '*to bed . . . to bed . . .*' sending shivers down everyone's spines.

Miss Terry crouched at the foot of the stairs, and tremblingly blew out her lamp's flame. There was but a blink of solid darkness, before all the lights went back on and the crowd exploded in cheering and applause.

I had to take a deep breath, and so did McGray.

Like a phoenix, Miss Terry rose to her feet, dropping the white cape and revealing her majestic green dress. Next to those iridescent beetle wings, all the other ladies' beads and spangles looked cheap and dull.

She stood tall and proud, her arms outstretched, receiving the cheering as it if were a life-giving force, and Irving joined her from nowhere and held her hand to kiss.

'Welcome, ladies and gentlemen!' he bellowed, smiling and looking more jubilant than I'd ever thought he could. Tonight he was not the monster everyone in the theatre feared. Tonight he was a patrician figure with the grace that can exist only in dreams: welcoming, charismatic, buoyant with joy, and so was his speech. His voice was deep, his enunciation perfect, the sound masterfully projected from the depths of his swollen diaphragm.

'Honest, steadfast work is almost sure to bring rewards and honours,' he was saying, 'and Edinburgh's warm welcome has given us all a renewed zest for existence! A distinction which will be remembered for as long as the annals of our stage will last ... Sir John, for instance! Many a time you have honoured us with your presence! And I believe the illustrious Lady Anne is also here tonight ...'

I shook my head at the pomposity of his words. No wonder people fell for his charm.

While Irving thanked and lauded every person under the Scottish sky, I drew closer to McGray and muttered, 'Are you all right?'

He gave a quick nod, struggling to collect himself. He had to pat his cheeks to recover some colour.

'Where's the brat?' he asked, his eyes looking for Freddie. 'We should ask one o' the waiters to go fetch him.'

'I'd be more interested in keeping Miss Terry within our reach. She is our strongest lead right now.'

We both looked at the staircase, where Irving's flattery continued. 'You cannot think it strange,' he said, 'that every fibre of my soul throbs, as my lips try to utter the truest, warmest, most earnest thanks to –'

He hushed all of a sudden, just as a butler hurried in, walking so stiffly I doubted his knees were jointed. He approached Irving and whispered in his ear. I was close enough to make out the words 'entrance' and 'not invited'.

Irving's face betrayed him, his bushy eyebrows contorting and his frown deepening like cuts into his skull. There was horror on his face, as if the ghosts in his brain were taking shape before his eyes.

People began to gossip, and then there was a general gasp coming like a wave from the main entrance. All our heads turned to find two thin, very young men, around Elgie's age, coming in as if they owned the entire building and everything inside it. They certainly wore expensive dinner jackets and sparkly cufflinks.

They were Irving's sons.

One needed but a glance to realize it. They were both the spitting image of their father: the same long face, the cheekbones just as sharp, the thick eyebrows and even the stern way they beheld everything. Irving could not have denied his parenthood even if his wife had entertained as many lovers as Miss Terry.

They approached slowly, parting the silent crowd like a knife does soft butter, and planted themselves right in front of their father, one of them even brushing his arm against McGray's.

I could not tell who was the more mortified, Irving or Miss Terry. They could have been playing Macbeth beholding Banquo's ghost, and Lady Macbeth at the exact moment before her wits snapped.

Worse, more painful than a scandalous rant, was the boys' silence, which seemed to last a lifetime.

'Good evening, Father!' said the elder brother – Harry – as mordantly as only a handful of people on this planet are capable of. Curiously, I saw Catherine in the background, standing on her tiptoes and stretching her neck like a meerkat. 'You look well.'

'Our invitation must have got lost in the post,' added the slightly younger one – Sydney.

Amidst the paralysed crowd, Miss Terry was the first to move. She pulled up her hem, turned her back on everyone and left the room with brisk steps. It was as though the ruffling of her skirts was the only sound left in the world, and in her haste some of the beetle wings ripped off and fell on to the carpet.

There were cruel smiles creeping upon the Irving boys, their teeth as white and sharp as their father's.

Stoker stepped ahead, as if appearing from thin air. 'Sydney, Harry! You are so welcome.' He had to grasp the boys' hands to shake them, and then made a gesture to the musicians, who began playing a lively polka. 'You boys need no invitation.'

'Of course we don't!' snapped Sydney. 'Our inheritance is paying for all this extravagance.' His eyes went from the champagne bottles to the piles of oysters and the enormous wheels of French cheese.

The music somewhat covered his words, but the people who did hear would pass them on to all the other attendants within minutes. I saw King Duncan, elderly and regal as he looked, beginning a dance with one of the witches, and some of the actors followed his lead in a pathetic attempt at diverting attention. However, even *they* kept watching the Irvings out of the corners of their eyes.

Henry Irving finally faced his sons, but he spoke awkwardly. Suddenly he was the teenager and his offspring were in charge.

'Boys, I've not seen you in . . .'

'A few years,' said Harry.

'How's the wench?' asked Sydney, finally setting Irving's temper on fire.

He leaned towards them and hissed something at them. Unfortunately, I did not manage to hear, but it must have been something truly spiteful, for the young faces became distorted with anger.

Sydney was the colour of parchment when he answered back. 'Never.'

'We are staying right here, at the Palace,' said Harry, holding his brother back, for the teenager looked as if he could have punched his own father's face there and then, 'we are right next to your suite, in case you haven't noticed. Come and see us when you've returned to your senses. We want to have a little chat.'

Sydney pulled away from his brother and stormed off, once more parting the crowd. Harry cast his father an intense, hateful look, before leaving too.

Irving was both enraged and terrified; an expression I had seldom seen. Stoker tried to rest a hand on his shoulder, but Irving brushed it aside, and as he did so his eyes fell on McGray and me.

Embarrassment was added to the mix. How could a single man's face show all those feelings at once? Rage soon took over them all though, and he barked at us, spitting with every consonant.

'*A pox on you!*' and he turned on his heels and rushed away.

Stoker's eyes followed him. The Irishman looked as perturbed as if someone had just dropped dead. 'You'll want me to explain this scene now, I suppose?'

'Nae,' said McGray, 'but thanks, lad. I'd rather go to the source itself.'

'Miss Terry first?' I asked. 'Or Henry Irving?'

'Terry,' said McGray. 'Better to approach Irving with some prior knowledge.'

'That bitch sent them!' Miss Terry spluttered as soon as she saw us step into her parlour. Her eyes were wrath itself. 'And it's not the first time she has done such a thing!'

She covered her mouth swiftly and lowered her voice, pointing at her bedroom door. I assumed Susy was sleeping there.

'You mean Mrs Irving, do you not?' I said.

'Of course!' she hissed.

McGray poured her a liberal measure of whisky – Miss Terry had a nice stock of decanters. 'Here. Ye better sit down.'

Miss Terry welcomed the tumbler but chuckled. 'I can't sit down in this dress! Mrs Harwood is in no shape to mend it again.'

Instead she paced nervously up and down the room until McGray seized her arm.

'What d'ye mean when ye say it's not the first time?'

Miss Terry sniffed the drink and made to have a sip, but did not actually drink. 'She *uses* them – her sons. That woman has poisoned her boys' minds against Irving.

They hate him yet they don't even know him! I would not expect them to like me, of course, but their mother has made them abhor me!' She realized she was not making much sense, forced a deep breath and gave herself a moment to reflect. 'When Charles, my second husband, passed away, that woman had the gall to send her boys to the funeral. She sent them to spy on me! I could not throw them out, being Irving's sons, so they just stayed around, staring at everything like police officers. Charles and I had been separated for a while, but his death *did* take its toll on me. His drinking worsened as soon as I left him, so I've always wondered if —' Miss Terry rocked her drink so anxiously some of it spilt on the carpet. She held her wrist with her other hand. 'And on top of Charles's death — these boys came to judge me as if I were a street woman . . . Oh, it was a black, black day.'

'Why would they want to spy on ye?' McGray asked.

'I don't know!' she cried back. 'Perhaps their mother wanted to know how miserable I was . . . or maybe she thought I'd be joyful, finding myself finally free to snatch her husband from her.'

'Miss Terry,' I said softly, 'I need to ask you these questions, if only to understand Mrs Irving's behaviour.'

She smiled with acrimony. 'Is it not a little too late for you to ask me whether I am Irving's mistress? Or are you going to ask me whether I'll try to instigate his divorce?' My silence was clear enough. 'At some point we *did* love each other, Inspector. Very much. We still do, but it's a different kind of love these days. I couldn't live without him and I'm sure he couldn't live without me — yet I cannot possibly see us married.'

There was no hesitation in that sentence. I had the

impression she had either rehearsed it a lot, or had told herself that line so many times she now believed it was true.

'Did he ever offer to divorce?'

Miss Terry raised her chin but a fraction of an inch, her neck as tense as her lips.

'No, he *never* would, but even if he had, I am not a marrying woman any more. Not after what I've been through.'

Her tone was sour, but just as earnest, and I remembered Catherine's gossip. If Miss Terry had been a child bride to a middle-aged man, and then had married an imbalanced alcoholic, it was no wonder she'd lost her faith in the institution.

'Ye sure?' McGray asked.

'What does one marry for?' she said, sneering. 'For money? I make two hundred pounds on a working week. To have children? I've already raised the most wonderful son and daughter. For *love*?' Her smile grew more twisted. 'Love is a rotten apple; it comes cheap and never lasts.'

'It might come cheap to the likes of you,' I whispered, not realizing I'd spoken out loud until it was too late.

'If Mrs Irving exerts full control over her sons,' McGray said, 'then ye think they were here tonight following her orders.'

'Of course.'

'And cannae ye think of a reason for that?'

Miss Terry assented. 'I know they've had some frictions recently. Sydney wrote a while ago saying he wanted a career in the theatre, but Irving refused to support him.'

I remembered the old Mr Haviland mentioning precisely that, the first time I'd questioned him.

'Really?' McGray asked. 'D'ye ken why?'

'He believes they'll never be respected,' said Terry. 'They will always be under the shadow of their father. They'll always be *Irving's sons*. He told me so himself, not two months ago. Many people think he's being selfish or mean, that he doesn't want someone stealing attention from him, but I understand him perfectly.'

That struck a chord in my memory. I produced my small notebook and went through the pages, not being quite sure what I was looking for.

'So all this commotion could be out o' jealousy?' McGray said.

I reread the statements of King Duncan; he *had* mentioned the children's issues. I pressed the spine of my notebook against my lips.

'Irving,' I said, 'has not shown the same scruples towards *your* children, has he?'

Miss Terry frowned. 'What do you mean?'

'I have been told that your daughter . . . pray, her name is?'

'Edith.'

'Yes. I have heard that she joined Irving's company last year, and that Irving sent her to Germany to train in costume design. And your son . . .'

'Ted.'

'Ted. Is he not meant to train with Irving in preparation for your autumn season?'

Miss Terry bared her teeth. 'Why do you even bother to ask me any more questions? You seem to know everything about us already. I was a theatre-child, Inspector. I was happy, but only too late did I realize the disadvantages of lacking a formal education. It would have been hard enough had I been a man, but for a woman on her own . . . Gosh! It was hell sometimes. My accountants used to trick me and laugh behind my back; so did the tradesmen. They loved making all manner of lascivious jokes about me, and the idiots thought themselves so bloody manly and witty for it. And there is, of course, the disdain and the condescension one gets from the jealous snobs we so frequently have to perform for. I didn't want that for my children, and neither did Irving for his. We *never* put ideas about acting into their minds. They have chosen this path on their own and I will not hinder their careers. I'm their mother and I'll help them, especially since I know everyone in the business.'

'Speaking o' help,' McGray said, 'Irving seems to be supporting *them*, instead o' his own kin.'

'That is Irving's choice, not mine. Even if he wanted to help, he is completely cut off from them – and that's his own wife's doing! She is the one who hasn't let him see them; she is the one who's read every single letter Irving's ever written to them before passing it on; she is the one who insists on dealing with Stoker instead of Irving.'

Out of habit McGray tried to stroke his stubble, but grimaced at the smoothness of his skin. 'Where's *yer own* children's father? What does he think of Irving's – patronage?'

'Edward Godwin,' I said, recalling Catherine's gossip.

There was a dark expression in Terry's face; one I had not seen before. She made to sit down but remembered the dress, and when she rose again she nearly stumbled. 'I sometimes forget there are people in the world who don't know. He died.'

'Oh, I'm sorry,' said McGray. 'When?'

'Not three years ago. Complications from kidney

stones; he was very ill for a while.' She finally brought herself to drink.

'It seems to have affected you a good deal,' I remarked.

Miss Terry blinked tears away.

'Yes,' she said. 'I did not know how terribly it would alter me; for months I knew nothing but rage and despair. I tried to continue my work but it all felt meaningless. I . . . I should have never left him. He loved me so.' She shook her head, her eyes fixed on some point on the empty wall, and for an instant I saw Lady Macbeth's madness taking hold of the real woman. 'If only the dead could find out how to come back and be forgiven . . .'

Miss Terry said nothing more for a moment, again her stare lost somewhere, a twitch in her face.

'I need to have a rest,' she said, wearily taking the ginger wig off. 'At least try to sleep. I have to pose for a portrait tomorrow.'

'Unfortunately,' said McGray, 'there's still one question I need ye to answer.' He nodded, seeing Miss Terry's understanding. 'Aye, the leather bag.'

She hurled the wig on to the floor. 'Oh, that blasted bag! Do you think I have the clarity of mind to remember something so trivial right now?'

'Ye better do.'

'I have no idea!' she growled. 'And I couldn't give a damn. I might have thrown it away or given it to Irving's dog to chew on, and it would have been so trifling it never even imprinted on my memory. No matter how many times you ask, that's the only answer you'll get. Are you happy?'

McGray stepped closer, in that imposing manner of his. Miss Terry would have been undeterred, had McGray not said what he did.

'Then it's time ye ken, Miss Terry: the bag in question was found under Regent Bridge right after the banshee appeared. The bag was soaked in blood; the very substance used to write the message. D'ye understand its relevance now?'

With her blonde curls dishevelled, her mascara running and wrinkles suddenly appearing from nowhere, the majestic Ellen Terry seemed to be no more.

She gulped, gently placed the tumbler on the little table, and whispered with barely any breath left in her.

'I'll try to remember . . .' Then she drew in a deep, rasping inhalation. 'Please, gentlemen . . . leave me now. I beg you.'

29

'That was rather gruelling,' I said as we left Miss Terry's apartments. 'Do you think Irving will want to talk?'

'Don't care. I'll make him if he doesnae.'

We found the ballroom in a gloomy mood. Couples still danced, people still chatted and the musicians still played, but it looked as though they were all tense and simply playing their parts.

Stoker was nowhere to be found, neither was Irving. We were about to inquire after them when Miss Ivor approached us.

'Inspectors, are you looking for Mr Irving?'

'Aye.'

She covered her mouth with her fan. 'I heard one of the waiters say they saw him refill his hipflask and go to the roof. To the roof!'

'Thank you, madam,' I said, rushing ahead.

We went up through the servants' stairs, which were the only way to the roof. They did not resemble at all the luxuriousness found at the front of the hotel: they were narrow, steep and damp, and the paint was falling off the walls and the handrails. There were oil lamps at regular intervals, for all the landings were windowless, except for the one on the fourth floor. Through that window I saw the grimy, battered roofs of the backstreet buildings – a sight the illustrious guests were never meant to see.

Rose Street, which ran right behind the opulent Princes

Street, should in fact have been called an alley. It did not even have proper street lamps, and the moon and the weak lights from shabby windows barely described the outlines of narrow, unkempt buildings, crammed against each other like sad people on a frosty train station platform. I was happy to see the white gleam of a bull's-eye lantern carried by one of our men.

We ascended to the topmost storey, where the servants slept, and from there on to the narrow, rusty steel steps that led to the roof.

We found Irving there, seated on a box, his elbows on his knees and his long, pale fingers interlaced under his chin. He was wearing the black cloak we'd seen the other night, for the evening had become quite cold, and as the fabric waved in the soft breeze it made the man look like a crouching bat.

Very slowly he turned to face us, and I felt an inexplicable shudder. Perhaps it was the brandy, or the recent shock, or something entirely different I would never fathom, but he spoke without us even asking a question.

'My poor, silly sons . . . When they attempt to act, they make utter fools of themselves; when they don't act, they steal the damned limelight.'

There was an entirely different quality to his voice. A certain roughness we'd not heard before. He was not attempting to modulate his speech or exalt his emotions, like he did on the stage. He was being *himself*. And a hint of his old Cornish accent had also come to the surface.

'Attempt to act?' I echoed.

Irving assented, produced a small flask and drank a mouthful of what smelled like brandy. He looked so dejected I thought it improper to bring out my notebook.

'They have attempted,' he said with a wry smile. 'At their school in Marlborough, of course. I secretly went to see Harry's Hamlet.' Irving covered his brow. 'I was expecting him to be raw, but not quite what I saw! The poor boy was abysmal: juvenile, wooden, poor diction . . . but the worst part is that nobody seemed to notice! There was a review in the local paper. All they did was compare him with me! Damn it, I memorized that bloody line: "His face, figure and especially his walk are more or less those of his great father." That was exactly what I'd warned him would happen!'

'Have ye spoken to them?' McGray asked.

'No. I went to their suite but they're not there, and Bram can't find them. My boys don't like him; they think he's my spy. I cannot say Stoker feels too much sympathy for them either, but he's too loyal to say so.

'From time to time I sent good Stoker down to Marlborough, to see them, simply to make sure they were coping well in college. What happened during their meetings I do not know; Stoker always came back telling me they were doing outstandingly well, but later we found they were miserable.

'I visited them once and they were just as insolent as they were tonight. I learned from their professors that Harry and Sydney hated all the school sports – no surprise, they were always glaringly inept at anything that involved moving their limbs, acting included. Other boys hit them and Florence visited so often the boys were the school's laughing stock. And she'd write to each of them daily – *daily!* – and addressed Sydney as *Wee*. Can you imagine the fuss a horde of mocking adolescents would make out of this?

'I heard that Harry himself put an end to it. He had to ask Florence to write no more than one letter a week and . . .' Irving could not hold back a scornful grin, 'the woman was distraught. Eventually she understood her place and found new ways to entertain herself: parties and' – a chuckle – 'I hear she is very fond of attending the criminal courts and public inquests. She yawns at Shakespeare and the Greek tragedies, but adores a good street scandal.'

Irving emptied the hipflask in just a few gulps, and it was perhaps the drink burning his throat that made him say all that followed.

'I would have divorced Florence long ago. On the very day she told me what she thought about my "foolish" career. But my sons . . . What I would not do for them!'

McGray cackled. 'Ye really love the brats? Ye've done nothing to prove it! Everyone tells us ye've done more for Miss Terry's children than for yer own!'

Irving punched the box and the tattered wood cracked under his fist. *'How could I do anything for them?* They have been trained since birth to hate me! Florence reads all my correspondence to them; withholds any letters she pleases; makes it almost impossible for me to meet them. And when I do, or when I have a gesture to them, they treat me with suspicion; they send my presents back! They don't see what I *have* done for them: paid for the best education, the best housing and the best lifestyle they could have in London – they moan because Ellen's children are in Germany, but Harry reads law at Oxford and Sydney has been learning languages in St Petersburg, to someday train as a diplomat. I have arranged all that! That's all I can do from a distance, and I do it gladly. What I'd give up to win them back; to love me but a tenth of how I love them! And I cannot even let them know. Good Lord, my sons who now hate me because of *her*!

'But Florence was right in calling me a fool. I was indeed a fool for marrying her. Now I think I wouldn't have, had her snobbish father not forbidden her to see me for a year. The bastard lived in India, yet he controlled everything and everyone! He had never met me, yet he thought a silly actor wasn't good enough for his precious daughter!

'Alas, I was young too, and the prohibition just made the affair the more exciting. Florence would write me letters and used her grandmother as go-between. How thrilling that all was: to have the forbidden fruit, even though the rest of Eden was in my grasp. We even disguised our hand-writing and developed codes – I'd forge her father's hand; she'd forge her cousin's – in case her mother found our letters lying around. The fool . . . Th-th – the fool I was . . .'

He blushed after that sudden stutter, which I instantly recognized as the vestige of an old speech impediment. Irving tried to get the last few drops from his flask, then interlaced his fingers and looked upwards, the bright moon reflected clearly on his dark eyes.

'I have reached the highest point of my career,' he said, again in control of his voice. 'I know it. From now on I'll just gradually head to my sunset: I shall fall, "Like a bright exhalation in the evening, And no man see me more." And when I die and I am forgotten, as I *shall* be, I will have left nothing in this world but a pair of resentful sons, a monstrous wife who only loved my money, a wounded Bram, and an Ellen who never loved me as much as I did her.'

He said no more, as if drained of all energy. McGray and I stood there in silence, but that did not last for long.

There was a howl on the street. Sharp and high pitched, clearly a dog, but McGray lifted his face, his bright pupils moving to where the sound was coming from. Then a second, and almost immediately a third dog joined in from across Castle Street.

'What is it?' I asked. There had been other noises from the streets – carriages, men walking to and from the pubs, officers checking on each other – but the dogs had sent Nine-Nails into something like a trance. He pressed a finger on his lips, bidding me to be silent, and then moved cautiously to the north-facing side of the building. He grasped the low brick parapet that encircled the roof, and looked down.

A sudden draught, quite chill even for Edinburgh, hit me just as I joined McGray, and the breeze seemed to send the dogs into a louder frenzy of barking.

I tried to follow Nine-Nails' eyes, but it was very dark down below, the building itself blocking the moonlight. Only a small corner of the backyard was lit, quite dimly, and we could see the floor: a thin triangle of grey slabs, closest to the wall by Rose Street, the wet stone reflecting –

'There!' McGray spluttered, pointing down just as I saw it too.

Emerging from the darkness – a red spot. A hand. Trembling and smearing the stones in the colour of blood.

30

'*Banshee!*' McGray hollered, his voice resounding through the night like a rolling thunder. People on the street turned their heads up; our officers too. '*In the backyard! There!*'

He pointed down and then sprinted to the stairs, all before I could even look away from the floor. The hand had retreated, leaving nothing but an auburn stain. Now the air reverberated with our chaps' shouting, boots on cobblestones and the screech of their whistles, and the world became a commotion.

I ran after McGray but clashed against Irving.

'Did you really see –'

'Don't stay here on your own!' I barked at him before running down the creaking staircase. I instantly yelled: 'How can anyone rush on this death-trap?'

The steps were steep and smaller than my feet, and with each stride I pictured myself falling on my face, rolling down and breaking every bone in my body. I'd never reach McGray in time.

There were screams from the streets, and then a gunshot.

'*There!*' McGray was shouting. He had kicked the one window open and half his torso stuck out.

'They're running away!' someone on the ground yelled back. At once McGray hurled himself out through the window and disappeared in the darkness.

'*McGray!*' I screamed, expecting to see him crushed on

the backyard's flagstones. Instead I found him dexterously sliding down along the drainpipes, the lead joints cracking under his weight.

I put a leg out the window, then –

'No, I cannot possibly do that,' I mumbled, and ran back to the stairs, grasping the handrail so tightly my hands burned. I darted ahead, tumbling and grunting yet unable to move as fast as I wished, and each moment I spent in those blasted stairs I reproached myself for not following Nine-Nails.

There was a second shot, and this time I was close enough to hear the cries that came from the ballroom and the hotel rooms.

Upon reaching the ground floor I met a sweaty cook, ghostly pale, pointing towards a corridor which I followed. I rushed past the steaming kitchens, where more staff pointed, and then through a large pantry that led to the backyard.

I felt a trickle of sweat roll down my forehead as I leaped out. The place was cold and dark, but I saw the wide back door rattling, as if someone had slammed it an instant ago. McGray had gone, but I saw the shadow of an officer struggling to get on his feet, swaying clumsily and with a hand on his temple.

'I thought you were guarding every entrance!'

'Someone hit me!' the chap whimpered.

A very brave maid came out right behind me with an oil lamp, shedding light on the floor. I glimpsed at the red smears only enough to recognize it was a written message, the light drizzle already blurring the edges. I did not have time to decipher it, for there was a third gunshot from the street.

'*Somebody write that down!*' I shouted as I dashed towards the exit.

Right then a big hand grasped me by the shoulder, pulled me backwards with mighty strength and made me roar in frustration.

'*What the —*'

It was Bram Stoker, sweating profusely and his mad eyes open like perfect circles.

'A banshee can also appear as a black dog!'

He stuttered some other nonsense but I did not even reply. I ran to the narrow street and followed the racket of the pursuit. I could hear McGray swearing and more whistles blowing frantically, the noises moving like a physical mass around the corner.

I ran there, to the wide road that descended to the busy Princes Street and on to its sunken gardens. There I saw three policemen and McGray's wide shoulders; they were all running south, towards the castle.

I went after them and just as I made it to the well-lit Princes Street I saw a black, cloaked figure entering the leafy park.

'*Call for help!*' McGray was yelling as he crossed the busy road. 'Get men on every exit!'

One of the officers went away, whistling frantically, while the rest of us ran ahead into the gardens.

I descended across the lawns, which were so steep I felt I was falling forward, bouncing on legs no longer in my control. The momentum toppled me over and I fell on all fours, leaving the skin of my hands and knees on the gravelly path. I jumped up and looked ahead.

'Damn!' I grunted. The gardens were in full bloom, the canopies of birches and chestnuts blocking all the light from the road. Even under the midsummer dusk and the bright moon we had lost the running figure.

I only recognized McGray amidst the darkness because his lustrous jacket reflected the beams from the officers' lanterns.

'What did you see?' I asked as I caught up with him.

'Barely anything. They hit that Cooper lad and – *There!*'

McGray snatched the lantern from the officer and ran ahead, directing the light to the base of Castle Rock, where I saw a fleeting movement. We all followed Nine-Nails, even if we were not sure he'd seen anything at all.

We jumped on to the railway that went along the gardens, the tracks made muddy and slippery by the rain. My utterly inappropriate ballroom shoes skidded all over the gravel and I nearly fell on to the steel rails. One of the officers pulled me up just before I did, and very soon we reached the black lump that was Castle Rock. The jagged mount was surrounded by dark shrubs, its rocks covered in moss and undergrowth, and we soon lost sight of the cloaked shadow.

McGray went on undeterred, through the thorny bushes and up on to the rocky hill, which at points was as steep as a wall.

'Always in my best suits!' I grumbled, but I could not hesitate. I had to follow him, my eyes straining to see as McGray and the other chap swung their lights from left to right.

'Have we lost him?' I asked, as we all looked in every direction, and I tried to hear footsteps or a frantic breath. There was none of that.

The yellow gleams from the castle windows loomed

above us, and higher above, the rainclouds threatened to block the moonlight.

'*Stop!*' McGray hollered, raising his gun and shooting to the air. 'We see ye!' I did not know if he lied. If he'd spotted anything the rest of us were at a loss to see.

We climbed on, the sharp, cold stones cutting my skin, my shiny shoes slipping on the wet stone. My hands then landed on a very large nettle.

'Oh, for goodness' sake!'

'*Stop!*' McGray shouted right then, directing the light beam to a small shelf of rock on the western side of the hill. My heart jumped as I had a clear sight of shoulders and a male head, but the silhouette soon went back into the darkness.

We rushed in that direction, moving on to the steeper side, where the hill became a vertical crag. I saw the lights of the city beyond the gardens as we went up and up. We were so high I shuddered: at least fifty feet above the garden's lawns. Just as I realized it my feet slipped again and I had to clasp an overhanging rock. McGray had gone on but stopped a few yards ahead.

'Dead end!' he said, looking all around.

I joined him then. We were standing on a cleft barely wide enough for our feet, before us nothing but a precipice.

'Where did the bastard go?' I cried, looking back to retrace my own steps.

'He's vanished!' McGray shouted. 'He must have –'

I did not hear the rest. The cloaked shadow landed right before me, jumping down from the rocks just above my head. Under the moonlight his face appeared before mine, so close and so familiar I lost control of myself for one disastrous instant.

'*It's you!*' I shouted, just as his fist hit me in the chest.

I felt a tingling wave of vertigo, flailed my arms in wide circles and felt my feet slide, my entire body falling backwards and into the void.

McGray grasped my collar and pulled me back up, hoisting me on to the hill. The stone wall hit my face and I saw an explosion of stars, just as Nine-Nails sprinted around me, towards that blasted man.

The sparks blurred my vision, but I still caught glimpses of Nine-Nails and the young officer, both struggling and throwing blows. I saw the black cape billowing, blacker than the sky, and then, just as I clung to the slick rocks with all my might, I recognized that thin, pale face one last time, before McGray threw a blow at him. The man waved to dodge the fist, but then lost his balance and fell into the darkness.

I heard his panicked scream and how abruptly it ended, somewhere down there in the garden's grounds. I thought I'd heard the crack of bones. And I felt sick.

I remained dizzy for a good while, so I had to put an arm around McGray's shoulders as he guided me down the hill. The one thing that felt perfectly clear was the acute pain on my face, as if the rock had split my cranium in half.

'Are ye all right?' McGray asked as we descended, and I grumbled something that sounded vaguely affirmative. 'Good,' he said, wiping a trickle of blood from my face. 'Ye'll look really ugly in the morning – that wound will swell.'

By the time we set foot on the smooth lawns there were four more peelers rushing in, all with blinding lanterns and pointing in our direction. With the additional light we very soon found the black cape, all crumpled and wet – sadly, not with water.

One of the officers knelt before the body and turned it over quite brusquely – there was no hope anyone would survive that fall.

McGray gasped, utterly shocked, but not I. Again I saw the face that had startled me and nearly made *me* fall to my death. I'd recognized him too well: the lean features and the gaudy moustache of Alan Dyer, the journalist from *The Scotsman*.

He was now soaked in blood, the flesh on his face contorted in the most disturbing manner, and I thought with a shiver that, had my feet landed a few inches in the wrong direction, that could have been me.

'We have to go back,' McGray urged, shouting orders at full speed: the body was to be taken to the morgue, his colleagues should be informed, his belongings searched. There was a slight quaver of panic in his voice.

'What is it?' I asked as McGray virtually dragged me across the gardens.

'He wisnae the banshee, Frey. He was there just for gossip. That thing might still be around the hotel.'

'Dyer could well have been the one doing the writing,' I protested as we crossed the street, the ground still feeling a little wobbly under my feet.

'Don't think so,' McGray said with laughable conviction. 'I'd bet my life he was just lurking around to get stories. He must have found the writing – perhaps he even saw who did it.'

'Then why run? Why would he risk being arrested – or killed?'

''Cause he was at the wrong place at the wrong time. He must have been frightened; must have thought we'd blame it all on him. *Ye* would have!'

'Nine-Nails, may I remind you that you threatened to stuff his mouth with newspapers? If anything frightened him —'

'Och, d'ye want me to pat sleazy suspects on the back and buy them a pint and beg them to be *cooperative*?'

I snorted. 'Well, the man is dead now, which is most inconsiderate of him. And all covered in blood. It is impossible to tell whether it is his own or a spill from what he used to leave the message.'

'Aye, but there might be other ways to find out.'

On our return the Palace Hotel was still in turmoil, but Millar had done a very good job at keeping — almost — everyone inside. The officers who'd not followed us had stayed and guarded all entrances, aided by a handful of other policemen who had approached after hearing the gunshots. Now they were keeping a dozen reporters at bay. Clearly, they had all been spying around, just like I believed Dyer had done, and now they'd emerged like earthworms in disturbed soil.

'Did you see the apparition?' a daring newsman asked McGray. 'Was it the same banshee as —'

Nine-Nails pushed the man, who fell backwards and knocked over another two who'd planted themselves in front of us. Nobody yet seemed aware of the death under Castle Rock.

'Only four people came out o' the building through the main door in the past half hour,' said Millar as soon as we stepped into the foyer. 'Two young men, very haughty looking, only a few minutes before all the fuss began.'

'Irving's sons,' McGray grunted. 'Who else?'

'The Lord and Lady Provost. He called for his carriage just in the thick of it. Of course, we couldnae stop them.'

'Of course,' I echoed. Edinburgh's Lord Provost could not have borne being spotted at a scandalous crime scene – particularly not one that involved ghosts and stage celebrities.

I forced myself back into my full senses, and managed to walk into the ballroom without McGray's aid, but we still caused a stir: our suits were torn and muddy and my face was bleeding.

McGray jumped on a chair and announced, with a roaring voice, that nobody was to leave the building until we'd carried out our search. There was a rain of protests, and immediately I had Catherine and my father in front of me.

'How could you involve us in this dreadful scandal?' Catherine whimpered, blind to my wounds, pulling Elgie by the arm. Conversely, my brother could not have looked more excited.

Father (who had spilt half a glass of claret on his white shirt front) grabbed my arm as if I were still a naughty eight-year-old and hissed at me, 'Make haste, Ian! Pull some strings and let us go at once.'

I snorted. 'I will do no such thing. You are all witnesses now and will have to be properly questioned.'

'*Oh!*' Catherine seemed to faint, placing the back of her hand on her forehead and 'falling' slowly enough so that a passing gentleman could catch her.

I let go of my father's grip, and McGray and I rushed to the backyard.

The place was fully lit now but the entire image was an attack on my senses, and for an instant I did not know which way to look: on one side was Constable Cooper, still slightly stunned, now being aided by a colleague and a maid who'd brought him tea. On the other side, glimmering under the lanterns, was the red writing.

'Ye all right, laddie?' asked Nine-Nails. Once young Cooper nodded, McGray took a few steps towards the bloodstains. He shook his head and covered his mouth; I could sense his anxiety without even seeing his face. I feared to look, and when a cold finger tapped my shoulder I started.

'Here, sir,' a young maid said, offering me a piece of paper. 'The head cook wrote it down as you wanted.'

I thanked her and took the note, although I would not really need it. The soft drizzle had not managed to erase the words; it had only smudged the edges of the letters, making them look as if the blood had oozed from the slabs themselves.

11 JULY SIGHTING

Chase not the voices and the spells they write
For only death and blood your hand shall spread;
One falls on the stage, maybe one tonight
If you hunt whispers that concern the dead

Bram Stoker's Journal

Extracts from the final entry for the evening of 11 July. Transcribed by I. P. Frey, given the poor handwriting.

[...]

Tried to warn them about the banshee shape-shifting, but the Inspector left and shooting ensued. Didn't know what to do.

Read those horrendous words and could scarcely recollect myself — then something queer happened. As outlandish as the following lines seem, I swear on everything I hold most dear that all here described is truthful.

Heard a voice. Rasping, guttural. Male or female? Impossible to tell, but came from outside. Made me tremble to my core. I tremble even now when I put it on paper.

'Bram,' it whispered. 'Bram. You know it is time.'

God — My blood curdled.

The policeman next to me was oblivious to it. I pushed the door and looked at the street. Trembled again when a shadow lurked there, short but broad, that very massive dog, as black as night itself. The very animal I saw at the Lyceum in London; the same red eyes, staring at me hungrily as if waiting for a treat. It walked away, then looked back at me, as if bidding me to come after.

Reckless, but I went out. The policeman gave me some warning but I felt I must follow and the small man couldn't stop me.

In the alley I lost the dog. Too dark.

'Bram.'

That voice – it drew the heat, the life out of me. But still I followed!

How my heart pounded, how my whole body felt pierced by pins and needles.

Turned around a corner. A long, narrow backstreet opened before me, entirely deserted except for one tall figure, patiently waiting for me a hundred yards ahead.

Rubbed my eyes to convince myself. It was really there. A black cloak, much like Irving's. Faceless. Dear Jesus, <u>faceless</u>. Only deathly pale hands, long fingers interlaced.

The dog was there, its dark body hugging the equally dark shroud.

Walked cautiously to it, as though pulled by some force I cannot ascertain. What was I doing? Was I walking to my death?

Then I saw that second shadow join the first. Smaller, trimmer, cloaked as well, but as it drew nearer I saw something glint under the hem. The iridescent –

Note:
The two following sheets have been torn out from the journal, and there is only a short paragraph scribbled on the subsequent page. – I. P. Frey.

Hand hurts now but <u>had</u> to write down these happenings. I can finally res–

Note:
This is the last known entry in Mr Stoker's journal. – I. P. Frey.

31

'What these verses say . . .' McGray mumbled, looking as pale as a ghost. 'This is what just happened. There's been one death . . .'

I could not repress a gasp. I'd never believed in omens, but this had been written merely minutes before Dyer's demise.

'We cannot yet refute that Dyer did this,' I mumbled, if only to reassure myself.

McGray kneeled down and again tasted a drop of blood from the tip of his finger. Not that we had many doubts as to its nature.

'Real blood, just like before.' He stared at the lines for a moment, mouthing them once and again. Then he rose and went to the junior officers. 'Oi, baby-face! Go get another laddie to help ye. Look for any traces o' blood in the building and around it.'

'Aye, sir,' said the perky young man, and left us with poor Cooper.

There was a mighty bump on his head, and a flirtatious maid was pressing a damp cloth to his scalp.

'How did that wretch get out?' McGray barked, his loud voice making Cooper squint. 'I told youse to lock every damn exit! And take the names of everyone going in and out.'

'Sorry, sir. The door was unlocked.'

McGray could have smacked him again had the poor chap not looked so shaken. 'Who unlocked it?'

'Dunno, sir. I – I didnae see.'

McGray made to slap him with the back of his hand, but then took a deep breath. 'How could ye not see? Ye were s'posed to be guarding the damn entrance!'

The young man pleaded. 'I only went for a quick piss about an hour ago. But it was just a minute!'

'One bloody minute too fuckin' long!'

'I'm really sorry, sir.'

'When did ye notice the padlock was open?'

'About a quarter of an hour later. Not five minutes before all the hubbub started. I leaned on the door and it opened! I hadnae seen it before 'cause it's too dark back here. I was looking at the padlock, my back to the hotel, when someone struck me on the head. Brought me down, the blow. I fell on my face 'n' was all woozy 'n' couldnae scream.'

'Did you see anything?' I asked, pointing at the smears of blood. 'Did you see who did that?'

'Nae. My head was turned to the wall. I only heard the rustle o' clothes. And then the dogs went mad, and then I heard Inspector McGray climbing down the pipe and I saw him getting out. And then I saw ye, Inspector Frey, and then that ginger Irishman.'

My jaw dropped.

'Stoker?' asked McGray, his frown growing deeper.

'Aye. He went out, sir, right after Inspector Frey here spoke to him.'

'Did he come back?' I prompted.

'Nae, sir. At least not this way.'

I scoffed. 'I do *not* like this at all. McGray, he came to me all distraught, crying that banshees can also take the shape of black dogs, but all I could think of –'

To my surprise – though I should not be shocked any

more – McGray took the news as if I'd announced the doors of hell had just opened.

'That's what made me look down,' he said, 'I was reading that this morning. The banshees also come as huge black hounds that follow whoever is about to die. With red eyes. They're called the *Auld Shucks*. Remember that dog howling when we were up on the roof?'

'Yes, but –'

'That didnae sound natural.'

'It was just a dog howling,' I stressed. 'Perhaps the smell of blood made them uneasy . . .'

'Och, I cannae argue right now,' McGray said. 'We must find Bram. The sooner the better . . .'

'You look more concerned than I expected,' I said, looking at the tendons bulging on his neck. 'Why do you fear for him so much?'

McGray did not reply, but he called two officers. One was instructed to look for a very tall, sturdy Irishman in the neighbouring streets. The other chap was to look for him at the hotel. And if their searches were not thorough enough, Nine-Nails was to 'suspend them by a rope tied to their ———' (here the reader should fill the gap). And he also asked them to keep their eyes open for a huge black hound.

'A hound indeed,' I said scornfully as they left.

'Frey, don't make me regret I saved ye from getting splattered.'

'McGray, as much as I appreciate the favour, this is all very clear: There was no banshee cry because we had the entire building surrounded by policemen. The perpetrator attempted to do the writing discreetly to then be able to flee, and would have succeeded had you not looked down at precisely the right time.' McGray inhaled, ready to defend his theory, but I had to stop him. 'We will not agree on that right now. I'd rather focus on that padlock. It was on this side of the door; whoever opened it did so from within the yard. That someone must have been spying on Cooper, waiting for him to get distracted.'

'Sirs, I swear I didnae –'

'Oh, shush, Cooper!' I said. 'It does not seem logical to unlock the door, leave it open and only *then* strike the guard. If someone tried to get out unseen, you'd think they'd strike the policeman first, and then unlock the door.'

McGray nodded. 'It's good when ye put yer brains to work, Frey, ye should make a habit of it. Aye, it must have been two different people. One person unlocked the door and sneaked out – he didnae come back or he would've locked it again to cover his tracks – I'd bet more than just ten years' worth o' whisky that a second blasted bastard hit Cooper afterwards; most likely someone not connected at all with the one who unlocked the door.'

I pondered. 'That makes a lot of sense. And the second party, the one who hit Cooper, was most likely the one writing the verses. Perhaps they went back to the hotel and did not even need the door.'

'A banshee wouldnae need –'

'Nine-Nails, for the love of God!'

After that we looked carefully into each nook and cranny of the backyard, but found nothing of relevance. We also looked into the pantry that adjoined the backyard and the kitchens. There was a pile of flour sacks in utter disarray, jars knocked over, and potatoes and almonds scattered all over one corner of the room. However, the cooks and scullions said all that was perfectly understandable: the place had been mayhem since the morning, everyone rushing to get things ready for the dinner and reception.

Nearly every servant, maid and guest was questioned, and this time Superintendent Campbell spared no resources. As soon as he received word of the sighting, he sent us a dozen men, both constables and sergeants, who helped us do the leg work.

Still, it was three o'clock in the morning when we finally dispatched the last witness.

My father, Catherine and Elgie were amongst the last to leave (McGray might have had something to do with the delay), and my dear stepmother could not stop moaning about how roughly they'd been handled by 'the most vulgar, impertinent of police pigs'. She would never let me or my father forget the episode, and I knew it would be decades before she stopped recounting the incident.

Tired as we were, McGray and I had to go through the list of people questioned. The statements had been compiled neatly by the constables and were stacked in a tidy pile, waiting for us on the ballroom's main table. Nine-Nails went through it while helping himself liberally to a marzipan parapet, chocolate rocks and brandy, the latter kindly brought to us by the equally sleepy headwaiter.

'Besides Stoker, was everyone accounted for?' I asked, giving in to a most ungentlemanly yawn. When I opened my eyes I saw McGray's mouth half open, crumbs of chocolate falling on to the table. 'What is it?'

'Ye won't believe this. We cannae find Ellen Terry.'

'Why were we not told immediately?' I leapt to my feet as I saw a slender figure coming in. I was so tired I had to blink twice before recognizing the smug face of Freddie Harwood.

'Young man, we have *no* time for your impert—' McGray smacked me in the stomach with the back of his hand. Only then did I remember that Freddie had begged to talk to us before the pandemonium began.

He approached us rather gingerly, nothing like his usual self, although he'd soon come back to his ways.

'Can we speak now?' he said in a whisper.

McGray looked at him gravely. 'Depends. D'ye have something useful to tell us?'

Freddie nodded vehemently. 'You cannot tell anyone you heard this from me.'

I arched an eyebrow. 'Why?'

'If they knew I told you . . . It could ruin my career.'

It struck me as ludicrous that a fourteen-year-old put so much emphasis on the word 'career'.

'We won't tell a soul, laddie,' said McGray. 'Honest.'

There is something about McGray's countenance that always works at these moments. Whenever he assures discretion, or appeals for trust, there is complete earnestness in both his voice and features. Even the spoiled, insolent brat Freddie responded to it. The boy looked alternately at each of us, and all of a sudden spurted out the words he'd been so afraid of.

'I saw someone walk out of Miss Terry's rooms — just before the ball. A man I had never seen before.'

32

McGray grasped the boy's arm. 'Ye swear it's the truth?'

'Yes.'

'And it was a complete stranger, ye say?'

'Yes.'

'What did he look like?'

Freddie writhed like a worm, harming himself more than the hand gripping him, so McGray had to let him go.

'I didn't see much of him. The man ran away very quickly and I only got a glimpse of his working-class clothes. Oh, and he had dark hair – very greasy.'

'Is that all you can remember?' I asked. 'Any detail might be of help.'

Freddie did not need to ponder for long. 'Well, he ran with a funny gait and he . . . he left behind a hint of a ponging whiff, something I have never smelled before.'

'Was it chemical?' I asked. 'Or body odour, perhaps?'

Freddie had a good thought this time. 'Not sweat, I am sure. I would say chemical.'

McGray pondered. 'If ye smelled it again, d'ye think ye'd recognize it?' Freddie nodded, but there was not much else he could tell us. We told him to stay at the hotel at all times, in case we needed to ask more questions, but he did not receive the instruction with much enthusiasm.

'You won't tell anyone, will you?' he said before leaving us, but once again he sounded arrogant: commanding rather than requesting.

'Treat yer mother 'n' sister better and we'll see,' said McGray.

'Don't talk to me as if I were a silly little –'

'*Get out!*' McGray hollered. Most people would have rushed out, or at least started, but Freddie smirked in the most arrogant way imaginable, and very slowly and insolently dragged himself to the door.

'And now Miss Terry,' I groaned. 'Shall we send someone out to look for her too?'

McGray waved a hand indifferently. 'Aye, but I'm sure Terry will be back. She cannae miss her big opening night, or posing for her portrait tomorrow morning.'

'What about Stoker? He has not come back yet.' I looked at my pocket watch. 'He went out right after I saw him, so he has been gone almost four hours.'

Nine-Nails bit his lip, a dark look on his face, and as he rubbed his eyes he snorted. I wanted to ask what the matter was, but I was too tired to argue. Again I yawned, yearning for a warm bed and a sound sleep, but we were not done yet.

After McGray sent out two more men to look for Stoker and Miss Terry, we received a note from the morgue. Dr Reed was already there and had begun work on Dyer's body. He told us he wanted to see us, and that Constable McNair had left news from the butchers he'd visited through the night (I had completely forgotten about them).

Before heading to the City Chambers, McGray wanted to have one last look at the backyard. We found nothing, but on our way out I recognized the dim corridors we'd seen when first visiting Mrs Harwood. I realized how close to the kitchens her lodgings were.

I took a quick detour to check on her door, which one of our men was still guarding. The officers had changed shifts, so the current chap looked much fresher than us.

'No one's come in or out, sir,' he told us, but I was not satisfied and knocked at the door. Mrs Harwood did reply, albeit with a rather throaty voice.

We went in and found her sitting up in bed, wide awake despite the hour, with a small trinket box on her lap. From it she was withdrawing iridescent beetle wings and lining them up meticulously by her side.

'I should have enough,' she told us, smiling, before we had asked anything.

'Enough?' McGray asked. 'To do what, missus?'

'To repair Miss Terry's dress. She came to tell me a few had fallen off. But I have enough! I'll mend it for her . . .'

I tried to sound as casual as possible. 'At what time did Miss Terry speak to you? Before she went to bed?'

'Oh, yes. Before all that noise from outside. Told me she had to look fresh for Mr Sargent. The painter. He's coming all the way from London just to finish Miss Terry's portrait. It is very, *very* important her dress looks its best.'

As she re-counted the little wings I approached the window and pried the curtains apart with two fingers.

Though locked, the window overlooked the now busy backyard, where I saw a few maids mopping up the red writing.

We left the Palace Hotel at half past four in the morning.

I would have happily rented a cab, but McGray decided he needed some cool air and a stroll to refresh himself. I remembered he seldom slept more than a couple of hours, so this night would have felt almost normal to him. By the time we made it to the City Chambers my eyes itched with drowsiness.

Luckily, the seemingly pubescent Dr Reed had a large flask of very strong coffee, which his mother had forced him to take with him. I welcomed the caffeine more than a sweet lady's kiss.

'Constable McNair left you this message,' Reed told me with his now usual antipathy. 'He was adamant he'd tell you in person, but he looked so worn-out I told him to go home.'

'You hardly have the authority for that,' I mumbled, proceeding to read the message.

McNair had a quivering, rather childish hand, yet quite legible, and since most of the officers cannot read or write, I was quite pleased. In a message with atrocious spelling and not a single punctuation mark, he told us of all the butchers' shops he'd visited, and then listed a handful of merchants who'd sold either blood or blood sausages to customers who were not regulars. That narrowed the possibilities to a manageable number.

'He has done an excellent job,' I concluded, folding the note and shoving it into my pocket.

'Reed,' said McGray, 'what did *ye* have to tell us?'

'I'd better show you,' he replied, guiding us to his work area. 'These are Mr Dyer's belongings . . .'

A muddy, bloodstained coat had been stretched on an operating table, and next to it an assortment of items had been lined up in a meticulous fashion, from the largest to the smallest. Besides the common articles (a watch, a comb, a small tin of wax which Dyer had surely used to shape his moustache) there was an object that instantly caught my eye: a very small notepad. McGray picked it up and had a close look at the covers.

'Looks brand new,' he said as he opened it.

'His notes are in shorthand,' said Reed, 'so I've not been able to read a thing.'

'Give me that,' said I, reaching for the small pad.

'Can ye read shorthand?' a surprised McGray asked me.

'Some. I learned a little while studying law. I thought it would be useful if I ever practised at the courts.'

Reed frowned. 'I thought you'd started a medicine degree. Did you read law afterwards?'

McGray cackled. 'Nae. The soft dandy tried, but he abandoned that one too.'

'*Two* unfinished degrees?' Reed cried.

I hate it so much when those two join forces against me. 'Indeed, Reed. That is infinity times the number of degrees Inspector McGray has *ever* started.'

The notepad was indeed new, for only the first few pages had been scribbled on, and I went straight to the last lines, dated the night before. Despite my rusty training, I had no difficulties in making out the meaning.

Hid in little alley behind hotel.
Heard person going out & door flapping.
Found back door open! Got in.

Saw guard coming back. Hid in pantry.
Shadow walked past me. Someone wrapped in white.
Shadow's out. Hit the Peeler. Must look out when shadow's gone.
Blood! In the yard ——

33

'D'ye need any more proof?' McGray asked as soon as I translated those lines. 'The poor bastard was innocent. He was only looking for a story.'

He was right. The meaning was clear, and I instantly felt a pang of guilt.

'Good Lord, we chased that man to his death . . .'

McGray patted me on the back. 'Nae, don't blame yerself. The rascal shouldnae have run like that.'

I assented. 'Indeed, but he would not be dead had we not been investigating – Nine-Nails, do not grin so triumphantly!'

'Say what ye like, but the prophecy was clear. Chase nae the voices, for only death and –'

'*Sod the prophecy!* I'd as soon visit those butchers and show you how blasted bloody wrong you are!'

'All right, all right,' said McGray, his hands up. 'I think ye better rest. Yer getting grouchier than when I caught ye having yer lavender bath.'

I took a deep breath, massaging the bridge of my nose. 'I suppose tiredness *is* getting the better of me.'

'Aye. Go home, have yer beauty sleep and come back – say midmorning.'

'What about Stoker? And Miss Terry?'

'I've nae forgotten about them, but I'm much fresher than ye. I'll help the lads' search. I won't leave a bloody flagstone unturned. And I'll make sure someone wakes ye up if anything develops.'

Feigning more reluctance than I actually felt, I made my way to the door, yet pointing at Reed. 'Do examine Mr Dyer properly. There's clearly no need for a post-mortem, but make sure you do not miss anything he might have carried in his pockets or –'

'Och, just get out!'

What odd dreams I had.

My mind was a whirl of witches, theatre fires, men falling from cliffs and beetle wings being crushed. And they all mingled with the faces of my father, the deceased Alan Dyer garishly wounded, Miss Terry cackling at me, Henry Irving reciting from *Hamlet* with a blood-dripping skull in his hand, McGray and Caroline Ardglass promenading by the arm, and finally Bram Stoker on his knees, begging for mercy from a howling banshee that swirled around him, her white rags floating in the air like trails of smoke.

A strip of those rags touched my skin, so cold it felt like a sting, and the fright made me jump up and open my eyes.

It had been Layton's hand. He looked mortified. 'Do, do excuse me, sir. I tried to wake you but you were too fast asleep.'

I wiped some cold sweat from my face and inhaled deeply. Suddenly my bedroom felt strangely cold. 'What is it? What time is it?'

'It is a quarter past ten, sir. I would not have disturbed

you, but there is a gentleman at the door who claims to be the head of Edinburgh's police.'

I groaned. 'Oh, good Lord! By any chance does he look like a grumpy, scruffy, undernourished old lion?'

Layton cleared his throat. 'Your depiction is most accurate, sir.'

Begrudgingly I left my bed. Had it been any other visitor (or had I been one year less embittered) I would have at least tried to flatten my hair and my shirt. Superintendent Campbell, however, deserved no such gallantries.

I found him pacing nervously in the downstairs parlour, his walking cane leaving deep marks on Lady Anne's Turkish rug.

'Would you please not do that?' I said bluntly. 'This is not my property.'

Obstinately, Campbell dug the cane firmly into the weave. 'Where is McGray? And for both your sakes I hope he is at work whilst you take the morning off.'

'Are you unable to find him or simply did not want to face him?'

'Answer the bloody question, Frey!'

So it was the latter, I thought. 'Inspector McGray is leading the investigations as we speak. You may have heard by now that a reporter from *The Scotsman* perished last night.'

By the speed at which his faced turned white, I realized he had not.

'What the –'

I briefed Campbell on everything that had occurred the previous night, and by the end of my telling his left eye was twitching.

'The scandal . . .' he mumbled, pressing his walking stick even harder on the material.

'Dyer was in a very compromising position,' I added. 'Trespassing, far too close to the banshee writings for his own good, attempting to flee, resisting arrest and putting policemen's lives at risk – mine included. I doubt the newspaper will want to admit publicly that a member of its staff was up to such dubious deeds. If you still need further guarantees, I am sure McGray can *charm* the editor into silence.' Then something struck me as strange. 'Sir, if you knew nothing about last night's affairs, what on earth brings you here?'

I realized I had never spoken so brusquely to a superior – even those I'd heartedly disliked. I had spent too much time around McGray.

'Mr Irving came to me less than half an hour ago. He is distraught.'

'Distraught?'

'Yes. Somebody's gone missing. Abraham Stoker, or whatever his name was. I damn well hope McGray is looking for him as we speak.'

'Indeed. As I told you, he is taking care of it. Half a dozen men are helping him.'

I rubbed my eyes, feeling another hour in bed would have worked wonders. 'Do you want me to assist the search right now?'

'If it is not too much bloody trouble to Your Majesty! I have told you, Henry Irving is distraught!'

'Did he mention Miss Terry being missing too?'

Campbell nearly lost his balance. 'No. What do you mean? Did she also . . . ?'

I shrugged. 'She disappeared briefly in the small hours,

but she must have returned to the hotel by now. Otherwise Irving would have also bleated on about her to you.'

There was the bluntness again. I did want to keep my good manners, but polite language felt like an impossibility right then.

'Just find him,' Campbell snapped as he made his way out. 'Preferably before you have to file yet another report about a mutilated corpse found in New Town's sewers!'

'Excuse me, that has happened only *once*!'

But Campbell was already gone.

Without a clear plan at hand, I first went to the Palace Hotel. It was much nearer than the City Chambers, and if Stoker had already appeared he'd be most likely to be there. Besides, I could as well inquire after Miss Terry, whom I was almost sure would be back in her rooms.

As Philippa took me in a south-west direction, and with all those thoughts flashing through my head, I felt my heart pounding from the coffee and the brandy I'd drunk in the past ten hours.

'I deserve a quieter life,' I told myself.

A young officer recognized me at the entrance and told me that Stoker had not yet been found, so McGray and a good number of men were still searching the breadth of New Town. He'd heard nothing about Miss Terry, but shared my suspicions of her being back.

I rushed to the lobby and demanded to see the manager. The pompous man appeared swiftly.

'Remind me of your name,' I said.

'Josiah Clarke, sir.'

'Have you seen Miss Terry?'

He went ghostly pale. 'Oh, well . . . I haven't had the pleasure myself, but one of our maids served her breakfast.'

'Do you know what time she came back?' I asked, but the man stammered, his eyes flickering in every direction. 'You *do* know she was missing last night,' I pressed. 'When did she return?'

'Oh, Inspector, I'm a true professional. I could not possibly divulge one of my clients' most intimate –'

'Miss Terry is suspected of illicit behaviour, so your refusal to "divulge" would de facto turn you into an accomp–'

'Quarter past five. Almost to the exact minute. I had it from one of our sweepers. She saw Miss Terry come through the main door.'

I smiled. 'Thank you, Mr Clarke. Is she in her chambers?'

'Oh! You're not thinking of . . . Might it not frighten her terribly? It is highly inappropriate to break into a lady's room!'

I raised a hand. 'I am not planning to break in. Simply tell Miss Terry that she is not to leave the hotel before I speak to her, unless she wants to be arrested.'

'*But, sir!*'

'As to when that will happen, I am not sure; I want to search Mr Stoker's room first. Will you kindly give me a key?'

Mr Clarke obliged, still scandalized at the prospect of Miss Terry going behind bars. I truly hoped that things did not have to go that far; one does not want to be the man who imprisons the nation's most beloved celebrity.

As I made my way to Stoker's chambers, I was reached by a very distressed Miss . . . I could not for my life remember her name, only that she played Second Witch (I recognized her as the most wrinkled of the three).

'Oh, Inspector, thank goodness you're here!'

'Miss . . . Erm . . . Are you all right?'

The woman, whose name I then recalled was Desborough, did not look it. Her face was set in a grimace, the skin around her eyes as creased as stone-beaten linen. She grabbed me by the arm.

'Excuse my being so forward, sir, but something really odd has happened.'

'Pray, speak, good woman. I am in a rush.'

'Well, ever since I had my savings stolen during a tour around Somerset . . . gosh, that was twenty-five years ago! It was not a vast amount, you see, but I was young and making very little from my acting. Those few shillings meant the world to –'

'Do you have a point?'

'Of course, do excuse me. I meant to tell you, since then I always keep with me . . . well . . .' she bit her prune-like lip, 'a gun.'

'A gun? You?'

She could not have looked any meeker. 'Well, yes, but only a little one. A four-shot Derringer; point three-eight calibre. It's a darling thing with an ivory grip and my name engraved in gold on the barrel.'

I inhaled deeply. 'And why is that relevant to me?'

'Oh, Inspector, it has gone missing.'

I groaned with exasperation. Things were getting more tangled before I had even undone a single knot.

'When did it happen?' I asked with a sigh.

'Not half an hour ago. I kept it under my pillow, like I always do when I travel. I only came down for a late breakfast, went back to my room and it was gone! And I've looked everywhere.'

'Did you lock your room?'

'Of course not, Inspector. This is still Britain!'

I had to lean on the wall, my eyes shut and reaching for my last shred of patience. 'Ma'am, allow me to summarize: you keep a gun underneath your pillow – yet you do *not* care to lock your doors?'

'Well, if you say it in that tone, of course you'll make me sound like a lunatic!'

Count to ten, Frey, I told myself. 'Did anybody else know you had it?'

'Oh, yes! One wants people to know one's not defenceless.'

I rubbed my face in utter frustration.

'I doubt this is a petty theft,' I said at last. 'And if it is, this is the most fiendishly ill-timed burglary.'

I asked one of our officers to attend Miss Desborough and have some of the hotel staff looking for that gun. I would have liked to oversee it myself, but Stoker's whereabouts were a far more pressing matter.

His suite was one floor below those of Irving and Terry, in a rather secluded corner of the building. I noticed that the servants' staircase was not too far away.

I stepped into a spacious room, not as luxurious as Miss Terry's but still very neat and comfortable. The view from the small window, however, was rather grim, over that infamous backyard.

One could read Stoker's character from that room as if it were an open book. The bed had not been slept in, there was a large trunk only half unpacked, and every surface – table, side tables, desk and some of the floor – was covered with a disarray of books, bills, ledgers and loose sheets packed with handwriting. This was the dwelling of a hyperactive man, one whose work never stopped.

As I stepped forward my foot landed on a book that lay on the floor. It was a tatty penny-dreadful, cheaply bound and tastelessly titled *Varney the Vampire or the Feast of Blood*. I did not bother picking it up. Instead I went to the messy desk. On top of everything I saw a piece of old correspondence, dated December 1888, but not specifying the day:

> *My dearest, dearest Bram,*
>
> *I know the grand Macbeth premiere will fall on little Irving's birthday and how very busy you will be, but could you please come home, even if for just a moment, to see him? The poor thing is already turning nine. Are you to miss his entire childhood?*
>
> *Yours always,*
> *Florence*

The names in that letter made my heart skip a beat. Had Stoker named his son Irving? And who was this woman writing to him? Was Stoker's wife also named Florence? Underneath there was another letter which answered the question: it was written in the exact same hand, which also matched the sender's address on its envelope. It read *Mrs Stoker*. What a coincidence that Irving's and Stoker's wives shared the same Christian name! Or . . . could there be more to it?

This second letter was much more recent, dated but a couple of days ago:

Dear Bram,

I must beg you again to come home. It has been days since we last talked, and your little Irving sorely misses you, as I have told you before.

Yours,
Florence

I also found a handful of unopened letters, all from Mrs Stoker, which probably contained similar messages, and Bram, knowingly, had not even bothered to read them.

Besides his wife's name, there was a detail that caught my eye: Stoker had indeed christened his own son Irving.

'Bram, oh Bram,' I muttered. 'I am only beginning to understand you . . .'

I searched the room from end to end and then rummaged through the contents of the large trunk. Neatly piled in a corner was a stack of odd books. The titles alarmed me.

Treaties on Irish faeries, anthologies of old European folklore, compendiums of superstition comparable only to those in McGray's library. There were sixteen tomes there, and they were all underlined and profusely annotated in the margins.

I realized with a thrill that Mr Stoker was obsessed with the occult.

'Damn,' I said out loud, sitting on the floor as I leafed through a particularly well-worn volume about Eastern European legends. 'If only I'd known this before!'

Could he be orchestrating it all? Drawing the police's attention to his own made-up apparitions? He certainly had knowledge of such things.

I tossed the book aside, and only by chance did I see the corner of yet another smaller one, sticking out from underneath the bed. I reached for it and saw that it was in fact a little leather-bound journal, dark reddish brown in colour, its corners rounded with wear.

A photograph fell out from between the pages and landed on my lap. I nearly gasped when I saw it: a portrait of Irving. The man looked as dignified as at his best moments on the stage, but also somewhat younger — remarkable he'd not aged that much, given the portrait's date, which I found on the back of the picture. It was signed and dedicated with a nearly illegible hand:

My dear friend Stoker
God bless you! God bless you!!
Henry Irving
  Dublin
  3 Dec. 1876

A peculiar memento to keep in one's journal for almost thirteen years, I thought, although this behaviour was making increasing sense in my head.

As soon as I opened the journal I found another piece of paper. Upon unfolding it I saw it was a meticulously traced family tree: Bram Stoker's, going as far back as the 'O'Donnell clan Chieftains'.

'I can see where this is going,' I mumbled, now turning the pages at full speed.

The journal was almost completely full – understandably so, for the first entry was dated July 1882 – and I noticed that Stoker kept very regular entries, all dated methodically and some of them very long. I sat on the bed and turned the pages to 30 June 1889, the day after all the mayhem had begun.

I was in for a riveting read.

ACT IV

MACBETH

    Is this a dagger which I see before me,
    The handle toward my hand? Come, let me clutch thee.
    I have thee not, and yet I see thee still.
    Art thou not, fatal vision, sensible
    To feeling as to sight? Or art thou but
    A dagger of the mind, a false creation,
    Proceeding from the heat-oppressed brain?

Bram Stoker's Journal

Fragment from the first entry marked as significant by I. P. Frey.

> *29 June. London. 11.45 p.m. – Before the day dies, before I describe the ghastly happenings at the theatre, let me say here what has to be said of myself.*
>
> *In my earlier years I knew much illness. Certainly till I was about seven years old I never knew what it was to stand upright. This early weakness, however, passed away in time and I grew into a strong boy.*
>
> *I was Athletic Champion of Dublin University. I won numerous silver cups for races of various kinds for rowing, weight-throwing, and gymnastics.*
>
> *I spent ten years in the Civil Service, engaged on a dry-as-dust book on The Duties of Clerks of Petty Sessions. I have edited a newspaper, and exercised my spare time in many ways as a journalist; as a writer; as a teacher.*
>
> *I am no hysterical subject; no green youth; no weak individual.*
>
> *My words are true. I write nothing but the truth.*

34

'I hope he is still alive,' I muttered, my pencil hovering over my own notes, 'I have a thousand questions to ask him.'

I ran my tired fingers through my hair. It had taken me two hours of intense reading, annotating and sorting Stoker's accounts – some of them so hastily written I'd had to transcribe them myself. With Stoker's statements interspersed with the happenings of the previous days, things now felt a little clearer in my head. But just a little. Like in my dream that morning, there was a torrent of names, personalities and situations swirling in my mind.

Would all the pieces somehow fit together? Or was this tangle of loose ends the direct result of dealing with so many people, so many lives and so many stories converging in this one play?

Two facts had struck me most forcefully: Stoker's suspicious ancestry, and the many recent passages that were either obliterated or torn out (something which did not occur at all in the earlier sections of the journal).

It was almost certain he'd witnessed (or thought he'd witnessed) something, both last night and after our tense meeting with him and Irving atop Calton Hill. Then again, why was he defacing his own words? Why had he not talked to us? Why hide such facts?

Stoker could either be protecting someone, or – more worryingly – he could be mentally disturbed.

I had seen such behaviour before: unbalanced people acting out their own fantasies, leaving traces and statements that blurred every investigation until they were proven unreliable. The dog sightings, traceable back to their last London performance, were particularly suspicious.

I thought Stoker could be embarrassed about believing to have seen something otherworldly; then again, he had confided such things in McGray (no wonder they'd seemed so secretive around me) and he had tried to warn me about the dog last night.

Could Stoker simply be a particularly shrewd fellow, orchestrating the publicity stunt I'd suspected all along? Could he even be enacting his own disappearance, after skilfully hinting at a hound-shaped harbinger of doom?

I thought of the brains found in Miss Terry's dressing room, and her missing leather purse. Stoker, as the theatre manager, would have had plenty of chances to place the former and take away the latter. Could he have done it all without telling anybody, so that the affair seemed more realistic?

I had to push those theories back, for there was something far more immediate I could infer from his writings: Stoker *had* returned to his chambers. He'd ventured into the dingy alleys, 'following' whatever he'd thought was calling him, but then he'd come back and written it all down. He had disappeared *after* doing so.

There were no signs of violence in the room, so it was likely Stoker had left of his own accord, whether willingly or tricked into it. Unless, of course, he'd been attacked so swiftly and unexpectedly he'd had no chance to defend himself.

As I gathered the sheets with my notes, a sweat-covered Sergeant Millar burst into the room.

'Sir!' he screeched, 'we know who took the gun.'

'Who?'

'That mad seamstress. Mrs Harwood.'

'I thought someone was guarding that corridor,' I said as we walked briskly towards the main entrance.

'We were running out of men,' said Millar. 'Inspector McGray wanted more officers out there looking for the Irishman.'

'And who saw her?'

Right then we entered the lobby. There was quite a commotion.

'She did,' and Millar pointed at Miss Ivor – Hecate – who was prostrated on a chair, all colour gone from her face, and grasping a cup of tea one of the chambermaids had just offered her. 'This lady says it all happened about ten minutes ago.'

I leaned closer to her. 'Miss Ivor, pray, what did you see?'

The poor woman looked up, her lips and hands trembling, the tea beginning to spill.

'Mrs Harwood was in the hall,' she said, but barely managed to utter the words.

'And she had the gun?' She only replied with a nod. I had to rest a hand on her shoulder to try to calm her down. I wished McGray was around; he is very good at managing distressed witnesses. 'Where is she now? Where did she go?'

The maid encouraged Miss Ivor to have a sip of tea. Miss Ivor gulped painfully but the drink seemed to help.

'I tried to reason with her,' she said, 'but she looked so frightening with that gun; she was caressing it with mad eyes. I asked her where she'd got it from and she barked at me. Said it wasn't my business. She said we should have told her about . . .' Miss Ivor clutched a hand at her chest. 'Well, about the little girl's trouble.'

'Oh, Lord,' I hissed. 'Who ever told her?'

'I don't know,' replied Miss Ivor, 'but it made her lose her wits! She said she was looking for Mr Wheatstone.'

There was a general gasp at those words, and I realized we were surrounded by half the cast of *Macbeth*. The three witches, Banquo, Macduff . . . I could not see Freddie or the assassins though.

'Is he at the hotel?' I asked them.

Mr Haviland – King Duncan – stepped forwards. 'No, he cannot be. I saw him this morning at breakfast. He was leaving for the theatre.'

'I saw Mrs Harwood run down the corridor,' said Miss Ivor. 'It looked like she was heading to the kitchens –'

I immediately ran there, Millar and another officer following me. We found the now familiar kitchen in even greater turmoil than the lobby. The head cook, a rather overweight individual, was sitting on the floor, and the scullery maids were fanning her with rags.

The cook, whom I'd questioned myself the night before, recognized me at once.

'Crazy lady!' she cried. 'With a gun!'

'Did she go into the street?' I urged, and the chubby

woman assented, pointing at the door that led to the pantry and on to the backyard.

'She must be going to the theatre,' I told Millar. 'We must get there before her.'

I had Philippa fetched at once, and as I mounted I saw an enormous canvas being unloaded from a wide carriage. A small crowd had gathered as some workers took it into the hotel, and before darting east I caught a glimpse of the unfinished, larger than life, full-length portrait of Ellen Terry in her beetle dress.

What a frantic race it was! I took Philippa straight into Princes Street Gardens, scarcely believing I had chased the now-dead Dyer across those very lawns a few hours earlier.

We passed the gardens' sumptuous fountain. Then the gravel of the railway crackled under my mare's hooves as we galloped across it, and we circled Castle Rock so swiftly I feared Philippa would fall on her side.

Millar's horse, a dark and mangy beast, very soon lagged behind.

I groaned out loud. I would have to face Mrs Harwood alone.

As I galloped I thought the matter through: if she had gone on foot I would reach the theatre much sooner – and I'd be waiting for her. If only things could be so easy.

I ascended the lawns on the south-west side of Castle Rock and rushed through the garden's wrought-iron gates, then cut the path along the narrow Cornwall Street, which led directly to the corner where the Lyceum

Theatre stood. I felt an immense relief when I saw its blindingly white façade emerge, but the respite would not last.

The first thing I saw upon rounding the corner was a cart loaded with jute sacks, being unloaded by three men: two young workers and – I gasped when I recognized him – Mr Wheatstone himself.

'*Get inside!*' I hollered, well before I reached them. Wheatstone, loaded with a sack on his shoulder, looked at me with incomprehension.

Behind him a cab had just stopped. I would not have noticed it had it not halted so violently, and before its wheels went still – my quarry jumped down.

My heart skipped a beat then.

I cannot believe the striking detail that has been imprinted in my mind: the pattern on her white dress, the slight trip of her first step on the pavement, the little blue purse she clenched, but more than anything else, the feral expression on her face. She opened her mouth as if to roar, but not a sound came out.

'*Behind you!*' I yelled as I dismounted.

Mr Wheatstone did turn, and as soon as he saw the woman his legs trembled and he dropped the sack. The jute burst on the pavement and a thick cloud of white lycopodium powder engulfed the scene.

As I ran to them I saw Mrs Harwood open her purse and pull out the little gun, its ivory glimmering in the sun despite the explosive dust suspended in the air.

'*It's all your fault!*' Her voice caught all eyes on the street, people screaming at the sight of the weapon. She was pointing it directly at Mr Wheatstone's chest, the barrel but a yard from him.

I leaped forward, stretched my arms desperately, and at the precise instant my fingertips brushed her lace-trimmed sleeve, a bullet was fired. The detonation resounded across the road, the cloud of powder ignited instantly, and the world became hell itself.

35

I felt the flames on my hand and the heat burning my eyes. I instinctively covered my face and jumped back as I heard the piercing, anguished shouts of Harwood and Wheatstone.

The ball of fire ascended like an eruption and dissipated in seconds – only the floating powder had burned, not that in the sacks piled up all around; not even the white heaps scattered on the floor – but Mrs Harwood's sleeve was ablaze and she yelled madly, jerking her arm uncontrollably. She had dropped the gun. I seized her and had to smother the flames with my bare hands, which already felt scorched. As soon as the immediate danger had passed she began writhing and trying to pull herself free.

I tried to control her, and as we struggled I saw Mr Wheatstone.

The man lay on the pavement, his clothes singed and a splatter of blood on the side of his grey beard. The two younger workers had knelt by his side.

'Wounded badly?' I managed to say, still struggling.

'Shoulder!'

Mr Wheatstone himself spoke, and pressed his blood-soaked hand on the injury. I had managed to push Mrs Harwood's arm just enough to save the man's heart.

'Take him to Chalmers Hospital,' I told the men. 'That's the nearest.'

'Where's that, boss?' asked the cockney worker. 'I don't know the city very –'

'Just south from the Cattle Market. Do you know that?'

'Oh yes, that we know.'

They helped Mr Wheatstone rise, and then climb on to the same cart they'd been unloading. Just as they did so I finally managed to twist Mrs Harwood's arms and hold them firmly against her back.

'*He burned my child!*' she howled when she knew herself subdued, and she became a dreadful thing to behold. Her eyes burst into tears, her voice was an unbearable wail and people on the street were covering their ears. '*You demon!* If there was any justice you would've burned right now!'

Despite her fits I felt her misery, just as much as I felt the guilt on Mr Wheatstone's face. He was a wretch as the cart took him away, wincing from both pain and remorse.

I dragged Mrs Harwood to the cab. The driver had initially stayed there waiting to be paid, but now he was petrified.

'I've nothing to do with this!' he cried when I approached. 'I just carry passengers! I never thought she'd –'

'*Shut up!* Take us to Morningside. Now!'

Right then I saw Millar arrive on his sweating horse, and a street peeler had come running upon hearing the gunshot. At least I would not have to escort Mrs Harwood to the asylum on my own. As it transpired, I would not go at all.

With Stoker still lost, the situation was now nearly out of hand, so I decided Millar and the other officer were perfectly able to take Mrs Harwood to the caring hands of Cassandra Smith at Morningside. In the meantime I rushed back to the Palace Hotel, where I'd left Stoker's journal and all my notes, determined to question Miss Terry once and for all. However, when I stepped into the lobby I found Nine-Nails.

I could tell he'd spent all night looking for Stoker: he was still wearing the borrowed black suit, but it was so creased and muddied it could have belonged to him for years. Arms crossed and looking as alert as if he'd slept for seven hours, McGray was questioning the hotel manager, Mr Clarke, who looked as if he were about to pass a kidney stone.

McGray saw me out of the corner of his eye. 'Where the hell were ye? I've been looking for ye everywhere.'

'We had a little bit of a situation here,' I grunted.

'Aye, just heard it all from this one.' He nodded at the manager. 'Did ye find Mrs Harwood?'

I told him everything in five sentences, seeing the concern grow on his face.

'Jesus, Frey! I cannae leave ye on yer own without everything blowing to smithereens! And ye sent poor Wheatstone to Chalmers Hospital! Everybody kens that place is a shite hole.'

'Excuse me, it was an emerg—'

'There, there, ye did well. But if Wheatstone needs

stitches his shoulder's gonna look like a sock darned by a blind donkey.' McGray's tone suddenly shifted. 'Frey, something happened on my side too. That's why I was looking for ye. And Irving.'

'What was it?'

McGray cleared his throat. 'We just found Stoker.'

36

Was he dead? Was he alive? In what state had he been found? I asked those and many more questions in a single breath, but before McGray managed to answer, Henry Irving came to us.

The man had not slept either, sporting dark rings under his eyes and very little colour on the rest of his face. With the black jacket and tie he was wearing, as if assuming he'd be mourning someone soon, Irving looked like a spectre.

'Well?' he spat. 'They told me you had news.'

McGray took his time to reply. 'Aye, we found yer man. Alive.'

Irving's chest went down in the most relieved exhalation, a bony hand drawn instantly to his heart. For a moment his stare lost all its arrogance and I caught another glimpse of the real, almost fragile man we'd seen last night. He would not let that impression last; Irving blinked and any trace of compassion was gone.

'Is he well?' he demanded. 'Where did you find him?'

McGray sneered. 'He's *quite* shaken, Mr Irving. Broken leg, michty blow on his head and bruises all over his arms and legs. We found him lying under some bushes in Queen Street Gardens. Unconscious.'

'My dear Lord . . .' Irving muttered after a gasp. 'Where have you taken him? I must see him.'

McGray had had to borrow the only mount available at the City Chambers: a flea-ridden nag with patches of mange, which looked even more pitiful next to my snow-white Philippa. Irving followed us in a black carriage, and very soon we reached Edinburgh's Royal Infirmary.

Everything on that street was either grey or lacklustre: the cobbled road, the buildings' stones and the wrought-iron fence surrounding the hospital. And my mood was just as gloomy: during the ride I'd begun to feel utterly spent, as if my mind and body had suddenly become aware of the dreadful happenings of that morning.

My right hand was growing blisters from the fire, and I could barely handle the reins. I should ask a nurse to bandage me whilst we were here.

We must have been the oddest trio to enter that hospital: three very tall men, each as different from the others as the imagination could conceive. A nurse guided us to a small waiting room, telling us the doctor was still with Stoker, but that we'd be able to talk to him in a few minutes. It would have been awkward in the extreme to sit there with Irving, and he must have thought just that, for he went back to the corridor to pace.

The same nurse kindly applied an unguent and bandaged my burns, and when she left I seized the chance to talk to McGray in private.

'Why did you not tell me about all the nonsense Stoker confided to you?'

McGray looked downright puzzled. 'What?'

'The black hound, his cursed ancestry and all that gibberish he believes.'

'Who told ye that?'

I pulled the journal from my side pocket, my notes now crumpled around it, and handed the lot to Nine-Nails. 'I found this in his room. He wrote everything down. Everything about –'

'*Notes by I. P. Frey*,' he read. 'I didnae ken ye had a middle name. What is it?'

'That is not important now. What *does* matter –'

'Is it Petunia?'

'*McGray!*'

'Is it Peaches?'

I brought a hand to my exasperated face. There was no way he would let it go. 'Very well. It is Percival, could you now –'

'Och, yer a Percy! This is priceless!'

I rolled my eyes. 'Could you please bloody focus?'

'Aye. Sorry, Percy.'

I grunted, though thinking that Percy was still better than Nine-Nails' original nickname for me.

'How could you not tell me about his ancestry?' I snapped as he looked through my notes.

'What for? Ye would've mocked him and me, and given us one o' those shite-sniffing faces o' yers.'

'I do *not* know if I would have –'

'Percy . . . ye would've. Yer doing it now!'

'Very well, I definitely would have. But had I known he is a direct descendant from Irish chieftains I would have looked at him under an entirely different light. I could tell he believed in all that superstitious Irish folklore, but I never imagined how obsessed he really is. I just went through his belongings; he is as mad as you! He has the knowledge and skills and resources to piece together all this banshee nonsense.'

McGray arched an eyebrow. 'Him behind the banshee sightings? Ye've nae seen him yet. The man was battered quite badly. He wouldnae've done that to himself.'

I opened the journal at one of the blotted pages. 'Look at the intentionally masked passages. Then these missing pages. It is as though Stoker was censoring himself. Why do that?'

McGray looked at the sections in question and pondered.

'He must have seen the banshee.'

I closed my eyes in exasperation, just as a middle-aged doctor came to us. After McGray introduced me as 'Inspector Percy Frey', the doctor told us that Stoker had regained consciousness, but the pain in his leg had been unbearable.

'I gave him some laudanum,' the man said, 'but I might have overdosed him.'

'Overdosed him!' I was incandescent.

'I gave him twenty drops, given his size, but it did nothing, so I gave him another five. Which sent him to the clouds.'

I drew a hand to my frustrated face. 'How long did you wait between doses?'

The doctor just bit his upper lip. 'Erm . . .'

'Oh, never mind. Take us to him.'

He led us to Stoker's room and we saw that Irving was already there.

On the bed beside the window lay Bram Stoker, his face flushed and breathing heavily as though in a stupor.

And by his side stood the tall, thin Irving, clad in black and leaning over the bed. His spine was curved in a way that made him look like a vulture watching over a dying animal. With his left hand he held both of Stoker's, as he spoke softly.

'I am so relieved, Bram. So relieved!'

Stoker smiled. It was a tired, yet comforted gesture.

'The doctor says you'll be fine,' Irving went on. 'Do your best. I need you tomorrow at the premiere.' He leaned a little closer. 'And if you recover promptly we might have time to go for a nice Angus steak before we leave Scotland.'

Amidst the drug-induced euphoria, there was a pathetic spark in Stoker's eyes – that of a little boy who is promised toffee if he behaves – and I felt deeply sorry for him.

'I'll try,' Stoker mumbled, his voice slurred as if he were terribly drunk.

I cleared my throat. 'Mr Irving, we need to have a few words with Mr Stoker.'

Irving rose to his full height, pushing back his shoulders and casting me the most disdainful stare. 'Have them, then.'

'In private,' I added, but Irving stood his ground.

McGray intervened. 'Get out! Or I'll pound ye 'til the winter o' yer bloody discontent!'

Irving had to oblige. The doctor, wisely, had already left the room, so I shut the door.

Nine-Nails whispered in my ear, 'I quite like to abuse that auld crook whenever there's a chance, but why d'ye want to question Stoker right now? He's in no state –'

'He is overdosed with opiates. He will never be more cooperative.'

McGray looked alternately at Stoker and me. 'Good lad! Yer starting to think like me.'

'That is rather worrying.'

I pulled up a chair and sat by the side of the bed. McGray remained afar to avoid crowding the man.

'Mr Stoker,' I said, 'we know you are in pain.' I recognized he was not, but it felt like a good first line. 'However, there are vital questions we need you to answer.'

Stoker sighed. From his eyes I could tell he was quite aware of my words, even if his speech seemed unconnected.

'Flo – Florence . . .'

'Mrs Irving?' McGray asked, quite shocked.

'No,' I told him. 'Mr Stoker's wife, curiously enough, is also named Florence. He must be calling for her.' I turned to Stoker. 'I promise to telegram your wife and tell her you are quite all right; I will give her no reason to worry.'

Stoker exhaled loudly. 'I once knew a little boy . . . he put so many flies into a bottle that they didn't have room to die.'

'He's bloody well drugged,' McGray said through his teeth.

'Mr Stoker, we need to know what happened to you last night. Who did this to you? Did someone attack you in your room?'

Stoker tried to raise a hand, but then dropped it, as if not sufficiently bothered to move. 'I saw nothing. I was writing my journal, minding my own business. Knock on the door . . . I opened and there's no one . . . Someone hit my leg – from the side – and I dropped on my face. I felt a blow to my head. After that . . . nothing. Nothing until I woke up here.'

'Are you certain you saw nothing? Could you perhaps have heard a voice . . . smelled someone's perfume . . . anything?'

Stoker wrinkled his nose. 'Smell? I think . . . I think . . .' he gathered breath. 'There are funny smells in the theatre. I once met a young actress who only washed her hair with –'

'Mr Stoker, I need you to remember.'

He groaned again, turning his face away. 'I was . . . I think I was lying on the ground . . . already beaten, and saw a thin man walk away. He walked queerly.'

'Queerly?' I asked. 'What do you mean? A limp?'

'Ye– yes, maybe.'

I pressed for more details, but that was all he could tell us.

'Just what Freddie said,' McGray mumbled.

I asked Mr Stoker a couple of questions but he did not reply, as if his thoughts had drifted for good. Fortunately, I knew how to get his attention back.

'I took the liberty of reading your journal,' I said, and Stoker turned his face to me so quickly I feared for his neck. 'I do apologize if I invaded your privacy,' I added promptly. 'You were missing and we feared the worst. I thought that your writings might give us clues – and they did.'

Stoker's eyes fixed on his journal, which I had just pulled from my pocket.

'You saw something,' I insisted, opening the book at the relevant page. 'Or should I say – someone.'

Nine-Nails took a small step forward. 'Was it the banshee?'

Stoker groaned again, as if his own writing and the smudged ink were the words of the Devil himself.

'Why did you do this?' I asked, pointing at the obscured lines. 'What is this you wrote that you decided it was best to conceal? And why did you tear these pages out?'

Stoker frowned when I showed him the remaining strips of torn paper. He then closed his eyes and exhaled as if letting out his final breath. He was experiencing a pain, a conflict which even the opiates could not alleviate.

'I tried to protect them. Oh, God, I did!'

I leaned forward. 'Protect who?'

Stoker shifted his weight as if suddenly bitten by a bug, and the bed creaked. 'Oh, I don't like that Terry woman . . . I tell everyone I do, but I don't. Bloody harpy. She forgets her lines and people call her *endearing*. She has children out of wedlock and people admire her for her *independence*, when any other woman would be called a – Lord, she could commit murder on the stage, in everybody's plain sight, and people would still applaud her for her good performance!'

'Mr Stoker, could you please simply tell us –'

'What annoys me the most – she knows the world loves her and has become bored of it. *Bored!* She didn't realize she was madly in love with Godwin until the poor wretch died. Although . . . I don't even think *that* was true love . . . Rather . . . she knows she can never have him back, so now she wants him like nothing else. Oh dear, we're all like that, aren't we? How desperately we crave what we cannot have.'

'Did ye see the banshee?' McGray asked again.

'Was it Miss Terry?' I pressed. 'Was she the person you saw last night?' I looked through the pages. 'You mentioned the word "iridescent", and Miss Terry was wearing her beetle dress at the ball.'

Stoker shook his head. It was terribly sad to see such a tall, well-built man about to whimper.

'I couldn't denounce her! I thought I saw her in Calton Hill that night, when Irving and I met you, but I wasn't sure, so I kept quiet. I didn't even keep those lines in my journal lest someone should read it. And then last night . . . I *know* it was her! The dog has, *has* to be hers . . . I tried to conceal it all, right before someone knocked at my door and attacked me.'

'Why would ye do that?' McGray asked, though he already guessed the answer.

'I did it for Irving! I wanted to keep it all quiet for him. He loves her so much, God only knows why!'

I gave him a moment to collect himself. Then I whispered, 'Mr Stoker, you have just said you know it was her. Are you absolutely certain? More importantly – can it be proven?'

He nodded and pointed at the back of my chair, where the nurses had hung his muddy jacket. 'Pocket – right-hand pocket.'

I flung my hand in, and as soon as my fingers felt it I knew what Stoker meant.

It was an oval, delicate, iridescent beetle wing.

37

The ride from the infirmary had felt like an eternity. We ran past Irving without even looking at him, and only heard him roar at our backs. He'd surely asked Stoker what had happened, and by now must be travelling frantically to the hotel in his rented cab, but he would certainly not beat us.

We stormed into the Palace Hotel, inquired for Miss Terry, and were told she was in her rooms but had commanded not to be disturbed. I would rather not transcribe what Nine-Nails told the manager.

McGray climbed the stairs like a dart, and when I caught up with him he was pounding Miss Terry's door so hard the wood creaked.

A young bellboy opened the door a crack, but before he could say a word McGray pushed his way in and the boy scrambled backwards. We walked into the vestibule, but there was nobody there. Then we heard voices from the sitting room, and McGray stepped in so swiftly its occupants needed a moment to take in what had happened.

The room was filled with the pungent smell of oil paints and white spirit, and at the very centre stood the enormous canvas I'd seen being carried in. The portrait was so imposing one had to stop and admire it, even at such dire a moment.

Clad in her striking green dress, Miss Terry held the

Scottish crown up high, about to place it on her head. Her pale skin had an almost ghostly glow against the dark background and the heavy fabrics. The portraitist, however, had not attempted to be flattering: Terry's large nostrils and strong jaw were there, depicted most accurately, but so was the fire in her eyes, which not even photographs were able to capture with absolute fidelity – the sensibility of the artist succeeding where the cool lens of the camera could not.

I recognized the man who'd painted the portrait of one of my stepmother's distant in-laws (Mrs Henry White), and whom I'd seen in a social gathering a few years ago, when his career was only just taking off in England: John Singer Sargent.

From the seconds it took him to acknowledge our entrance, I saw that the man painted with staggering dexterity: a single stroke from his brush, charged with bright green and yellow and white, suddenly became a perfect beetle wing; then a winding line, on its own nothing but a dark green smear, expertly positioned became part of the intricate yarn weaving.

He turned to us and spoke with the strangest accent I'd ever heard, not quite English, not quite French, and with a few American slurs here and there.

'May I help you, gentlemen? I am quite busy, if you don't –'

'Shush!' said McGray, stepping sideways. The canvas had obscured the real Miss Terry, who was posing at the end of the room, standing on a low side table that acted as a platform, each fold of her shimmering dress carefully draped. And when she saw us there was sheer panic in her face. I thought it would be impossible to describe it, yet –

'*There!*' Mr Sargent cried, sprinting back to his set of brushes. 'Freeze there, Miss Terry! That is perfect!'

Even though the painted eyes were already flawless, their colour and shape an exact match to the model, Sargent began retouching them with his finest brush, his nose almost rubbing the canvas. I cannot tell for certain what he did – some tiny lengthening of the dark eyelashes, some touch of titanium white added to the sparks on the pupils – but in seconds the expression of the portrait had changed entirely. Suddenly there was all the fear, all the shock we had unleashed, as if Miss Terry were staring at the gates of hell.

The woman was frozen, the only movement the slight tremor of her parted lips, staring at us and unable to conceal that fright, now immortalized by Mr Sargent. What a bizarre moment . . . and McGray stood there in silence, as if savouring the tension. I, on the other hand, was spellbound.

'That is superb!' cried Sargent, taking a step back to admire his work. 'Simply superb!'

Another male voice came from one of the adjacent chambers, quite pompous even to the likes of me. 'Why, I would like a peek, dear Sargent!'

Another face I recognized from society gatherings. Mr Oscar Wilde himself: tall, large, dreamy-eyed, arrogant to the marrow and holding a glass of port as he approached with a light tread. Before he could look at the painting he scrutinized us.

'Oh, my! Who are the two Dickensian characters?'

'Nine-Nails McGray,' he grunted, as if attempting to appear even more Dickensian. 'CID. Who the fuck are ye?'

Mr Wilde chuckled; quite condescendingly and standing dangerously close to McGray.

'You obviously do not move in the cultivated circles I –'

'*Get out!*' McGray snarled. 'Both o' youse. We need to talk to Miss Terry.'

Mr Sargent put his palette and brushes down, but Mr Wilde again chuckled, brushing imaginary specks of dust off his velvet jacket.

'Oh, my raggedy policeman, I would like to know what on earth Miss Terry could have to do with the –'

McGray growled. 'Mind yer own business, ye sleekit beastie!'

'Why, my own business always bores me to death; I prefer other people's.'

McGray looked at me quite wearily. 'Och, and I thought *ye* were the worst.'

Then, startling us all, he grabbed Mr Wilde by the collar, and the round-faced man dropped his port on the carpet. Mr Wilde was but a couple of inches shorter than McGray, but where the Irishman had pomposity, the Scot had sinew.

'Give me wit again, ye braggart, and I'll punch yer wobbly stomach 'til ye soil yerself from both ends.'

'Lord, you are quite the brute, aren't –'

Mr Wilde would not finish his sentence, for McGray dragged him out like a stray cat. I shall never forget the sight of Wilde's long, dark hair flailing about as he was being so roughly handled.

Upon Nine-Nails' return, Mr Sargent gulped, stammered a fearful 'excuse me' and then left the room with hasty strides. Before shutting the door he waved at Miss Terry, his face full of concern. I remembered Stoker's words: everyone was in love with that woman.

Right now, though, she looked at us with the eyes of a cornered fox. She did not move or speak as McGray walked around the painting.

'So lifelike,' he said. He offered Miss Terry a hand and she stepped down from the makeshift plinth, clasping the crown. 'Are ye happy with the result, miss?'

Terry blinked nervously and made to sit down, but must have remembered she could not whilst wearing that dress.

'I've not seen it,' she murmured. 'Not until it's finished. I like to be surprised.'

'You cannot be surprised right now,' I said. 'You must know very well why we are here.' Miss Terry said nothing, but she held my stare quite bravely. I produced the mucky beetle wing from my pocket and put it in the palm of her hand. 'I believe you dropped something.'

Terry received it and stared at it for a good while, looking puzzled.

'Where did you find this?'

'Not us,' McGray intervened. 'Mr Stoker.'

Terry's eyes, if possible, opened wider. '*Have you found him?*' she gasped. 'Is he well?'

'Well enough to tell us he saw *you* on the street last night,' I told her, and her chest swelled. 'He found this wing while following you.' Miss Terry opened her mouth to say something, but McGray jumped in.

'And we ken ye were out last night. We questioned everybody in this building and ye were nowhere to be found. What were ye doing out there?'

For the first time Miss Terry blushed. She was lost for words, and McGray had to tap her on the shoulder.

'Ye better talk, hen. We also ken that some stranger

walked out o' yer rooms earlier yesterday. Very likely the same person who attacked Mr Stoker.'

'Very likely! What do you mean?'

'He was recognized by Stoker and by . . . one other witness.' I preferred not to mention it had been Freddie Harwood. 'We know the man walked with a strange gait, and also that he left behind some sort of chemical smell.'

Terry shook her head so fervently that every beetle wing trembled. There it was again, the expression of doom in her eyes. 'Who told you that?'

'Nae need to expose the sinner,' McGray prompted.

'He did smell funny . . .' she said in a whisper. I could almost feel the cold fear she was experiencing.

'So ye've met that man,' said McGray. 'Who is he? What was he doing here?'

Ignoring the dress, Miss Terry sank on a sofa, covering her mouth, the crown falling from her hands – from the soft thud on the floor I could tell it was made of painted wood. The beetle wings cracked beneath her.

'He brought me letters . . . *But I've been deceived!* My God, I must have been deceived!'

'Deceived?' I asked.

Miss Terry spread her fingers all over her head, as if containing her skull from exploding.

'*What a fool I've been!* And now Bram . . . what happened to him?'

'Before we tell ye more,' said Nine-Nails, 'ye tell us yer story. What letters was this man bringing ye? Who deceived ye?'

'*I wish I knew!*' cried Terry, clasping her head so tightly I thought she'd plunge her fingernails into her scalp. 'I thought I – I thought I was exchanging letters with . . .'

She blushed intensely, and then rose all of a sudden, went to the table at which we'd had tea with her and brought her copy of *The Adventures of Alice in Wonderland*. That was the same small book I'd seen young Susy Harwood bring back, the one Lewis Carroll had dedicated to Miss Terry.

She pulled out a letter from within the pages and showed it to us, unable to say more.

McGray grabbed it and unfolded the expensive cotton paper. His eyes flashed across the sheet, and then he saw the dedication on the book's first page, which Miss Terry was holding up for him.

'Lewis Carroll?' McGray asked. 'Did he send ye this?'

Miss Terry could not contain angry tears any more. '*I thought he had!*' And she dropped herself on the sofa again.

McGray handed me the letter. It was clear that the hand matched that of the dedication. It read thus:

My Dearest Ellen,

I must appeal to you for help. It is all very, very sad, and there are things I cannot put on paper. I must say them face to face. Do meet me at the arches of Regent Bridge, a quarter past midnight. Not a minute later, <u>I beg you</u>!

Charles

'Why did Mr Carroll sign as Charles?' I asked her.

'His real name is Charles Dodgson. Lewis Carroll is just his pen name, and I've always called him Charles.'

'Youse two were very close,' said McGray. 'I remember ye telling us so.'

'Yes. He is the dearest gentleman and he was very fond

of my sister as well. I also told you we had to cease all con-nections after I had my two children illegitimately.'

I again blushed as she mentioned such a thing so nat-urally. 'That was many years ago, was it not?'

'Yes.'

'Yet . . .' I added, raising a brow, 'all of a sudden he asked you to meet him on an insalubrious city street, in the middle of the night?'

Her chest heaved. 'It was not all of a sudden. We resumed correspondence recently. Well, only a few weeks ago, to be frank . . . although now I'm not sure he ever wrote me anything at all!'

McGray and I exchanged sceptical looks.

'So someone deceived ye,' said Nine-Nails, 'into think-ing Lewis Carroll wanted to renew his friendship.'

'That's what must have happened! In his letters he mentioned he would come to Scotland to see me on the stage, away from all the London gossip, and that we might even meet in person. After all these years! Then yesterday he sent me that damned note asking for my help. I could not refuse! There I went. I risked it all to be there at the precise time.'

'Even after the mayhem we all witnessed last night?' I said. 'Were you aware of what your little jaunt would make us think?'

Miss Terry gulped. 'I wasn't. I wasn't thinking. You've seen the note. It seemed dire, and Charles is such a dear friend, taken away from me because of – *propriety*!'

I recalled Stoker's words: *How desperately we crave what we cannot have.* He knew Miss Terry very well indeed.

'So what happened?' asked McGray. 'I guess ye made it to Regent Bridge?'

Again Miss Terry blushed and looked sideways.

'And?' Nine-Nails pressed.

'I saw no one,' she spat, her face still askew. 'I was there at the right time, not a minute late, but there was nobody around. And I waited for almost two hours.' She saw our disbelief and cried: 'That's the truth!'

McGray stroked his still incipient stubble. 'We don't want to destroy ye, miss. If this deceit took place I'm sure ye can give us evidence. Did ye tell anyone about Carroll sending these messages?'

'No . . . I . . .'

'Did ye take a cab there? We can get a statement from yer driver.'

Miss Terry began fidgeting with the yarn of her dress. 'No. I walked. I didn't want even a coach driver to see me.'

'And then the alleged Mr Carroll did not use the post,' I said, 'but that mysterious man that was seen lurking around here . . . only to attack Mr Stoker a few hours later.'

'I'm not lying!' she snapped. 'I remember his face. I could identify him!'

'We will have to find him first,' I said, producing my notepad. 'Miss Terry, tell us more about this man's characteristic smell.'

Miss Terry ran shaky fingers through her ginger wig, so intently I thought she'd tear it out. 'Yes . . . he . . . He always left a little nasty whiff. I would always spray my scent of camellias when he left. That was the only perfume strong enough to get rid of his trace.'

'Pray, describe the man, to the minutest of details.'

'Oh dear . . . Forty-something, though he might have been older, with leathery skin. Very thin, with pronounced bags around his eyes. And he wore very threadbare clothes, even though he sounded a little too refined for them. He had the peculiar gait, as you mentioned; as if he'd had an old injury, but it had not been treated properly.'

As I jotted down her portrayal McGray asked more questions.

'D'ye ken anything about him? His name? Address? Any means to contact him?'

Miss Terry shook her head.

'So how did you summon him when you wanted to send a message to – Lewis Carroll?' I asked.

'I didn't. He came to me with messages and waited until I wrote my replies. That's how it worked from the beginning.'

'And he didnae want to be seen,' McGray added.

'No . . . he said that Charles – Mr Carroll – didn't want his servants to be seen around me. He said it was because people would talk!'

'So ye kept it all quiet,' McGray added again. 'A wee bit *too* quiet.'

I went to the first entries in my notebook. 'And Miss Terry, there is the issue of the brains you found . . .'

She covered her mouth, as if the mere memory of that day made her retch. 'He'd just delivered a message, right before I found the ghastly parcel.'

McGray raised a brow. 'Is that the reason ye were washing yer hands in the middle o' the corridor? To allow for the man to go?'

Miss Terry nodded. 'Yes. I had just sent him out with a small present for Charles.'

It was curious that she mentioned that. I remembered Miss Ivor's statement: that night Ellen Terry had brought a bag ostensibly full, and Miss Ivor had seen it empty after the brains had been found.

'Had you carried that present in a . . .' I read aloud: 'blue, pouch-style handbag?'

There was no need for a reply; her eyes confirmed it all.

McGray paced around her. 'Miss Terry, how come ye didnae suspect the man?'

Miss Terry shook her head, her face all confusion. We could tell she'd been dwelling on the fact all along.

'I . . . I did . . . a little. But he had just brought me a very loving letter from Charles. And he was so charming! If someone brought you letters from your dearest friend you'd not suspect him capable of something like that. That's the reason I didn't want the matter investigated by the police. I'm sure Irving would have had people guarding my dressing room at all times; I wouldn't be able to receive more messages.'

McGray and I exchanged incredulous looks.

'Miss Terry,' I said, 'you arrived in the theatre with a bundle, left without it *after* the brains appeared, *and* you were seemingly desperate to keep people away from your dressing-room door. If I had to speculate, I'd say you put the brains there yourself.'

'*What?*'

'Now you tell us this rather implausible tale –'

'*I am telling the truth!*' Miss Terry insisted, her eyes now bloodshot. There was a hint of madness in her pupils. 'I wouldn't even dream of touching that filth! It was all very stupid of me not to suspect him, I know that much now! But I'm telling you the truth!'

Neither of us replied.

347

'What about his letters?' Miss Terry appealed, pointing at the book. 'That's his hand!'

I chuckled. 'How can we be certain you did not sign that book yourself?'

Miss Terry's jaw dropped. 'How dare you imply that? Many people know his hand. He's signed countless books! You have but to look for one. Or better still, ask him in person to write you a damn limerick!'

Her voice had become raucous.

'Miss Terry,' I said, 'please calm down. You must see how suspicious this all seems to us.'

'I do, and I'm just as baffled. This must be a trap!'

'Trap?' I echoed. 'I am afraid I find it somewhat difficult to believe your story. Nobody knew of these communications, and apparently nobody saw you where you claim you went. But Mr Stoker did. He saw you in that very dress you wear now, and which you wore last night at the ball, in everybody's sight. And we know for fact you were not on Regent Bridge, because Stoker also found that missing beetle wing on Queen Street.'

'I told you I went to Regent Bridge. I walked a straight line on Princes Street, no detours there or back.'

'Stoker thinks otherwise,' said McGray.

'Then Bram lied!' There was more animosity between those two than either openly admitted.

'He says he saw ye and he gave us this beetle wing,' Mc-Gray said, 'which he could have picked up from anywhere, I admit, but his story rings true to me. *Yers*, Miss Terry, doesnae. And ye have no witnesses to support what ye've told.'

'It cannot be . . .' she whispered. There was true despair in her features. And then, like the flip of a coin, her expression changed. 'Unless . . .'

Her stare fell on some spot on the wall. For a moment I feared she too was losing her wits.

'What is it?' I asked.

I could see a spark glowing in her pale eyes, the epiphany forming in her head. She looked straight into McGray's eyes, and her mouth was dry when she spoke.

'There are two dresses.'

Right then the door burst open, almost falling off its hinges, and the dark figure of Henry Irving stormed in.

'*Leave Miss Terry alone! I will not allow –*'

McGray turned to him, unsheathed his gun and pointed at the floor. 'Shut yer gob now, or I'll *accidentally* shoot yer bloody clown feet!' Irving said no more and McGray, gun still at the ready, looked back at Miss Terry. 'Go on. Two dresses.'

If the actress had seen the gun, she was too absorbed in her own thoughts for it to sink in. Her eyes moved from side to side while she spat words at full speed.

'Of course! We always make two dresses – one for me and one for my understudy. Our measurements are not the same, you see.'

'Yer understudy?' McGray repeated. 'Who's that?'

Ellen's mouth was dry. 'Miss Ivor. You . . . you know her. She plays Hecate.'

'Miss Ivor, of course!' I could hear the exhilaration in my voice. Miss Ivor, the disillusioned, middle-aged actress whose only scene had been cut out following Miss Terry's wishes; the woman who'd been so keen to give evidence against her.

The woman from the same town as the manufacturer of the bloodstained leather purse.

I was about to air those thoughts, and I could tell from

the spark in McGray's eyes that he was coming to the same conclusions, but then Irving spoke.

'Ellen, I have no idea what this is all about, but I thought that dress had been taken apart.'

Quite innocently, Irving himself had just thrown the scent back on to Miss Terry. She'd seemed momentarily relieved, but now her chest had swollen.

'Oh, Henry . . .' she mumbled, almost coming to tears.

'So it wisnae in Miss Ivor's hands?' McGray jumped in.

'No,' said Miss Terry. 'We left that dress with Mr Sargent, so that he could finish the portrait without me having to pose for so long . . .'

'Mr Sargent?' I asked. 'Could he –'

'No, no,' said Miss Terry. She moved her fingers nervously, as if tying invisible threads in the air. 'This dress I'm wearing was damaged on the train, on its way here. That was a couple of days before we travelled here. We were in such a rush to mount the play for Edinburgh we had to take beetle wings from Miss Ivor's dress, so we had it fetched before leaving London. That's why John – Mr Sargent – had to come all the way here with that mammoth canvas. He wants to exhibit that painting very soon at the New Gallery in London – apparently there's a very important patronage at stake, so he needs it finished. Dear Oscar heard of his conundrum and funded the trip.'

'All that *is* traceable,' I said, remembering the telegrams mentioned in Stoker's journal. 'But it does not clear you entirely. We could –'

Irving leaped forwards. 'What do you mean, not entire–'

McGray raised the gun but an inch and Irving went quiet.

'Who was the last person to handle that second dress?'
I asked.

Miss Terry's frown deepened. I had seen that expression before: the first time we'd met her and I'd thought she looked riddled with guilt. Only now it was amplified a thousand times.

'Well, I wrote the necessary letters to Mr Sargent, but I never touched the dress myself. I had it sent directly to . . . God forgive me . . . It was delivered directly to Mrs Harwood.'

Final letter from the partially burned stack found at Calton Hill

The top of the sheet was completely charred. – I. P. Frey.

[. . .]

and I will cry and count my tears and I'll collect them in a thimble, and then in a wine glass, and then in a tureen, and I will count them one by one, and I shall always know how many tears I've shed for you.

I'll cry like Ophelia before she drowned herself in that ghastly Danish brook.

I'll cry like Romeo when he found the corpse of Juliet in that icy grave.

I'll cry like Lavinia when the Goths raped her and then cut her hands and tongue.

I'll cry like Othello when he realized he'd been tricked into smothering his beautiful wife to death.

And I will count those tears and I shall always know how many tears I've shed for you.

Love,
X

38

Once again I found myself looking through Mrs Harwood's window. The backyard's floor was now completely clean, and one of the scullery maids was there, sitting on a tiny stool peeling a mountain of potatoes.

'It would not take much agility to go in or out through this window,' I said. 'If Mrs Harwood was silent enough, our guards would not have noticed.'

McGray pulled the curtains to have a look. 'Aye. And she had a very good view; could've seen when that chap Cooper lowered his guard – and then strike him. She's proven she can be violent.'

I noticed the undertone in his voice. Being reminded of his own tragedy had brought McGray's spirits to a dangerous low, and now he dragged his feet and moved lethargically. He had no energy to defend his banshee theory any more, but he seemed so crestfallen I decided not to boast about all the whisky he'd soon owe me.

Avoiding my eyes, he searched the room slowly but conscientiously. The silence was oppressive, but fortunately it did not last.

'Here it is,' he said, on all fours and looking under the unmade bed. He pulled what at first sight looked like green rags, but then I realized it was the torn remnants of tinsel and yarn.

'The second dress!' I gasped. As I spoke, McGray pulled the full garment from under the bed, and we heard a metallic clink. A little golden thing fell from between the folds, and McGray caught it as it rolled across the floor. I saw it was a thin, cheap wedding ring, too small for a man's finger.

'Mrs Harwood dropped something,' McGray said, pocketing it, and then he spread the spoilt material on the bed. There was no doubt; it was a perfect copy of Ellen Terry's dress.

'How anticlimactic,' McGray said.

'Two dresses,' I muttered, suddenly recalling my first encounter with Mrs Harwood. 'Her only alibi for the night of the first sighting was Miss Terry's dress. Everyone saw a torn dress in the evening, and the following morning it was restored. That is how she attempted to prove she'd not been at Regent Bridge, but busy at work at the Lyceum. Of course, if there always were two dresses . . . That changes it all.' I shook my head. 'And I consciously avoided mentioning the dress alibi in front of Miss Terry . . . perhaps that would have sent us in the right direction from the very start.'

McGray sighed deeply. 'We should ask the lads to take this to the City Chambers and store it. This is proper evidence.'

We stood there in silence for a moment, simply looking down at the few cracked wings that were still attached to the weave.

It could have been the end of it, both of us satisfied that enough clues pointed at Mrs Harwood, but right then something happened in my mind; something shifted in me and it would never go back.

'No,' I mumbled. 'There is something here I do not like at all.'

'What d'ye mean? Ye won! Ye were always right. It was the mad Harwood woman.'

In the vast majority of cases I've dealt with the culprit is always the most obvious person. There is always glaring evidence; everything pointing at a sensible truth. And it looked like the rule also applied to this case: all the clues and evidence pointing at the seamstress. However, there were still many unexplained details, and it bothered me.

I told McGray all of this, and he laughed wryly. 'Are ye saying – ye *do* think there was a banshee?'

'No no no. Step back. I am saying I believe there is something odd here.'

'Do ye doubt what yer seeing? Do ye doubt Mrs Harwood was the figure Stoker saw last night?'

'My most rational side says it can be the only answer – however . . .'

McGray let out a sour laugh. 'Are ye having a hunch? A premonition? I can ask Madame Katerina to give ye a beginners' course.'

'McGray, think about it. The anonymous messenger, Miss Terry's illogical tale, the blood – God, I still need to trace who bought the blood from the butchers! And remember that sonnet predicting somebody's death tomorrow. Could an unbalanced woman have the wits to write those lines? I refuse to believe this is it. This case is far from over.'

But first we had to tell the children. It was a dire prospect, but it was our duty.

Miss Terry had requested the deed be done in her chambers, so we headed there.

Mr Clarke, the hotel manager, intercepted us. 'Inspectors, this nurse here insists on seeing you.'

Miss Smith came behind him, looking rather grim, but I truly welcomed the sight of her. She'd be invaluable when breaking the news to the children.

McGray cast Clarke a killing stare and the man had the tact to retire at once.

'How bad is she?' I said.

'I had to sedate her, Inspector. I knew she was on the edge, but I didn't expect she'd crack so soon.'

McGray told her we had found the torn dress and that everything pointed at Mrs Harwood being responsible for the 'apparitions'. 'Looks like she should remain under yer care,' he concluded.

'That would be the best, and Dr Harland agrees. Now I only need to wait for Dr Clouston to return and give the second opinion. You mentioned that Mrs Harwood doesn't have any family or next of kin?'

'Only her two children, as far as we know,' I said. 'We were just on our way to tell them about their mother's situation. Do you think it is the right thing to do?'

Miss Smith's face went sombre. 'Sadly, yes. In my experience delaying this type of news only makes things worse.'

McGray rubbed his eyes, looking terribly tired.

'Dr Clouston should be back in a few days,' said Miss Smith. 'He sent a telegram saying so. I'm sure he'll have news for you then.'

McGray did not answer immediately. He lowered his face but could not bring himself to look at his mutilated hand.

'Let's get it done, then,' he said at last.

Just before I knocked at the door, a long, pale hand, as cold as a corpse, held me by the wrist.

It was Irving.

'Inspectors,' he whispered, 'I must ask you – well . . .'

'Speak,' McGray huffed, not a trace of patience left.

Irving took a deep breath and spoke with a most supplicatory tone. 'I know what you are going to tell them, I'm not an idiot. Mrs Harwood can't leave the asylum.'

'Yer so clever,' McGray said in a monotone.

Irving had to take a deep breath. 'Could you possibly – tell them *after* the premiere?'

I frowned at the request. 'I beg your pardon?'

'Inspector, please, they are going to find out anyway. But if we tell them now . . . it might ruin their performance. Particularly the girl's.'

McGray threw his head back in the loudest cackle imaginable. 'Ye unbelievable piece o' scum!'

He pushed Irving aside and banged at the door. When we stepped in we found Miss Terry already there. She'd changed into a lilac muslin dress, and sat at her parlour table which was full of biscuits, cakes and tea. Susy and Freddie were on the sofa, at the foot the imposing oil painting.

Freddie was lounging on the cushions, carelessly munching on a large slice of cake, spilling crumbs all around. Susy, on the other hand, had a dark expression on her face: her skin was pale, contrasting starkly against her reddened scars. Besides her troubles – God, it had happened just the day before! – she seemed to anticipate what we were about to announce.

The reality suddenly hit me: those two children had

no one. Ellen Terry was now the closest they had to a guardian – if only a guilt-ridden one.

'What is it?' Freddie asked from the sofa, bossy and impatient.

Miss Smith took a deep breath and went to the children. Irving tried to take a step forward, but I held him by the shoulder. Ellen Terry, who also knew what was about to be said, was chewing her lips and squeezing her handkerchief so intensely I thought she'd soon tear both cloth and flesh.

McGray pulled up a chair and Miss Smith sat in front of the Harwoods. Her expression was solemn, yet reassuring.

'Susy, Freddie – I have been looking after your mother. I am sorry to tell you this, but she is very ill. I'm afraid she can't take care of herself any more.'

That tableau would have made a heartbreaking oil painting. Susy opened her eyes wide; not with surprise, but with the anguish of seeing that the ghastly outcome she'd probably feared for a long time had finally arrived. Freddie, on the other hand, became red with anger.

'What do you mean?' he snapped. 'Where is she now?'

Miss Smith tried to hold his hand but the boy pulled it away. 'Freddie –'

'Frederick!'

'Frederick, we are looking after her.'

'Where is she? *Tell us!*'

Miss Smith took another deep breath. 'Right now we need to care for her at the asylum, but –'

'So she's finally gone mad!' Freddie shouted, jumping on his feet.

'Freddie!' cried Miss Terry.

'You think we're stupid and don't notice things, don't you? You think we couldn't see her losing her marbles!'

'*Frederick!*' Miss Terry also stood up, furious. 'How dare you be so cruel! She is your own mother!'

'And what's going to happen now?' Freddie went on, smacking the air about. 'I'll have to work like a mule just to pay for the mad woman's asylum! And to maintain this monstrosity!' He pointed at his sister and the girl burst into tears, burying her scarred face in her hands. 'Why do you cry? It's the truth. You only have *one* scene and it is as a monster! What else can you play these days?'

Amidst the general gasp, McGray went to Freddie in huge strides, and smacked him so hard it sounded like the crack of a whip.

'Listen to Miss Terry,' he hissed, in a tone that made my blood curdle. 'Have some respect, ye spoiled brat.'

We were all paralysed. Even I, after having witnessed terrible things throughout my career, felt a horrid tingle in my chest.

Freddie was about to touch his cheek, where McGray's incomplete set of fingers was artistically imprinted, but he contained himself. Instead, he made his way out and slammed the door with a strength seemingly impossible for his flimsy arms.

'Irving,' I said, 'go and make sure he does not do something silly.'

Irving welcomed the excuse and left the room swiftly.

Miss Terry, trembling from head to toe, went to Susy and embraced her tightly. As she ran her fingers through the girl's hair, it appeared to me that she was trying to console herself more than she was the child.

'I'll look after you, my dear,' she whispered, her voice broken. 'Don't you worry about a thing, I'll look after you.'

And as the two wept, resting their faces on each other, I thought I would have rather heard the deathly cry of a banshee.

39

Decidedly out of spirits, McGray and I sat languidly in the hotel's smoking room, where the very accommodating headwaiter poured us each a large brandy.

McGray stretched his long legs, crossed his arms and stared at the wide windows. He was not looking at the bright, clean dusk, or at the dark silhouette of Castle Rock, which rose right ahead of us. His eyes were devoid of any expression. Once again I found his attitude strikingly similar to that of his sister, as if both Amy and Adolphus suffered from the same dreadful, paralysing melancholy.

In vain I tried to spur his brains, for there was a mess of facts in my mind which I must untangle. Nine-Nails, however, replied to my speculations only with grunts, which became louder and angrier each time, so I retreated to the safety and coolness of my own notes.

I first noticed that my entries right after the ball had become sparser – no surprise there, with one death and all the mayhem that ensued – and I wondered whether I might have missed an important fact since then. I felt I had, but could not pinpoint what. I read statement after statement, turning back the pages until the very start of my battered little notebook, to the first apparition under Regent Bridge. I had written down the banshee's words, and I read the four lines a few times.

'You are not random words,' I mumbled. 'There is some dark wit in there . . .'

I produced my pencil, tore three pieces of paper and wrote down the three messages left by the alleged phantoms. I placed them in front of me, rearranged them, read them in every possible permutation.

'The death-Macbeth rhyme has to go last,' McGray said rather unexpectedly. Not out of interest, but frustration at my shuffling. 'And the other two seem to be in the right order.'

Rather than refute him, I tried to engage him further. 'What makes you think so?'

He shrugged. 'Cannae tell. It's poetry. It just feels that way. And it also matches the order of the events. So far it's been truthful. The more we plunge our hands into it, the more people get hurt.'

I growled from the bottom of my stomach, 'I refuse to sit down and do nothing, like a hostage to some silly rhymes!' When I looked up everyone in the room was casting me baffled looks. I turned to whispers. 'I have the awful feeling something terrible is about to happen, and that it is all slipping through my fingers!'

McGray nodded at the sonnet. 'Well, don't fret so much on those. They're not giving us the final clue, and that's on purpose. We cannae tell what's going to happen.'

'We should be able to infer it,' I said stubbornly. 'We are supposed to be smarter than this.'

I could feel McGray's acute stare on me, as if challenging me to find the right answer.

'They do tell us it will happen on the stage,' I said. 'We can take things away from them. We can cancel the play.'

McGray chuckled. 'Irving's not going to like that.'

'Irving does not tell us what to do.'

'Nae, but he's got Campbell eating from his mucky hand.'

'I am happy to at least try.'

McGray shifted his weight on the seat, grumbled, and then, very slowly, with the tired look of a father who is humouring a child, he pushed himself up. 'Fair play, but let's not waste our time going to Irving. Let's go directly to Campbell.' He looked at one of the ornate pendulum clocks. 'He'll be having his tea by now. This'll be fun; I've never seen his house.'

I gathered my notes quickly. 'Please, oh please, do not punch him this time.'

'Cannae promise, Percy . . .'

To my complete astonishment, Superintendent Campbell lived in a very modest dwelling in the Old Town, just around the corner from the City Chambers.

His house, one of the oldest on Blair Street, and to my eyes fit only for demolition, looked downright medieval, with a front wall that had bowed after the centuries, and a door that opened directly on to the road, without any garden or porch. No wonder the man was so bitter about his wages.

McGray knocked at his door, but as soon as he lowered his hand we saw a wide, black carriage halt next to our horses. Its roof was folded back, and the long, pale figure of Henry Irving stuck out like a mast.

The man alighted nimbly, swaddled in his black cape, which the mild evening did not justify. In his gloved hands he carried a bottle that I recognized as some of the most expensive French wine.

'What the hell are ye doing here?' McGray demanded, even though we both understood already.

A young maid attended the door and Irving spoke to her, completely ignoring Nine-Nails. 'Tell your master Henry Irving is here to see him.'

He had hardly finished the sentence when Campbell himself came out, as if he'd been listening behind the door (perhaps he'd seen us through the window, and had instructed his maid to send us away).

'Mr Irving!' Campbell cried, with the jolliness of a sixteen-year-old girl called upon by her beau.

'Good evening, Mr Campbell. What a delight to find you home! I took the liberty to bring you a small token, for you and your fine wife.'

'Oh, such kindness, sir! Do come in. Frey, Nine-Nails, go away.'

McGray raised an arm between Campbell and Irving. 'We've come to talk about this very man.'

Campbell growled through his teeth. 'I said, *go away*!'

Irving smiled contemptuously at us. 'Come, come, my dear Mr Campbell, I'm sure these gentlemen are just doing their duty. I believe –'

I saw a long speech coming, so I went straight to the point.

'The play must be cancelled.'

'*What!*' both men yelled in perfect harmony.

Irving cleared his throat and then smiled, but his inner actor struggled to take over.

'Your staff have an unorthodox sense of humour, Mr Campbell,' he said. 'They obviously have no idea of the costs, the effort and the expectations that revolve around my art.'

'Frey, go away!'

'I'm surprised ye don't suspend the play yerself,' said McGray. 'Yer manager is in hospital with a broken leg, yer effects expert was shot in the shoulder, yer head seamstress is in the Lunatic Asylum and yer two main child actors are distressed beyond their wits.'

Irving chuckled. 'My company has pulled through worse, I assure you.'

'And,' McGray continued, 'there's the prophecy!'

Irving shook his head. 'I thought you were done with that! Weren't you two certain that poor Mrs Harwood had done it all?'

'We have not completely confirmed that –'

'You have *not*?' Campbell interrupted me. 'Frey, I thought that you, out of all people, would be keen to declare this case closed. Now you are telling me you think those "omens" deserve more investigation? Based on what?'

'There is a mysterious messenger we still know nothing about, and the blood writings, and the possibility of someone dying tomo–'

'Oh, these two can be unbelievably tiresome!' Campbell interjected, making Irving chuckle.

'You hardly need to tell me that. Mr Campbell, may I take advantage of your hospitality and join you for a cigar – and perhaps a brief word?'

'Why, I should be delighted!' he exclaimed, inviting Irving in.

McGray shook his head. 'Campbell, ye sad, sad piece o' shite!'

'*Shut up, Nine-Nails!*' Campbell snapped. 'And get your sorry carcasses away or I'll have you both arrested for insubordination! *Now!*'

Irving raised his hands. 'There, there, Mr Campbell, I hate to see you thus altered. And I'm sure your officers will understand they *do* need to leave.'

I drew air in, ready to shout on, but McGray seized my shoulder and pulled me back.

'Come on, Frey. We've lost here today. Don't give him the satisfaction o' feeding ye prisoners' porridge.'

The anger burned my insides. I could not believe how the roles had inverted: on a regular day it would have been *me* begging McGray for equanimity.

As they shut the door on us, I saw Irving's hand rest on Campbell's shoulder. He had fine, gentle fingers, but with the power of iron chains.

And he cast us a mordant smile.

40

'I am surprised you refrained from kicking down Campbell's door and punching him to a pulp.'

'Och, why always me? Time ye got yer own hands dirty.' He patted the bony neck of his borrowed horse as we rode back to New Town, and did not speak again until we passed Princes Street Gardens. 'For the first time in years I feel like I'm goin' to have a good night's sleep.'

The statement puzzled me, but then I realized it was well past eight o'clock in the evening. With the still-bright sky I had not realized the hour.

'What shall we do now?' I asked, seeing that McGray was heading to his house in Moray Place.

He shrugged. 'We've done all we can, Frey. We are almost certain Mrs Harwood's responsible. If that's the case, she's in the asylum now. Everyone's safe. And ye'd be right: it was all a hoax. Not the kind ye were expecting, but still a hoax. We could call our wee bet a draw, if ye get fastidious.'

He sounded exhausted, his face so spent I thought it was a miracle he did not fall from the saddle. And I understood why. The case, which had come to remind him so much of his sister's misfortune, was clearly taking its toll on him. I could not demand more; I could not expect McGray to be perennially determined and driven. It was already remarkable he'd endured this long without crumbling.

'*Nine-Nails!*' I struggled for the words to explain myself. This must be what he felt like whenever he described his theories of the odd and ghostly to me. 'Something will happen tomorrow! I am certain! I can feel it in my gut!'

My voice carried across the road, over the carts and horses and the distant echoes of the steam trains. McGray was quite a few yards away already, but I still managed to see the tired smile on his face. 'I've been just as certain of so many things . . .' he said, 'and so far I've been mostly wrong.'

Again he looked ahead, but then, just before the famished horse turned around the corner, McGray shouted over his shoulder. 'Try Madame Katerina if ye really are so desperate!'

'I cannot believe I am doing this,' I muttered, 'I cannot believe it, I cannot . . .'

The sky had darkened in less than half an hour, blocked with clouds so thick the summer dusk was now as gloomy as my hopeless thoughts.

Philippa was quite restless, as if foreseeing what was to happen that night, but she still took me quickly to the deserted cattle market.

I dismounted carefully, trying not to drop the fine bottle I'd retrieved from my cellar, and after another 'I cannot believe it', I knocked at the gypsy's door. The wood was sticky and stank of stale beer; she'd probably had a very profitable night.

It took her chubby, grubby manservant a good while to open, and when he did so the stench of his sweat made me cough.

'What d'ye want? We're closed.'

'I am friends with one of your mistress's main patrons. I –'

'Aye, aye, yer the dandy always running after Nine-Nails McGray.'

'I do not *run after* –'

'Madame Katerina can see ye, but nae for long.'

He bid me in and I climbed the – by now – sadly familiar staircase that led to Katerina's *divination* room. I found the woman herself already there, lit by only a solitary candle on the centre of her little round table.

'I cannot believe this!' she cried too, her grin as wide as that in the engravings of the Cheshire Cat.

I grimaced at her customary vulgarity, her garish make-up (which, given the late hour, she would probably not wash off before going to bed), her pierced nose and earlobes and eyebrows, her claw-like nails covered in black varnish . . . and her crude, walloping, impossible to ignore pair of breasts. Thankfully, tonight she'd covered them with the folds of thick dressing robes.

'Good evening,' I said, forcing a smile so deeply my face ached.

'Oh, you brought me a present!' she added, her green eyes on the bottle. 'Or is it a down payment for one of my tricks?'

'May I sit, ma'am? Thank you. This, in fact, is meant to be uncorked right now. And I do have a few questions I would like you to answer. *Without* resorting to your – special gifts, if at all possible.'

She chuckled, snapped her fingers, and a moment later the stinky servant brought us a corkscrew and two surprisingly fine glasses. He opened the bottle, poured the wine, and I raised my drink.

'May we toast to –'

'Oh, don't be so coarse, boy,' Katerina said. 'Put that thing down and let it breathe.'

I raised both eyebrows. 'I am all astonishment. I thought you only drank those nasty ales you brew downstairs.'

'That's your problem, boy. You think. You assume. You give your senses more credit than they deserve, and then think we're all idiots for not seeing things through the same glass as you. That's why I have never liked you.'

'I cannot say I have ever liked you much, either. Every time I have been coerced into your premises I have thought I'd rather be anointed with honey and set on by a beehive.'

The woman laughed heartily. 'You have some wit, boy. I grant you that. But if you didn't work for my Adolphus I'd have sent you home with a few hexes every time.'

'Ha! The only hex I could catch here are rashes and fleas.'

'Oh, don't challenge me, boy!' she concluded with a wide smile – joking or warning me, I could not possibly tell. 'Now, let's try that bottle you brought – to see if at least you have good taste.'

We clinked our glasses and drank; the most unusual toast in my entire life.

Madame Katerina savoured the wine and felt the bouquet like an experienced oenologist.

'Not bad, but I don't need to use my inner eye to tell you didn't bring the best.'

I smiled. 'Indeed I did not. You could not expect me to waste my finest Cabernet on the likes of *you*.'

Again, she laughed.

I put my glass down. 'Now, ma'am, as enjoyable as this has been, I must get to the point, and since we have both been quite sincere so far, I hope we shall remain so.'

'Ask, boy,' she said, one chubby finger caressing the rim of the glass.

'Madam, tell me, and *please* tell me the truth …' I looked intently at her feline eyes, neither of us blinking. 'How do you do it?'

She raised an eyebrow. 'How do I do what?'

'You know what I mean. Your divination tricks.'

She chuckled. 'I have no tricks. I have *the eye*.'

'Please, madam, Detective McGray is not here, nor are any of your gullible clients. You and I know better. You have told us, Nine-Nails and me, things you could not possibly have known. How do you do it? I can tell that you have a means to elucidate secrets, for certain, but I do not believe it has anything to do with your – inner eye.'

There was a long silence, a motionless duel of stares, lit only by the dim flame of the candle.

'Please, madam, I am a gentleman. I give you my word of honour, not a single soul shall ever know what you tell me.'

I replenished her glass before she had the need to ask. She enveloped the drink with both hands, reclined in her chair and gazed at the shifting shadows on the ceiling.

'Do I sometimes lie?' she shrugged. 'Yes, of course, I'm a businesswoman.'

'*Now* we are being sincere.'

'Do I sometimes observe and guess correctly?' she went on. 'Again, of course, and very often! Most people come here with glaring problems, Inspector, and not everyone is as cryptic as you or me; we all wear our masks, true, but most are very easy to lift. And I do have a "special eye" for that. One look at a simple person and you can tell most of what's wrong with them. Then ask them a careful question and they'll reveal more than they think . . . or want.' A derisive chuckle. 'Although most of the times they *want* you to know. They want you to guess correctly and tell them what to do. They don't realize it themselves, but the stronger their wishes and their longings are, the easier for me to spot them.'

'And you take advantage of that?'

'Of course. I told you, I'm a businesswoman. But don't think I'm a monster. I never charge a pauper more than they can afford, and I never tell them anything that does them harm. A widow comes, I tell her her husband's in heaven and wants her to move on; a drunk comes asking if he'll ever be rich, I tell him the bottle stands in the way. I speak common sense to them, but they find it enlightening.'

'And what do you do when – Adolphus McGray comes to you?'

'Oh, that boy is an entirely different business. He has a good heart.'

'But you still lie to him.'

Katerina leaned forward, swigging once more, her eyes ever fixed on mine. 'No. I don't.'

'But you just said –'

'I said I *sometimes* lie.'

'And then you said that you make an exception for McGray, which I think is simply one of your lies.'

'Adolphus has read his books. He sometimes knows more than I do. I couldn't fool him if I wanted to!'

'So, only for McGray, you do use your – supernatural powers.'

'Mock me as much as you want, boy,' she retorted, helping herself to more wine, 'but don't ask the questions if you won't like the answers.'

'Where does that *inner eye* come from?'

'My grandmother had the gift. My ma didn't. It usually skips a generation. I can't tell you why.' She saw my sceptical smirk. 'Doubt all you want, but there are things nobody can prove. Not in the way you want.'

'If that is your answer . . .'

'It is.'

'Very well,' I granted. 'I was not expecting to uncover all the mysteries of your trade in one evening.' In fact, she had told me more than I thought she ever would. She might have tried to convince me of her powers, but she'd achieved the complete opposite. I was now certain there was some kind of trickery underneath; secrets that Katerina would, of course, not volunteer so casually. 'Now I can ask you these other questions with a little more confidence.'

'More questions? You should bring two bottles next time.'

I smiled. 'We had another message left by the alleged banshee: *Chase not the voices and the spells they write, For only death and blood your hand shall spread; One falls on the stage, maybe one tonight, If you hunt whispers that concern the dead.*'

'I heard of those. It may not have been in the newspapers, but the gossip travels fast.'

I produced my notebook and looked for the lines I'd jotted down whilst reading Stoker's journal.

'You also told McGray and this Irish gentleman that – at least one will die tomorrow, and there's nothing we can do about it . . . Now . . .' – I closed the notebook with a flap – 'I do not like the sound of those two omens together.'

'I don't like them either, but that's what I saw. You two won't win this time.'

I grunted and rubbed my face. 'Let's assume, just for argument's sake, that I believe you. Have your . . . visions been wrong in the past?'

'No. Well – yes. But not when the feeling is this strong.'

'Can you tell me anything, *anything*, no matter how trivial, that you might *think* you have foreseen?'

'Oh, yes. I can see you'll blame yourself if you fail. Don't. You're already doing your best.'

'*Who* is going to die?' I snapped, banging a fist on the table. 'Stop the cryptic games. Tell me!'

Madame Katerina smiled, but not the sardonic, horrible smirk she usually had for me. She understood my desperation, and the woman had enough grace not to mock me for it. She put her hands on the table and pushed herself up, then walked into the shadows and produced a little sprig of lavender, which she ignited with the candle's flame.

A trail of white smoke danced and spiralled as she moved the twig from left to right, her green eyes following it. She traced some fleeting figures in the air, and waited until the aromatic smoke had dissipated.

'Not an innocent one,' she whispered.

'Pardon?'

'You asked me who is going to die. I'm telling you: not an innocent one.'

I chuckled. 'That hardly narrows it down!'

Before I said more Katerina clasped my head, her nails pressing against my scalp and my forehead, and I felt a tingle, as if a cold draught had come from nowhere to chill my blood.

Her words came then, low and sombre, almost as if uttered by someone in the rooms below.

'All the pieces are set. Like a game of chess. Move your queen and your rooks and your knights, but it is all set: the ones you'll save . . . but also the ones you'll have to let go.'

41

The skies broke again as I rode back to New Town. I realized too late the sheer stupidity of venturing into the streets of Edinburgh without an umbrella. By the time I reached Great King Street I was soaked to the marrow, my clothes stuck to my back and the brim of my hat dripping copiously. Layton welcomed me with a towel and received my drenched overcoat, hat and gloves.

'Where is everybody else?' I asked, drying my hair vigorously.

'Mr Elgie and your good parents are dining out. They were invited to the Palace Hotel, where your eldest brother is staying. They asked me to inform you.'

I grunted. 'At least the weasels did not have the audacity to show up in my house . . .'

As it usually occurs in Scotland, the rain stopped as soon as I was properly settled at home.

I changed into sleeping clothes, and Layton poured me a glass of the good brandy, which he brought to my bedroom along with some biscuits. The old butler knew me very well already.

He left swiftly, but the house and streets were so silent I could hear his steps echoing across the staircase.

I thought I would welcome the solitude, but instead I found myself longing for some company, wishing I could pour someone a brandy, or offer them one of those excellent butter biscuits – or even Joan, chattering some useless gossip. My evenings would become this quiet as soon as Elgie left for London, so I'd better get used to my own company.

My spirits had plummeted since the incident with Mrs Harwood. I could not help feeling so terribly sorry for her, and even worse for her children. What a difficult, gloomy life awaited them. Frederick I could only call the true monster. I still shuddered at his words for Susy; I could not believe that so much poison could come from the mouth of such a youth.

And his poor sister . . . cast as a ghoul. My stomach went on fire thinking how Irving used Susy's scarred face to enhance the drama in his witches' scene. How little he must care what that would do to the girl's psyche, or to Mr Wheatstone – who had already been driven to alcoholism out of sheer guilt – having to see the girl every day, and even *helping* set the scene to make her appear more like a soul in purgatory.

All for the glory of Irving's *art*. Or rather his own glory. He used everyone around him, he played them all to his own benefit, and he did it with such mastery: even Superintendent Campbell had been made to forfeit his duty and was now reduced to a pathetic admirer. I also wondered if Miss Terry's affair with Irving – though now clearly over – had had anything to do with her first joining his theatre company.

The saddest case, however, was Bram Stoker. That portrait of Irving, which apparently he always carried in his journal, had shown me the true source of his loyalty, and I could not help feeling a particularly strong pang of sorrow for him. I remembered the scene at the hospital: the spark in Stoker's eyes when Irving showed the smallest drop of concern for him. Even through the laudanum – or perhaps enhanced by it – Stoker had shown his true feelings. Irving knew this, and he knew it too well. He fed Stoker with crumbs of appreciation; hardly any, but just enough to keep him within his grasp, like a hungry puppy longing for more. And he used that power like a leech, sucking all of Stoker's energy, both physically and emotionally.

I'd seen that happen before – to me. Eugenia Ferrars, the young woman with whom my father and brothers must be dining and cheering right now, had once treated me like that. The petite girl, blonde, fair and wide-eyed, needed but to stamp a foot and I'd move mountains for her; and I had been too blind to see it back then. Perhaps her ending our engagement had been a blessing in disguise. Not that something like that could happen to Stoker; as long as he was useful to the theatre, Irving would not let him go. A real shame, for Bram seemed bright, diligent and talented . . . but he devoted it all to somebody else.

I sighed and silently raised my glass for poor Bram, hoping he would someday manage to free himself from the shackles of Henry Irving.

I then thought of Ellen Terry. The woman seemed to have it all – comfort, a career she adored, talented children with promising futures, the love and admiration of her colleagues and the entire nation – yet she felt compelled to lurk in the darkness, like a pitiable street woman, when she thought an impossible lover messaged her. Stoker, indeed a smart fellow, had put it plainly: *How desperately we crave what we cannot have.*

What a collection of misery we all were, I thought. McGray and I too.

I raised my glass again, this time for all our trials and tribulations. It was depressing to think of us all, at once feeling so lost, so cut off and so alone; all of us terrified in our own ways. What a cruel, desolate place the world could be. I gave myself nightmares with those thoughts.

I dozed off in my chair, and suddenly found myself in one of the royal boxes at the Lyceum Theatre. I knew I was dreaming, but I was as frightened by what I saw as if I had been awake.

The theatre was empty, except for Irving's two sons and me – and the pit of the orchestra, which was full of dark demons playing only violins.

The shrilling notes rose, just as bright flames climbed high on the stage, burning the fake trees and the wooden castles and the velvet curtains. Henry Irving stood there, amidst the fire, not in Macbeth's attire, but swathed in his black cape, reciting lines from the play's final act.

And as he uttered *she should have died hereafter*, his skull cracked open like an eggshell, pierced from the inside by the glistening legs of a black scorpion. As the fissure grew wider more insects followed: hundreds, then thousands of creatures with iridescent shells, crawling and swarming across Irving's face and body and on to the stage floor, as the man continued, impassive, his dark soliloquy on the futility of life. 'Tomorrow . . .' he said, 'and tomorrow . . .

'And tomorrow . . .'

ACT V

LADY MACBETH

Come, thick night,
And pall thee in the dunnest smoke of hell,
That my keen knife see not the wound it makes,
Nor heaven peep through the blanket of the dark,
To cry 'Hold, hold!'

From The Scotsman, *13 July 1889*

A CALTON HILL MYSTERY

The neighbourhoods surrounding Calton Hill are just at present exercised with an event which seems to run on lines parallel to the mysterious hauntings around Henry Irving's production of *Macbeth*.

Yesterday night, under the midsummer full moon, several unconnected individuals concurrently reported the sight of what was referred to as a 'bloofer lady', wandering around the columns of the National Monument.

Depictions as to the looks of the lady are as varied as there are witnesses – our correspondent naively says that even Ellen Terry could not be so winningly attractive – but the general agreement is that the female was of singular height, slender waist and white attire, as if dressed in the cerements of the grave.

There is an even stronger agreement as to the ghostly figure's voice, for the most piercing, desolate wails were said to have been heard all across the east end of New Town, and as far as the outermost houses of Regent Terrace.

The lady was seen strolling across and in between the columns for a number of minutes, as if in deep distress. According to a keen observer, the lady never ceased to raise up her hands, tear her hair and beat her chest, until she finally stood at the northern edge of the monument, where her final agonized cry curdled the blood of countless residents. That sound rose even the heaviest of sleepers, and was said to be terrible enough to drive any man insane.

A pair of very brave tradesmen ventured to the top of Calton Hill, where they found no trace of the tormented lady.

The police of the division have been instructed to keep a sharp look. Whether this sighting is in any way connected to the portentous happenings reported three days past under the nearby Regent Bridge, it remains to be seen. Nevertheless, the mystery might well be clarified tonight, at the grand opening of the most lavish rendering of The Scottish Play the world has seen to date.

42

I tossed and turned in bed for hours, the snoring of my father in the adjacent room as annoying as a constant drip in a Chinese torture chamber.

It was a quarter past six when I peeped through the thick curtains, only to find the sun already high in the grey sky. My day, for all practical purposes, had begun. And a hellishly long one it would be.

I had a wholesome breakfast by myself. The rest of the Frey family would be either too tired or hungover from last night, and I thanked Providence for that. I could not have endured Catherine remarking on how pretty Eugenia looked, or how excellent Laurence's venison had been. It was bad enough that I might see the blasted couple tonight at the theatre.

Layton came by rather gingerly, clearing his throat so nervously I thought he'd expectorate something on to the carpet.

'Layton?' I said. 'What is it?'

He leaned over. 'Sir . . .' he said as if about to tread on red-hot coal. 'You might be interested in reading the paper.'

And he unrolled a copy of *The Scotsman* in front of me.

🐞

The monstrous Peruvian carving startled me again as I stormed into the cluttered office. I was so angry I kicked it aside, bringing down yet another tower of moth-eaten witchcraft books.

McGray was already there, which I was truly not expecting, given his apathetic looks last night.

I held the crumpled newspaper high. 'Have you seen this?'

'Seen it! McNair knocked at my door last night 'n' we went there to investigate.'

'*And?*' I felt a rush of anticipation. 'Was that another banshee apparition? Did she leave the last part of the sonnet? We are only missing four lines now.'

'That's what we first thought, but there was not a bloody, manky, buggin' trace o' blood. The grass around the National Monument was as clean and pristine as yer bed sheets.'

'What do you mean by –'

'However, we found these.' McGray was spreading a few half-charred pages on his desk. '*The Scotsman* doesnae say it, but the woman fled when a reckless young lad came close. She had a wee bonfire going on. When we arrived it was still burning. Looks like she was trying to get rid o' these. What ye see is all we could salvage, but there must've been much more; there was a big pile of ashes around.'

I perused the sheets swiftly. 'These are all undated and unsigned . . . Are you sure they are linked to the theatre at all?'

'Must be. This one mentions a dog . . .' McGray said, tapping the central sheet. 'How seeing a dog can foretell death.'

I picked it up and read it. 'Indeed, but . . .' My eyes combed the other texts. 'This prose makes little sense.

Necklaces made out of teeth . . . Coffins full of "lies" . . . And look at these scrawls, as if written by a mad pers–' I looked up instantly. 'Is Mrs Harwood –'

'Still at the asylum? Aye. I sent a laddie to check. As far as we can tell she was there all night. It's very unlikely she'd escape only to lock herself back.'

'If Mrs Harwood was accounted for . . .' I felt a twinge. 'Lord, could it have been Miss Terry, trying to get rid of her "Lewis Carroll" correspondence?'

'I thought o' that too, but this hand doesnae match his.'

'Could she have been communicating with someone else, and just using the Lewis Carroll story as an excuse – in case she was ever discovered?'

'Aye. That's a possibility. And that would explain why she wanted to burn them precisely now.'

I sat on my desk, looking at the headline for the hundredth time. 'I suppose the woman was not identified.'

'Nae. None of the witnesses saw her face. At least not close enough.'

I let out a tired sigh. 'And there is no way to prove it was Terry. If we confront her she will just deny everything.'

'Indeed.'

'I do not like this, Nine-Nails. Not at all . . . And the bloody play opens tonight!'

We remained in silence for a brief moment, but then there came a tapping from the stairs. I thought it would be Superintendent Campbell, coming to scold us for some ludicrous transgression, but I was wrong. The door opened and I saw Bram Stoker himself, looking as if he were on the verge of death: the poor man was supporting himself on crutches, his left leg wrapped in a heavy cast. His skin was dry and pale, he had bags under his eyes (which were almost as orange as his hair and beard), and as soon as he walked in he also brought a powerful waft of laudanum (which he probably needed to withstand the pains of the beating and the nasty fracture).

'Mr Stoker, I hope you are not overdosed again!' I said, wrinkling my nose.

'Why would you care?' he snapped. 'Do you want to question me against my will again?'

I cleared my throat. 'Without the laudanum you would have never told us you thought you'd seen Miss Terry after the ball – or after our midnight meeting at Calton Hill.'

'It transpired that it was Mrs Harwood after all, did it not?'

'That is still debatable,' I quickly said. 'And if you had not kept it quiet we could have questioned Miss Terry about it much sooner. Our line of investigation could have been completely different and God only knows what we might have already found –'

'There, there, Frey,' McGray intervened, 'yer sounding all screechy again. And Mr Stoker's clearly come to ask for some help. Haven't ye?'

He assented, rather nervously.

'I cannot understand Irving's attitude,' he finally admitted. 'He is adamant the play goes on as scheduled. I have never seen him this obsessed – and I've seen him at his lowest, *believe me*! It's as if his life depended on it.' He saw *The Scotsman* in my hands. 'And now that sighting makes me fear the worst.'

McGray sat back, his fingertips pressed together, the fourth finger on his left hand without a partner.

Since he said nothing, I sighed again. 'What do you want us to do, Mr Stoker? We were just discussing we have not solved much to speak of.'

'Be at the Lyceum tonight,' he asked most keenly. He looked at Nine-Nails. 'You know about these things – otherworldly things. You have followed this case since the beginning; you know us and what's going on at the theatre. If something were to happen, you two would know how to act better than anybody else.'

McGray leaned forward. 'In that yer right, laddie, but what if Campbell doesnae want us there?'

'Oh,' Stoker looked down, 'I know for fact he definitely doesn't want you around. But you'd be there as my guests and Mr Howard's. The police cannot ban anybody from our premises without a warrant.'

I grunted. 'Do you want us to defy the wishes of the head of police? As ridiculous as that man can be, I would not like to . . . Nine-Nails, why are you grinning like that?'

'This lad's very well versed in law. I like him.'

'Inspector McGray,' said Stoker, now rather gravely, 'I am already indebted to you. I wouldn't have been found so promptly had you not redoubled your efforts. Do us this favour and you will have my gratitude for ever.'

McGray nodded, a hint of enthusiasm glowing in his eyes. It was impressive what a good night's sleep had done for him. 'Say no more, laddie. But Percy here might be harder to convince.'

I immediately looked at the brighter side.

'As long as this keeps me away from the Freys' theatre box . . .'

43

Grindlay Street was all abuzz.

Undaunted by the unexpected drizzle and fog, enthusiastic pittites began to gather outside the Lyceum irrationally early. At about four o'clock the crowd was so large and the weather so bad, that Henry Irving arranged for hot tea to be sent out to warm the masses.

Later in the evening, a glittering assembly of personages descended from their carriages into the torch-lit portico, passing through the great doors to be greeted, as was customary, by the well-rehearsed charm of Bram Stoker. I do not know how he managed, but his countenance was completely different from that of the morning, and he welcomed people with such amiability some did not even notice the crutches under his arms. Mr Howard stood by his side, albeit looking dwarfed and monochromatic next to the tall, grinning, ginger Irishman.

Edinburgh's most notable audience had gathered that night. The cream of the social, artistic and literary classes were all there. Again I saw the Lord Provost, and even Lady Glass herself, the white plumes of her hat rising up well above the average head. Fortunately I managed to avoid her gaze.

They all claimed to be there for the play; swore they adored their Shakespearean tragedies, and unanimously and most condescendingly dismissed the morbid, baseless scandal that had brought all those smelly bourgeois to the theatre. Stoker told me he knew better.

The press, of course, was out in unusual force, and not only for the Scottish papers. Stoker told me he recognized reporters from the *Herald*, *The Times* and the *Tribune*, all come up from London, surely, to report the accuracy of the banshee's prophecy. They would all be wiring reports of the performance, whether the spirits appeared or not. Until that moment I had not quite appreciated how precious, how potent, a supernatural scandal could be.

All the security had been discussed the previous night at Campbell's dinner table, over that bottle of fine Merlot, sadly wasted on the man's rough and vulgar taste buds. No one but him and Irving had been heard or even consulted on the matter of safety, and it showed: there was a good number of officers (McNair amongst them) guarding both sides of the entrance and several key points of the vestibule and the auditorium. Instead of uniforms they were all wearing medieval soldiers' costumes and fake beards, and some of them sported smug faces, fancying themselves Cids or Lancelots

Looking less than comfortable was Nine-Nails, who'd been forced not only to shave again, but also to wear another suit from Stoker's wardrobe. I found him standing awkwardly in a corner of the crowded vestibule, pulling at his collar as if it were made of poison ivy. A trio of young ladies were staring lasciviously at him, but were utterly disenchanted as soon as he spoke.

'Once wearing this dandy shite was bad enough. Twice is a bloody bad joke!'

'At least you are not wearing orange facial hair,' I

whispered, looking at the poor McNair. 'I cannot believe that this city's police is commanded by a dim-witted buffoon who can be smitten with a glass of liquor and a box at the theatre.'

'Och, it's as if ye called the bastard,' said McGray, pointing at the entrance, at a sight I would have never expected to behold: Superintendent Campbell's *wife*. She was a chubby, rubicund lady of around fifty, with a hairstyle and a sour expression that both very much reminded me of Queen Victoria's.

'Let's get in,' McGray mumbled. 'The longer it takes him to see us the better.'

I welcomed the suggestion, as right then I also saw the wide figure of the old Mr Frey, and recognized the receding hairline of my brother Laurence sticking out above the crowd. Next to him there was a bunch of pink feathers; surely the flamboyant hat worn by Eugenia, although the people around her blocked my view of her face.

We rushed into the auditorium, where the bustling spectators were taking their places in the half light. The place made me think of an enormous mine, its darkened walls encrusted with glittering gems from the magnificent chandelier, and also from the raised boxes and galleries, where the beautifully dressed and bejewelled ladies could see and be seen.

I looked around and my attention fell on the royal box, raised and right next to the proscenium's gilded frame. There, looking utterly put out, sat Irving's sons, Harry and Sydney. There was an empty seat next to them, and the next place was occupied by the pudgy Oscar Wilde. Harry's eyes met mine, and the boy started and looked away.

'All normal,' said McGray, with an unashamed note of

exhaustion. Except for a brief pause to shave and change clothes, he had been around the theatre almost all day, along with a few other officers. They'd patrolled every corridor and entrance, along with the back and the understage. Nothing suspicious had occurred as yet.

'So it seems,' I answered, spanning one last look. I saw that under the red velvet curtains the orchestra were tuning their instruments. 'Give me a second,' I told McGray, making my way to the pit. I waved at Elgie, who frowned as soon as he saw me. He was angry at me (apparently everyone knew we'd attempted to have the play cancelled), but he came to greet me nonetheless.

'Nervous?' I asked. He only shrugged, so I patted him on the shoulder. 'You will be fantastic, I am sure.'

'Ian,' he said just as I had turned away. 'Look after yourself,' he mumbled, and I managed to smile at him.

McGray was clicking his tongue. 'What a lovely scene. Let's get to work now.'

The orchestra burst forth with a powerful chord, so loud and so sudden it made me jump, even though McGray and I were descending the creaking stairs that led to the understage, and the sound was muffled. Three stabbing chords, and then the dark, foreboding melody I'd heard at the rehearsals.

The understage was boiling hot, and no wonder, for the initial scene with the witches required a lot of fog. In Mr Wheatstone's absence, the man in charge was the foul-smelling cockney chap I'd seen assisting him during rehearsals. He looked far from comfortable in the role: his face was contorted in a panicked grimace that would last throughout the play, and he stank mightily of perspiration, which dripped on to everything as he jumped to and fro.

There were piles of lycopodium powder all around him, and he jumped over them to reach the crank of the rheostat. He turned it with one hand, slowly increasing the light on the stage; with his other hand he poured water on to an enormous bucket of red-hot coals. The embers sizzled as rolling clouds of steam ascended towards the actors.

He was not the only one having a bad time. The three witches stood by the wooden steps that led to the proscenium, and it astounded me that they looked less ugly with their frayed rags and their facial prostheses than they did in their evening dresses. The music was raging out there, but instead of going ahead to begin their act, they faltered.

'What's going on?' McGray asked, and I then noticed that Miss Ivor was amongst them, attired as another witch. *Not* as her usual character, Hecate.

'We can't find Miss Desborough!' she cried.

'What do you mean?'

Miss Marriott, the first witch, stepped forward. 'She came with us from the hotel. We shared a cab. But now we can't find her.'

'I'll have to take her place,' said Miss Ivor.

'Isn't Desborough the one who kept that wee gun under her pillow?' McGray asked, and I nodded.

Stoker came by just then, along with Mr Howard, whom he used as a human crutch.

'I just heard! Have you found her?'

'No, Mr Stoker,' replied Miss Ivor. 'But I'm ready. Shall we go up?'

Irving, in full medieval attire, arrived just as the woman said this. There was panic in his eyes. 'What are you waiting for? *Get out there!* You're already ten bars late!'

The ladies ran up the steps, tripping on their rags, and in no time I heard Miss Marriott quickly recite '*When shall we three meet again?*', trying to get back in synchrony with the music.

'What will we do if she doesn't appear before the fourth act?' Stoker asked, sweat trickling down his temples. 'Miss Ivor has to play Hecate then, in front of the three wi—'

'*I know the damn play, Bram!*' Irving hollered, exactly as a deafening thunder resounded above the stage. 'If it comes to the worst we'll have to do with two witches. Now you better try to find that old crow!'

So engrossed was Irving, he did not even notice McGray and me. He stormed away swiftly, for it was barely minutes before his first appearance.

Stoker stumbled, as if he'd forgotten his injury and wanted to sprint forward. Mr Howard's face now looked blue under the Irishman's weight, and McGray had to help support him.

'Is Miss Desborough the one with Irish blood?'

Stoker went white for an instant, but he soon breathed out. 'No, no. That is Miss Seaman.'

'Good,' McGray assented. 'Were the witches the last to see her?'

'I believe so,' said Stoker. 'I know no more than you.'

'All right, ye stay here and wait for the hags to get their hurly burly done and make them tell ye all they can. In the meantime we'll get our chaps searching; I don't like that auld hag disappearing just now. Frey, go tell the men in

395

the front doors and the hall. I'll organize the ones backstage.'

I nodded and ran back towards the auditorium. The quickest way was through the orchestra pit (where Elgie cast me a puzzled look), and then through the crowded lower seats.

The witches, I heard, were just telling Macbeth their damning prophecies.

As I trotted across the rows of people, now in almost complete darkness, I felt dwarfed by the task. There were more than nine hundred spectators, dozens of actors and just as many theatre staff, all gathered in a labyrinthine building of colossal proportions. We would never find the woman.

Katerina's words, written down by Stoker, appeared in my head: '*At least <u>one</u> will die on the thirteenth, my son. There's nothing you can do about it.*'

The light, already scarce, became dimmer and dimmer. I turned to the stage and caught a last glimpse of the Weird Sisters as they seemed to vanish into a cloud of mist.

Irving and his Banquo were about to speak, but their voices would be overpowered.

My heart went cold as everyone at the theatre heard the otherworldly sound we had feared all along.

The banshee's final cry.

44

That was the sound of terror itself.

I instinctively stooped and covered my ears, finally believing the statements of all the people I'd mocked. It was a drilling, shrilling sound; a hysterical voice that stabbed at the body as it did the soul.

Panic took hold of the entire building, and anguished screams from the audience joined the already unbearable shriek. The lights went on and Irving pleaded for people to stay in their seats. His deep, commanding voice at least had some effect on me. I had to focus.

It is not omnipresent, I told myself. The voice had a source. And I must find it.

Painful as it was, I forced myself to uncover my ears, squinting at the horrible sound, and just as I did so the voice faded away, as if the banshee's lungs had run out of air. I'd had only a split second to work out where it came from, but it had been enough: it had come from behind my back, from the front area of the theatre.

I dashed in that direction, whilst Irving laughed nervously on the stage, raising both arms.

'My dearest friends, I hope our little joke has not scared you out of your wits!'

'Preposterous!' I grunted, but let him work his charm. A panicked mob was the last thing we needed.

I crashed against someone, nearly knocking the man over, and recognized the voice of Sergeant Millar.

'Inspector, I think I saw her!'

'Where?'

'At the rotunda, sir. And she left another message.'

Millar guided me there, an overwhelming feeling of déjà vu taking hold of me. My heart pounded as we arrived: the polished marble floor was the perfect frame for a smear of thick blood, the horrendous red letters standing out like an open wound on magnolia skin. As McGray had predicted, this was the final part of the sonnet:

> *The dead that travel fast, the opening door,*
> *The silent room, the heavy creeping shade,*
> *The murdered idol rising through the floor,*
> *The ghost's white fingers on thy shoulders laid,*
>
> *All hail! These tragic marks await Macbeth*
> *All hail! The Scottish stage shall see your death*

I was speechless. Never had any words made me feel so cold, so confused. All I could think of doing was to kneel down, touch the viscous liquid where it spelled *death*, and put it to my tongue.

Again, it was genuine blood.

'They repeated the final couplet,' I mumbled, my mind an uncontrollable swirl. 'As if to confirm the order of things . . .'

Young Millar said nothing, but he was almost panting with fear.

'Let no one come here,' I said gravely. 'And bring Inspector McGray, right away.'

'Aye, sir.'

A very tall man in a black suit came by. I had to blink to recognize him as Nine-Nails.

'Fuck!'

'Indeed.'

'Is there a trail?' he asked, trotting around and looking in all directions. There was none; not even a little red spot to tell us where the banshee had gone to or come from, and on the marble floor it would have been impossible to miss.

'Somebody must have seen something!' I spat. 'This is the main bloody entrance!'

'Everyone's watching the play,' said McGray, 'our lads are searching for Desborough everywhere and all the crew are backstage . . . Makes sense – this spot was deserted.' He came back to the sonnet and saw my stained fingertip. 'Real?'

'Yes.'

He read it intently, his eyes scanning each and every letter. 'That makes nae sense!'

'The murdered idol,' I mumbled. 'It will be an actor . . . or actress.'

McGray was frowning. 'The whole stanza feels wrong . . . as if written by someone else.'

'What do you mean?'

'The style is different. The others had a narrative or gave a clear warning . . . This one's vague, almost amateurish; loose sentences only tenuously connected . . . Yet the rhymes are still perfect.' He knelt and hovered his fingers over the third and fourth lines. 'Rising through the floor . . . The ghost's white fingers . . . That has to mean something.'

The doors to the auditorium opened abruptly and we heard the echoes of Irving's voice, who'd successfully resumed the play. I was expecting a swarm of attendees to come out, but was relieved to see it was only Bram Stoker and Mr Howard.

'Oh, God!' both Irishmen said in synchrony.

'We need to clean this up before the interval,' Mr Howard whispered, covering his mouth and suppressing a retch.

My attention, however, was entirely on Stoker. He looked white again, whiter than he'd been that morning, and perhaps whiter than he'd been when McGray had found him unconscious on the street.

'What is it?' McGray asked him.

Stoker shook his head, as if refusing to let the words sink in.

'*What?*' McGray urged.

'I know the sonnet that's taken from,' he mumbled. 'I read it not too long ago . . .'

'What d'ye mean, ye read it?'

Stoker's voice had gone dreamy, and when he exhaled I perceived a slight hint of laudanum.

'Mr Stoker, I hope you are not intoxi–'

'It was written for Irving,' he let out, his eyes back to reality all of a sudden.

'For Irving!' I cried. 'By whom?'

Stoker looked at the lines again, perhaps still begging for this not to be true. When he looked up, however, there was not a shadow of doubt.

'Oscar Wilde.'

We burst into the royal box, McGray tossing the curtains aside so violently they almost came off their hoops.

The cries of Mr Wilde and the two Irving boys were

overwhelmed by a booming ovation, for Miss Terry had just appeared on the stage for the first time, holding Macbeth's letter and displaying her iridescent beetle dress in all its glory. The box was so close she must have seen us, but managed to conceal any hint of recognition.

As she recited 'they have more in them than mortal knowledge', Mr Wilde stood up to confront us. His velvet-lined chair fell backwards and his tall, wide frame nearly lost balance. Had Harry not grabbed his jacket, Wilde would have fallen into the central pit.

'What in heaven is this? I *demand* that you –'

McGray grabbed him by the collar as he'd done before and dragged him to the corridor, where we could question him a little less publicly. The Irving boys followed closely.

'Leave him alone!' cried Sydney. 'We'll call the police!'

McGray slapped him in the back of the head. 'We *are* the police, ye silly sod!' He turned back to Wilde and showed him the piece of paper where I'd hastily copied the sonnet. 'Did ye write this?'

Mr Wilde was perspiring. He held the note with his white gloves and took a strand of bushy dark hair from his face, as his eyes flickered on the paper at unthinkable speed.

'Why, I did, my good Scot. But I fail to see how this would –'

'I truly doubt he was involved,' I said, looking at his snow-white gloves and the sheer incomprehension in his eyes.

'Involved in what?' Wilde asked, and then his eyes opened wide. 'Oh! Was that dreadful cry not part of the –'

'Did ye write this?' McGray jumped in, closing his fist around the crumpling paper.

Mr Wilde stammered. 'Well . . . yes. Yes, I did, but –'

'No wonder I thought it was shite! Why did ye write it?'

'Well, it was all but a little frolic between friends. I did a full sonnet: "With the shrill fool to mock him, Romeo – For thee should lure his love –"'

'Och, save it! Nae need to recite yer excretions to me. When was this?'

'Oh, dear, it was a good few years ago – for a private party. Only a handful of people kept a copy.'

'Och! Finally! That's what we needed to hear. Who were they?'

'My goodness, I cannot possibly recall so suddenly –' McGray raised his fist and hovered it an inch from Wilde's face. 'Irving, of course! And good Bram asked me to copy it for him too . . . And Miss Terry, who commissioned me to write it in the first place . . . and . . .' He rolled his eyes, desperately trying to remember.

McGray was terribly close to punching him so I had to step in. 'Did you say Miss Terry commissioned it?'

'Indeed, as a present for Irving, and she was highly delighted by it. Although . . .' Wilde tilted his head, his eyes going slowly from side to side. 'Now that I remember . . . it is based on a sonnet I originally wrote for *her*. She later asked me to rewrite it and dedicate it to Irving! May I see it again?' McGray gave him the paper and Wilde smoothed it out. 'Oh, yes, I remember, these last two were the only lines I did not change. They were identical in my original for dear Ellen . . .'

McGray at last let go of him. 'Miss Terry's dad was Irish, right?'

Harry Irving sniggered. 'Yes. The wench has a lot of Irish in her.'

I looked into McGray's eyes, and he returned the most flabbergasted gaze.

'It's her!' he hissed. 'Miss Terry. The sonnet ends with lines dedicated to her!'

'You're right!' I said, and we instantly dashed down the narrow stairs.

We found Irving in one of the stage wings, chatting with Campbell as joyfully as if they were at a garden party. Obviously, permission to nose around the backstage was part of Campbell's bargained perks.

'It's Ellen Terry!' Nine-Nails blurted out, panting. From there we could see the back of the actress, still delivering her murderous speech.

'What are you talking about?' Irving cried. Campbell looked more embarrassed than alarmed.

'The banshee cry you just dismissed as part of your act,' I said, 'was in fact the very thing we have been chasing.' I looked at Campbell, showing him the sheet. 'These words appeared in the rotunda, written in blood. This couplet is from a sonnet that Oscar Wilde originally dedicated to Miss Terry. We now think that the omens might have been about her from the very start.'

'Give me that,' Irving demanded, snatching the paper. 'Well, this proves nothing!'

'Are ye willing to stake her life on that?' McGray asked.

Irving's mouth twisted in a cruel smile, which made me feel a prickling on the back of my neck. He said nothing, but simply turned on his heel and walked on to the stage, where Miss Terry received him with a deep reverence and exclaiming, 'Great Glamis! Worthy Cawdor!'

'How can you let this go on?' I cried out, but Campbell would not be intimidated.

'You two are *not* supposed to be here! Get out right now!'

'Sod off!' McGray retorted, about to step on to the stage and end it all.

'*Stop right there, Nine-Nails!*' Campbell wielded his walking cane, his eyes bloodshot. 'Keep off that bloody stage or I'll have you both incarcerated! In fact, I shall order all the officers out of the building right away.'

I planted myself in front of him. 'You will do no such thing.'

He stared at me in utter puzzlement. 'What – what did you say?'

'You will do no such thing, Campbell! A murder is about to be committed! Someone is going to die. *Die!* Are you familiar with the term? That is what happens when the thumping in your chest stops for ever. Is it so difficult for that mouldy slime inside your head to comprehend it?'

There was an instant of silence. I caught a glimpse of McGray's mouth, open as a perfect O.

Campbell's chest swelled. '*How dare you talk to me like that, Frey?* This will be the end of your career in –'

'*Oh I am so sick of your threats!*' I let out. 'Your hogbeast of a wife has more allure than my poxy, dead-end post in your rotten force.' I looked at Nine-Nails. 'No offence.'

'None taken.'

'But someone is going to die, you stubborn dimwit. We know it. And I shall do everything I can to avoid it!'

'Let me through!' Campbell tried to walk round me but I blocked his way. '*Let me through, you –*'

He made to hit me with his cane, but I snatched it from

his clammy hand and tossed it aside. I felt exhilarated. 'Why, if I'd known it would be so easy I would have voiced my opinion of you a good while ago!'

'*Get out of my way, Frey!* Or I shall impale you, roast you in a pit and eat you for my dinner!'

I chuckled. 'Then you'd have more brains in your belly than you do in your head.'

Campbell was so flushed with fury we could have fried an egg on his face. 'McGray, get this foppish English flower out of my way!'

His command was so deliciously laughable I nearly felt sorry for him.

Nine-Nails looked sideways, pretended to dust his lapel in Oscar Wilde's nonchalant fashion, and cleared his throat.

'Erm . . . Nae.'

'*I'm giving you a direct order!* Do as I say or I'll see that your murderous slut of a sister —'

But I never knew what he had in store for her, for Nine-Nails punched him with uncontained wrath right in the centre of the face. As if time itself stretched, I saw Campbell's nose burst as the man fell on his back, thrown by the blow like a child's rag doll.

I looked at Nine-Nails, utterly staggered.

'*What?*' he asked with mocking innocence.

'What do you mean, *what?* You have just assaulted the head of the Edinburgh police force! – *Again!*'

'And? Did ye want to do it yerself this time?'

'Indeed I did!'

45

'What now?' I was saying as we strode away from Campbell's writing body. 'The complete sonnet seems to –'

'Frey, hold yer horses. I'm happy to go on, but ye just heard Campbell. He'll try to send us to jail. I ken yer soft ways and I'd hate to see ye surrounded by angry convicts.'

'Let us cross that bridge when we reach it. Right now I am rather worried about Miss Terry.'

'Aye. The final part o' the sonnet pointing at her – and the last loose ends we've not managed to tie also have to do with her. The messenger definitely; the burned letters probably.'

'Shall we confront her about those?'

'Aye, but first let's see if we can find out a wee bit more about the bastard messenger who attacked Stoker.'

'Stoker does not remember –'

'I ken, but we can call that whimsy brat Freddie and see if we can get anything else from him.'

Stoker had been told about Campbell's threat to us, so he suggested we waited in Mr Howard's office. Given the state of his leg, he stayed with us while the theatre manager fetched Freddie. McGray helped Stoker into one of the leather armchairs, the Irishman's face distorted with pain.

'Could you pass me some water, please?' he pleaded, pointing at a carafe on Mr Howard's desk.

I poured him a glass. As soon as I put it in his hand Stoker produced an amber bottle and added a few drops of laudanum.

'That is highly addictive,' I warned him. 'You should stop taking it so liberally.'

He nodded. 'I will, Inspector. After tonight, I promise you.'

He slurped rather anxiously, his eyes shut hard, and I could only hope he would keep to his word.

A few minutes later Freddie Harwood stormed in, strutting like a small Irving. 'You do this quickly! I need to get ready for my next scene! And the horse –'

He stopped mid-sentence, all arrogance gone from his face, his mouth open.

'What is it, Freddie?' asked Stoker, leaning forwards.

Freddie pointed at him, his wide blue eyes suddenly alarmed. 'That's it! That is the smell!'

'What smell?' asked Mr Howard, utterly puzzled.

'The man who you saw coming out of Miss Terry's room?' I asked. 'Are you certain?'

Freddie assented, sniffing the air. 'Yes, it has to be!'

Impatiently, McGray snatched Stoker's glass and put it in front of Freddie's nose. 'So this is what he smelled like, laddie? If yer telling us lies, I'll –'

Freddie was sniffing at the water, wrinkling his nose, his face distorted. 'No, no! I swear! This is it! The chemical smell!'

The boy's words, for the first time, came out so truthfully we could not doubt him.

All our heads, in unison, turned to Stoker.

'Ye didnae tell us if ye smelled the man who attacked ye,' Nine-Nails said at once.

I looked at my notes. 'Indeed, he did not. Even though we asked him that very specific question . . .'

Now it was Stoker's mouth that had opened wide. His face moved spasmodically from the little amber bottle, then to the glass, then to McGray and me.

'I was overdosed with laudanum when you asked that!'

I raised an eyebrow. 'The doctor who attended you said the first dose did not work on your pain at all. That could have been because of your size – or because you have developed resistance to opiates. Through overuse.'

'This –' he mumbled, 't-this is clearly a misunderstanding! I had not taken laudanum in years! Not since my bedridden times as a child!'

'That's the smell,' Freddie said again, all his conceit back.

'Was it Mr Stoker you saw?' I asked. 'I understand you have known him for years. Would you have not recognized him?'

'I only caught a glimpse,' said Freddie, 'and he could have been in disguise.'

Stoker was livid. 'How dare you accuse me of that, you little scoundrel? After all we've done for your family!'

'But I don't know what he could be doing in Miss Terry's room,' Freddie added. 'We can tell he doesn't really like her.'

Stoker pushed himself up, but then growled and fell back on the chair, clasping his broken leg with both hands. He could have torn the boy apart otherwise.

'Get out, laddie,' McGray commanded, and he did not wait for a reply; Nine-Nails simply pulled him by the arm, tossed him out and shut the door. 'Now, Bram,' he said, 'tell us more about yer laudanum.'

'You can't possibly believe it was me! Miss Terry would have told you so!'

'Well,' I said, 'you tried to protect Miss Terry, out of consideration to Irving. Could Miss Terry be doing the same for you?'

'Or,' McGray prompted, 'could youse *both* be partners in crime? Miss Terry bringing the brains in her purse and ye helping keep the affair quiet? Youse two leaving the ball at around the same time for some dubious purpose?'

'You're talking nonsense!' Stoker cried. 'I brought the case to you! Why would I –'

'I might have mentioned it a hundred times now,' I said. 'Ticket sales!'

Stoker stammered for a moment, but then there was a frantic knocking at the door.

Mr Howard rushed to open it and we saw McNair, drenched in sweat and the fake ginger beard about to fall off.

'Inspectors!' he panted. 'We have found Miss Desborough.'

McNair stood aside as the Second Witch was brought in by two other officers, barely conscious. The poor lady had half her head covered in blood, which had also stained her neck and her extravagant yellow dress.

'Dear Lord!' cried Stoker, again trying and failing to stand.

McGray pulled the other armchair over and the men carefully deposited the frail woman in it. Thankfully the laudanum was at hand; McGray still held Stoker's glass, and he delicately fed Miss Desborough a couple of small sips.

'Ellen Terry's still on the stage?' he asked whilst still bent over the woman.

'Aye, sir. They just killed the auld king.'

'Good. I want some o' the chaps looking after her. Someone follow her 'n' someone should guard her dressing room too.'

McNair bit his upper lip. 'Sir, Superintendent Campbell told us to ignore anything either of youse said – Then again . . . if the order came from Mr Howard . . .'

The theatre manager took the hint. 'Of course. Do as the inspectors say.'

'And somebody arrange a transport to take this woman to the hospital,' I said.

The officers left us and again Mr Howard shut the door. I looked back at Miss Desborough and gasped when I saw there was now a stain of blood on her chest. For an instant I thought she'd been stabbed, but as I looked down I understood.

I whispered, 'Her hands are stained with blood . . .' thinking that, ironically, at that precise moment Ellen Terry would be washing fake blood off Irving's hands.

'Shite!' cried McGray, thinking what I was thinking: could she have done the writing and then faked her injury?

I gently tilted her head to have a better view at the splatter of blood. Her grey hair was caked with half coagulated bleeding; there was a genuine wound there.

'Someone gave her a powerful blow,' I said. She could not have done that writing after being stricken like this.'

'Nae,' said McGray, 'but she could have *before*.'

Miss Desborough moaned, stretching her bony hand for the laudanum. She had another sip, her face wrinkling like an old prune at the medicinal taste. She was conscious enough to understand she had become a suspect, disappearing at the worst of times, but she was still too stunned and we had to extract the truth from her drop by drop.

I leaned closer and spoke softly. 'Miss Desborough, are you able to assent or shake your head at my questions?' She nodded. 'Good. Did you write anything at the rotunda?' She did a vehement shake, her head turning violently from one side to the other. 'Very well, so this is your own blood on your hands, I suppose.' She nodded again, a solitary tear rolling down her creased cheek. 'You were attacked, were you not?'

She drew air in and moaned, and after a moment managed to speak again. 'Yes! They hit me! *Hit me!*'

'They! So more than one? Did ye see their faces?' asked McGray

Miss Desborough looked up, breathing heavily and drawing a hand to her wounded head.

'Two of them. One taller . . . but too dark . . .'

'Where was this?' I asked her.

We had to give her another helping of medicine.

'Back gate. Went back . . . left my purse in the cab . . . wanted to see if the driver was still there. As soon as I opened the gate there they were, and they hit me and left me there on the floor!'

She leaned forward and we had to push her gently back on the chair.

'Did any of them smell of this?' I asked, looking at the glass of laudanum.

'I don't know, sir. It was all too quick. But . . . I saw a dog . . .'

We all seemed to lean towards her.

'Big, black animal?' McGray asked, and Miss Desborough assented. I could tell we were straining her a little too much.

'Try to rest,' I whispered to the lady. 'Someone will take you to the hospital shortly.'

She hinted at a smile, then rested her head on the back of the chair and closed her eyes.

'Any thoughts, Percy?' Nine-Nails asked me.

I went through the facts, trying to order them in my own head. 'Miss Desborough is attacked by two people who were perhaps trying to enter the building. Her coming out would have given them that chance. And that blow on her temple seems too strong to be the work of another woman. Then there was the banshee cry . . .' I raised an eyebrow, things slowly fitting together. 'The malodorous messenger, the black hound and the banshee are all together in this, I would say. In which case there would be no doubt now that –'

'That they've been messing with Miss Terry,' McGray jumped in. 'If yer musings are right they're definitely after her.'

'Which means we have a potential murderer in the theatre as we speak, hidden amongst hundreds of other people . . . and we do not even know what the man looks like! Still the only clue we have is that the man stinks of laudanum – so possibly someone addicted to the stuff.'

'*Oh! Oh!*' cried Miss Desborough, and I thought she was about to have a fit. She was again leaning forward, her jaundiced eyes so wide I feared they'd roll out on to the floor, and her hands once more stretched up. She'd never looked more like a witch about to throw a curse.

'I know someone! I know someone addicted to laudanum!'

'Well . . . I used to know,' she groaned a minute later, when she saw us all surrounding her chair.

'Who was that?' I asked. 'Anything you can tell us.'

Miss Desborough bit her lips, suddenly looking unsure. 'I heard the story . . . Backstage gossip, you know, of this man who used to work with Irving – many years ago. Before Mr Stoker's time.'

'Well, that's no use!' said Stoker, but McGray raised a hand.

'Nae, nae, let her talk.'

'An actor, of course,' said Miss Desborough. 'The man broke his hip after Irving pushed him from the stage in a tantrum,' the woman suddenly bit her knuckles. 'Confound it, I cannot remember his name!'

There was a general uproar of frustration, but I did not join in. I felt a rush of excitement as I looked in my notebook. 'Dear Lord, I think I have heard of that! Somebody mentioned it . . .' I passed the pages so eagerly I tore a few sheets, my eyes scanning the notes as quickly as I could. Suddenly each second felt like an eternity, my mind too slow to get through all the useless entries.

'Told ye, ye take too many notes,' McGray said, which did not help my focus.

'The story does sound familiar,' Stoker mumbled, but looking sideways, and with a dark, fearful tone.

My heart skipped a beat when I found the entry.

413

'Here it is!' I cried. 'I had it from Mr Wheatstone; he was talking about Irving's temper . . . He mentioned one man . . .' I looked up, fervently pointing at the lines, 'who broke his hip and developed an addiction; his career ruined!'

'D'ye have the name?' McGray urged.

'Yes. John Tarvin.'

Bram Stoker instantly covered his mouth.

'Ye ken the lad!' Nine-Nails cried.

'Well, I never met him,' he said, rather defensively. 'Miss Terry never met him either. He worked with Irving in his early years, in the Theatre Royal in Manchester. The accident happened when they were rehearsing *Hamlet* – if I remember correctly.'

I smirked. 'Is there anything else you might risk to remember correctly?'

Stoker tensed his lips, glaring at me, but he did speak. 'Mr Tarvin played Horatio, and from what I've heard showed real promise – although Irving says he was utterly hopeless at remembering lines, and *Hamlet* is Shakespeare's longest play. It *must* have been frustrating to work with him.'

Mr Howard raised his chin then. 'That was in the sixties, wasn't it, Mr Stoker? It must have been the first time Irving played Hamlet?'

'Yes,' Stoker mumbled.

Mr Howard's face was now illuminated. 'I think I remember that play. They brought it on tour to the Theatre Royal here in Edinburgh. I used to work there at the time – this theatre hadn't even been built back then. I remember it particularly well because that was the first time I saw Irving on stage.'

McGray chuckled, all bitterness. 'I doubt ye remember someone in a play ye saw more than twenty years ago.'

'Well, no, but . . .' he then grinned. 'Why, I might have a photograph from that production!'

Mr Howard dived into his files and soon produced a photograph album. I recognized it instantly: that was the album he'd been leafing through when I'd first met him. He opened it on his desk and passed through the black cardboard pages as quickly as his stumpy fingers allowed.

'There!' he exclaimed, pointing at a very old, slightly faded photograph of *Hamlet*'s entire cast. It was dated 1864.

At last we would have a first glimpse at the face of the man we were chasing.

46

Irving stood proudly in the centre, holding the play's emblematic skull. Quite strangely though, like in Stoker's picture, his face did not look much younger, as if his sharp cheekbones and deep brow were immune to the passage of time – as if he'd been a middle-aged man all his life.

'Which one's Horatio?' McGray asked.

'Must be this one,' said Mr Howard, pointing at a young man standing behind Irving, sporting a plumed hat, like in that famous lithograph by Eugène Delacroix.

The man had the haughtiest expression imaginable, his mouth turned upside-down, his eyelids half shut and his eyebrows raised. Even Irving looked humble by his side.

'Is this yer messenger?' McGray asked Stoker, showing him the album.

'*My messenger!*' Stoker cried. 'I've never seen that rascal in my life!'

McGray snorted. 'Well, even if yer lying, I have nae time to beat it out o' ye. Mr Howard, I hope ye don't mind,' and he tore the photo from the album, half the page coming with it. He looked at me. 'Frey, let's go. We have to find this man.'

Stoker protested, but McGray pointed at him with exasperation. 'Don't ye move from here! Yer not completely cleared yet!'

And we left Mr Howard's office without glancing back.

Just as we walked out a couple of theatre clerks came in to take Miss Desborough to the hospital.

'Miss Terry will be able to confirm if that Tarvin man was her messenger,' I said as we made our way to the auditorium.

'Aye, but I feel we're just glimpsing the surface of it . . .'

We met a couple of officers, showed them the photo and asked them to detain any man who looked like that, only twenty years older. I even sighed as I gave the instruction, realizing how ambitious our quest truly was.

McGray found his way across the theatre very easily. In no time we were at the stage wing that led to the dressing rooms. Two horses were being held by stage assistants, as the brawny men who played Macbeth's assassins stepped on to the stage.

Freddie was there too. This was the scene where he fled, right after Banquo's brutal murder.

'Did Mr Stoker confess?' he asked with scorn.

'Sod off!' McGray spat.

Behind the painted scenery people were frantically laying Macbeth's large banquet table. Meat joints of papier-mâché, piles of wax fruit, as well as empty jugs and goblets were being flung into place with extraordinary precision. Torches were being lit in the background to complete the medieval feel.

There was no need to walk to the dressing rooms: Miss Terry appeared in front of us, and what a vision she was! She had now changed into her queenly dress, the one I'd seen before: white material embellished with pearls and silver threads, and on her back a thick, heavy cape embroidered in intricate Celtic knots. With a gleaming crown on her head, bejewelled with more pearls and fine coral, she looked the perfect Queen of Scotland. Even I found her beautiful then, but she was not in a pleasant mood.

'Could you please tell your men to get out of my way?' she barked at us, for there were two officers virtually stepping on her toes. 'I'm trying to do my work!'

McGray only held the photograph before her eyes.

'Is this the man?' he asked, no need of further explanation.

Terry's cheeks were suddenly blanched with fear. She recognized the face immediately; McGray did not even need to point.

'He is not so young any more,' she whispered, drawing a trembling hand to her chest. Then her eyes fell on Irving's image. 'Not many people age as well as Henry, I suppose . . .' and she shuddered from head to toe.

'*We told you to get out of here!*' Henry Irving cried, timing his voice with the neighing of the trained horses and the fearful cries of the audience, now watching Banquo getting slaughtered.

Irving too was in full kingly attire, wearing the wooden crown Miss Terry had used to pose for Mr Sargent.

'We think this man has been sending those spurious messages to Miss Terry,' I said at once. 'And we now know that you broke his hip years ago.'

Irving could not have looked more astounded. He, the great actor, could not disguise his shock or emit a sound.

'John Tarvin,' McGray added. 'Sounds familiar?'

Irving looked at the picture, then at Terry. She was just as speechless, and could only give him an affrighted nod.

That was clearly not the reaction of someone plotting for ticket sales. Terry was aghast, as if seeing the bundle of blood-dripping brains again.

'So those omens . . .' Irving muttered.

'It's Miss Terry we fear is in danger,' said Nine-Nails. 'Like we told ye before.'

I have no words to describe the desolation, the sheer dread in both faces. All the crew around us had heard McGray's sentence. We'd brought the entire backstage to a standstill.

The floorboards under our feet trembled with the horses' hooves, the scene behind the immense canvas coming to its dramatic end. It was now time to lift the painted landscape and reveal the interior of Macbeth's castle.

The stage assistant, however, did not proceed. He approached Irving with meek steps.

'Shall we – shall we raise the curtain, Mr Irving?'

He did not reply, but took a step closer to Miss Terry, who recoiled. 'Can you go on, my dear?' Irving whispered.

Her bosom heaved and her eyes flickered from him to the back of the painted canvas.

Irving clasped her by the arms. 'I need you!'

And then, to everybody's shock, he kissed her full on the lips, so fervently and so anxiously I blushed and had to look away.

A flushed Ellen Terry stepped back, pulling herself from Irving's grip, looking utterly confused.

The orchestra was now playing the majestic cue to the banquet scene, the trumpets and French horns in all their glory.

I saw a fleeting glow in Miss Terry's eyes – tears pooling. She raised her hand, clumsily adjusting the crown on her head, and then she blinked the tears away.

'I am Lady Macbeth. We shall go on.'

As soon as she said so everyone except the actors left the stage. McGray whispered at her:

'The banshee said "the Scottish stage shall see your death".'

Miss Terry took a deep breath, her eyes indomitable fire once more. 'Then so be it, Inspector McGray!'

We ran across the theatre as Irving cried and writhed in fear, his Macbeth falling into madness, the guests at his banquet jumping to their feet.

By now all the officers had seen the photograph, and we were conducting a systematic search of the place.

I walked up and down the rows of seats in the Grand Circle – to me, the seats which offered an even better view than the royal box – and I looked into the face of every single spectator. Thankfully, the stage was ablaze with torches, shedding crimson light all over the audience. I worked my way from the back to the front, ending at the gilded banister of the raised platform, and had a spanning view of the entire auditorium.

Irving was now on his knees, before a sharp ray of light symbolizing Banquo's ghost. Miss Terry bent down and tenderly embraced him. She lifted her face to the audience and happened to look me straight in the eye. It was the only time her voice seemed to fail.

'This is the very –' she exhaled, 'this is the very painting of your fear!'

Then a frantic waving caught my eye. To my right, in the royal box, I saw Mr Wilde gesturing hysterically, but not at me. His white gloves almost glowed under the torchlight. He was desperately trying to catch the eye of

McGray, who was searching the pit. I noticed that Irving's sons were no longer in the royal box with Wilde, so I instantly ran over.

I found Harry and Sydney in the corridor, both boys reading intently from a small piece of paper.

'What is the matter?' I asked, and Mr Wilde and McGray joined us just then. 'Why, you look like parchment!'

Harry, the eldest, handed me the piece of fine paper, but he did not speak. Neither boy looked at us.

'This sheet was thrown into our box!' Mr Wilde told us.

'What the hell?' exclaimed McGray, who had already read the scant words:

Dearest boys,

Tell your silly mother to meet me as agreed. I shall not be laughed at.

ET

'What does this mean?' I asked.

Mr Wilde's mouth had gone dry. 'That is Miss Terry's hand. I – I am speechless.'

'Good,' McGray snapped, and he grasped Harry's collar. 'Why would Miss Terry send youse this?'

Harry again looked down, pulling his head back as if Nine-Nails were a wolf about to bite him. 'She has been sending Mother letters. She wants money.'

'Money? Why?' McGray asked.

Harry gulped, his lips trembling.

'She has been blackmailing our mother,' said Sydney. 'The wench said she would leave father's company for ever if Mother gave her a pension as recompense.'

'She demanded *a lot* of money,' Harry whispered, 'practically all our grandfather's estate . . . which is more than she could ever make as a performer.' His eyes drifted to the sliver of stage visible from where we stood, just as the curtains closed on the doomed regents of Scotland.

47

The corridor was suddenly full of people, everyone moving to the rotunda for the interval.

'If we find yer telling lies –' McGray hissed. I thought Harry Irving would soil himself there and then.

'That's the truth!' Sydney spluttered. 'That's why we're in Scotland. That Terry woman asked Mother to meet her on the night of the ball, and it was then that Mother agreed to most of the viper's terms.'

'Is Mrs Irving in Scotland?' cried Mr Wilde.

'Yes,' said Sydney, 'but she didn't want to stay at the hotel, where she could stumble across Father or that horrid woman any time of the day. She stayed at a friend's home in the Georgian East End.'

'She did ask us to stay close to Father,' Harry added. 'Part of the deal Miss Terry offered was that she'd convince him to give us a chance in the theatre, and Mother thought our presence might influence him.'

'And she must have been right,' said Mr Wilde. 'The boys sent Irving a note telling him they would be here tonight, and now he is giving the performance of his career!'

Harry spoke rather bitterly. 'Mother has not allowed us to see most of his plays.'

I immediately thought of Irving's fraught speech on the hotel's roof; his desperate yearning to gain his sons' affections. No wonder he was manically determined to go ahead with the play.

I massaged my temple, my head overloaded with information. 'Good Lord, everything has just turned upside-down!'

McGray had another quick look at the note. 'If Mrs Irving's here tonight I'd like to talk to her.'

Harry shook his head. 'She refused Miss Terry's invitation, even though she was offered that empty seat in the royal box. She didn't want to be seen and spoil father's performance.'

'But she insisted we came,' said Sydney, with a note of pride. 'She asked us to watch carefully and learn from Father.'

It all felt genuine, logical, simple enough; unlike Miss Terry's story about receiving letters from Lewis Carroll. Still, and perhaps out of sheer surprise, I remained suspicious.

'Tell us,' I said, choosing my words carefully, 'how were the messages delivered?'

Harry answered swiftly. 'She used a horrible, stinking old actor as a servant,' and he wrinkled his nose as if he could smell the man right now.

'Is that why yer mother was in the theatre on the night the first banshee appeared?' McGray asked.

The boys nodded. 'Yes. They were supposed to meet right then,' said Harry, 'but they couldn't, because of all the commotion after that scream was heard. The next day the wench sent another letter to Mother, asking to meet her in Scotland.'

'And tonight our mother was supposed to deliver the first payment,' Sydney concluded. 'No wonder the wench became so pushy!'

'For the love of God,' gasped Mr Wilde, 'will you stop calling her *the wench*? What a dreadful word that is!'

'Wait a moment,' I said. 'Why did you not tell us this before? Why was this kept a secret?'

'This is a family matter, gentlemen,' Mr Wilde intervened. 'And from what I have heard from the boys, Irving himself is not aware of Miss Terry's messages.'

Just as their words began to settle in my mind, a dark, threatening logic began to emerge from all the noise.

'We must –' I began to say, but then saw the expectant faces of the boys and Mr Wilde, and restrained myself. 'You all stay here, do you understand? Stay here until we come back.'

I bid McGray to follow me. By then the corridors were deserted, all the people enjoying themselves in the rotunda, and as soon as Mr Wilde and the Irving boys were back to their seats, I was free to speak at ease.

'We really do need to keep an eye on Miss Terry.'

'Are ye thinking the same I'm thinking?' McGray's expression was enough for me to tell we were formulating the same theory.

'Miss Terry tries to blackmail Mrs Irving,' I whispered. 'The lady, who has abhorred her husband's lover for years, finds it a trifle too much. Mrs Irving puts together the banshee act as a distraction. She sends out all these omens . . . to ultimately get rid of the nuisance Miss Terry has become – before having to pay her a penny. Perhaps she even implicated Mrs Harwood along the way.'

McGray looked down for a moment, and then, so suddenly he startled me, he growled and stomped angrily.

'What?' I asked.

'D'ye have any idea of all the damned whisky I've just lost to ye?'

'Lewis Carroll my arse!' McGray mumbled grumpily as we rushed downstairs. We had to fight our way against the crowds, everyone walking and pushing us in the opposite direction, going back to their seats for the play's finale.

We dashed into the stage wing, where I saw half a dozen men arranging the rocks of the witches' cave, and up in the rafters was the sweaty effects assistant, positioning sacks of lycopodium.

The instant I looked down my heart stopped, the blood supply to my face became blocked and my brains froze: I found myself clashing against none other than my eldest brother – and the woman who'd jilted me last November.

'*Damn!*' I shouted, more affected than upon seeing Dyer's mangled body at the foot of Castle Rock. 'What the hell are you doing here?'

McGray whistled. 'Yer brother, is it? Och, youse two *do* look alike!'

Indeed we do, but Laurence seemed a good deal wider around the waist, and showed off his arrogant, ever smug expression. Eugenia, as annoyingly beautiful as ever, was smirking.

'Oh, Ian,' cried Laurence, more pompous than Mr Wilde, 'how very good to see you! – I do have manners, you see . . .'

'I have no time for this!' I snapped.

'We have just met Mr Irving,' Eugenia boasted,

tucking an imaginary lock of hair behind her ear, if only to show off the garishly large diamond of her engagement ring.

'I owe the introduction to one of my wealthiest clients,' said Laurence. 'Mr de Whittaker manages the textile company that supplies the canvases for –'

I walked on, but Laurence held me by the arm. 'Oh, please, little brother, will you not introduce us? Are you still working under this ... Nine-Fingers Malone, or whatever his name is?'

I was about to unsheathe my gun in pure Nine-Nails style, but I did not need to. Right then, as if sent from the heavens, a thick cloud of white powder landed on them.

'*Sorry!*' the effects man yelled from the flies high above, some of the powder still falling from a torn sack.

The powder expanded in a cloud so thick that for a moment I could not even see Eugenia and Laurence. As the lycopodium began to settle their faces emerged, but as white as London's newest stucco walls. The fine powder had stuck to everything like charcoal, and I shall never forget how it clung to Eugenia's eyelashes in thick clumps, the young woman coughing and shrieking like a mouse in a trap.

I regret not having laughed as earnestly as McGray, whose cackle must have been heard all the way to Arthur's Seat.

'Oi, youse better wash yerselves soon! That stuff's highly flammable!'

'This is my best suit!' Laurence hollered, oblivious to his fiancée's sobbing – her angry tears rolling on the hydrophobic powder like flour-coated dewdrops.

McGray's laughter stopped abruptly. So much so that even the distraught Eugenia lifted her chin to look at him. Nine-Nails had a doomed expression as he stared at the powder. He prodded Laurence's shoulder, where the stuff had formed a small mound, and then looked at the thin layer that stuck to his fingertips.

'*The ghost's white fingers on thy shoulders laid . . .*' he muttered.

I was about to say something, but then a young officer came running to us, stumbling and panting.

'*Inspectors!* We just found a woman hiding in the store-rooms! Come quick!'

'Mrs Irving?' I said aloud, but McGray was already running after the policeman, and I had to follow. Desperate as the situation was, I indulged in one last glance at the floured Laurence and Eugenia, wishing one could carry Gandolfi cameras in one's pocket.

The shortest way was through the understage, where the two remaining witches – the scene would have to do with two – and the horde of apparitions waited to be lifted up to the proscenium. McGray nearly tripped on the young Susy, who looked at us with confusion.

Miss Terry was also there, already changed into Lady Macbeth's nightgown, and perhaps looking for someone to fix the wig she had in her hands.

McGray pointed harshly at her. 'Go to yer dressing room! *Now!* And wait for us there!'

'Excuse me! I need to –'

'*Shush!* This lad will escort ye there,' Nine-Nails turned to the young officer. 'At gunpoint if ye need, laddie. We ken where to go from here.'

Just as we left, the trapdoor let in the red glow of the hellish witches' cave.

***

We could hear the woman's cries long before we reached the stores. As we ran along the lines of costume rails the voice became eerily familiar.

'That is not Mrs Irving,' I said.

Four officers, McNair amongst them, were struggling to contain the punches and kicks of a rather short lady, dressed in a white nightgown and wrapped up in a dirty overcoat.

Mrs Harwood.

'*I want to see my children!*' she yelped, again and again. '*I want to see them!*'

'How did she manage to escape?' McGray asked to the air. 'Wasn't she s'posed to be locked in the asylum?'

She saw us – or rather, she saw *me* – and her rage instantly turned into misery. Her limbs fell passively, except for her right arm, which she stretched pleadingly in my direction.

'Please, good sir, *please!* Let me see them!'

How distorted, how terribly sad her countenance was, her cheeks already drenched in tears.

I gulped painfully, and McGray, seeing my affected face, leaned closer to the poor woman.

'We can bring them to ye,' he said softly, surely remembering Dr Clouston's approach. 'But they're on the stage right now. Ye don't want to ruin their performance, do ye?'

Mrs Harwood's face trembled, her gaze still manic, but she seemed to accept his argument.

'And ye don't want them to see ye in this state,' Nine-Nails went on. 'It would worry them sick. Do me a favour; let these gentlemen make ye a cup o' tea while ye compose yerself. All right?'

Mrs Harwood did not appear to acknowledge those last words, but she did not protest either, which was enough for us.

Two of the officers gingerly led her to a nearby seat, while we and McNair stepped a few yards away.

'Brilliantly handled,' I whispered to McGray.

'Let's hope it lasts,' he answered, his brave façade crumbling for an instant. He let out a long sigh before addressing McNair. 'Go to the asylum and tell them where she is. They might be looking for her already. And be quick; she might become unhinged again at any time.'

McNair bowed and we left the officers with the poor woman, who was now keenly biting her nails.

'She could have been the banshee,' I said in a low voice. 'Only her hands are clean . . .'

McGray rubbed his eyes, perhaps to wipe pooling tears. It was so unfortunate he'd had to deal with madness at such close quarters these last few days. 'Perhaps, but now let's focus on Miss Terry. She might have something to say about it.'

⁎

Young Constable Cooper was guarding Miss Terry's door with concerned eyes.

'She didnae want me in, sirs,' he told us as soon as we appeared. 'Nearly slapped me with one o' those wooden swords!'

'That's all right, laddie,' said McGray. 'We'll take it

from here, but stay close in case we need ye.' Then McGray knocked at the dressing-room door.

'I told you to go away!' Miss Terry shouted.

'It's us,' McGray answered. A long pause. 'If ye don't –'

'Oh, come in if you must!'

So we did, and we found her in front of a large mirror, painting dark rings under her eyes. She did not turn, but looked at us through the glass, all her former charm gone. 'What do you want now? Have you come to incarcerate me, perhaps?'

McGray chuckled. 'Well, that depends on ye. Why did ye send this to Irving's sons?'

He produced the message and passed it over Miss Terry's shoulder.

There was a slight frown on her face as she took the note, but nothing compared to the sheer alarm as she read its contents. I could not tell whether she was immensely concerned, or if it was the effective make-up augmenting her dismay.

'I never wrote this!' she hissed.

'Is that not your hand?' I asked her.

She finally turned to face us. 'It seems so, but I have never –' she struggled for words. 'Who – who gave this to you? Harry and Sydney?'

'Yes.'

Miss Terry threw her head back and laughed. 'Are you two so gullible? Those little brats *lied* to you!'

'Madam, they gave us a very convincing account of your correspondence with Mrs Irving.'

'What are you talking about?' She was outraged, standing up and wrapping herself more tightly in her white costume. 'Why would I contact that horrendous woman? And even if I wanted to – she thinks herself so high and mighty she wouldn't even bother to open my letters!'

I did not wish to volunteer more of what we had been told, but rather gauge her reactions.

'Are you planning to stay in this company for long?' I asked.

The question threw her off balance. 'Why? Why would you ask me that? Of course! I shall stay with Irving until they have to drag me off the stage in a stretcher.'

'Did ye ken Mrs Irving has been in Edinburgh all these days?'

Miss Terry bit her lip. 'Well – no, but . . .'

'Well?'

She spat the words. 'I suspected she was! The smothering harpy never lets her babies go anywhere on their own. She writes to their boarding school daily!'

There was an unusual thump on the door, soon followed by commanding knocks.

'That's my call,' said Miss Terry. 'If you'll excuse me, I have a final scene to play.'

McGray planted himself in front of her. 'Ye'll go nowhere 'til ye tell us what's going on.'

Miss Terry again laughed. 'Why should I have to speak? You two have concocted a brew the Bard himself would have envied. Now let me through!'

Again the frantic knocking.

'*Sod off!*' McGray shouted.

'These people are counting on me,' Miss Terry snarled. 'And I have no idea what you want me to say. Pray, let me out!'

Nine-Nails and Ellen Terry exchanged irate looks; a

silent battle of wills, whilst the knocking got more and more insistent, until it became a constant clatter.

Irritated, I pulled the door open, and as I did so I received a mighty blow on my head that left me sprawled on the floor.

48

I caught just a glimpse of an elongated figure sprinting down the corridor, and upon hitting the floor I saw the motionless body of Constable Cooper. He'd been struck with even greater force and we were now lying side by side.

'Ye all right?' I heard McGray ask. I saw him leaning over me, but neither my voice nor my limbs would obey me. The entire world spun madly, and I believe I managed to mumble a 'yes', but only because McGray assented and jumped up to chase the attacker.

With splitting pains all over my head, I managed to roll on my back, only to see Miss Terry step out of her dressing room, looking in all directions.

'Sorry,' she said, sneering at me, 'this is my call,' and she ran off to the stage.

I pressed a hand on the top of my head, trying desperately to stand, and a moment later felt two pairs of arms lifting me up.

'Inspector Frey!' said McNair's familiar voice, as a second officer helped the now semi-conscious Cooper sit up. 'Miss Terry just told us that you allowed her to go and –'

'Forget about her!' I snapped, fighting to regain control over my senses. 'The attacker . . . That way . . .'

I must have pointed in the right direction, for McNair dashed there immediately. I had to lean on the wall, taking clumsy steps forward at a frustratingly slow pace. I heard McGray shouting in the distance, along with some other scared voices, but I failed to make any sense out of it. All I could do was move towards the racket, feeling utterly useless, but then a white figure bumped against me and nearly knocked me over.

'Mrs Harwood!' I shouted, for it was she, running like the wind, her arms and legs flailing about like a disturbing spider.

A black hound, larger than any hunting beast I'd ever seen, came behind her, but it was not chasing her. The dog turned in a different track, perhaps down the corridor McGray and the others had followed.

That image suddenly brought me back to my senses.

'*Stop!*' I shouted, turning in her direction, my trembling legs barely allowing me to keep up after her.

'He said he'll help me!' the woman cried as we ran through the maze of corridors, taking turns and rushing through doors I had not seen before. 'He told me the banshee's here!'

'Madam, stop!' I cried, as her voice receded further and further away. 'We can help you too!'

I heard her steps descending through a narrow, steep staircase, barely lit by sparsely placed lamps, before I lost her.

I was lost myself, and still slightly stunned, as I emerged from the stairwell into what I thought must be the lower painting room. Line after line of gigantic canvases hung from the ceiling, a section of which was open to the upper storeys, and countless ropes dangled vertically like vines in a rainforest.

Mrs Harwood could be heard no more; neither her

steps nor her voice. I grunted in frustration, looking between the paintings as I unsheathed my gun.

I then heard other voices, screaming, and a man howling. It all came from the adjacent room and I rushed in that direction, not even knowing if there would be a connecting door.

'Everybody out!'

The voice came loud and clear, and in the darkened basement it was my only guide to a small wooden door. I crossed it, but halted immediately, my heart pounding so hard I thought it would break free of my chest.

I was facing the understage, and saw all the effects assistants sprinting away from their equipment like scared pigeons.

Tarvin was there, standing in the middle of the room, between the rheostat and the bucket of glowing embers. His back was towards me, and he was sweeping a gun from left to right. The black hound was now next to him: enormous, filthy, its eyes savage and baring its fangs at everyone it saw. No wonder Stoker had thought it an apparition.

'Everybody out, I say!'

The sweaty cockney tried to strike Tarvin, but the wolfhound instantly darted ahead. It caught the man's left arm in its jaws, biting with all its might. The man threw a swift punch to the dog's head, making it release its grip and fall back on all fours, and then he ran to one of the adjacent corridors. After a brief whimper, the dog went after him.

The only figure that remained still was McGray, standing defiantly by one of the side doors, pointing at Tarvin with his gun. He must have become separated from the officers, for he stood on his own. Somehow he saw me, even if the only light came from the central trapdoor open to the back of the stage.

I drew a finger to my lips, getting myself ready to shoot. Everyone had left by then, the place now so silent we could hear Miss Terry's monologue from above.

'Gimme that, lad,' McGray commanded, if only to keep Tarvin's eyes on him.

I would have shot then, but, still feeling dizzy, I feared I'd miss. I had to get closer.

I took a step ahead, afraid to breathe, afraid of the rustle of my clothes, and rested my weight on the floorboards as if treading on eggshells, fearing the wood would creak under my weight.

It did not, but I could not exhale yet. The only other sound was the soft sizzle of the embers that had been used to produce the stage steam.

'We don't want any bloodshed,' McGray pleaded, stretching his hand. 'Gimme that.'

'Oh, there *will* be bloodshed tonight,' Tarvin said, savouring each word. Were they all mad in this theatre? 'Get away or I'll blow your brains out!'

I used his voice to cover the sound of my steps. I could smell the laudanum already: he perspired it, along with the hint of other drugs.

It must have been a creak on the floor, or my breathing, or the man simply felt my presence somehow, for he turned on his heels in my direction, and all I could do was point down and shoot at his legs. I missed, Tarvin shot too, and I hurled myself towards him, yelling and reaching for his weapon.

The world became a blur of shouting and struggling,

McGray joining us, until somehow I was pushed and fell on my back.

Still struggling with McGray, Tarvin managed to throw a kick at my ribs and my gun slipped from my fingers. I curled up on the floor and then rolled about, trying to avoid the stomping feet of either man.

I heard the thump of a gun against the floor, but could not tell whose. Right then I saw Tarvin reach for the embers, pick up a handful of red-hot chunks with his bare hand and throw them at McGray's face. Nine-Nails had to bend sideways, protecting himself with nothing but his forearms. Some of the embers fell on the rheostat's uncovered wires, showering the whole area with sparks. Some landed on my clothes and I had to roll again to smother them. Suddenly I pictured the entire building burning to its foundations with every one of us inside.

Tarvin ran up the trapdoor stairs, McGray a few steps behind. I thought I saw steam rising from his face.

I managed to muster the last of my strength, got back on my feet and followed them. I dragged myself up the creaking wooden steps and then on to the stage. The painted scenery again concealed us, the shadow of Miss Terry projected sharply on the canvas, and I saw that Tarvin and McGray were already climbing a ladder that led to the flies and rafters. I realized neither carried a gun. McGray must have dropped his when Tarvin threw the charcoal at him.

More recklessly than bravely, I followed, regretting it halfway up, for my ribcage throbbed with pain at every movement, and my hands and feet were still slightly numb, barely feeling the rungs I clung to.

I saw that Tarvin's hands were about to grasp the bridge that ran across the stage, some thirty feet above the floor. From that height – I could not help looking down – I could see the other side of the canvas. Miss Terry was down there, a single light on her, pretending to wash her hands. She had everyone captivated.

Just as Tarvin was jumping on to the bridge Nine-Nails seized him by the leg. Tarvin let out a strange groan, as if trying to be as silent as possible, and then threw Nine-Nails a well-aimed kick in the chest. I saw his torso lurch backwards, McGray grasping the ladder with nothing but the very tips of his fingers.

I rushed upwards and managed to push the back of his thigh, just enough for him to recover his balance.

'We're even now!' I said, but McGray had no time to reply. He reached the top of the ladder and sprang up, tossing dangling ropes aside as he strode forward.

Tarvin seized a rope tied to an iron pulley, and began whirling it in the air as if about to throw a noose on to a colt. The bolt fanned swiftly towards McGray's face. He jolted sideways and grasped the bridge's low railing, nearly falling over it. I thought the pulley had hit him, but he'd simply dodged it so quickly that his own momentum had almost toppled him.

I went closer, and just as McGray regained his balance we saw Tarvin trip on something. He fell backwards on to the creaking wooden boards, lifting a little cloud of white powder. He'd stumbled over the very same sack of lycopodium that had spilt half its contents over Laurence and Eugenia.

McGray ran towards him, ready to seize him before he got hold of the rope again, but then we all halted.

There was a terrible female wail: long, anguished and rasping, and I immediately thought of the banshee.

It was Miss Terry, though, finalizing her act and then whispering 'to bed, to bed', which was followed by an ovation that made the very walls of the theatre tremble.

We'd looked down for a second, but by then Tarvin had grabbed a handful of lycopodium, produced a little lighter from his pocket, and ignited it in front of the hump of white powder. Tiny sparks of unsettled dust burst around the flame, like an ominous halo.

'*Get away!*' he shouted, as if he'd waited for the ovation to conceal his voice. He blew over the hump of powder, turning it into a cloud of hellish fire that made us jump backwards.

When it dissipated I saw Tarvin grinning like a fiend. He'd picked up a second handful and was staring at it with wicked eyes. He spoke eerily, almost father-like, at the explosive.

'Curious that you should be here . . . as if by design. So small yet as deadly as the strike of thunder.'

He glanced at the stage. Miss Terry was leaving now, glowing with satisfaction, but instead of going to the stage wing, the natural choice, she walked around the canvas towards the trapdoor; the same one through which we'd just ascended.

'*Choose who shall burn!*' Tarvin snarled, his eyes moving maniacally from Terry to us, holding the lycopodium up high. 'The enchantress of fools – or *you*?'

The cheering was deafening, dragging on and on like a downpour. Terry would never hear our warnings. Her own admirers would be her doom.

'There's a fucking third option!' McGray shouted, stepping forward.

Tarvin turned the powder to us. 'Then this is the end of the applause! After this –' he bellowed, '*Only silence!*'

It all happened at once: the orchestra burst into a fateful chord, Tarvin dashed lycopodium in every direction and waved his lighter around, and as he kindled intermittent balls of fire Nine-Nails and I charged against him.

Engulfed in fleeting flames, shouting and kicking under the uproar of the music and the persistent clapping, we pushed him backwards, desperate to get him away from the sack.

It's just a handful of powder, I told myself over and over, feeling the flashes of fire on my hands and through my clothes.

Amidst the frenzy I thought I saw a pair of bright eyes by the end of the bridge, glowing in the dark like those of a cat. It was only for an instant, for right then Tarvin ignited his last fire, mere inches from my face, and I instinctively thrust myself on my back, feeling as if my eyelids had been singed.

Through streaming eyes I could still discern the blurry outlines of Tarvin and Nine-Nails.

McGray's shoulder was ablaze, but he somehow found the strength to throw one last blow at Tarvin's cheek, hurling him to the low railing. He still had some lycopodium in his hand, but before he could ignite it McGray hit him squarely on the nose, and the man fell backwards into the void.

It was as if time itself stretched; as if I was looking at a man slowly sinking into the depths of the sea. His final terrified shriek sounded grave in my ears, mixed with the chords from the orchestra, and at last Tarvin landed on the back of the stage, his body bursting in a ghastly mess of red.

And I mumbled, '*One falls on the stage . . .*'

I pressed a hand against my sore eyelids, but I'd barely have time for a deep breath.

'Och, it was just a wee scorch,' said McGray, thumping his jacket's seared shoulder.

He offered me a hand, pulled me upwards and then rushed down at unthinkable speed. I do not know how I faced that dreadful ladder again, but I managed to make my way down as the stage filled with soldiers preparing for the final battle.

A dark shape, crawling timidly out of the shadows, reached Tarvin before us. It was the enormous hound. For a moment I thought it would have us by the jugulars, but the animal was now whimpering like a lost puppy.

It sniffed Tarvin's lifeless body, from his stomach to his neck, and then began licking the blood that had spilled from its master's face. Its moans became louder as Nine-Nails and I approached.

Only then, after the man was dead, did I have a proper chance to look into his face. There was the handsome actor I'd seen in that picture merely minutes ago, the main features still there; a face undoubtedly fit for a Hamlet or a Richard III. His skin, however, was now dry and leathery, not so much from age, but eaten away by strain and substances. His eyes were wide open, so piercing it was as if his bitterness would last beyond death.

'Poor wretch,' McGray mumbled, kneeling down and

gently closing the man's lids. As he did so, on the other side of the scenery, Irving was receiving the news of Lady Macbeth's death, followed by his 'Out, out, brief candle . . .' I remembered my nightmare the previous night, and I felt my entire body giving into a nasty shudder.

McNair and a couple of theatre assistants arrived then.

'Do youse want us to move him?' McNair asked, the only composed one amongst us, for all the theatre men around him were either sickened or terrified.

'Aye,' McGray whispered. 'No need for everyone to see him in this state.'

I was about to say something religious, before the men set to do the messy work, but then we heard another female voice, one I'd never heard before, coming from the trapdoor.

'Ellen! No!'

McGray jumped to his feet and hurled himself down the trapdoor. I followed as quickly as I could, saw him descend the steps in only two long strides, and then my eyes went to the rheostat, where a woman was screaming. Ellen Terry, swathed in her white nightgown, was standing in front of her like the angel of death.

'No, Ellen! Don't!' the other woman cried as she stumbled backwards towards the rheostat, her elegant grey dress billowing as she approached the bobbins of naked wires. The electricity running through them would be enough to light up an entire street.

I realized, unable to do anything from where I stood, that I would see all that power strike her body, burst in blinding sparks and burn her flesh to charcoal.

And then McGray caught her.

He thrust himself like a locomotive, pushing the

woman away, and they both fell flat on the floor a good six feet away from the machine.

The sweaty effects assistant came back right then, pressing a cloth against his forearm where the hound had bitten him, and he resumed operating the rheostat. So stunned were we all that nobody even looked at him for more than a second.

Miss Terry came to me, ghastly pale and pleading for protection. Her eyes were filled with a mix of fear and rage that would have made Mr Sargent's masterpiece look like a mediocre doodle. She gripped my arm so tightly it hurt.

'*There she is!* The Mrs Irving you claim I've been messaging! She lured me in here. She was calling my name after the scene! When she heard you approaching, she pretended I had pushed her towards that . . . that infernal device.'

McGray helped the battered woman stand up, and I recognized Sydney's haughty brow in her. Right now, however, she looked dumbfounded, every inch of her body trembling violently.

McGray told her we were CID inspectors, the formalities sounding odd at a moment like this, but it did help Mrs Irving come back to her senses.

'You . . .' she whispered, finally focusing her gaze on McGray. 'She tried to . . . You just . . . saved me . . .'

I could not possibly tell what emotion, other than surprise, underlay her words. Was she glad? Could she not believe her good luck? And then her eyes fell on Miss Terry, and her astonishment turned into blind rage.

Both women glared at each other, their eyes hotter than the red embers next to them, and they both cried at once: '*She wants me dead!*'

49

The sounds of the battles taking place on the stage were nothing compared to their slanging match. Florence Irving and Ellen Terry began shouting obscenities I would have never believed could have emanated from a lady's mouth.

'*Shut up the both o' youse!*' McGray roared, so fiercely that even I started, but the women only reluctantly obliged. Nine-Nails then paced around them, his blue eyes analysing both faces.

'Youse both cannae be telling the truth ... So ... Who's the lying bitch here?'

Mrs Irving was still so shocked she did not notice the insult. 'But it is all so clear!' she babbled. 'This harlot wants me dead! She wants my husband and knows he'll never divorce me for our children's sake!'

Miss Terry showed a little more composure, though from her grip on my arm I knew she wanted to tear Mrs Irving apart. 'This – lady has always hated me. She thinks I'm responsible for the hell of her marriage, but she did it all to herself!'

'Mrs Irving,' said McGray, 'how did ye end up here right now?'

'She brought me in with deceit! She sent me letters promising my sons would have the career they've always wanted. She promised she'd finally leave Irving alone. All I had to do was to maintain her for the rest of her life!'

'I have no idea what this harpy is talking about!' Miss Terry screamed. 'She is sick and mad!' and I had to pull her hand from my arm, as her nails were about to break my skin.

'Oh, but I have your letters!' Mrs Irving argued, a sneer on her face. 'Go to my rooms in New Town and you'll see all the letters she sent me! I have one with me which I received just this afternoon. This so-called doyenne asked me to meet her here, right after her performance!'

She looked at the floor, where her purse lay. McGray reached for it and opened it himself, pulling out a sheet of paper. Again, it was good paper, and the writing looked neat and refined.

'What happened to the other note?' asked McGray, looking at Miss Terry.

She stammered. 'I . . . I still had it in my hand when I left my dressing room. I must have dropped it on my way to the stage. *God, I can't remember!*'

McGray looked dubiously at her. 'Were ye sending letters to Mrs Irving? Were you using John Tarvin as yer messenger?'

'Of course not, I was telling the truth!' She clasped her stomach, 'I thought they were real! I thought they'd come from –' Nine-Nails raised a hand to make her stop.

Mrs Irving cackled, the echoes bouncing throughout the understage. 'Another lie! What a pathetic woman you are! Why would a respected gentleman like Mr Carroll want to resume friendship with a – with someone like *you*?'

Nine-Nails looked up sharply. Once more I could tell we were thinking the same, but neither of us spoke immediately.

'I do not need your money,' Miss Terry snapped. 'I have more money than I need! And don't wish to marry ever again . . .' She turned to me. 'And if I wanted to kill her, I wouldn't play these foolish games – she'd be long dead.'

McGray was still pacing, stroking his cleanly shaven face. 'Perhaps I should've asked this first. Miss Terry, did ye push this lady? Where ye perhaps trying to get rid o' her and make it look like an accident?'

'Of course not!' she retorted, although I could see doom growing in her eyes. 'I didn't lay a finger on her!'

'So . . . she just tripped?'

Miss Terry began to shed copious tears, now sheer terror drawing in her face. 'No . . . she – she . . . she jumped backwards!'

McGray smiled. 'Miss, d'ye expect us to believe that?'

Miss Terry had difficulty breathing, and I struggled to interpret her following sobbing words: 'That's the truth.'

'She's a terrible liar!' Mrs Irving spat, showing her teeth in a wide grin. 'She makes no sense! Why would I want to jump to my death?'

McGray had to reach for her hand, for she looked as if about to lose her mind. 'Mrs Irving, come, come, give me yer hand, look nae so pale. Here, have a seat.' He pulled a crate, dusted it and helped Mrs Irving sit down. 'There. Miss Terry told us ye've slimmed a lot lately. Ye've been ill?'

'No. Will you –'

Most indecorously, McGray kept Mrs Irving's hand in his, looking at it and stroking it gently.

'I remember after my wee sister became – well, ill, I lost a lot o' weight in a matter o' weeks. All the strain, just like ye. And somethin' I hadn't realized 'til then is that when you slim down, ye slim down everywhere. Waist, neck, face, and ... fingers – well, I was one the poorer in that section! But the annoying part is, things won't fit ye any more. Important things, like, say, yer wedding ring.'

Mrs Irving tried to pull her hand from McGray's grip, but he brought it closer to his face.

'Aye, ye ken what I'm talking about, don't ye?'

'Let go of me, you brute!' she growled, showing her teeth again, but not in a grin any more.

It was McGray's turn to smile. 'It was ye wearing the beetle-wing dress on the night o' the ball. Ye who helped Tarvin lure Stoker out to the streets. Youse needed a witness; someone reliable to believe he'd seen Miss Terry around yer lodgings that night. It would all have supported yer tale, wouldn't it? And youse also kent Mr Stoker wouldnae speak straight away; he's so loyal to Irving he wouldnae ruin the reputation o' the company's leading lady. But ye did bet on him talking once ye were dead and the inquiries began. Right? Ye kent he wouldnae keep quiet if he also suspected Miss Terry was a murderer.'

Miss Terry then brought both hands to her face.

'Yes,' I told her. 'It is just what you are thinking.'

'Good God!' Miss Terry mumbled. 'Florence was actually willing to kill herself ... and make *me* appear a murderess!'

There was fire, thunder, the yells of warriors, frenzied music and the roaring voice of Henry Irving. None of which reached our ears. We were all looking at Florence.

Her muscles reacted very slowly, stretching her lips in a crooked smile, completely at odds with the horrified expression in her eyes. What an eerie image it was; an empty, almost idiotic smirk, under a pair of doomed, terrified eyes.

'That's why ye lured Miss Terry down here,' said McGray. 'Like she said, ye jumped on the electric wires to kill yerself. Ye expected people to find Miss Terry standing right next to the rheo-thingy, and we would all think she'd pushed ye!'

'Nonsense,' Florence mumbled.

'Ye were wearing that dress,' said McGray, still holding her hand. 'Ye lost yer wedding ring. I can see the tan line in yer finger.' He raised the hand for us to see. 'And it didnae happen long ago, I can tell the line's quite sharp. A thin tan line too, which tells me yer ring was a cheap one; of course, since Irving didnae have much money when he married ye, and as youse fell out he never got ye a better one. We found that ring and thought it was Mrs Harwood's. And I'm sure ye ken where we found it.'

'*Nonsense!*' Florence repeated, trying to pull herself free.

McGray held her by the arm before she had a chance to do something silly. 'How did ye ken Miss Terry claimed to receive letters from Lewis Carroll?'

'Indeed,' I added. 'She told no one but us. The matter was so embarrassing that not even Irving himself was aware of it. How could it then reach your ears? Unless you . . .' I inhaled deeply. In a blink, like clockwork suddenly falling into place, all the events of the last few days reshaped in my head. 'You *forged* the letters,' I said triumphantly, at last recalling Irving's words on the night of the ball. The very words I'd not had time to write down because of all the mayhem that immediately followed.

'You have done it before: you forged many love letters to Henry Irving during your courtship with him.'

'And how did *you* come to know that?' she spat.

'Yer husband told us himself. He also told us ye like attending the criminal courts to amuse yerself. Plenty of inspiration to gather there!'

Mrs Irving looked around, as if desperately trying to find something misplaced in the darkness.

'My sons!' she said. 'My sons can testify! They can tell you –'

'Tell us what?' asked McGray. 'I doubt yer sons were aware of yer true intentions. Ye surely made them believe yer story about Miss Terry blackmailing ye, right?'

'Indeed,' I added. 'So their statements would sound truthful – and to spare them the pain of knowing their mother had committed suicide.'

'You're all mad,' she hissed. 'Of course you're all mad!'

'Have ye ever met Lewis Carroll?' McGray asked her.

'He used to be a mutual acquaintance,' Miss Terry jumped in. 'He dined many times at Henry's house – back when he lived with this woman, of course.'

'So you would have known his handwriting,' I said. 'And it was you who attacked Miss Desborough today – you and Mr Tarvin, trying to get into the theatre without being seen.'

'By the way,' said McGray, 'the poor lad's dead.'

He'd said it upon seeing McNair and two officers bringing the body down the steps, wrapped in a thick blanket, which had nonetheless turned red with the man's blood.

Miss Terry looked away, but her aghast expression was nothing compared with Mrs Irving's.

McGray let go of her wrist. Florence instantly pressed

both hands against her face, her quivering fingers moving in a way that made me think of the snakes on Medusa's head. She sank on to the floor as she saw the body being taken away. The hound, tied by the neck with one of the stage ropes, was following its master's corpse, attempting to sniff his dangling hand – and still whimpering.

'Sorry, sirs,' McNair said, clutching the dog's rope. 'We didn't want to disturb the ladies, but this was the quietest way out.'

Behind them came a sickly looking theatre assistant, carrying a stained mop and a bucket. Mrs Irving let out a harrowing moan when she saw the contents.

And just as they carried the real corpse away, another man in medieval costume brought in Macbeth's severed head, impaled on a long spear, looking unnervingly authentic. Syrup dyed red dripped from the false neck, and I could no longer tell which stains on the floor were actual blood.

We then heard the clash of steel against steel. Irving must be locked in the final sword fight against Macduff.

'There's one more thing,' said McGray. 'What about yer attack on Stoker? Why did youse batter him so badly? Was it even necessary?'

Something had shifted in Florence. Upon seeing Tarvin's dead body she did not seem to care about defending herself any more. All of a sudden she spoke candidly, and I suspected her connection with Tarvin had been far from platonic. I would soon confirm that.

'It *was* necessary. I got rid of the dress that very night, right after Stoker saw what I wanted him to see. I had only thrown it over my own clothes – that cow and her understudy are much bigger than me these days, so I could easily pull it out and give it to Tarvin, who took it to that mad woman's room.

'When I was back in my lodgings, only after I'd calmed down, I realized I didn't have my ring on. It never even occurred to me it might have been caught in the dress, but I *had* seen something that terrified me. I saw Stoker pick something up from the floor when he followed me. Something shiny, so I thought Stoker had found my ring. That's why Tarvin followed him back and searched his room and his clothes – we didn't have to be too careful; his room was already a mess. When he found nothing he thought we were safe . . . we assumed I'd lost the ring somewhere on the streets, and that Stoker had perhaps picked up something else.'

'He had,' I said. 'A beetle wing that fell off your dress, which led us to suspect Miss Terry, just like you expected.'

McGray arched an eyebrow. 'Why did ye have to plant the dress in Mrs Harwood's room? Why not burn it?'

'That's where we took it from originally, but that was not the only reason. There was always the risk that someone had seen Miss Terry where she really was that night. And she would defend her story to the death. The dress just guaranteed that, should everything else fail, the attention never went back to me. Vanity. All vanity. I would have been dead by then, but I didn't want the world – my sons! – to know what I had truly done. We actively tried to make sure everyone thought that the woman was losing her mind – which she was! Although . . . I never thought he'd be so close to killing one more person in the process.'

'Mr Wheatstone was indeed very nearly killed,' I said, and Florence nodded. 'So it was Tarvin who gave the little gun to Mrs Harwood. He told her about Susy's situation and set her against him.'

'Yes, but that was Tarvin and Tarvin alone!' Florence spluttered. 'He went too far. He always went too far when he had his beer and laudanum. I told him we needed Mr Wheatstone away from here. We needed the coast clear when I faced this trollop after her stupid monologue. All we needed was a distraction, nothing more, but Tarvin gave that mad seamstress a gun! And tonight he helped her escape from the asylum, God knows how, and brought her here only so that the police would have to chase her around.'

'He did a good deal for ye,' said McGray. 'He helped ye send the messages, mount this spectacle . . . Why? Were youse two – *close*?'

Florence looked away at once. 'I refuse to answer that.'

A pathetic reply, I thought. I remembered my stepmother mentioning that people had seen Mrs Irving on the arm of a 'pauper-looking scarecrow'.

'Did he ken ye were planning to take yer own life?' McGray asked.

'He did . . . though not from the start. I promised him a sweet revenge on Irving and he was all too happy to help. But when I told him my true intentions – his resolve crumbled. He wanted to kill this trollop with his own hands.' Her eyes for Miss Terry were poison. 'He abhorred the filthy hussy who was forcing me to scheme my own death . . .'

'*Forcing!*' Miss Terry exclaimed, but I had to contain her. Mrs Irving was not done yet.

'Poor Tarvin tried to convince me otherwise,' Florence continued, 'time and time again. He wrote me the most agonizing letters pleading that I should change my mind. Usually while overdosed. I was trying to burn them atop

Calton Hill. I knew my possessions would be searched after my death, and those letters revealed too much . . . But I was seen before I finished.

'I was terrified – terrified of my fate. I saw the letters burn and the fire only made me think of what might await on the other side. I saw myself burning in hell, and I felt this wave of horror, and before I knew it I was howling. *Howling!* And I went on even when my throat scalded. I only stopped because I saw people approaching and I had to flee.'

'Was it Tarvin who left those ghastly brains?' Miss Terry demanded, making Florence grin.

'Of course, you witless crow! Right after handing you a message! It all arose from an impulse: a parcel he'd just bought to feed his dog! And I thought you would realize it immediately, but you were desperate to ensnare yet another man, weren't you? You're far more stupid than I gave you credit for! I was furious when Tarvin told me what he had done; I thought he had ruined my plan; but when that didn't happen I was only sorry I didn't get to see you when you found them! What a face you must have pulled!'

I had to hold both of Miss Terry's arms.

'Tarvin didn't just want to help me. He wanted Irving to see his company destroyed. Utterly destroyed. And everyone in it as well: Wheatstone, the seamstress, the old hag who plays the witch, Stoker . . . He targeted them all in one way or the other. He would have seen them all dead just to bring Irving down.' She shuddered. 'I aimed for much less. I only wanted the legendary Ellen Terry ruined and behind bars . . . and my sons to have what they've always yearned for – even if I had to die to accomplish it.'

We heard steps coming from the trapdoor. Heavy and slow.

It was Henry Irving, still sweating from his fight, dragging the blunt metallic sword designed to emit electric sparks whenever it hit his opponent's.

He'd heard it all, and all the colour seemed to have drained from his face. Rather fittingly, he'd just died on the stage and his chest was drenched in fake blood.

'You were willing to *die* for this?'

'I don't fear death,' Florence retorted. 'I would have gone to a better place, unlike you and your whore!'

'You've been hovering over us all like the damned vulture you are!' And he threw the sable against the wall. 'You damned beast from hell!'

'Why, did you expect me to sit quietly while you spat on your kin?' Florence cried. 'My sons – *your sons* – only wanted a chance in your theatre, but instead of helping *them* you kept stuffing the goose with bastards of the Terry breed!'

Both Terry and Irving took a step ahead, their hands set to tear the woman apart.

'There, there,' said McGray, pulling Florence away, but she would not keep silent any more.

'You abandoned me when I was about to give birth to Sydney! Only because I thought your career was a fool's! Only because I didn't bow to you and praise your "genius"! *Look at yourself!* A middle-aged man still dressing like a buffoon, playing at swords and calling himself a prodigy for that!'

'*Quiet!*' McGray snapped, handing her to a couple of officers who'd just arrived. 'Ye'll have plenty o' time for this at the inquest . . .'

'Oh, there will be no inquest!' she said, jubilant. 'Am I right, my dear husband? For the boys' sake?'

I could almost feel the heat emanating from Irving's body. Ellen reached for his arm but he pulled it away.

'Damned she-wolf! How dare you use them as your shield? I love those b-b . . . !' Henry covered his mouth instantly, and Florence let out an awful cackle.

'Oh, is it coming back to you? The p-p-poor Henry can't sp-p-p-p-peak?'

Irving leaped towards her. McGray and I both had to restrain him, and the technician had to join us too. Irving threw fists and kicked about with such fury that even Tarvin's hound would have recoiled.

We did not let go of him until Florence was out of sight. Every inch of Irving's body quivered with a wrath that, I was certain, would not cool for years.

'Shall I go on stage now?'

Only then did we notice Freddie Harwood, who was supposed to emerge right behind Macbeth's ghastly head. Finally, the play was drawing to a close.

'There's still blood up there, sir,' said the man with the bucket, who had lingered to hear the gossip. Irving waved a hand dismissively, still shaking.

'It'll look like b-b-battle . . . b-blood,' he said, then turned his back to everyone.

The boy was looking intently at him and Miss Terry, even as he climbed the steps to the stage. And he was smiling! As if it was all part of a farce and he found it terribly amusing.

We were all too drained to speak, or even move. We

heard the ovation from the auditorium as the curtains came down, an uproar unlike any I'd ever witnessed, but it all seemed so trivial now. Even the ears of the mighty Henry Irving were deaf to his followers' acclaim.

And then, when I thought we had reached the end of it all, a scream came from above, so piercing it chilled my heart.

No banshee this time, but a male voice.

Something terrible had just happened on the stage.

On the night the blood runs thick and freely
Some fiend here comes, replete with too much rage
Announcing death and doom and infamy
Like a poor player, sentenced on the stage

Chase not the voices and the spells they write
For only death and blood your hand shall spread;
One falls on the stage, maybe one tonight
If you hunt whispers that concern the dead

The dead that travel fast, the opening door,
The silent room, the heavy creeping shade,
The murdered idol rising through the floor,
The ghost's white fingers on thy shoulders laid,

All hail! These tragic marks await Macbeth
All hail! The Scottish stage shall see your death

50

Elgie looked utterly shocked, his lean cheeks pale and his eyes red from lack of sleep. His night had been difficult, of course, but not nearly as bad as mine; I must have looked like a living corpse as I walked into the house, my body battered, my face scalded from the fire and my heart still heavy.

It had been such a consolation to step out of the City Chambers, after having spent hours at the morgue, and to be received by the fresh air, the clear summer sunshine and the bustle of people preparing for their daily chores. After the horrors of the previous night it was a relief to see that the world was still turning.

My good brother helped me to the upstairs parlour, and Layton immediately brought me strong coffee and toast. I forced myself to eat, even if my mouth was still so dry I had to down it all with two cups of the brew. Elgie was kind enough to butter a second slice, but I barely managed to eat half of it.

'I hope it was not as bad as people are beginning to say,' he ventured.

It had been a thousand times worse, but I would not tell him so. At least not right then.

'What did you see?' I asked him, before volunteering anything.

Elgie sat back. 'Well, that boy who played Fleance came out, with a little candle, like at rehearsals. We finished with the last chords and the curtain came all the way down as usual. There was a standing ovation – I even saw Mother and Father on their feet . . . and then we heard someone scream and the bottom of the curtain caught fire. Mr Stoker and Mr Howard appeared then, pleading for everyone to leave immediately. I cannot take Mr Stoker's gesture out of my head; he looked horrified, but there was something else. I cannot really put it in words . . . There had always been a certain spark in his stare; some – zeal that never went away, even when he seemed in every other way exhausted. But it was gone then, as if everything around him had lost lustre . . . As if the whole world had darkened.'

Elgie got lost in his thoughts for a moment.

'Go on,' I encouraged.

'I was about to reach the main entrance when I heard that female cry and I thought it was all part of the act, like the first banshee scream, at the beginning of the play. I thought we would be asked to come back and Mr Irving would give us a speech, or at least all the cast would come back out for the cheering. But it never happened, and I heard some people waited for hours on Grindlay Street.'

I thanked heaven he'd not seen more. I closed my eyes, for they burned with exhaustion, and I tried to recall the events in chronological order. I could hardly go through them in my head, let alone tell them aloud.

The worst part was that Mrs Harwood had witnessed it all from the stage wing.

She'd been standing there, staring with pride at the glorious last scene of her son, when the cloud of lycopodium had fallen on him. The powder had ignited with the little flame of Freddie's candle; the poor boy must have been engulfed in flames in no time. We heard his screams from the understage and rushed up there.

I will forever shudder at the memory of his thin body turned into a ball of fire. The amount of powder around him must have been a hundred times what we'd faced on the rafters. McGray jumped on him and rolled him on the floor, extinguishing the fire with his bare hands. Somebody came with a thick blanket, but by the time they smothered the flames the damage was . . .

Thank goodness the boy had not lived for much longer. Death by fire is something I would not wish on anybody.

His mother had run to him, and I am afraid she had the closest possible view of the injuries. That scream she let out, the one Elgie had just mentioned, was terrible. No banshee, no fury, no mythological being could ever utter anything as sharp and unsettling. Not one, but her two children victims of fire. I cannot imagine what went through her already perturbed mind. Poor Mrs Harwood ran away and could not be found for the next twenty minutes — I am secretly relieved it was not I who did so.

McGray and I were on the street when we first heard of the next tragedy. We were looking at the bodies of Freddie and Tarvin being carefully placed on the cart that was to take them to the morgue, when McNair came running and shouting. I cannot believe he still had energy to feel the terror so deeply: he had found Mrs Harwood at the back of the very basement into which I'd followed her. Half hidden between the vast canvases, and tangled in the ropes used to lift them, she appeared to have hanged herself.

I must have appeared insensitive, but as I said, I was too drained for further emotion. Quite frankly, a part of me is glad Mrs Harwood is finally at rest, for her future could only have been grim.

At least little Susy was spared those scenes. Miss Terry had already taken her to the Palace Hotel, after finding the girl in her own dressing room, washing off her make-up, so she was not even aware of her brother's fate. The dreadful news was piling up for her. We sent word to the hotel about Mrs Harwood's passing, and the messenger came back with Miss Terry's immediate reply. Apparently the actress had reacted much like me; too tired and beaten for a proper display of emotion. In her note she told us she'd be the one to break the news to Susy, but not before morning, after the child had had some rest.

I reached for my coffee and looked at the grey yet bright sky through the window. Susy Harwood would probably be receiving the news at that very moment, and I could only wonder how she'd react. Would she be distraught? Would her wits endure? Or, like me, would she also be a little relieved?

I thought of her prospects. Unless Miss Terry took her on, the girl would probably be sent off to her relatives in New Zealand – the distant cousins mentioned by her mother. Given the circumstances, that was perhaps the best possible outcome for her. Distance would be the best balm, and in this case half the world would be scarcely enough.

Elgie had waited patiently while I pondered, and I realized how surprisingly soothing his company was, even if we both were silent. Again I thought how sad it would be to see him go.

'Have you slept at all?' I asked him.

'I went to bed, but did not sleep. This all brought back bad memories.'

Indeed, it must have. Perhaps Elgie would welcome his return to London, after all.

I took a deep breath, stood up and patted Elgie on the shoulder. 'Thanks for keeping me company. I should lie down for an hour or so. There is still plenty of work to do at the City Chambers.'

So much, in fact, the mere idea made me want to scream.

There would be a full inquiry, and it would be a very long one, although I could already tell it would lead nowhere: whilst we attempted to bring Mrs Irving to justice, her very victims would be making every effort to absolve her. This was a scandal Henry Irving would never allow to become public, and he'd pull every string at his disposal, just as Florence had predicted.

She *must* have weighted all those factors long before embarking on her suicidal plot. And now, having dragged three men and one woman to their early graves, she'd simply walk away, alive and well, and most likely having accomplished what she wanted for her sons from the very start. What a conniving woman she was.

In the end I would have to write all that down in a hefty report that would be read with suspicion by everyone; then not a single party would be found guilty, and after long days of arduous work the entire affair would be filed away. Forgotten. Never to be spoken of again.

But before that, of course, I would sleep.

*(fragments from a carbon copy underlined and annotated
by Detective Inspector A. McGray)*

From the investigations preceding and following the tragic events of Saturday 13 July 1889,
we can deduce the following:

Mrs Florence Irving, aided by former actor
J. R. Tarvin, intended to commit suicide in a
manner that would directly incriminate actress
Alice Ellen Terry. To this end she devised two
parallel sets of lies: one to be believed by Miss
Terry and one to be believed by the police after
her death.

Miss Ellen Terry was meant to believe that
an estranged friend – Mr Charles Lutwidge
Dodgson, popularly known as author Lewis
Carroll – was renewing correspondence with
her. The police forces, on the other hand, were
meant to believe that Miss Terry had been
blackmailing Mrs Irving, and had ultimately
murdered her.

which the sneaky shrew used during her secret courtship with Irving

and who perhaps played the horizontal hornpipe with Florence

The brats had also been told Miss Terry was blackmailing their mother

Mrs Irving resorted to <u>an enviable talent for forging letters</u> in order to trick Miss Terry. Given the plausibility of Mrs Irving's carefully created story, combined with the two women's juxtaposition at the moment of her intended death, it is doubtful those documents would have been subject to thorough analysis.

All the cited correspondence was delivered by <u>Mr J. R. Tarvin, a former actor with a long-held grudge against Mr Henry Irving</u>.

A stranger to Ellen Terry, Mr Tarvin was able to act as a simple servant. Irving's sons, ignorant of the ultimate intentions of their mother, were part of the charade, allowing Mr Tarvin to hide in their rooms whenever and for as long as required, in the belief that he was carrying correspondence between Miss Terry and Mrs Irving.

That is how the man managed to come and go without being sighted by guests or hotel staff, whom he could wait out and avoid.

The clear purpose of these letters was simply to place Miss Terry at the wrong place at the wrong time, to further support the idea of her involvement in Mrs Irving's death.

[. . .]

On the night of 11 July, in an attempt to create more suspicion around Miss Terry, Mrs Irving summoned her to a meeting in the middle of the night; a meeting she was to believe had been arranged by said Lewis Carroll. Miss

<u>Terry's rather foolish decision to accept the summons will not be commented on.</u> ← *Aye, must have been expecting a night o' passion . . .*

Again the correspondence was delivered by Mr Tarvin. It is most likely that he was the person who left the door to the backyard open during the ball [. . .] However, <u>the perpetrator of the attack on Constable Cooper, which took place only minutes later, remains unknown.</u> ← *That was the banshee, you stubborn mule!*

This person must have been seen by the late Mr Alan Dyer, reporter of *The Scotsman* and sadly deceased on the same night.

[. . .]

Mr Abraham Stoker was intended to become another witness against Miss Terry. He was lured into the streets by <u>Mr Tarvin, who played cruel games fuelled by Mr Stoker's unfounded beliefs in Irish folklore.</u> *don't omit the details, Percy: Stoker thought Tarvin's wolfhound was an omen of his death*

Mr Stoker was guided in the direction of Mrs Irving's lodgings, and according to his own journal he caught a glimpse of two cloaked figures. One was Mr Tarvin; the second was Mrs Irving herself, <u>wearing the second beetle dress.</u> *which, it later transpired, they'd taken from Mrs Harwood's room*

The purpose of this act was to convince Mr Stoker that Miss Ellen Terry had perambulated in the direction of Florence Irving's lodgings. This would have suggested the two ladies had indeed met whilst in Edinburgh. Miss Terry would have only had her word, and the very implausible tale about Carroll's invitation, to deny it.

[. . .]

Even though Mrs Irving's actions were criminal in nature, the lady cannot be prosecuted for 'attempted suicide'. She could indeed be tried for insidious stalking, but this would only proceed if Miss Terry were to press charges against her. Unfortunately, Miss Terry, through legal advisors, has categorically refused to do so.

Charges could have also been pressed by Mr Abraham Stoker [. . .] His case would have had solid grounds at court, given the physical assault, plainly orchestrated in the interest of Mrs Irving's schemes. Mr Stoker, just as Miss Terry, will not take further action. His personal *to put it nicely* allegiances are all too clear.

[. . .]

Mrs Irving has denied any involvement in the banshee sightings, despite confessing to much graver deeds [. . .] She herself could not have acted as the apparitions, having been amidst the audience at the time of the first sighting, and on the other side of New Town during the second (her lodgers can avow to this).

She has, however, admitted to having been at Calton Hill on the night of 12 July, when attempting to destroy incriminating correspondence from Mr Tarvin. On this night her determination to commit suicide failed her. Mrs Irving abandoned herself to raucous despair, which was witnessed by the entire neighbourhood and reported in the local newspapers.

[. . .]

We will never be able to ascertain — beyond

reasonable doubt, at least – that Mrs Harwood acted as the banshee, although that is <u>this author's preferred theory.</u>

Aye, Percy couldn't contain himself

Her whereabouts were certainly not accounted for during any of the sightings and, as a member of the theatre company, the lady would have had plenty of opportunities to hear or read Mr Wilde's now infamous sonnet [. . .] Aided by Mr Tarvin, who assaulted an orderly at Edinburgh's asylum earlier that evening, Mrs Harwood was able to escape and make her way to the theatre. She would have been in the building when those last verses were written, and her mental breakdown would explain why she borrowed poetry from Mr Wilde, rather than continue delivering her own. Nevertheless, this is all circumstantial evidence. [. . .] The mention of one person 'falling' on the stage and one on the night of the aforementioned ball, which would coincide, respectively, with the deaths of Mr Tarvin and Mr Dyer, <u>must be mere and unfortunate coincidence.</u>

You unbelievable moron. . . .

To purchase and transport the amounts of blood required to write the cited rhymes may have been beyond Mrs Harwood's mental state [. . .] particularly for the very last instance [. . .] With Mrs Harwood sadly perished, it is doubtful that this particular mystery will ever be solved.

[. . .]

Had we not been involved in the investigation, Mrs Irving would most certainly have succeeded in her suicide attempt and Mr Wheatstone would have probably not survived his encounter with Mrs Harwood. Furthermore, Mrs Irving's plot against Miss Terry was so carefully orchestrated that this witness doubts the actress would have had much chance of acquittal in court.

[. . .]

The recklessness of Superintendent George Campbell must be pointed out and urgently addressed.

Lynch the bastard!

His blasé attitude and perennial obstruction to our investigations unquestionably resulted in the three aforementioned deaths, all of which might have been avoided had the play been cancelled. The superintendent's approach was that of a narrow, biased, ignorant, selfish, bigoted – [. . .]

Aye, takes one to know one . . .

(The contents of this report, alongside the testimony of other affected parties, led to a subsequent internal enquiry and the immediate dismissal of Superintendent G. T. Campbell.)

then again, had we NOT been involved
- Mr Dyer would not have plummeted from Castle Rock,
- Nobody would have chased Tarvin on the rafters and he wouldn't have fallen to his death.
- Tarvin would not have kicked the sack of explosive powder into a precarious position and so the boy Freddie would still be alive.

self-fulfilling prophecy?

Epilogue

I tightened my dressing gown as I walked downstairs. I would have stayed a little longer in bed, it being my last day on leave, but the rattle of carriages on the street woke me, and when I opened my curtains the sun was already quite high in the sky – rather than *sun* I should call it the slightly lighter spot behind the grey clouds, for the weather had lately turned for the worse.

I was tempted to pour myself a small glass of port, but refrained from doing so. Ever since the entire Frey family – Elgie included – had left, fortified wine had become my customary breakfast. That had been nearly a week ago, so I decided I could not go on like that.

Before I reached my parlour I heard a knocking.

'Who is it, Layton?' I asked from the top of the stairs. A moment later I saw George, McGray's old butler, come in with a crate of whisky under his arm. Behind him came Nine-Nails himself. He sneered at me.

'Och, ye lazy sod! Freshly out o' yer four-poster, are ye?'

I must say McGray did not look that well – and not only because his stubble was as prickly as ever and he again wore his preposterous tartan trousers and cheap overcoat. His hands were still bandaged, for he'd received some nasty burns while trying to help the unfortunate Freddie, and he'd taken the worst while fighting Tarvin on the rafters. There was a particularly bad burn on his cheekbone, where Tarvin had thrown hot charcoal. Most of my burns were only superficial and would clear soon enough, though the ones on my hand, from saving Mr Wheatstone, would probably leave a permanent scar.

'Is this a social visit?' was my incredulous question. I noticed McGray carried another bottle of whisky, the label old and faded.

'Take those to Percy's cellar,' McGray told George. 'We'll start with this one.' He looked at me. 'Aye and nae. I'm sort of paying a gentleman's debt.'

Before I could say anything McGray was already in the upstairs parlour, pouring the golden drink into two of my cut-glass tumblers.

'McGray, it is nine in the morning.'

'Nah! A wee dram or two for breakfast once in yer lifetime won't kill ye.'

Since I could not refute his argument without mentioning my recent morning-port addiction, I simply took up the tumbler and we toasted.

'To unsolved cases,' said McGray.

'Unsolved! McGray, it is so clear it was not a banshee. I thought this was the first delivery of my ten years' supply!'

'*Ha!* Ye cannae prove there was nae banshee. Ye only have yer theories. I read the report ye sent to that Monro in London.'

'Oh, McGray, the evidence –'

'*Circumstantial.* Yer own word. Neither of us can convince the other, so I thought this was a good compromise. I'll let ye keep yer mare, but only out o' the goodness o' my heart – and 'cause I still miss my good auld Rye.'

'Oh, I cannot believe what you are claiming, simply to save yourself some whisky.'

'The omens came true, dandy. Somebody fell on the stage, and more than one died on the thirteenth. The more we delved into it, the more people died, and remember that line: *The ghost's white fingers* –'

'*On thy shoulders laid,*' I completed. 'Yes, as always, obvious only after the fact in question has occurred. Excuse me if I find your theories a little far fetched.'

'Och, just shut it and drink up yer ill-gotten whisky.'

We drank in silence for a moment, and Layton brought some cold meats to avoid me becoming inebriated on an empty stomach.

'I had a letter from Stoker,' said McGray, helping himself to cured ham. 'He told me all that's been happening in London.'

'Did he? How very solicitous.'

'Aye, and he asked me to lend him a couple o' my books. For a play he's working on, or something. He says that Susy is already on her way to New Zealand, the poor lassie. And Miss Terry is spending a couple o' weeks resting in her country house – Stoker doubts they'll be doing any Shakespeare plays for at least a couple o' years.'

'I cannot blame them.'

'Also, Irving has "all of a sudden" been allowed to see his sons. The laddies might be breaking into the theatre, after all.'

I raised an eyebrow. 'Mr Stoker seems strangely keen to keep us well informed.'

'Nae strange at all. He finished his letter begging us to keep all the evidence of the case – statements, reports, newspapers, his confiscated journal, the lot. He wants us to file it all properly and keep it safe, in case Irving's bitch of a wife ever attempts anything against him or Miss Terry.'

I nodded. 'He is a clever man, that Stoker.'

'Indeedy. He'll probably keep in touch, if only to make sure we're protecting those documents. Can ye take care o' the filing tomorrow, first thing?'

'Of course. I shall be well rested, and I doubt we will have any more pressing cases so soon.'

McGray laughed loud. 'Ye never ken, Percy!' He downed his glass and stood up. 'I should go now. Dr Clouston is back. I want to ask him how Pansy's been doing.'

It was good to see he managed to talk about his sister without being overwhelmed by gloom, and I sincerely hoped the doctor had brought good news from the Orkneys.

'By the way,' said McGray, before crossing the threshold, 'Joan will bring ye some o' the scones she says ye love more than ye do yer dad. I offered to bring 'em but I think she didnae trust they'd make it here. As if I were such a gorger . . .'

Nine-Nails left soon afterwards but I lingered in the parlour, alone with my thoughts, and there was one I could not postpone any longer.

There *had* been somebody else on that bridge above the stage. I had seen those cat-like eyes, I was sure of it, and even though I only regarded them for a split second, they will forever remain imprinted in my memory. I could mull on that image for as long as I wished, yet I would never come to a satisfactory conclusion.

I sighed, thinking I'd better follow Lady Macbeth's advice: *Things without all remedy should be without regard . . .*

And I drank the last drops of whisky left in my tumbler – the spirit was far too precious to be wasted.

🪲

Joan did arrive, but a few hours later, bringing a mountain of the promised scones. Larry, her twelve-year-old helper, also came along, carrying a basket with several jars of jam.

Just before leaving, Joan came to my parlour, where I'd been reading all morning. The good woman replaced the lukewarm pot of tea with a freshly brewed one.

'Oh, sir, I nearly forgot. I've been meaning to tell you this for days. Do you remember when you came to Mr McGray's house, asking me about them butchers and pints of blood?'

I closed my book at once. 'Yes. Why do you ask?'

Joan smiled. 'Just yesterday I was chatting to Mrs Sandson, the wife of my favourite butcher. He told her that last week a very odd gal came on market day to buy a gallon.'

'Odd? In – in what respect?'

'Well, she covered her face with a strange shawl all the time. They never saw her full on, but Mrs Sandson says her husband thinks the girl had a very nasty scar.'

Before Joan finished the sentence I was already picturing that little face, half sweet, half mangled, embarked towards the South Pacific, enveloped in the sea mist, satisfied by her revenge against her brother and grinning back at the now-distant old continent.

The real banshee.

Historical Note

The idea of a *Macbeth* case came to me well before completing the first draft of *The Strings of Murder*, and it originally involved a fictitious theatre company on the verge of bankruptcy. It was a really happy accident that Henry Irving and Ellen Terry (the Judi Dench and Ian McKellen of their day) were presenting this very play exactly at the time my Ian Frey was solving his first cases in Scotland, and that their manager turned out to be none other than Bram Stoker.

Irving's *Macbeth* is one of the best documented productions of Victorian theatre. The material available well after a century (correspondence, sketches, photos, paintings, reviews, etc.) is outstandingly detailed, to the point we are able to tell on which words of her lines Ellen Terry paused for breath. This is, of course, a double-edged sword, so I must begin this note with a little expiation.

As the well-learned Irvingites will be quick to point out, he did not take his *Macbeth* to Scotland on the dates this novel takes place. The play, however, did premiere in London on 30 December 1888, with its last performance on 29 June 1889, the date for my overture. According to the Scottish Theatre Archives, the Royal Lyceum was in fact closed from 1 July to 22 July for their summer holiday. As I was not going to allow this 'minor' detail to get in the way, I interweaved this in the dialogue as an apology to historical fact (and to prove that I had indeed done my homework!).

As mentioned in my initial note, I hardly had to make anything up with regards to Bram Stoker, Henry Irving and Ellen Terry. In fact, the more I delved into their lives, the juicier the novel got.

Sir Henry (not yet knighted in 1889) did court the upper-class Florence partly in secret, since he was not considered a suitable match for her. Ultimately, he did walk out on her when Florence was heavily pregnant, in the exact circumstances described in chapter 15. Their unhappy marriage was common knowledge, and so was Irving's on-and-off affair with Ellen Terry. Florence and her sons – quite understandably – abhorred the actress, and in their letters did refer to her as 'the wench'. The Irving boys were not so keen on Bram Stoker either, whom they saw as their father's spy. Irving tried to keep his sons away from the theatre, for the reasons here mentioned; however, father and sons did reconcile, rather inexplicably, from the summer of 1889 onwards, and both Harry and Laurence (the latter I have recast as Sydney, his middle name, to avoid confusion with Frey's brother) went on to have careers in the theatre, one as an actor-manager and the other as a playwright (Laurence's plays, however, were not financially successful and eventually forced Irving to sell the London Lyceum). The fictitious events in this book would have explained this sudden change of heart. Florence Irving, as far as we know, never spoke to her husband again, but she did make people address her as Lady Florence after Irving was knighted (the first knighthood ever bestowed upon an actor). Her having a lover is the one fictitious element in the story – as far as we know she remained faithful to Irving – but she did enjoy attending public trials.

Dame Alice Ellen Terry (again, not yet honoured in 1889) was so ahead of her time she even seems anachronistic in this text, but her background is entirely real. She married three times (twice by 1889), had an incredibly long list of romantic liaisons (all the names mentioned by Catherine are real) and her two children were indeed born out of wedlock from a relationship in-between her first two marriages. Her friendship with Lewis Carroll did end at some point due to Terry's reputation, and the acquaintance would not be resumed until much later in their lives. Terry's children were very fond of Henry Irving, who gave them many opportunities in the theatre; this gave even more grounds for Irving's two sons to become jealous.

Much has been speculated about Bram's Stoker sexuality and his relationship with Henry Irving. Stoker managed Irving's company for twenty-seven years with so much dedication he became estranged from his wife and only son (whose names were indeed Florence and Irving, though the latter preferred to be addressed as Noel, his middle name). Stoker's commitment to the theatre did not diminish even after the success of *Dracula*; upon Irving's death Stoker wrote a lengthy biography, which includes very suggestive passages. Noteworthy is the line he devotes to the signed portrait (the one Frey finds in Stoker's journal), which Irving gave him on the night they first met, and which Stoker kept for the rest of his life: *And the sight of his picture before me, with those loving words, the record of a time of deep emotion and full understanding of us both, each for the other, unmans me once again as I write.* It is my personal interpretation that Irving recognized this and used it in his favour, though I am not the first one to suggest so. I do, however, doubt that Stoker consciously based his Dracula on Irving (which has also been suggested by many scholars); having said that, it was a treat to the imagination to pour all those vampiric traits into my depictions of him (my heartfelt thanks to actor James Swanton for his comments on the first draft).

Other curiosities worth mentioning:

Stoker's family tree and his connection to the most ancient Irish chieftains are real.

The cast list was copied word for word from one of the play's souvenirs (just like the one Frey picks up). Lady Macduff really was cut out, and the fact that Fleance and one of the apparitions were both played by children named Harwood was the initial inspiration for their backstories.

The 'ladder of angels' mounted for their 1886 production of *Faust*, and Ellen Terry spotting the top girl in the audience a year earlier are real anecdotes. Though *Faust* was truly plagued with all sorts of accidents, the fire on the last performance is fictitious.

Every fact regarding John Singer Sargent and his painting of Ellen Terry is accurate (except, of course, his being in Edinburgh on those dates). The portrait, now part of the Tate collection (and now on display at London's Tate Britain), is still considered a masterpiece. I loved being able to insert an explanation for Ellen Terry's alarmed expression in that painting. The striking beetle-wing dress has been restored recently (reconstructed from two damaged dresses!) and is now in permanent display at

Smallhythe Place, Ellen Terry's last home and now a museum devoted to her life.

The other portrait by Sargent mentioned by Frey, that of Mrs Henry White, does exist: it was painted in 1883 and I like to imagine that the woman in question could be a distant relation to Ian's horrid stepmother.

Oscar Wilde, one of my most loved authors, was a very close friend of Irving and company, and did write the sonnet partly quoted in the text. I might have tweaked it to fit the Shakespearean metrics, but that is fine between *tocayos*. My apologies if anybody thinks Nine-Nails treated him too roughly, but that meeting could not have gone any other way.

Edinburgh's Royal Lyccum is said to be still haunted by Ellen Terry's ghost. The auditorium is virtually unchanged and still looks as grand as it would have back in 1889 (special thanks to Ruth Butterworth and Jack Summers-McKay for organizing the private tour). The back- and understage, naturally, have undergone the necessary modernizations to keep the theatre functional, and for these spaces I took inspiration from a nineteenth-century cross-section of the Drury Lane Theatre in London.

Lycopodium powder is still used for special effects, and it is one of the strangest substances I have encountered in my studies as a chemist: it ignites only when it is suspended in the air, while a heap of the stuff lying still on a table will never catch fire.

The rheostat, great-grandfather of modern-day dimmers, was invented by Sir Charles Wheatstone, hence my insertion of a fictitious nephew of his.

The first man in charge of painting the scenery for *Macbeth* was a major let-down for Irving's company. Long after commissioning the work, and after asking repeatedly as to a date of completion, Stoker found that the painter (one Keeley Halswelle) had not even started the 'charcoal outlines'. One of the men who rescued it all as a last-minute job was indeed named 'J. Harker'. I suppose Bram Stoker remained forever grateful.

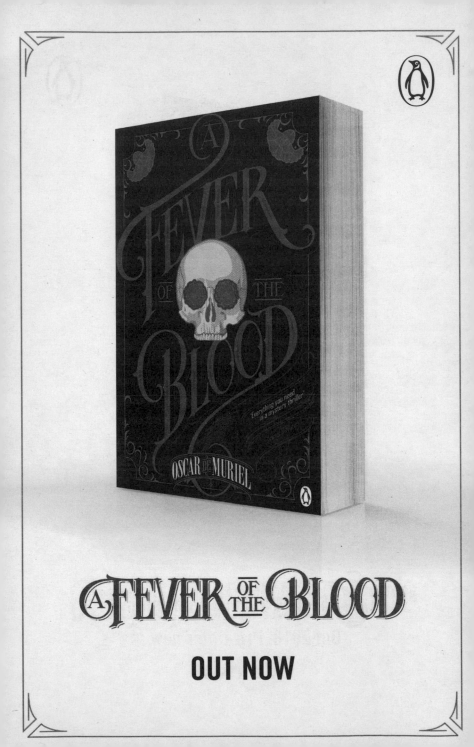

OUT NOW

THE
LOCH
OF THE
DEAD

Frey and McGray's next adventure.

Out 2018. Pre-order now.